P9-BUG-698

LUX

ALSO BY MARIA FLOOK

Invisible Eden: A Story of Love and Murder on Cape Cod
My Sister Life: The Story of My Sister's Disappearance

Open Water
Family Night
You Have the Wrong Man

Sea Room
Reckless Wedding

LUX

MARIA FLOOK

LITTLE, BROWN AND COMPANY

New York Boston

Little, Brown and Company
Time Warner Book Group
1271 Avenue of the Americas, New York, NY 10020
Visit our Web site at www.twbookmark.com

First Edition

Library of Congress Cataloging-in-Publication Data

Flook, Maria.
Lux / Maria Flook.—1st ed.
p. cm.
ISBN 0-316-00092-2
1. Cape Cod (Mass.)—Fiction. I. Title.
PS3556.L583L895 2004 813'.54—dc22 2003026613

10 9 8 7 6 5 4 3 2 1

Q-FF

Book design by M. Kristen Bearse

Printed in the United States of America

MY THANKS TO GAIL HOCHMAN
AND JUDITH GROSSMAN.
TO MY EDITOR
PAT STRACHAN—THIS BOOK, WITH GRATITUDE.

LUX

1

IT WAS THE END OF HER SHIFT and the rain was falling. In the half dark, Alden switched on her desk lamp. A silhouette from its finial loop cast a noose across the ceiling. She unscrewed the dreary ornament and got rid of it. She enjoyed hearing it clang in the metal wastebasket at her feet.

Her moods often pounced on her at quitting time, and she hurried to finish last minute items. She had been having some trouble with a married man she had met in her office at the National Seashore Visitor Center on Cape Cod. He was scouting locations for an Internet travel agency that booked "wilderness tours" and "nature vacations" and had come to collect information about the outer peninsula. He showed up when Alden was surrounded by schoolchildren as she monitored a stranded sea turtle, a creature about the size and shape of a pressure-cooker lid. The turtle had been found on First Encounter Beach, stunned by a sudden drop in the water temperature. During their autumn migration, these stragglers sometimes washed ashore, numbed by the cold. The New England Aquarium retrieved the endangered turtles for observation and eventual release into warmer Florida waters, but the research truck had been late to collect this one.

He had tried to make small talk about the turtle and other wildlife attractions within the National Seashore, but Alden said that she was just the "bookstore manager" and he should try to find the director at the other end of the corridor. The man went away but soon returned to her bookstall. He wasn't fazed by her initial brush-off and he asked her about her perfume, seeming quite pleased by it. He was surprised, he told her, that "a book clerk" would bother wearing scent, but he was handing it right back to her.

"This perfume?" she said, tugging her cuff to extend her wrist. But she withdrew her arm before he could have a closer inspection. The French scent was a subversive incorporation of musks and spicy florals, bergamot spitballs and gingers. "Like a hothouse on fire," her husband had once told her in his typical ridicule. But her husband was out of the picture.

The travel agent told her his name was Mr. Ison. She thought "Ison" had a clear, ringing note, like the name of a steep mountain or a famous skyscraper building. The Prudential, the Chrysler, the Hancock, the *Ison*. She kept busy, charting the sea turtle's progress. It had not yet reached room temperature. Ison lingered with the children, pretending to be interested in the stranded animal. He had recognized something about Alden, a willingness or desperation that made her seem receptive.

Alden sometimes looked unraveled, a little akimbo, like a sticky door that needs planing, or a window propped open by a book when its sash weights are broken. She was still trying to regain her footing after her husband had disappeared two years ago.

Alden thought she saw her husband everywhere.

She sometimes saw Monty coming out of the automatic doors at the supermarket just as she entered with an opposite river of shoppers. She turned around in an instant and tried to follow him back outside, but the electronic sensors were slow to signal the mechanism, and the door didn't sweep open until after he was gone. Once, she drove past an alley and saw Monty standing beside some garbage cans. She turned the car into the private lane to confront him, but it was just an apparition—a bicycle had been left standing vertical on its handlebars.

Or it was a rake propped in a barrel with a blue jean jacket draped on its tines. Another time, it was a pair of bibbed overalls luffing on a clothesline. Never Monty.

After Monty disappeared, she visited a therapist a few times. The MSW had told Alden that there is the "imagination of hope" and the "imagination of fear." Imagined fears accelerate to a finite disaster scenario. The building burns. The bridge collapses. The 737 nose-dives. The lover cheats on his beloved. Fear eventually climaxes, thank goodness, but hope just escalates. Hope is an ascending fever; hope is the one-and-the-same unfounded expectation that spikes hotter and hotter.

The therapist slapped Alden's hand to get her to stop twisting a loop of hair around her index finger. The woman told her, "Uncontrolled anxiety can eat you up."

He'd been less than a perfect husband, but Alden still hoped Monty would turn up. When she filed a missing-persons report, the police officers looked at her as if she was crazy. They were certain that the schoolteacher had jilted her. If only her husband had remained in town with his new conquest, Alden might have got over him. When she pestered the officers too often, they nicknamed her "Miss Bride Interrupted."

Left on her own, Alden had opened her door to suitors, but they were just "filler" until Monty returned. She sometimes believed that she brought out the predatory and, even worse, the *scavenging* instinct in these men. Men would gladly pick over her bones, feeling no responsibility for what had befallen her. That was her husband's fault.

ALDEN HAD YET TO TRANSCRIBE MESSAGES from the Audubon hotline, 349-WING, a duty she saved until the end of her day before locking up. She sat at her desk with a pad of paper and pressed the play button on the answering machine. She listened to the tape rewind, a lisping shiver of magnetic plastic that promised a long list of reported sightings. There were a couple of national counts in progress, and Alden logged these notations in different registers that required she keep running tallies. The callers were often regulars, and Alden recognized their voices. A familiar oldster reported a Townsend's solitaire at the old railroad bed at Corn Hill; and three Lapland longspurs were spotted in the wrack line off First Encounter Beach. About seventy northern gannets were plunge-diving just off the beach in front of the Watermark Inn in Provincetown. A flock of eighteen common redpolls. One sharp-shinned hawk. Two marbled godwits. Nine whimbrels. Two more Kemp's ridley sea turtles were seen paddling sluggishly between moorings in Wellfleet Harbor. They should be picked up before they were too numb to swim. She penciled in each sighting, noting its numbers and exact location. She added up any repetitions to get the final counts for migrating waterfowl and songbirds.

Then it was Sarah Calhoon, a fiftyish retiree who often visited the National Seashore bookstore. She wasn't calling to report a sighting, but said, "Alden, did that order of ladybug thumbtacks come in?" Ladybug thumbtacks. Arachnid cocktail napkins. Killer whale shot glasses. These items had come to represent the "good life" for some people. Alden couldn't find solace in animal figurines and trinkets, although she tried to match the enthusiasm of the knee-jerk naturalists and tree-hugger types who came into the bookstore to buy badges. Real naturalists don't have to wear it on their sleeves. But her favorite regulars assembled the way farmers mobilize at the local Feed-and-Grain just to rest their dogs and shoot the breeze. Alden sold them wildlife coffee mugs and tote bags, ladybug thumbtacks in plastic tubs.

Alden reset the tape machine, locked her cash drawer, and left her desk at twilight. A minor storm hit the coast in a typical Cape Cod "sea squall makes landfall" hissy fit. The rain stopped as soon as it started, but a Stephen King–caliber fog rolled across from Chatham Bars. The wind was clammy and the short walk to her car was like fighting through a shower stall of wet Hanes and panties. She got into her Jeep but could hardly see the road. Landmarks disappeared.

The outer peninsula had a chaotic, fiddlehead topography of dunes and swales that curled around in a spiral. Sometimes, when Alden stood on the breakwater at Land's End, she lost her sense of direction entirely. What was supposed to be due west was actually looking south, and northward could be east. Living at the inverted tip, a person needed a heightened kinesthesia or a cartographer's intuition, especially in sea mists.

But the whiteout made her nervous. She tried to remember what the Weather Channel announcer had said: "Fog is just harmless cloud." Mothering cloud that sinks down on its clan to enfold and nourish, the way a white pullet sits on her brood. Its white banks swept across the windshield, closing around her. Alden couldn't see six feet in front of her. No backward, no forward, just the instant interior.

After hours, Alden worked with the U.S. Fish and Wildlife Service, which had started a project to exterminate an overpopulation of seagulls. The herring gulls bred on Monomoy, a barrier beach sanctuary two miles offshore. At first, the extermination project seemed to be working; the gulls were eating the poisoned bait. Heaps of sliced table bread were sprayed with Avitrol and systematically deposited across the sand dunes. The plan backfired when, in their death throes, the gulls flew inland and dropped like flies into the densely populated vacation resorts of Chatham and East Orleans. At the height of the summer season, gulls were falling onto people's decks as men in barbecue aprons grilled swordfish and burgers. Gulls were going belly-up in motel swimming pools. It was Alden's job to collect the carcasses.

Just the other week, Alden was in Snow's Library on Main Street when a crazed gull crashed through the skylight, somersaulted to the carpet, then took wing again. It flew out through the same jagged starburst.

"I guess he's not a bibliophile," a senior told Alden. Together they watched a steel blue flight feather that the gull had lost in its crash test flutter down and stab the carpet. The woman seized it, twisted the feather before Alden's face, and said, "I think it's criminal, what you're doing to those poor birds."

Alden had always thought that seagulls were the rats of the sky, but she told the Audubon crone, "The project will help endangered piping plovers reclaim their nesting grounds. We need to increase the plovers to at least ninety nesting pairs in the next five years." Alden often saw these baby plovers, tiny birds of speckled fluff racing in tight zigzags across the tidal flats. They pecked the foam necklace at the wrack line, chicks hardly bigger than the tufts on a chenille bedspread, searching for immature sand shrimp and beach fleas. It's a baby-eat-baby kind of thing. These wildlife babies tweaked her heartstrings. She told the senior, "But I'm not in charge of this gull project. I just work at the bookstore."

"Plovers. Seagulls. Let nature decide who's king of the mountain," the woman said.

"Like I said, don't blame me. I'm not the mastermind."

As a National Seashore employee, Alden had been enlisted to help collect the scruffy seagull corpses *after the fact*. She was given a canvas rucksack for toting the poisoned shorebirds to the transfer station, where she put them in a predesignated Dumpster stamped with the peculiar, postmodern toxic-waste cartouche. Next to the gull bin was the recycled milk jug bin with the missing children's faces lined up in forlorn rows just like in a Romanian nursery. It wasn't her idea of a posh moonlighting gig.

She was assigned to the Orleans rotary at dusk to patrol its traffic island for any sick or dying birds. Alden parked her car on a service road and crossed against traffic. She entered the tangled moat of underbrush, briar and scrub pine, careful to skirt hummocks of poison ivy. Alden was highly allergic to the pesky vine and just had to look at it for her skin to erupt in seeping welts. She had a fresh lesion where the noxious plant had twanged her bare leg and left a flaming check mark.

On her patrol, she didn't find any stricken birds, but she disturbed a red fox bitch. She watched the startled fox weave across the busy rotary traffic and disappear into a deep belt of spartina growing along Cove Road. She fretted that the fox would get hit, leaving its little kits motherless.

She imagined rescuing these kits.

But fox litters usually come in the spring. Audubon do-gooders might move in on dens, thinking the kits were orphaned, when the mother was probably just out hunting rabbits. These naturemongers and wildlife collectors look for their opportunities wherever they might claim one.

Alden sympathized with the fox's denning ritual. She imagined the secret bliss of retreating to a dark parlor with such glorious offspring. Her aunt had had a fox collar jacket, its fur pelt a soft velvet choker. She imagined snuggling in bed with a whole row of these fox collars. Alden often examined her feelings about the maternal ethos—how it can be nurtured or shattered in an instant. She had recently submitted an application to the Department of Social Services for a foster-care license, but she hadn't received word that she had been approved. They told her to send proof of her current residence and employment status and a copy of her marriage license. She had bristled at the suggestion that her marital status remained unconfirmed without the live item or the appropriate paperwork. Single women could often adopt babies; why was she being scrutinized?

Finding no seagulls, she waited on the island for the traffic to thin out so she could get back to her Jeep. Cars cruised nonstop past the big topiary clock that greeted tourists at the Route 6 rotary in Orleans, a mock timepiece carved from a circle of ornamental hedges planted on an incline. All twelve emerald digits were sheared across the top and sides and checked with a spirit level. The clock's green hands were set, in perpetuity, to five o'clock.

Five o'clock. Quitting time.

Outsiders driving onto the outer peninsula passed the clock at the rotary circle, and from there they entered the circus of leisure and R & R, retirement and recreation, of life without work. Even locals who held regular jobs at the fish piers, resort hotels, antique shops, and souvenir outlets found some reassurance in the "Quitting Time Clock" as their workday began. They'd have their respite, too, in just eight hours.

Cars rolled past the landmark and entered the rotary counterclockwise, as if in a prideful attempt to *reverse* time. Alden would be glad to go forward or backward just to lose the stigma that had clung to her since her husband ran off. She tried not to think of anything but her daily routine, the *here and now,* no matter how monotonous it was. When summer people crossed the Cape Cod Canal at Sagamore, they could plead instant amnesia, but year-rounders couldn't claim the same privilege.

At the canal bridge, the beloved steel-tied arch had a new suicide fence, tall metal tines hooked inward at the top. The fence had been built to enforce the familiar billboard sign "Desperate? Call the Samaritans," which for decades had greeted all traffic funneled into a bottleneck at the arch. When people moved to Cape Cod as a last resort, the geographical cure sometimes wasn't enough. She would read about these suicides in local newspapers. The *Cape Codder* sometimes reprinted excerpts from suicide notes, hasty scraps found tucked under windshield wipers on parked cars left on one side of the canal or the other. Alden was especially struck by the brevity of these notes. One victim had written the two words "Pain everywhere," and another jumper had complained that his life was just too much to bear, that it was "Everything—all at once."

These messages, "Pain everywhere" and "Everything—all at once," echoed in her head when she least expected. Bridge deaths seemed like blatant flag-waving from the damned, or perhaps these unhappy victims had gone too far in their bratty role play, enacting "Pierre, I Don't Care" syndrome with fatal consequences. Once, Alden saw an extension ladder left propped against the new suicide fence. She rationalized that perhaps bridge painters had forgotten to stow it. But the ladder was a mocking invitation to lost souls, and Alden tried not to think that someone had brought his own ladder to the site.

Each time she crossed the narrow span, she tried to empty her mind. The canal had even earned the nickname the River of Forgetfulness, like Lethe. On Cape Cod, the two poles of linear time lost definition. The Quitting Time Clock was disconnected.

Tonight the clock face was unreadable behind a fog screen of wet gypsum. Traffic was a smear of motion, with no distinction between vehicles. Alden watched inexperienced drivers enter the rotary and ride their brakes or freeze, using too much intellectual forethought and caution as they edged into the whirling gear. Old hands merged seamlessly, holistically, and rolled around the circle without decelerating. Natives just plowed through. The final destination: P-town, home to long-term nonprogressors, a majority now, since most everyone does well at first with the cocktail. Less-fortunate advanced cases also came back to die off one by one, at the same beloved seaport where they were infected. At the town line, there was a new HIV-positive billboard greeting. It was a large neon plus sign with the words "Welcome to Provincetown. Tolerance in the New Millennium." The PC sign was already weathered and bleached from the sun.

Alden wiped a monster mosquito off her cheek, bursting its rich sac under her fingertips. The wet weather had invigorated the dwindling swarms for a final feast before the first hard freeze. She rubbed the blood from her face. She had entered *their* environment at *their* dining hour. The swarm was famished.

Seeing an opening in the traffic, she ran across the pavement, only to be sandwiched between a grid of swollen high beams and the rosy daubs of taillights. Brakes screeched. She froze in her tracks as a pickup rear-ended a little Nissan. The tiny subcompact shot forward in Newton's "conservation of momentum" and plowed into the thick green band of hedge, into the town's beloved Quitting Time Clock. A wake of air tugged Alden's hair off her shoulders; she was that close to the impact.

The dense topiary treasure was damaged at the number seven. Its thick, sculpted branches were crushed, and the splintered stumps instantly emitted a sharp juniper musk. Traffic halted behind the pileup. Alden trotted up to the crumpled Nissan to hear the radio still chugging a Janet Jackson single. A girl had been thrown out of the driver's seat. Her torso was flopped forward at the waist in a supple tai chi ritual or yoga prayer, her blond ponytail splashed over her head. Alden had never seen a girl like this.

Her nostrils glittered with gold soot.

Just then, a can of Krylon spray paint fell off the rocker panel and rolled across the berm and onto the blacktop, where it kept going. It was hard to tell if the girl was undone from the Krylon or from the shock of the collision, but she couldn't get up off her hands and knees. Her shirt was bunched above her bra strap, exposing a gaudy tattoo. It was the familiar image used so often on coffee mugs, posters, and tote bags: the girl had Edvard Munch's *The Scream* on the small of her back.

Alden looked at the young woman bent in half. The details thwarted all pity, but Alden felt pity for the girl anyway.

Rubberneckers got out of their cars and fanned out around the wreck. A truth seeker, dressed in soccer shin guards, joined the others. "Is it bad? Is she all right?"

The girl pushed herself up and sat back on her heels. She pawed her hair out of her face and squinted at the crowd. "Who hit me?"

The circle stepped backward as if her breath might ignite.

Then a baby wailed from the back seat of the wreck. Alden bent down to see a toddler drumming his heels, still locked into a safety seat. The car seat was secured upright in a lap belt, and the little boy seemed to be all right. A laundry basket of snowy white restaurant towels had spilled everywhere—perhaps the victim was a laundress for one of the big hotels.

Alden and the girl caused a ripple of hot feelings among the patrolmen and rescue teams arriving at the scene. The officers knew the accident victim and wouldn't have pampered her those other times if they had known she was still sniffing paint. Her name was Layla Cox, and Alden listened to the police rattle through some of Layla's little "off-season incidents."

She was piss and vinegar, one said. She was trash on fire. Layla had worked different jobs, including a modeling job at Princie's Peephole, a real-time, interactive porn site on the Internet. That was legal work, but the blister burst when the baby's father and Layla's boyfriend, Brooks McCarthy, was sent to the penitentiary at MCI-Plymouth. The couple had been running a meth kitchen in Layla's basement apartment at the Cape Breeze Motel. Police had found open containers of antifreeze, hydrochloric acid, red phosphorus, and lantern fuel lined up on the kitchen counter right beside bottles of baby formula. Boxes of Mini-Thins, the nonprescription ephedrine tablets used in the recipe, were left tossed around where the toddler could have swallowed them. Officer Francisconi said that Brooks could have killed Baby Hendrick. These meth kitchens sometimes even blew up.

And the gymkhana of law enforcement also knew Alden. Some had known her since childhood, others had seen her at the Seashore Visitor Center, but they'd all heard about her husband, the missing schoolteacher. The case for foul play was insubstantial, or it had been grossly mishandled from the get-go. Most of them believed it was more likely that Monty had run off with a skirt. Alden was high-strung, unhinged since her husband had disappeared, and few on the force had much sympathy for Miss Bride Interrupted.

It had been two years since she lost her husband. He was really, truly lost for good.

Monty had vanished from an authorized bus stop in Eastham, where he had worked as a bus monitor on a middle school route. At first Alden thought he might have gone on an impromptu "weekender" field study with Penelope Griffin, a woman he had met at the Xerces Society, a national group of butterfly enthusiasts. But to Alden's surprise, Miss Griffin herself turned up in a huff at the police station, claiming to know nothing. The two women were forced to meet for the first time in embarrassed solidarity. It seems that they'd both been ditched for a *third* ketty. The detectives couldn't erase their smirks.

Alden hated to be a victim.

She informed the officers that she had known about Miss Griffin all along. Monty and Miss Griffin had written environmental impact statements and had designed butterfly gardens for public parks and traffic islands. They worked together to identify inviting host plants that would attract the most specimens. "Mallow, buddleia, milkweed, glasswort, and amaranth. Fritillary butterflies like only violets," Alden told the officers. The detectives listened to her litany of shrubs and wildflowers. They recognized that Alden didn't want to imagine what else Monty and Miss Griffin might have accomplished after hours, one to one.

Neither woman had any knowledge of a different rival.

Alden gave Miss Griffin the once-over, trying to see what her husband had seen in her. Her inspection was arrested when she locked eyes with Miss Griffin, who was checking *her* over. She wanted to tell Miss Griffin, "Let's remember who was wife and who was mistress," but then she realized hers was the weaker station, after all.

Penelope Griffin explained to investigators that she and Monty had once gone on a working vacation together to a Caribbean island to collect exotic butterflies. Monty had told Alden all about his fruitful expedition with Miss Griffin and about the many unexpected discoveries they had made. Miss Griffin was especially interested in the glasswing butterfly, a glorious specimen with transparent wing segments. "Like tiny windowpanes," Monty had told Alden.

Of course, Miss Griffin's work as a lepidopterist was only part of her bond with Monty. Miss Griffin told the detectives that she had dated Monty for a year, almost as long as he had been married to Alden. Soon after meeting Miss Griffin at the police station, Alden learned that her rival had left town on a research junket. Alden was certain (since a bug fanatic in a push-up bra can't be trusted) that the tall drink of water had gone to join Monty somewhere in the tropics. Alden pictured her husband and Miss Griffin sitting in bamboo lounge chairs, a field guide spread before them, and in their hands they were holding frozen cocktails garnished with serrated paper umbrellas.

When police had found Monty's butterfly diorama on the shoulder of the road, Alden wanted it back, but it was tagged and stored away as evidence. "Evidence of what?" she had badgered the officers. Her husband's geeky pastime?

During her marriage, Alden had tried to learn butterfly lore to please her husband, but Monty didn't seem to want her to adopt his hobby. Two years after his disappearance, she still kept some of his pin-splayed insect specimens mounted on velveteen trays. She had saved the pocket notebooks that he took into the field, two pairs of his 7×35 binoculars, his widemouthed jars with panty hose lids, and the blunt-tipped tweezers he had used to safely pluck a butterfly from its host plant, careful to pinch only its forewings. She saved all his butterfly paraphernalia, fearful that Monty might yet be coming back. He would want his stuff.

"HEY, LET ME GO. GET OFF ME—" The girl with the gold-leaf kisser wouldn't cooperate when medics tried to make her recline on a backboard.

Alden saw that the policemen were upset. The girl was one of their little pets. Law enforcement professionals are exposed to the fallout from everyone's love troubles. An officer might be indifferent or have a predisposition for the said same. They scolded her or they clammed up to cover their own hurt and disappointment.

The girl tried to wipe a clump of hair out of her face, but it kept swinging down. Then she flopped back on the stretcher, happy to give up the fight.

Alden wondered if Layla was named for the mournful Eric Clapton classic. Her name alone tweaked things toward the melancholy for those nostalgic boomer officers who were close to retirement age. They made up half the force. Yes, "Layla" was a stamp of a bygone generation, but Alden thought that the appellation "Baby Hendrick" couldn't be more cunning.

During all the ballyhoo, Alden reached into the back of the car and unsnapped the belt on the little boy's safety seat. She lifted the squirming toddler in her arms and greeted him eye to eye. His smoke blond hair was kinked, but his skin was white as Elmer's. He could have been a white baby, or maybe he was half and half, Alden wasn't sure. His huge eyes drilled her with a point-blank look of unbridled, expectant innocence that she found instantly absorbing. The toddler held a rubber doll, a leprechaun figurine or gruesome troll. The toy was filled with sand particles in an elastic skin that stretched in every direction as the little boy worried it and pulled its limbs. She saw it was stamped "Mr. Squishy" by its manufacturer.

"Mr. Squishy? Is that your doll's name?" She sweet-talked the baby in a sugary singsong and marched the rubber figure in the air before the baby's face. Her moment of rapture came out of nowhere, and Alden didn't temper the game until a policeman eyed her.

She rested the boy on the waffled fender of the Nissan, taking the liberty to try to unhook his tiny nose ring. But the gold loop adorning the baby's nostril was seamless. It would have to be snipped.

Officer Francisconi walked up to her. "Miss?"

Alden remembered a children's story her mother had read to her about girls named Miss Bee Gotten, Miss Take, Miss Fortune, Miss Terry.

The officer waited for her to tell him Miss what? Miss who?

"Alden Warren," she said. "You know me."

"Yeah. Miss Warren? Warren—add a *t* to that and you've got yourself a 'Warrant,'" he teased her.

"Oh. That's good. I guess you're the *wordsmith* on the force?"

He didn't seem to enjoy his own joke or its aftermath. "Miss Warren, you say that you were jaywalking from the traffic island right as this happened?"

"I didn't say I was *jaywalking.* Shite."

"There's no legal access to that traffic island. There's no crosswalk—from here. To there." He scrolled his arm back and forth across the rotary intersection, jabbing opposing pindots on the accident-scene mural with his pointer finger.

For the first time she recognized that perhaps the officer believed that *she* had caused the wreck when she ran across the rotary traffic. She told him, "People drive too fast in this fog."

"They land 747s at Logan in this kind of fog. Fog doesn't kill people," he said. "People—"

"—kill people. I know," she said. "Jesus H."

The officer gave her his scalding once-over, eyeing the National Seashore ID patch on her jacket, an emblem that afforded her a bit of protection even as it stigmatized her. Local fuzz had a long-standing *thing* against the Seashore's Teflon coating. The officer might have been thinking, She's one of those *crazies* who volunteers for the Seashore. He said, "You were first on the scene, right? We'll need to get your phone number. You donate hours at the Seashore?"

"I'm a paid employee," she said.

"Oh, that's right. You get paid to count seagulls." The police officer was showing his mean streak. It was the end of the summer season and the beginning of the winter lull. He had had it with summer, but he wasn't looking forward to the dead months.

Another cop plucked the hotel towels off the car floor and searched through the back seat. "Layla's got Krylon *and* an open container in here. Shit. She'll be going to County tonight after she's checked out at the hospital."

Alden jiggled the toddler on her hip. "Are you arresting her? What happens to the baby?" Her own voice surprised her. It was at once cheerful and defiant, like when a child says, "Finders, keepers."

"What happens to the baby?" Francisconi repeated her question in an unreadable inflection.

Alden said, "I mean, since his mom's having a lost weekend, and she's getting arrested? You say his dad is in jail? I thought maybe I could help out," Alden said.

The police officer tipped his face to look at her. "You want to help with the baby?"

"I could bring him home with me. I mean for the in-between. I've got my application at DSS. I'm getting the license—"

"Are you on their hotline list? To be on that list you have to have an extra bed ready at any hour, any day of the week. You got an extra bed?"

Alden told him that she had the extra bed. She said, "DSS has all my forms at the Yarmouth office. They're just waiting for a CORI report and fingerprint clearance, all that red tape."

"Yeah, it's a lot of steps," the officer said.

"I attend meetings, the open houses. Those get-acquainted carnivals and birthday parties where I can meet these babies getting placed out. But I wonder what will happen to this one."

"Well, it's the typical story, I guess. It's always a mess until it's worked out. But nothing so bad as that Cuban kid in Miami, you always hope." Francisconi took out a pad of paper and wrote down a phone number. "This is for Hester Pierson, the DSS home finder. Call her in the morning to see if Baby Hendrick is on her list."

"Yeah, I know her. She's working on my file." Alden maneuvered the toddler onto her opposite hip and shoved the paper snip deep into her pocket. She felt a strange wave of heat rise through her center of gravity, through her diaphragm, and into her larynx. Next she heard herself cooing baby talk in a voice she hardly recognized as her own, the result of a knee-jerk maternal mechanism. She rubbed noses with Baby Hendrick, happy to accept whatever twist of fate had brought them face-to-face.

Another team rolled up in a sparkling white truck still dripping with soapsuds. The pickup driver who had rear-ended the Nissan refused to be transported to the hospital in Hyannis, but he agreed to wear a foam collar and stood still as a medic snapped its wide cuff around his neck. He was going scot-free because Layla was caught red-handed with the gold inhalant.

Alden bounced the toddler on her hip. The baby looked at the scene but didn't seem to recognize his mom without the typical spark of life. The gold pollen on his mother's upper lip gave her the appearance of a Tutankhamen treasure as she lay passed out on a gurney, mummified on Krylon.

A medic asked Alden, "You took the little boy from the car? You should have waited for Rescue. Has that baby been examined?"

"This baby?" She leaned back to study his adorable face, his dimples and pudges.

"That baby was a passenger in the Nissan, right?"

Alden looked at the accordioned sedan. Its trunk was crumpled and its fenders were gashed. The little car was a junker to begin with. That's when she saw the popular bumper sticker "Chatham: A Quaint Little Drinking Village with a Fishing Problem"—a tongue-in-cheek acknowledgment of the Lower Cape's number one doomed industry and its alcoholic aftermath.

Baby Hendrick began to fuss, and she rocked her pelvis in tight circles to soothe the toddler on her hip. She loved his compact weight; it had the comfortable heft of a flour sack or a canvas bag of loose silver. She was meant to have a baby of her own—maybe it was this one.

The medic said, "He needs to go with Rescue to Hyannis to get checked out."

Alden still didn't hand the child to the paramedic. The patrolmen and rescue teams watched her.

Alden was embarrassed that local law enforcement personnel thought of her merely as a wife who had been left behind. She wanted them to know that her husband's disappearance was a mystery beyond her control, just like those dramatizations on television shows that investigate paranormal events, shows that gave FBI profiles of weirdos, gigolos, and killers. Some of these stories were based on fact, but most were urban legends and contemporary rumors. Yet when her husband had disappeared, no scientists or FBI professionals had converged on the scene to speculate about whether it was a hoax, like those crop circles, or whether a flying saucer or an occult hand had reached down and snatched him.

The police seemed certain that Monty had disappeared of his own free will, and they had found nothing to suggest otherwise except for one small detail. Officers had discovered a shoebox diorama abandoned on the shoulder of the road at the stop where Monty usually got off the bus. Monty had often constructed insect dioramas with his students. The item was assembled with real monarchs, swallowtails, and sulphurs arranged in a diminutive kick-line and glued to a piece of two-by-eight. The papery creatures were pierced by toothpicks that held tiny protest signs saying "Butterflies on Strike!" Alden had told investigators that Monty would never have left the diorama behind, but the police didn't see much value in the item and shoved it in a storage closet.

The patrolmen all seemed to know about Alden's husband, and one officer recalled having recently stopped Alden. "Weren't you in that MVA at the stoplight last month?"

"No, but I think you stopped me once, remember? You gave me a warning citation."

Something on her dashboard had pulsed sun glare that blinded oncoming traffic. A carrot-sized prism shivered from her rearview mirror. The trinket had been a gift from her husband. At first she had displayed the ornament in a sunny kitchen window to see it shoot blurry rainbow daubs across the walls and ceiling. But one time Monty had tried to use the glass phallus to initiate their love act. He warmed the beveled rod under the tap, but Alden refused. Whether it was chandelier baubles or mail-order items, Monty had often tried to introduce foreign probes and gimmickry into their bedroom routine, and his requests had created some tension between them.

The officer had told Alden to remove the New Age trinket from her dash. He didn't like vehicles to have distracting bric-a-brac or bumper stickers. The toddler was beginning to unravel now, aware of new faces and the nervous landscape of blinkers, a throbbing cherry orchard with chirping radios scissoring on and off. He dropped his rubber doll when a paramedic took him from Alden. The toddler cried out, drumming his heels and arching his back. Alden tried not to imagine that the baby called to *her* as he was brisked away.

But without Baby Hendrick to hold, Alden's forearms felt weak and tingly, as if specific, involuntary nerve synapses had been primed and then abruptly disconnected.

One ambulance drove off with Layla Cox, and a second one took away the baby. Alden saw the Mr. Squishy doll on the pavement. She picked it up. She examined its weird mass in her hands. It had a sandy interior that migrated under the pressure of her thumbs. She stretched its putty arms and released them. The exaggerated limbs slowly retracted.

She would save it for Baby Hendrick.

ALDEN DROVE TO HER PLACE on the pristine back shore, a beautiful aquarelle wilderness. Her tiny house was perched on the Atlantic waterfront at High Head, where the glacial shelf abruptly ended. It was the last perch of solid land before the Provincelands, fifteen wind-torn miles of parabolic sand dunes that looked like the moon. Beneath her doorstep, the surf crashed forward or sluiced backward, a constant hydrorespiration that Alden liked hearing, even in violent weather. But to get home she had to navigate the sand ruts, skirting hillocks of shadbush and chokeberry; wide swatches of cordgrass scraped paint off the fenders of her used Jeep Wagoneer. Dune residents keep their car tires almost flat for traction, and Alden never bothered getting air unless she planned to drive up cape and off the peninsula.

Last summer she had entered her name in a drawing held for Seashore employees to compete for the few dune shacks secured for year-round occupancy on the National Seashore. She had won the privilege to rent the tiny but much-prized Victorian shack named Sea Call. Other dune shacks were named for different states of secular ecstasy and transformation—Euphoria, Transcendence, Simplicity, Reliance—and one was called Halcyon, named after the fabled kingfisher that was said to have the power to calm winter storms.

Her tiny Victorian shack was newly insulated against the pounding nor'easters she could expect all season. She had running water, a new well with a four-inch pump, and enough pressure to squirt water forty feet from a hose. The shack had a propane gas generator for her compact fridge, electric heat, and lighting. A high-tech composting toilet cleansed "gray water" before releasing it back into deep sand. She had purchased a mini–satellite dish and got permission from the park service to have it installed inconspicuously beneath her west-facing eaves.

When she got home, Alden dialed the number of the DSS home finder on her cellular phone. She left her name and number on the social worker's voice mail. "What's happening with my application?" Alden said, picturing Baby Hendrick's face. For the first time since Monty had gone, she felt connected to someone.

She buttered a piece of bread and ate it at the kitchen sink. She drank the last of the cranberry juice. Before climbing into bed, she placed the Mr. Squishy doll on top of the Panasonic portable. The stiff-armed homunculus cast an oversize shadow against the wallpaper, already working its juju.

Alden got under the covers and pointed the clicker at the satellite receiver box on her TV. The screen bloomed at the foot of her bed. A rerun of the mystery series *Unfinished Business* was just starting. She listened to the show's edgy signature music, a halting pizzicato that Alden liked. Next she heard the host's urgent voice-over as he introduced cherished segments from the series' archives: "Lost Loves." "Missing." "Haunted." "The Unexplained."

HE WAITED IN THE DARK until Alden came home. He imagined she must have been out on a date, but he cut away from that visualization. He didn't like to meet up with his challengers, not even in his imagination. Tonight she was alone in the dune shack. He watched her step out of her skirt and peel off her sweater as she walked back and forth before two narrow Victorian windows. One window had an oilskin shade drawn down, a buttery filter for her striptease; the other was unobstructed.

He stood just beyond the gold plank that fell across the sand. He watched as she nibbled a heel of bread and sipped a glass of deep red juice, After the Fall cranberry or cranberry apple, he noted adoringly. He felt sheepish, but he coveted every speck of secret information, even her modest shopping lists. Once, he'd found a tiny white envelope beside her trash bin. In three languages the envelope said "Extra Buttons. Boutons Supplementaires. Botones Extras." His mother used to keep odd buttons in a candy dish on her bedroom dresser; replacements were sometimes sewn inside the hem of a new sweater, or they came in a packet like this. Alden's button was a thin shell disk with four holes in a tiny grid. He put it in his pocket.

He followed her profile as she drank her juice. He admired her long porcelain throat as she emptied her glass in a succession of tiny sips, tipping her head back. He watched her tiny Adam's apple tug and contract. She rinsed the glass, swirling the water counterclockwise before dumping it out, and that, too, he admired. She completed her charming bedtime chores with blithe authority, and he adored every small movement she made.

Once more, she walked out of his view, maybe to brush her teeth. She returned, in full frame again, dabbing her knee with a cotton ball drenched in calamine lotion. Pink trickles ran down her leg, and she mopped them with a Kleenex. She picked up her alarm clock, tugged its lever, then set it down on her bed stand. Next, she lifted a stubby candle or rubber thing—he was jolted to see it was a sex toy she was inspecting.

But it wasn't what he had thought, just a funny little doll, a frog prince or troll. She centered the figurine on her TV.

He moved closer to the sill to see her climb into bed.

He watched her fold the hem of her sheet under one elbow as she opened a book and pulled it up to her chin. He usually waited until she clicked off her lamp, but the November night was increasingly bitter. November is the jaded month. Nothing sprouts but rime and frost flowers. He turned away from her shack and walked across the dunes, following the rutted car tracks. On the Outer Cape there was nothing to stop the east wind except the *north* wind. They often worked together to earn their fame, braiding their fluid fingers into one icy wallop. A storm was coming in. Whether it was a real nor'easter or not, he wasn't dressed for it. His quilted mac was a cheap item right off the discount rack and it didn't have the layer of Thinsulate he wanted. It was only a mile to where he'd left his car, but the loose pack was difficult to navigate on foot. The Provincelands wilderness was an all-in-one nightmare of repetitive landmarks. Back dunes sloped gradually westward, but the toe of the dune is a steep seaward cliff. He retraced his steps, following interdune swales, sunken forests, hummocks of snarled cedar, and scrub oak barrens. Even without a real moon, the track shimmered like a tin sheet. The sandplain glittered with magic pinpricks—quartz, feldspar, garnet.

2

LUX DAVIS STOOD IN A TEN-ACRE FIELD at Bay State Nurseries, where his supervisor had called a meeting. Tight rows of neophyte evergreen shrubs fanned out in a dizzying starburst until the optical effect challenged his posture, his balance, and his clear head. Lux preferred to work alone, edging green animals or in his pleaching arbor where he trained two lines of poplars into a tunneling hedgerow. He bound lateral twiglets with twist ties and braided opposing branches until their arms grafted together in seamless green arches and crowns. By late autumn, the bare knots looked like Jesus' thorns. A selectman had recently asked Lux to estimate the damage to the rotary clock. Lux inspected the scrambled topiary and suggested that the mascot clock needed new plantings and maybe some tricky grafts to save broken limbs where that Nissan ate up a section.

He rested his boot on his spade and leaned into its long birch handle as Mr. Nickerson explained the new project at Seacrest. It was the doomsday scenario Lux had imagined for two years. The teacher's "guide yellow" parka flashed in his mind; sometimes it was just the Nike swoosh that burned across like a fireball.

Nickerson had brought a cardboard tray of Starbucks coffees into the field to hand out to the crew. Lux accepted a cup, sloshing some coffee on his caked gloves. Panic caused a Novocain effect, and his lips felt numb as he tried to take a sip. It wasn't the usual dishwater java from the nearby Donut Den, and the premium dark roast was supposed to be a righteous little boost to the four men, who'd been transferring young shrubs into two-gallon containers. These buckets were going on a flatbed truck for a sale at the Pilgrim Mall. His boss halted that chore.

Nickerson told them, “Here’s the job. You know that new Seacrest development on Bearse Point? They’ve ordered a hundred and sixty trees.” He motioned to the west side fields. Those lines of hemlocks and cedars were not supposed to be touched for another five years. The trees had originally been reserved for a landscape contractor in Yarmouth who had wanted mature plants later on. Seacrest had bettered his bid. His boss said that they would start working those rows next week. It was a rush order, maybe involving some overtime pay. Nancy had a sign-up sheet in the office if they wanted the extra hours.

Lux snapped his quilted mac against the oncoming chill and said, “Wait a minute. Aren’t we doing the clock first? That’s high profile. It’s a brainless PR project. It’s advertising, right?”

Nickerson eyed Lux. He said, “Change of plans, Mr. Davis. Is that all right with you?”

“I’m just saying I think we should repair the landmark before doing anything. It’s got visibility.”

“The town has to vote on that before they plunk new money into it. We don’t do any work yet. That is, we don’t scratch our ass without cash up front. We wait till town meeting, and you know about that circus, so there’s plenty of time to move these trees out for delivery to that Seacrest project—”

“But if I’m remembering—I’m remembering that those trees are already sold,” Lux said. He wanted the whole argument. An argument can lead to a modification, a retraction, a forfeit. He rattled off his reasons for second-guessing his boss’s instructions. Nickerson walked off toward his 4x4 truck, and Lux was talking to the thin air. But Lux had heard right. The cedars on rows 77 through 82 were coming out.

The crew watched Lux.

He tipped his face to follow a Cape Air puddle jumper that buzzed overhead at a low altitude, making its landing approach with a minimum ceiling. He watched it disappear into a wall of fluff. Lux knew that the men stared at him, so he waited stone-still just for its antieffect. Standing erect and frozen, his secret preoccupations and unconscionable impulses surfaced against his will. Stirred up like this, his eyes narrowed in a startling Windex blue squint. Women often fell for the vision, *at first.* It was his alarming eyes coupled with his lanky physique, like buff runway models in Calvin Klein ads, boys stripped to the waist for that day-laborer look, agented beauties in boxer shorts that never saw a lick of real work.

But Lux did his share of monotonous digging. The men were used to his oddness but grew impatient with Lux's annoying requests. Just that morning, Lux had made them hike around an acre of rose canes to avoid disturbing a glossy ibis he had found sunning there. Whether Lux was a nature lover or just superstitious about the strange, prehistoric-looking shorebird, they couldn't be sure. They obeyed Lux's wacky entreaties just to avoid his edgy aftermaths.

Marty Stokes was first to trim his wick and told him, "Look, man, we dig up trees every day. Trees over *here,* trees over *there*—that's the fuck-ass job. If we start these rows or if we go to work on that goofy green clock, what's the difference?"

Lux said, "I'm just saying, 'Where's my bee, where's my honey? Where's my God, where's my money?' "

"Shit. Leave off with the poetry, for our benefit, okay?"

"That's song lyrics, actually."

"Keep it up, we'll leave you here to sort that baling wire."

"I'm just saying, you ever see Nickerson get his hands dirty? He can't wrap one fucking root ball. See his fingernails? No tar, not a speck of dirt, just the grime that rubs off his cash after taxes."

Marty Stokes recognized Lux's familiar serf-versus-master complaint. Lux didn't like taking orders. It was more than an attitude problem; they all had that, but Marty Stokes remembered that Lux had had a neuro-pathological affliction since childhood. His classmates had learned to live with it back then, and now Lux usually had it under control. The men beside him in the field saw he worked harder than most of them, but he could get touchy. It was something called "freezing" and "false paralysis." As a kid he'd stand stone-still in left field during a tense inning and let a simple fly ball land at his feet. In math class or history, he'd turn into a statue and wouldn't answer when the teacher asked him a question. In his attempt to break free of his frozen spell his face would contort like a gargoyle. He was trapped on some sort of neurological flip side, as if the needle couldn't drop onto the right band on the brain platter. Sometimes he wouldn't talk for days; then his mutism would evaporate and he'd talk a blue streak, reading road signs and miscellany backward and forward. He would read multisyllabic phrases back to front and invent palindromes. He could turn any word inside out in an instantaneous, knee-jerk reaction.

Lux's mother had nursed him at her breast and wondered why her baby would suddenly stiffen in her arms. He had sometimes stopped breathing until he turned blue. Then he would take a deep breath and scream in healthy bleats. His mother had plopped him into the kitchen sink several times a day, since baths seemed to soothe him. Doctors said his sudden freezing or "slowdown spells" might be some kind of comorbid seizure activity. PET scans could not detect true autism, and his charts said, "OCD and TS highlights are mild *now* but could accelerate." A team of neurologists and other specialists eventually concurred on a diagnosis. Lux was afflicted with a general anxiety syndrome and oppositional disorder that waxed and waned throughout his childhood. They warned his mother, there and then, to be vigilant, because statistics showed that anxiety disorders were a gateway to drug and alcohol abuse.

His third-grade teacher asked his mother to come into the grammar school to sit with Lux at his lunch table, because he would freeze in the cafeteria maelstrom with all its crashing silverware and kids' explosive laughter as they tossed apple cores and stomped on empty milk cartons to startle him. She sat beside him every day for a year. He stared at his sandwich. At last he would lift one half of the sandwich and nip the corners off to approximate a trapezoid; then he'd bite into the other half, executing another secret geometry task.

Every year, his mother sent him to school with the same form letter. "Dear teacher, coach, staff member, friend: Lux is very excited to be involved in the activity you will supervise. I hope you will take the time to read this sheet to help you understand my son's condition—" Taking the letter to school each fall when he tried out for team sports was more embarrassing to Lux than just keeping to himself. He crumpled the Xeroxed letters and stayed on the sidelines. One year, he joined the high school cross-country team. He could run miles on his own without any trouble. He liked competing against himself until the finish line. Left alone, in his independent tasks, he rarely had attacks.

A teacher in Lux's honors English class was sympathetic about his isolation, and he showed Lux Sophocles' play *Philoctetes*, about a hero at Troy who had a terrible stink from a festering snakebite that never healed. The teacher explained how Philoctetes was exiled for ten years because of his vile wound, but at Troy he was healed and was then victorious over Paris with the aid of a magic bow. The teacher said that the Greek drama suggested that a hero's superior strength was inseparable from his disability. He bookmarked a passage for Lux: "Genius and disease, like strength and mutilation, may be inextricably bound up together."

But his mother didn't read the Greek dramatists. She liked to tell Lux about a little girl his own age who had a disorder called uncombable hair syndrome. The girl's hair was so kinked that no one could tame it. Her hair grew in ferocious tight coils, higher and higher, like a towering cloud of poisonous nettles. Cutting it short only worsened the condition. "Imagine what a curse it would be to have all those snarls," his mother would tell him, trying to make him feel better. Lux didn't think snarls would be as bad as what he endured. But throughout his youth, he often thought about the girl with uncombable hair syndrome and imagined one day taking her for his wife. He still thought of her now.

Lux crumpled his coffee cup in his fist and tucked it in his back pocket. He levered his spade across both shoulders, his wrists crooked on either end. Carrying his spade like that, he looked like a man sentenced to a few hours in the stocks. Even worse, on the path before him, his silhouette shot forward like a life-size crucifix. He thought of the local nut who walked highways, dawn to dusk, hauling a ten-foot wood cross fitted out with a caster wheel. The weirdo often walked past Lux two times a day on Route 6.

He went back to work with Paul Swiss and Marty Stokes, using his spade to edge a circle around a hemlock sapling. He levered the heavy clump and the root ball lifted, healthy and dense; its fists of branching sucker roots looked like the clotted nerve clusters on an MRI. He went on to the next sapling, stepped on his spade, and let his weight sink into the slice. The earth was sandy and the trees weren't too difficult to extract, despite their bushy skirts. He cut new swaths of burlap from a big roll-out dispenser attached to the back of a flatbed truck. He wrapped each root ball in a coarse turban and soaked the fabric with the hose nozzle. He took his jolly time.

As he worked, Lux watched the office in the central barn, waiting until he saw the bookkeeper get in her car to drive to the post office, as she did every morning. Then Lux left his mates and went inside the empty office to call his sister-in-law.

GWEN ANSWERED THE PHONE after it rang six times. He told her, "Well, shit—thanks for finally picking up." He waited a moment before dropping the bomb. Then he told her, "It's the nightmare we talked about, Gwen."

"The nightmare?" she said, her mouth full of buttered toast.

"Gwen—it's the doomsday scenario."

"What are you talking about?"

"The teacher, I mean."

She stopped chewing. Lux heard her expectorate her mouthful of toast into the pedal trash can. He listened to its foot pedal chirp and the lid slap shut. The finality of that simple contraption made his muscles flinch.

"No. Don't tell me. I don't want to know—"

Lux said, "Nickerson says we start on Monday. We're wrapping hemlocks now, but next week we'll hit it—"

"Isn't it deep enough?" she asked in a tiny voice.

"It's trenched in pretty good, but in two years it could have heaved up. With every hard freeze the marl swells and shifts."

"Lux, are you saying it could have moved somewhere on its own?"

"I think we'll find it right where we left it," he said.

"Let someone else find it," she said.

"Look, Officer Francisconi knows I was driving that school bus. He's eyeballing me. Hear what I'm saying, Gwen? No one should touch it but us."

In Lux's night school class, the instructor had said there was a parallel theme in the Greek classics and every Martin Scorsese movie: *A corpse left unburied just causes trouble.* Lux thought he had honored that rule when he chose a row of landscape shrubs that offered a grace period of at least five years, but that was no longer the case. He had sweated every detail, but he hadn't foreseen Nickerson's change of mind. The trees were coming out early. Details weren't holding firm.

He remembered his nightmare dream about the candles. In low-budget movies, amateurish mistakes emerge on the screen. Props on the set might change frame-by-frame. Furniture moves around, or a glass is suddenly full when in the previous shot it was half-empty. It's a problem with what they call film continuity. Lux had first seen this in the classic movie *King Kong.* He noticed the shifting nap of fake fur on the King Kong model. Its tufted hair moved like wheat in a windstorm because each time the technician moved the ape doll to shoot a new frame, he mashed the ape's fur fibers left or right in unforeseen, random patterns.

In another film, candles on a dinner table are freshly lit and flickering. In the very next frame the candles are burned down to the saucer lip of the candlesticks; then *blink*— the candles are tall again. Lux had a recurrent "continuity nightmare" about the schoolteacher: First the teacher is buried; then he's unearthed. The dirt is mounded up beside the hole. Then the hole is covered and Monty is safely interred. The mound of dirt. The open hole. The body surfaces again as if it's rising on a hydraulic lift. Lux understood that the nightmare betrayed his escalating, fevered anxiety, but knowing this didn't stop him from having the dream almost nightly.

He lit a cigarette and watched its ashy worm wriggle and lengthen in sync with his sudden helpless feeling. When the trouble had happened, Lux had searched through medical stacks at the Boston Public Library. He had read forensic anthropology manuals, trying to calculate what was happening to the teacher month by month. He learned that medical examiners first identify a corpse by "sexing the skeleton." A man's bones are pitted, bumpy, irregular where major muscles and tendons were anchored, earning the male skeleton the descriptor *robustus.* A female skeleton, called *gracilis,* is smoother; her bones will look almost planed, beveled, except for her pelvis, which gets notched with each successive childbirth where uterine ligaments cause stress. Once he had learned the nomenclature, Lux started calling his secret trouble "Robustus." The Latin helped him to disentangle and disassociate from the teacher's real ID—a name he'd rather forget.

His sister-in-law said, "You told me those baby trees have to get bigger before they come out—"

"Change of plans." He was surprised to hear himself repeat Mr. Nickerson's exact words. They were the *exact words* but had a wholly different, snowballing feeling. Yes, he thought to himself, one person's change of plans can suddenly initiate another person's emergency maneuvers.

HE FIRST SAW ALDEN WARREN when she came to meet her husband at his regular bus stop, next to a dog breeder's compound. It was the last stop on Lux's route before he drove the empty bus to the lot. Alden was interested in the puppy farm on the corner and she always wanted to know if there was a new litter. The proprietor was grumpy and off-putting, and Alden didn't want to go through the kennels alone. She had asked her husband to take her, but Monty wasn't interested in dogs and never took the time. Lux built up his nerve to escort Alden into the compound. He told her to meet him there and he'd show her around the whelping pens.

She met him in front of the huge barn door, a heavy plank slider that was difficult to open. Alden watched him throw his shoulder against the panel and force the door down its track. It glided apart like a magic curtain, revealing the wonders within. Lux breathed the tangy scent of cedar shavings soaked from overturned water bowls and fresh urine. From several pens, puppies squeaked and tumbled, one over another, to greet them. He went ahead of Alden and started uncoiling hose to rinse the water containers and refill them. Next he sprayed the dirtied concrete pens. She watched his face. He looked Apollonian, almost like the Greek example, except his fresh-bitten mouth was surprisingly, nervously red.

When their eyes met, he looked back at her with a built-in reaction, nothing menacing, but it wasn't a neutral expression.

Alden said, “So, you come here after your bus route? Every afternoon?”

He nodded.

“You have two jobs?”

“Three, actually. I drive the bus route twice a day, but my real job is at Bay State. You know, the nurseries on Mill Pond Road? I do their ornamentals. Landscape architecture. Green rooms.”

“Green rooms, really? But you must like taking care of these dogs. I’m jealous,” she said. She waited as he unscrewed the cap from the blue neck of an antacid bottle and sipped its contents. Embarrassed that she watched him, he tightened the cap and put the plastic bottle back in his coat pocket. When she didn’t see any telltale chalk on his lips, she asked him if it might not be a stomach remedy, after all, but a makeshift flask of something. She said, “Did you know my father, Dane Baker? He put vodka in a yellow plastic mustard bottle whenever he drove on car trips. If traffic annoyed him and he wanted a stiffener, he squeezed the bottle to get a squirt of vodka.”

“French’s mustard and vodka, I don’t know,” Lux said.

“He’d rinse the bottle first, you silly—he said vodka doesn’t have a reeking smell if a cruiser pulled him over.”

Lux didn’t know what to say, so he brought her over to a new litter, tiny mitts of golden fluff staggered along their mother’s milk line. “Who doesn’t love a puppy?” he said.

In the puppy barn she didn’t need Monty.

She followed Lux from one brood stall to the next. The rich vapor of puppy shit, like cooked rye grass and hops, was a strong curtain between them.

Then he stopped at a grain bin to grab handfuls of dog food, stirring up its branny scent. From across the aisle, he started pelting Alden’s coat with Science Diet, one little nugget, then another. The dog chow glanced her face and snagged in her hair. He teased her until she protested; then, of course, he pitched the pellets faster. He didn’t stop even when she was laughing and couldn’t catch her breath. Pens of bitches and their pups were yipping and barking in excitement. Lux taunted her as if she was a baby sister—or something—until the manager of the puppy mill showed up. The man wasn’t pleased to see them. He was surprised to note that the water bowls had been refilled, but he told them that they were trespassing and could be charged with breaking and entering. He ordered them to leave the premises. Lux watched Alden's face to see if she understood. Lux wasn't authorized personnel at the puppy farm. He was an impostor.

Soon after they had toured the puppy farm, Lux saw Alden on TV talking with the news reporters about her missing husband. She was holding the teacher's butterfly diorama, which the police had found at the bus stop. The camera zoomed in on the insect figures glued to a plank. The bugs had diminutive toothpick signs that said "Butterflies on Strike!" The vision unnerved him. Here was his sweetheart holding something precious and surreal like angels on a pin.

Lux studied Alden's face on the fourteen-inch Sony until it was painted by memory. Yes, she was a pretty thing. Even in her sleepless trauma. Her tousled, neglected hairstyle streamed over her shoulders, tight ringlets shiny as screw bits spilled everywhere. She had the same pleasing, slightly trashy veneer of the feral urchin who had matured in Lux's imagination, the girl with uncombable hair syndrome that his mother had told him about. There she was—the secret cameo he had clung to for years and years.

In the news clip, she had recounted her brief married life in two or three ringing sentences. "Monty and I got married last year. We were so happy until—" Her voice was fearful and tinged with unresolved jealousy.

From that moment onward, Lux was in a spell. His fixation had volume and scale. Like a photo-realist painter filling in a wall-sized grid, he colored in every notch of blank canvas with idealized information. He had her heart-shaped face, her looping ringlets, her ivory neckline—the rest he was all too eager to fill in with his own trembling conjectures and needling ideas. Through no fault of her own, she was connected to him.

He wished he'd made a videotape of the evening news when she had addressed the Channel 4 Livecam. Then when she moved to the dune shack, he often went out to High Head after dark just to see that she was doing all right. She was his secret life. He thought of her morning, noon, and night. He pictured a family tree with himself on one side and Alden Warren on the other. Between them they had already produced one offspring. From their mysterious union was born something homely and unwanted; with neither forethought nor malice, their love connection had spawned Robustus.

HIS SISTER-IN-LAW WAS SOBBING on the other end. Lux listened to her sputtering, but there wasn't time to indulge her. He told her, "The trees are going to that swank development at Bearse Point in Osterville. Are you listening?" He tried to keep his voice flat. "We'll be lifting these trees out next week. We hit that row, and it's D-day."

"Lux, you said the teacher is safe where he is."

"Shit, it's a goddamn nursery business, isn't it? Nickerson is selling the stock. I can't stop him." Lux wished he had buried the teacher in his pleaching arbor. Those landscape trophies would never be dug up and sold. But Nickerson led customers on tours through the green animals near the offices. Someone might have noticed if the bed had been recently turned. Last summer, *Architectural Digest* had arrived to take pictures, and Lux was credited in the magazine for his masterly creations. Tourists were coming to see Lux's green animals and green rooms. The pleaching arbor had too much traffic.

"You think that body dissolved?" Gwen asked Lux.

"With all that ten-ten-ten we put down, the pelletized lime, and the sprinklers running, it should be just bones. And that nylon jacket—"

"What jacket?" Gwen said.

"Treated nylon doesn't break down. He'll still be wearing that." Lux knew that medical examiners calculate the time of death by how many generations of flies lay eggs on the body. Except for its polyester socks, a corpse doesn't last long in the dirt. An unembalmed corpse would be skeletonized in a matter of months if there was a source of water.

The nursery had a sprinkler system chugging twice a day.

He told Gwen, "The bones get ivory-clean like a piano keyboard."

"You're not bringing those bones back here," Gwen said.

He imagined his sister-in-law's face. Her wide-open eyes, mouth ajar, like her dead-ahead astonishment during sex, when she stared him down until he would shoot. His brother, Denny, was on a swordfish boat nine months of the year, so Lux was left with the delicate chore. He sometimes wished he wasn't afforded the obligation. But his only other steady lover had been a forty-year-old woman with elaborate tattoos across her backside. The garish tattoos were supposed to make her feel better about her flat ass, but for Lux it was like making love to a sheet of busy wallpaper.

Each midday he drove home to the duplex on Snow's Road where he lived with his brother's wife and two small nephews. "Going home? That would be for a *hot lunch,* I guess?" Marty Stokes pried, but Lux said nothing. The boys slapped their knees and hee-hawed, jealous of two things: the pretty girl waiting for him, and Lux's deadpan calm, which seemed glamorous or weird, just plain over their heads, when they would have bragged about doing her.

He pulled up to his house. One side of the duplex was vacant, but their side was always swarming. Gwen would be outside hanging wash on the umbrella clothesline that Lux had installed for her when he moved in two years ago. Gwen was thrilled to have the new contraption. She'd have his flannel shirts drying. His briefs. Even the ancient living-room slipcovers flapped in the wind. He looked at the umbrella clothesline filled with his shirts and jeans. She must have taken them out of his drawers just to wash them. When the old clothesline pulley had jammed, he bought her the new one. The box said "Automatic Clothes Dryer," and they had laughed about it.

"I guess the wind does all the work," he said.

Gwen acted like this umbrella clothesline was created by a genius, by Einstein or the Wizard of Menlo Park, Thomas Alva Edison. After Lux had assembled its center pole and spoked crown and tightly threaded its vinyl wires, Gwen had shown him every courtesy. She wiped his sweaty soda bottle with a dish towel before she twisted the top off. She served him extra portions at dinner, even when he couldn't clear his plate. She offered him the tough heel of the Italian loaf because he favored it more than the fluffy slices. He noticed her kindnesses because their life together had few pleasures and was usually all obstacles.

It was Gwen's idea to invite him into her bed whenever the boys were napping. At first Lux was a little spooked by her offer. Although his brother was fishing offshore, Lux didn't like anything too organized or pro forma when it came to sex. Gwen told him he wasn't hurting his brother's marriage pledge when her husband wasn't home to perform the role. She said Denny wouldn't really mind, but of course Denny shouldn't be told.

And in a crisscross agreement with Lux, Gwen promised not to tell anyone about Robustus. It was soon after the teacher disappeared that Lux was interviewed by detectives. They wanted to fill out the typical sheets, enough paperwork to satisfy office heads and the little woman who'd been left behind. Alden Warren had filed a missing-persons report and expected some sort of official feedback in return. Going through the motions, the detectives contacted Laidlaw Transit and discovered that Lux was the bus driver who would have been the last person to have official contact with the teacher. In their initial sweep-through, they had also learned that Lux had been seen with the school-teacher, sharing a pitcher at a local watering hole. Detective Milsky telephoned Lux at home for a five-minute feeler. The detective said, "Perhaps the teacher described a new attraction, someone besides Penelope Griffin? Do you know where they might be going? Was he searching for bugs, or maybe just headed for Vegas?"

Lux cooperated with the interview, hoping that the telephone call was in lieu of a full-scale raking over the coals. He confirmed information about his bus route and the drop-offs for the kids. He said that he had had a couple of beers with the teacher, but they had talked only about sports and how the Celtics had never come back to their glory level after losing Bird and McHale. It was a shame that Reggie Lewis dropped dead in a pickup game and his wife couldn't get a settlement. Lux told the detective that Monty Warren hadn't said where he was going. The detective saw that Lux had nothing to add to their research, which had stagnated at just the routine summations. The teacher had taken a powder from his matrimony chores, that was all.

But Officer Francisconi still nosed around, trailing Lux in the cruiser for weeks after the teacher disappeared.

Gwen had been watching Lux as he talked to Detective Milsky on the telephone. In her nervousness she stirred tomato sauce in a figure eight, shifting direction, clockwise, counterclockwise.

"They believe you?" she asked him when he had hung up.

"I don't know."

"Your voice sounded funny. Cops can read voices. They learn how at the police academy. Your voice sounded different."

"Shit. I'm me," he said. He took the wooden spoon out of her hand and slapped it in the china spoon rest. Lux stepped out of his muddy jeans. Gwen shoved the trousers into the hamper and followed him upstairs. She smoked a cigarette as he bathed in the claw-foot tub. He came into her bedroom with a jelly glass of bourbon because he feared getting even partly sober until the mess was over. He drank to keep from going to sleep until he reached the blackout level, when he wouldn't have dreams. But he fucked her for a good, long hour. He fucked her to flash-freeze his day in the standstill of his alcohol binge. Denny was coming in to offload the next weekend, and he wasn't going fishing again until later the next month. Lux would be back in the sofa bed with nothing but bottled distractions.

"TOMORROW WE'LL GO IN and get it after dark," Lux told Gwen. "Shit, I hope there isn't a moon. Is there a moon tonight?"

"How should I know?" Gwen said.

"Did you see a moon *last* night?" he said. "If there was a moon last night, it's going to come around again tonight. The moon's got no reason to hide out."

He was making it worse with philosophy. But this philosophy just kept flooding him from out of nowhere—little stabs and pinpricks of insight and poetic observation punctured a curtain of pure panic. As he tried to organize his thoughts, he pictured his victim's young widow. He couldn't get her out of his mind. She was working at the National Seashore office, like some do-gooder nature clerk. He remembered going there as a kid when his uncle wanted a hunting permit for antique musket season. Lux often phoned the wildlife hotline, 349-WING, just to hear Alden's voice on updated recordings: "Sixteen dunlins on Coast Guard Beach; one blackpoll warbler at the transfer station; one ruddy turnstone; twenty cedar waxwings in the power lines on Union Field

Road, in Truro. One Kemp's ridley sea turtle was seen between the spar buoy and the shoreline at Chequesset Neck in Wellfleet Harbor. Remember, Kemp's ridley and loggerhead sea turtles are still stranding on bay-side beaches. If you find one, haul it up past the high-tide line and call the Audubon emergency number at —"

Lux was convinced by her voice. She seemed to have a personal investment in that search-and-rescue mission. Lux began to notice the diverse flocks that swerved over the nursery fields like showers of black pepper. He watched for rare stragglers in the shad and beach plum along the perimeters. He noted songsters, their creaky warbles and trills. He had a dog-eared field guide and had learned to identify some of these birds, but he had never left a message on Alden's hotline. Sometimes he chased away grackles and crows that gathered conspicuously at the secret tomb site, as if they smelled carrion.

"Are you sure you remember which row it's in?" Gwen said.

"I know where."

"Lux, those were the old days. You weren't even sober yet. You were dead drunk. How can you remember where he went in?"

"It's not something you forget," he said.

It had happened in '99, the year before Y2K. As the millennium approached, Lux had hoped for massive global fuckups so that his own nightmare could get lost in the helter-skelter. But Y2K didn't amount to anything at all. No meteor impact, no power failures, no water shortages. None of the predictions had added up.

Suddenly he felt dizzy. He sat down in Nancy Silva's office chair. He saw the secretary's foam slippers, which she kept by her seat so she could remove her street shoes when she worked at her desk. He pushed his hand inside the plush stirrup of one slipper, its insole smoothed from wear and soft as hamster fur. "Look," he told Gwen, "I'll get ahold of King. We'll drive up to Vermont, into the boonies. Remember that von Trapp Family Lodge, where we had that camping trip?"

Gwen said, "You mean where those *Sound of Music* people are laid to rest? You want to bury it with them? You're crazy —"

"I don't know. We'll take it up there. Into the forest."

3

WEDNESDAY MORNING, Alden collected breakfast trays from the Council on Aging annex in Eastham and delivered the food to shut-in seniors. She didn't want the full-time role, but she filled in once or twice a week for the regular volunteer who ferried hot meals to loners. Alden was fond of her charge, Hyram Westover, and she liked to sit with him for a while before punching in at her bookstore job.

She found him watching CNN in the pitch-dark living room. His blinds were still drawn and the talking heads provided the only source of illumination. Alden liked taking over as soon as she arrived. She pulled the lamp chain beside Hyram's chair, and the messy room emerged. "On second thought, it's better in the dark," she said as she collected the disordered mural of socks, orange rinds, unfurled newspapers. Moldy sandwich crusts creeping across the upholstery like furred green caterpillars looked like the larvae of cabbage whites or long-tailed skippers in Monty's crumpled paperback *Butterflies of North America.*

He asked her to help him find his eyedrops. She found the little bottle and handed it to him. He handed it back. "You do it," he told her.

"I'm not a nurse," she said.

He tilted his head back and waited for her to administer the drops to him. She shrugged and unscrewed the tiny cap. She drizzled the medication in the corner of his right eye. "Ouch," he said. "These drops make it worse."

Alden had brought him to the optician's repeatedly to get the painful nose pads on his eyeglasses adjusted, but last week she had arrived to see Hyram wearing Looney Tunes Band-Aid strips crisscrossed over one eye. "What's wrong? Is it pinkeye?" she said.

"No. Dr. Glass calls it corneal erosion. The jelly dries up. When I go to sleep, my eye gets stuck to my eyelid. If I wake up, I can rip the same exact spot. Taping the lid shut keeps my eye closed until morning."

Alden never knew what to say in response to Hyram's graphic descriptions of his declining health. Thank goodness he stopped at his waist when he complained about his ailments. Hyram had asked her to help him tape his eye shut. Alden knew that he could do it by himself, but he wanted her to return each night just for the company. She had told him she couldn't show up all the time, but she went to the drugstore to purchase special paper tape that wouldn't irritate his skin.

When she came back some nights, he would sit at the kitchen table while she taped his eye using one horizontal strip and another strip to anchor the first one. In turn, he sometimes helped her sort through quarterly statements about her car insurance or her husband's TIAA-CREF retirement fund, which she couldn't touch without further proof of the shareholder's death or his whereabouts. When she and Monty were married, he had convinced Alden to put her own savings of four thousand dollars into his CREF money market, under his name, assuring her that she would be listed on all the paperwork as Monty's sole beneficiary. But her claim was still under review by the legal department. Hyram helped her draft letters to impenetrable institutions that withheld every resource from Alden, pending official signatures and paperwork to prove that her spouse was deceased. Alden saw that a fisherman's wife could get her husband's bank funds or open his safe-deposit box when her husband was lost at sea, but Monty had disappeared on dry land, and that required a body as proof of death.

Hyram advised her about her money troubles, and he had once tried to contact her sister-in-law to see if she had heard from Monty and might be in cahoots with him in a scheme against Alden. All of a sudden, Hyram was in her life. *Who* had adopted *whom* no longer seemed to matter.

Hyram was a noted conservationist in the area, an activist with full credentials and a scrapbook of newspaper clippings documenting his triumphs. Hyram had become active in environmental issues after he retired from the navy at forty-two, almost thirty years ago. He had spent his tours homesteading in Vietnam during a good chunk of the skirmish there. He saw the fall of Saigon.

The chaos of that frantic exodus seemed to debunk his whole career. He told Alden it was the final COMMFU or completely monumental military fuckup at the bitter end of a wholly doomed enterprise. He had watched women climb with their babies onto a helicopter tail boom and had seen the aircraft crumple like a taco shell as it tried to lift off. Other craft got airborne with refugees clinging to their bowed skids in two fragile lines like clothespins that popped off when, at last, they couldn't hold on. One by one they dribbled off, scissoring their legs and arms as they fell into the jungle or into the boiling surf of the South China Sea.

Hyram settled stateside and found his new niche as a mentor to Outer Cape worrywarts. He whipped things up into a froth and led the charge at every environmental melee, whether it be at the old landfill or at the harbor, where the Army Corps of Engineers were dredging a deeper channel in the Pamet River, disrupting a fragile shelf of samphire and glasswort wetlands. Or maybe they were invading acreage where a vernal pool was the sole home to fairy shrimp and the obligate wood frog, spotted salamander, and spadefoot. News media adored Hyram. He was a "lovable eccentric" in his repentant golden years, his shock of white hair recalling both Tip O'Neill and Andy Warhol. A brazen Green grandpa today, he had once mapped saturation-bombing runs that dropped Daisy Cutters and napalm across the hillsides of Vietnam. For that, he had earned fruit salad on his jacket. Now he wore a sweatshirt and pajama bottoms.

When his health had failed, he quit his fieldwork and directed preparations for sit-ins at the controversial Boston Harbor outfall pipe, conducting planning sessions from his kitchen table. Housebound, he sometimes took in wildlife survivors and nannied stranded sea turtles for Alden when she had more than she could handle at the National Seashore office.

Alden had first met Hyram when a pod of pilot whales had stranded at a Wellfleet beach and she had worked with volunteers to remove the stricken beasts. Hyram said that pilot whales, called blackfish by the native fishermen, looked like torpedoes, shiny bomblets, or "tin fish." Hyram often used military idioms and figures of speech. Workers hauled the whales onto flatbed trucks using block and tackle and hydraulic winches. From there, the odd caravan set off to Woods Hole Oceanographic Institute where the whales would be dissected. In the heat the whales had begun to smell rank, and Hyram had offered Alden his extra handkerchief so that she could tie a mask across her face against the stink.

But since Hyram's recent bout of congestive heart failure, his ankles had been badly swollen and he hadn't been down on the beach for months.

He told her, "We have to *get on message* now. We're finalizing plans for our second rally and sit-in at the outfall pipe. Can I count you in?"

"How can you organize a *sit-in* so many miles offshore?"

"We have a sign-up sheet for volunteer captains who'll take us out. We've got the *Cee Jay*, the *Kestrel*, dories, draggers, Zodiacs, Hobie Cats. Some Sea Rays and Mercruisers, dinghies with outboards hitched up, anything that'll get us out there."

Hyram had gained national attention for his "rowboat regatta," a sit-in staged in deep water, in rough surf, to protest the outfall pipe. The outfall pipe was a sudden-death waste management plan to save Boston Harbor by pumping sewage through a tunnel and discharging its suspect effluent in pristine open water. Hyram was a guest on morning TV shows, where he had explained, "The outfall plume will reach Cape Cod Bay and cause toxic algal blooms." Alden admired his determination; he just wouldn't give up when a cause was hopeless.

"We always need more crew; we have plenty enough wannabe captains already."

Alden said, "That's going to be a motley bunch out there."

"A first-class argosy."

"I hope you have good sailing weather."

"So, you want to come?"

"I don't know."

"Oh, that's right, you're not sticking *your* neck out for anyone. You're working for the government in this plover mess? They've killed off twenty thousand gulls already. We've got another rally happening this Thursday at Chatham Light. You're on the wrong side of that —"

"I'm not taking sides."

"You seem to be working with the agency on this, right?" he said.

"I'm just a bookstore clerk, shite. I've been collecting the dead birds. They're dead already. I'm not the one setting out loaves of bread sprayed with Avicide and Avitrol. Where do they get their bread, anyhow?"

"Crates of stale bread are donated by chain supermarkets. You know, like when Stop and Shop sends day-old bread to the soup kitchen? Gulls get some of that."

"Home Pride? Wonder bread? Well then, shouldn't your group picket those bakeries? They're accessories to the crime —"

"So you admit it's a crime?"

"Sure. It's a crime to waste good food on the rats of the sky." She had begun to feel better teasing Hyram. Her jabs were good natured and he liked to duel with her. It rejuvenated them both.

She watched Hyram eat his eggs and told him about the car accident and Baby Hendrick. "That little baby has a nose ring. I tried to remove it but it was soldered. I needed some snips."

"Was this baby American? Because ancient cultures used these tribal adornments for particular reasons, but today what are they supposed to mean?"

"Of course he's *American.* Where've you been? They have these piercing stalls at the mall."

"This was a wee baby?"

"Cute as a button," Alden said.

As Hyram ate his breakfast, she tidied up and rinsed his silverware in the kitchen sink. She noticed his empty prescription bottle on the windowsill. "Your nitro is all gone. Have you been having some angina?"

He shrugged. "Just a few episodes, not bad."

"Then why is this bottle empty? You're supposed to call the doctor if you have discomfort. Did you call? Has Mrs. White delivered your new prescriptions?" Alden said.

"Mrs. White? She's not my type. Now someone like *you*—" he teased her. His innuendos made her uncomfortable. He'd had a successful run as a lady-killer, and at seventy-two years old he still couldn't let go of his modus operandi. The usual volunteers who worked for the Council on Aging were older women in the chattering throes of "menopausal zest," and Hyram told Alden he hated those busybodies. "They keep bringing me these refrigerator magnets." He pointed to the GE, where someone had arranged a few diminutive tabby cats and parrots stamped out of magnetic tape. He didn't like these homey touches. He was still an outdoorsman, despite his confinement.

He enjoyed Alden's visits because she was always a little taciturn, almost affectless, and her sanitized moods interested him. "What makes you tick?" he asked her again and again. Hyram didn't try to cheer her up. But whenever he caught Alden thinking of Monty, he told her, "Find someone who *wants* to be found."

She looked at the old man. He might have been talking about Monty or he might have been referring to the married man she had wasted her time with lately. She didn't want him to know she was crazy about that new baby. Her maternal feelings were somehow much more personal than any fling she might be having. To throw Hyram off her new obsession with Baby Hendrick, she told him about her plans to take off from work that afternoon to meet Mr. Ison for a Dear John lunch in Boston.

"So you decided to dump the travel agent? Congratulations. Mission accomplished," he said. He lifted two fingers in the victory sign. Hyram had encouraged her to break it off with finality, with a "sweep of the scythe," so it wouldn't be mistaken for prolonged flirtation. He told her, "When the fire's out, you have to sweep the ashes out of the hearth."

The morning sun torched the sleeve of his flannel bathrobe, igniting its short golden nap. "Finish your breakfast," she said, "and mind your own business."

But Hyram could always tell when Alden was prisoner of her claustrophobic inner thoughts. Her introspections encircled her like snow fence, and he'd tell her, "Open up. Air out those cobwebs."

She sat across from him and shrugged.

He said, "Don't worry so much. Life is short. Life is a rope bridge with both ends on fire."

"Oh, nice," she said. But she had grown used to Hyram's wry, epigrammatic sayings. His needling always reassured her, like a meager strip of light under the hall door that used to mean that her mother was still awake and available to her if she needed her back rubbed.

He pointed to his eye. "After you get back from Boston, will you come over tonight?"

"You can tape your eye yourself, you know."

"But could you stop at PetCo to get some millet seed for Godzilla?"

"I guess I can," she said. She was careful not to accept too many extracurricular duties. Hyram had already asked her to get his toaster oven fixed, when she could see for herself that the artifact wasn't worth repairing.

She looked at Godzilla in his birdcage by the window. The tiny canary popped from one perch to a little swing, then popped to the next perch, then reversed direction. The songbird was a rare Gloucester canary, his plumage a handsome variegated green, what bird enthusiasts called lizard. The canary's repetitive flits back and forth in the tiny cage, perch to perch, sometimes halting to trill a rolling warble, all for the purpose of inviting amorous adventures that were never to be fulfilled, seemed absurdly poignant to Alden.

And Alden didn't enjoy some of the birders' vernacular Hyram used. He had told her that a female canary's sexual apparatus was called, in cursory summation, a vent.

Hearing the bird's relentless miniaturized power chords, she told Hyram that it was "like Aerosmith on helium." She threatened to buy a matching female just to shut Godzilla up.

"Oh, no you don't. If canaries find a mate, they might stop singing altogether," Hyram told her.

"You mean if they get a mate, they stop their serenade?"

"That's right. But when you women get hitched up, that's when you *start* your whining."

She was used to Hyram's jabs at the female sex; they sprang from his nostalgia for a little black book he kept in the sideboard, its leather binding cracked and taped. But keeping these canaries apart just to hear some avian Muzak seemed like a cruel hobby. Alden agreed to return that night to tape his eye and to bring the birdseed for the little voice box of fluff. She saw Hyram's relief when she promised. He invented errands, practical or not, just to make sure she came back.

ALDEN LEFT HYRAM'S PLACE and by nine-thirty was at her desk at the National Seashore Visitor Center, sunk in her same old routine. Alden sometimes thought no one knew she existed, hidden away in the little bookstore cubicle in the east wing of a hexagon pavilion built in the typical Mission 66 architecture of national park structures that were thrown up in the sixties, complete with its "Chinese hat" roof, same as a Pizza Hut. The visitor center was the hub of the Cape Cod National Seashore, a wilderness preserve of forty-three thousand upland acres on the outer peninsula, including forty miles of undeveloped coastline.

The visitor center offered programs, hosted guest exhibits, and housed permanent collections of marine zoology specimens in glass bins and display cases. It even had its own theater pit with plush upholstery seating like a real movie house, where you might watch films called *Tide Line Timeline* and *Cephalopods—Brains of the Sea.* For her break, Alden liked to sit down somewhere in the dark funnel of velveteen seats and put her feet up.

From her office window, she could see the water.

The sea was the same each day, but never exactly the same.

Revolving tides might daze or arouse tourists in short trances, but Alden was perpetually agitated, stirred—enslaved by the sea. Her shift was nine to five, like any working slob, but her desk faced a full-length window that looked out upon the Million-Dollar Marsh. Realtors had invented the nickname for a sales campaign that pitched Nauset Marsh as a local attraction. The untamed land increased property values. There was a building boom, and outsiders like Ison were building trophy homes that disrupted the waterfront vista. "It's like finding the Taj Mahal on Walden Pond," local editorials sniped. But real estate ads boasted, "Last lots to abut conservation land. Going fast."

Alden stared at the Million-Dollar Marsh, its complicated inlets and slurries, and the open water beyond. The astonishing view made her light headed. Maybe it was the sea air. The old saying went,

Cape air makes you sleep till noon,
Cape air makes you lazy.
Don't be surprised
when two *moons rise,*
because Cape air makes you crazy.

Hyram had told her that the Victorian rhyme romanticized their seaside paradise. The "*two* moons" merely described one moon in the sky and one twinned on the water; there was nothing crazy about it. But Alden believed that the moon, whether a full wafer or just a snip of rind or cuticle, was nothing to sneeze at.

She sharpened a few pencils and arranged them in a fan on her desk blotter; she sorted her money drawer, the checks and MasterCard receipts. She pounded a roll of dimes against the edge of her desk to tear the paper open, but she had made few transactions at the cash register that week. The bookstore was empty.

On top of her computer monitor she still kept a pair of baby booties Monty had given her when she thought she was pregnant. It might have been an "isthmic conception," or perhaps she hadn't been pregnant at all, but Alden believed she might have lost the baby after a doctor examined her. The doctor took a speculum directly from a warming drawer, but the instrument had rested too close to the lightbulb. When Alden said, "Ouch," the doctor replied, "You girls used to complain that these were too cold, now you say they're too hot." She wasn't really hurt, but Alden often wondered if this was the little insult that had caused her to get her period.

When Monty discovered her pregnancy was a false alarm, it didn't jinx his marriage commitment as it might have for a lot of men. They were married at town hall as planned, in a room recently decorated by workers from the Registry of Motor Vehicles. The state had launched a new campaign to encourage drivers to check the organ donor box when they renewed their driver's license. Alden married Monty beneath a banner that said "Be an Organ Donor—Give the Gift of Life." Actual marriage vows suggest a certain amount of sacrifice, but the unsettling poster seemed to be rubbing it in.

Monty had married her that day regardless of whether she was pregnant. But Alden realized, now, that Monty hadn't been serious about the tradition anyhow. He wasn't faithful to her. Sometimes Alden couldn't ignore her own suspicions. Sometimes she just *knew* that Monty wasn't lost, that he was hiding out with Penelope Griffin.

Alden had caressed the fuzzy piping on the little baby socks so often that they had become dirtied with nicotine. These booties were too small for Baby Hendrick. He had been wearing a diminutive pair of legitimate Converse cross-trainers. She dialed Hester Pierson at DSS and left a second message on her machine. "Is Baby Hendrick on the hotline list?" She didn't want to appear too anxious, and maybe she shouldn't have called twice. She didn't call a third time and decided to drive over to DSS on her lunch break.

She stared at the water. She couldn't take her eyes away, just as she couldn't resist the serrated flashes of a drive-in movie glimpsed through the slatted privacy fence. Stories were unfolding without her. Lovers were joined or torn asunder.

Her every waking minute since Monty had vanished had been in some way dedicated to self-management, but the sea outside her window mocked her daily attempt to find moderation, to keep her nose clean, her eyes dry, her mind clear. The water *rose* and it *sank*. Sloughs and gullies were alternately drained or brimming in six-hour cycles as if mimicking universal bipolar symptoms. At her fingertips, authoritative nature manuals provided reassurances: "Nature's dizzying routines are purposeful. In flux there is *constancy*. In change there is *regularity, precision*."

Alden read that some of the beasts and sea creatures described in these nature texts were doomed to be "artifacts in their own lifetimes." Yet another manual testified, "Wetlands *protect* like a rubber gasket on a revolving door."

Well, Alden could see this, the "rubber gasket effect." Nauset Marsh was a huge swirling sweep of spartina, eel grass, and sea lavender. Its five-hundred-acre bib was turning to rust by late fall. A few oldsters in hip waders raked the muck for bait fish; silver sand eels twisted like scraps of foil in the tines of their forks. By early November, the bluefish and sea bass had already migrated south, but the optimistic men still doodled in the muck.

Against rules, she had a cigarette at her desk.

In the off-season, the empty hours dragged on forever unless someone dropped off a stranded sea turtle or a shorebird struck by a car. Sometimes no one stopped in to the bookstore all day. It was a museum unless a nomadic tour bus pulled in, or a school group on a field trip from up cape, maybe from as far away as Boston. Alden catered to seniors or to silly grammar school students who purchased souvenirs, little plastic frogs and imitation scrimshaw rings. She dropped these trinkets into paper bags and handed them out to the kids. Then the store would be dead for hours.

A shopper came into the bookstore, and Alden waved away lingering drifts of smoke. The customer lurked somewhere in the tight pyramid displays, shelves crammed with science manuals, field guides, shipwreck diaries, and the beloved naturalist tome *The Outermost House* by Henry Beston, and Thoreau's *Walden* and *Cape Cod.* Monty had had many of these titles in his own collection. Once, Alden had opened a text from Monty's library to find a fancy self-stick bookplate printed with the name "Penelope Griffin." It was at about the same time that Miss Griffin had started leaving messages on their machine about a project at the Kennedy Memorial Park in Hyannis, a butterfly garden Monty had put on a fund-raising calendar. Miss Griffin had agreed to help him, suggesting specific publicity events and matching-fund strategies. Perhaps these messages about a butterfly garden were code for secret trysts. Since then, Alden had read in the paper that a new project had been funded to memorialize another Hyannisport celebrity. This time it was a garden for John-John. The committee argued about the commission. Some said the statue should represent the handsome magazine editor, and others wanted the figure to be the adorable cherub as he had looked when he played under the president's desk in newsreel footage.

When Alden had finally confronted Monty about Miss Griffin, he readily admitted to his indiscretion. He had been similarly blithe with the girl he had left behind to start up with Alden. Alden recognized that Monty had a system. He would never leave one warm bed until he had another boudoir fire burning. He didn't bother to make a clean break. He was careful to rev up the tachometer on a new engine before shutting one down. When Monty wasn't contrite about his imperious confession, Alden just felt inadequate. She must have failed a test as wife. As woman. Alden went into the bathroom and ran the water to the lip of the tub. She got in the bath and told Monty through the bathroom door that she might just slice her wrists, but she didn't really have a razor under the blanket of soapsuds. She soaked until the water was cold. At last, Monty came into the bathroom, reached into the water, and yanked the plug.

Monty was unruffled by Alden's emotional outbursts, having worked as an orderly at a mental hospital before getting his teaching certificate for the middle school level. He had met Alden at the Four Cs, Cape Cod Community College, where he had enrolled to get his ESL certificate in order to qualify for a pay hike in the public system. From the get-go he had often used his educator mask to enforce his upper hand with Alden. He used his hospital-orderly routine or his "I'm trying to be very patient with you" schoolteacher stare-down. He told Alden that she was too high-strung and needy and that she saw threats where there were none. He told her he believed her neurosis was within the limits of his expertise and that he could help her.

"Oh, really? What kind of *help* are you talking about?"

The first time he had asked her out, he took her to the Yardarm, a seedy bar in his neighborhood. A tourist trap in the summer, in the winter months it was a desolate warehouse of splintered rattan furniture. He led her to a corner table beside a white baby grand piano draped in a plastic drop sheet. Monty sat down at the keyboard and began to bang out a tune, Chicago's old hit "Color My World." He fingered the keys underneath the polyethylene covering. The notes were muffled and the chords smeared, strangely altered by the plastic sheeting. His performance was eerie, almost creepy. It reminded Alden of the zombie ballroom in the cult movie *Carnival of Souls*, where a zombie sits down at an organ and paws the keys in a rigid stupor.

The broken weave of Alden's Casablanca chair jabbed the backs of her knees as she endured the snowballing protocol that would lead her into bed with him. At his apartment, he showed her some butterfly specimens in display cases. The insects were mounted with their wings compressed tightly between two opposing glass panes. Monty explained that some of his favorites migrated thousands of miles, in relayed generations, all the way from Mexico to Massachusetts. Alden had once seen monarch butterflies migrating en masse, like a golden scarf drifting in swags across the open fields and foothills of the Berkshires. She thought it was particularly barbaric that these creatures should fly all the way to New England just to have their wings pinched between picture frames.

Monty took a tweezers, lifted a butterfly from his worktable, and dropped it into her hand. She held the butterfly in her palm as he started to unbutton her blouse. His hobbyist ruse was a good one, she wanted to say as she stood shivering. He continued to undress her and then shoved her gently down onto his rumpled bed. She let the fritillary slip to the floor like a scrap of smudged newsprint. There were plenty more bugs in Ziplocs on his worktable. Monty became suddenly more patriarchal and aloof as he fondled her. He seemed to have a condescending patience instead of a healthy *impatience*. He seemed to think he had all the time in the world and that Alden had nowhere in the world to go.

She said, "Is this a mercy fuck? Because I don't need you feeling sorry for me."

"A mercy fuck? Yeah, I'll have you *begging* for mercy," he said.

He thinks a lot of himself, she had thought.

But Monty's self-love rubbed off on her. She gladly mistook his commanding touch for matrimonial conviction, and her silk panties, tugged down, were already seeping.

But when Penelope turned up in the equation, even sex, their first and last connection, was threatened. Alden visited a marriage counselor and told the therapist that she wanted to work it out with Monty. The social worker said that Monty's poor record showed that the dominoes kept falling in a "classic pattern," and it might not be worth the heartache to try to turn it around. But the social worker encouraged Alden to talk to her husband and gave her a pamphlet called *Five Guides to Communication:*

1. Discuss, Don't Attack.
2. Keep the Voice Low and Pleasant.
3. Stick to the Subject.
4. Listen to His Complaints.
5. Don't Make Demands.

Before she could implement these "five guides to communication," Monty was gone.

Alden tried to reason why she hadn't been enough wife for Monty. Once, he had told Alden, "Making love to you is like trying to construct a geodesic dome," implying that it took a great deal of effort to please her. She wanted to say that it was *him.* When Monty made love to her, he was always preoccupied. His mind was somewhere else. Maybe he was thinking of Penelope.

Alden remembered Hyram's words, "Find someone who *wants* to be found." This meant different things to different people.

4

ALDEN BOARDED THE CESSNA TWIN PROP that took her back and forth to Boston. The commuter airline was a small, employee-owned operation that served the Outer Cape and islands. She grabbed the bucket seat beside the pilot. He was the same local kid who used to fly the "flightseeing" biplane before he was hired at Cape Air.

She had known him since they were classmates in grade school. Summers, they had dived off MacMillan Wharf for loose change that tourists threw into the harbor. Quarters dappled the sand floor. When her hands were full, she tucked the coins between her cheeks and gums, and she'd come up for air with her mouth full of silver. At thirteen she wore a string bikini for men who tossed dollars and larger bills. Bright snips of sea lettuce caught in her hair, and wet singles stuck to her bare skin like fish scales. She was half-mermaid, half–bank teller as she kneeled on the pier sorting her booty.

Alden felt safe sitting in the nose beside her old rival, because in the passenger aisle of the Cessna nine-seater there was a little Dutch door that easily sprang open. A chrome lever released a tiny staircase, just two treads, like the retractable stoops on mobile homes, but these treads unfolded into the empty air. In whiteout conditions the horizon was like blotter felt in all directions. If the door fell open, she wouldn't know up from down.

There was a dime-store copy of *Jane Eyre* crammed into the magazine pouch alongside a laminated drawing of the plane's emergency exits. The book had remained in the seat pocket, flight after flight. Alden picked it up once or twice, but when she felt herself getting sucked in, she shoved it away again. A bee was trapped in the cabin, and passengers shrieked until Alden used the paperback to collect it. She saw that the insect was of the harmless genus *Bombus.* So late in the season, these bumblebees are drowsy and not as industrious. It alighted on the cockpit panel, and Alden petted it with her fingertip.

The pilot scribbled on his windshield with a wax crayon. "What's that you're writing, Conrad?" she asked him.

"That's 'Captain' to *you,*" he said. But he told her it was his instructions for the twenty-minute hop to Boston; in fog he had to fly on instruments. He tapped the windshield where he had made his crayon marks. "These are my runway numbers at Logan."

"We're on time, right?" she asked.

"Another big-shot meeting downtown?" he said.

"Just lunch. Same as usual. I'm coming back to P-town on the four-thirty."

"Just lunch?" he said when he noted her perfume.

She had told Conrad she had business meetings in Back Bay, but he must have been thinking, Who goes to a corporate powwow smelling like a tropical drink? She didn't care what the pip-squeak aviator thought. The meticulous preparation for a love event is its own reward, in a way—even today, when she planned to ditch Ison. She adjusted half-glasses across the bridge of her nose. Alden didn't use reading glasses but had bought them at the drugstore, hoping that they might give her authority, an egghead aloofness that she needed to sort things out with Mr. Ison.

The pilot recited his ID to traffic control, yanked off his headset, and turned to smirk at her useless eyewear.

"What are you looking at, wharf rat?" she said.

He studied her face. "I love the new glasses. Really."

She didn't like him as a flirt, and asked him, "If that door fell open, could you keep flying the plane or would it cause a disequilibrium?"

"If the door was open? It wouldn't matter. This cabin's not pressurized."

She watched the wing tear through the ruffled clouds white as a wedding dress thrown down in a huff. There was no depth perception, no horizon, just white gesso. She could hardly read the familiar warning on the wing flap, "No step. Dismount in rear." It was worse than the blinding woolpack that caused the pileup at the Quitting Time Clock, when she found Baby Hendrick.

"God, how do you fly in this?" she said.

Conrad accepted every invitation to lecture Alden about nephology or aviation. He had once explained a theory called the angle of attack. He said, "It's how the wing meets or *addresses* the air." This angle of attack was what lifted the plane or allowed it to sink, or "mush." She had thought of this angle-of-attack theory when she was in bed beside Mr. Ison in a Boston hotel. "How the wing meets the air" merged with her ascending arousal, and she felt her orgasm loft and tangle, stronger and stronger. She couldn't describe how the physics of flying had worked as a sex mechanism, somehow. Ison wanted the credit.

Next, the pilot was explaining "vertical airspeed" to Alden. She interrupted his lesson and said, "I'm just asking how you can *see* in this soup."

"See? I don't need to see," he said. "I watch this ADI right here, my attitude director indicator. My artificial horizon."

"Your what?"

"Artificial horizon."

He tapped a tiny screen before him. She watched a winged silhouette line up against a lateral needle hair. The silhouette tilted slightly and readjusted as the Cessna purred forward. The instrument held steady as it pulled her into trouble again. If only she monitored her sympathetic nervous system like this, then maybe she could bow out of her luncheon arrangement and turn around. Instead she would think of the artificial horizon as she stood at the registration desk face-to-face with the clerk at the Dearborn Hotel.

The clerk always greeted Alden with a careful distance, a professional somnolence, after having pegged Alden for an out-of-towner who came into the city to flatback for a nameless executive. The computer screen flashed the conglomerate's acronym and its travel-agency affiliation, but it didn't implicate Mr. Ison, who left it to Alden to check in and do the paperwork.

"Of course, we will allow the same corporate rate," the clerk said, "and that's to be charged to TelTrek as before, correct?"

"No, no, I'll pay cash this time," Alden had said on her last visit to the hotel.

"You'll pay cash?"

"Yes." Alden didn't know why she insisted. She didn't always have that kind of money, but paying cash had made her feel in control of *something.*

The clerk smiled with such little affect that she looked like a Swiss maid on a chocolate box. Her two years in business school had taught her to be a discreet gatekeeper to a forbidden world—the world inside Alden, or any woman who showed up without a suitcase. The clerk's rote self-confidence as she monitored the hotel's hallways from behind her high mahogany console was a different version of the pilot's imperious comment, "I don't need to see."

At her first meeting with Ison at the Dearborn Hotel, she found her room, unlocked the door, and walked through the climatized dark to the window. She tugged the curtain wand across until the daylight washed in. She looked down to the street to see the famous *Make Way for Ducklings* bronzes in the Public Garden, surrounded by tourists. Children climbed on and off the backs of the knee-high burnished ducks as if they were sofa hassocks. She watched the chubby toddlers until Ison knocked at the door.

The sheets weren't yet turned down, and she yanked the spread open, wanting to be first to start the procedures. Then she tiptoed to the door to see his face through the peephole—troubled, handsome. He searched the empty hall, looking to the left and right, like a pup trying to avoid the dog officer's choke stick.

When he entered the room, he kissed her once and said, "It can't be anything serious, you know—I love my kids." As he removed his shoes, he described his beautiful vacation house in Chatham and told her it had two turrets on opposite ends. These turrets became a dreamy obsession of Alden's. She wanted to know, were they glassed in or open? Of course, they were nothing like the crowded sleeping porch of her childhood, where her parents had put her during their druggy parties, and where she had had to sleep even when the rain came sideways through the rusty mesh. In the morning, she helped her mother clean up. She rinsed her father's collection of bongs, tarry elbows of Plexiglas, and collected single-edge razor blades left out after Dane Baker had divided up the coke or meth. No, Ison's turrets seemed to be from a different world—a fairy tale where a princess, a willful sprite, has been wrongly mistaken for a madwoman and is locked inside a rose-briared campanile until her prince comes.

But Ison was merely talking about his trophy home with its "all-weather wicker" lounge chairs. A Ping-Pong table for his kids. A gas grill with a quilted mitt dangling off a hook. Elegant wrought-iron furniture that looks gorgeous after a snowfall.

Then he fell back on the bed.

After their first tryst, he began calling her at work.

"Got a minute?" he says. He calls from his desk and she hears his noisy office, girl talk vented up the hallway from the Xerox station or the fax machine, a jangle of fem bartering and bitching. His young assistant complains about her new belly-button ring; its cheap nickel loop gives her a reaction. Other girls are tearing sheets from a printer, serration upon serration, like days ripped from a calendar. Someone pounds a stapler in a monotonous crunching rhythm.

"Alden?" he says.

"Speaking." She shifts in her seat, crossing her legs. Her panty hose makes a silky friction and she wonders if he can hear it on his end.

He stands up to nudge his door shut. The heavy door sweeps closed and latches with a metallic hiccup. The hallway warble stops and there's silence on the line.

It's dead quiet.

That's his go/no-go decision, his countdown, like the ascending green lights on the starter pole at a drag race.

For these secret dispatches he uses his cell phone. Alden endures its maddening lisps and broken-off phrases. She scolds him, "Why don't you call your wife for a wireless quickie? Why me?"

He chuckles. Honey-clogged notes like a beehive in a pipe organ.

She hears his chair creak and its casters roll in furred rotations on the carpet. As soon as he sits down at his desk, she knows he's tugged his belt open. Her voice connects. She prowls through a tangle of heat-seeking verbs. Her voice is what gets to him. But she's going through the motions, as when she remembers to telephone a maiden aunt at Christmas, the same aunt whose bowl of ribbon candy has solidified into a garish hunk and has to be chiseled with a table knife.

He asks her, "Tell me what you'll do when you come to the city this week. Say everything, you know, in that excellent progression—"

"I've got a list of tasks to do in town," she says. "Are you ready?" Then she goes through the list thoroughly.

But at lunch that afternoon, Alden told Mr. Ison, "My commuter booklet is used up. I have only one ticket left."

"I'll get you another booklet," Ison said.

"That's very generous," she said, "but I don't have any more sick days. My paycheck will be docked each time I come to Boston. And on weekends, married men stay at home with their families. Isn't that right? At your house with two turrets?"

He nodded, stumped by her quiz. She asked him to stop calling her at the Seashore office. "There's always kids around. You saw them yourself—" She tried to sound wistful, not wanting to nick his pride, but her sighs were impatient.

Ison reached across the table to remove her faux glasses. He folded them shut and tucked them beside the rim of his plate. He said he was unhappy that she wanted to end it, but of course he would accept her verdict. He pressed her to agree to one final tumble, and they rode the elevator together, up to a luxury room. In the rising compartment, she gauged his mood. He was not yet resigned to his new status after the blow she had dealt him. She was thinking only of Baby Hendrick in her arms, his chubby fists and kicking limbs, when Ison asked her why she seemed distracted, so she tried to scramble his thoughts by asking about his own kids.

But as soon as he had her inside the darkened room, her clothes unbuttoned, she saw he would make good use of each final minute. As he hurried, Alden thought of the infinitely variable bumper-sticker slogan: "So many cheerleaders, so little time," or "So many cowgirls, so little time." So many *registered nurses, librarians, lacrosse teams*—et cetera. As much as you try to please me, Alden was thinking, it's not so easy to polish away a husband's touch—or a baby's squirming spell—try all you want, Mr. Ison.

ALDEN RETURNED TO CAPE COD that afternoon on the commuter plane and took her seat beside Conrad again. She told him about her decision to dump the travel agent. "I'm grounded," she promised.

Conrad said, "Well, what do you expect when you have sex with married men instead of having something real?"

"Something real? Sex is *too* real, if you ask me," Alden said.

Between furry dispatches from the controller, Conrad kept up the crossfire and said, "I think you see married men because they can't make a claim on you."

"But you're married. I'm not seeing *you.* That shoots holes in your theory."

"You're waiting for your husband to come back. Give up."

She said, "Look, don't wear your halo to analyze me. I won't listen to amateurs."

"Okay, how about this? I have to take some pictures for RE/MAX. They want aerials of that big house on Tom's Hill Road. You want to go up? We'll shoot some film and then fly over to Nantucket for lunch. Sound good?"

"Are you flying this Cape Air pea pod for moonlighting purposes? They let you do that?"

"No. Not the Cessna. It's that little Diamond single-engine. You know the one tethered at the far end, left of the hangar?"

"That itsy-bitsy thing—looks like a yellow jacket? Oh, Christ—"

"It's cozy as a La-Z-Boy. So how about it?"

She saw he was trying to compete with the travel agent, who had bought her expensive meals in Boston. On the island, lunch can be a little too quaint, B and Bs with checkered tablecloths and hand-carved napkin rings. "What does Nantucket have that I can't get at home?"

"I can think of several possibilities."

"*Im*possibilities," she said.

"Where's your imagination? I thought you liked love stories. You liked that *Jane Eyre*, right?"

"That's fiction. You're talking *science* fiction." She was stinging him. In turn he abruptly steered the yoke, banking so steeply it made her wince. He was acting like a jealous teenager, just like he did when they used to panhandle on the waterfront. He critiqued her mercilessly, but whatever it was, he'd have to get it all in before next month, when he was getting bumped up. He would start his training at American Airlines. Once, he had told her, "A commercial jet is the same as a Cessna. It's basically the same instrument panel, but with lots of repetitions."

As he needled her, she turned in her seat to find solidarity with the year-rounders onboard. There were two local gay men, beloved restaurateurs, and the counter help for the Cape Air gate at Logan, who rode up and back each day. One regular tackled the cabin copy of the Brontë classic as others were dozing.

Then, in midflight to Provincetown, the stowaway bee zigzagged up the aisle. Everyone tried to swat it. The pilot said its only chance was if Alden unlocked her small window vent. "*My* window? Why not yours?" she said as the insect bumped along the windscreen. But Alden obeyed captain's orders and forced open the stopcock. She watched the tiny thing, doom's busybody, sluiced away at three thousand feet.

THE MIST ATE INTO HIS COLLAR as he watched her undress. She bent at the waist and brushed her wild hair over her head; then she stood up and her hair swung back untamed. She smoothed her sheets, brushing a few loose grains of sand onto the floor with the palm of her hand. The hem of her T-shirt didn't cover her up as she leaned across to adjust her pillows. He saw the little pie wedge of jet-black frizz; just barely glimpsed, it stabbed him like an arrowhead.

He inched up to the windowpane.

It was the blurry hundred-year-old glass or it was the drain on him from his obsession—he felt dizzy just to witness each of her small gestures and routines.

She got into bed. Her room blinked once, twice, as she flipped channels. The TV churned tropical green colors, lighting the dune shack like an aquarium. He didn't think she'd get very far in her book with the TV on, but she waded through several pages before he decided that he had better head back to town.

5

Robustus

THE TEACHER WEARS A NEXT-TO-NEW GORE-TEX PARKA in blinding guide yellow with the Nike swoosh on its breast pocket. The waffle soles and leather uppers of his ankle boots are cinched by rawhide laces to the bony metatarsus of each foot, but his crew socks are rotted. His khakis have decomposed to gauzy leggings, long sieves full of sand and gravel. Only the nylon stitching along the inseams is intact, and the vinyl zipper teeth still intersect. His hat-rack bones are flesh-stained where there isn't flesh. At the crown of his head, his blond hair is thick, matted with dirt, but the swatch of scalp has separated from the marbled cranium. Two huge black orbits stare ahead with unbridled jocularity, like the wide, mocking eyes of cartoon spooks. Yet there's something staid and businesslike about him, his sum total indistinguishable from shellacked specimens displayed on tripod stands at premed seminars, the beloved Mr. Bones, greeter at the apron of every science hall.

THE CREW KNOCKED OFF FOR LUNCH. Lux said he was leaving for the afternoon. He collected their spades, rakes, and wire snips and volunteered to put them up when he usually left it to someone else. He immediately wondered if he shouldn't have offered. Today he should do everything *as per.* He thought he'd need a spade and wasn't sure he had one at the house. After he saw everyone drive off, he went back inside the barn. The John Deeres were dripping on the concrete floor. He wouldn't need the brush hog. He would have liked to use the Bobcat, except he couldn't be driving the Bobcat at midnight without making a racket. He selected a spade and a hacksaw and tucked the tools behind the hemlock hedge that flanked the storage barns. Nancy Silva, the secretary, was getting in her car as he toed his stash under the low shelf of hemlock. She didn't seem to care what he was doing. Nancy ignored the men in the fields, men who delivered gravel, pruned thorns, and drained motor oil. She thought she was a notch higher. Lux wanted to tell her that he was enrolled in night school, too, and would earn his degree in landscape architecture eventually, while she studied bookkeeping or pencil sharpening or how to line up her bottles of Liquid Paper according to their pastel shades. When she glared at him, he trilled his best, oily greeting, "Hi, beautiful." She didn't want to hear it. "You're killing me," he said. "I'm dying—"

He imagined the schoolteacher tangled up in the cedar roothold, and he went back for the snips and loppers to cut him loose. Each time he pictured Monty, the candles sizzled up and down in that disjointed movie scene with no continuity. This candle vision was all about his obsessive concern with *details,* but Lux recognized that candles are a corny euphemism, a symbol of man's mortality. Everyone is supposed to have his one candle burning, and then one day it's snuffed out. Monty didn't see it coming.

Lux worried about what hour to come back with his friend King. What *was* the blackest hour of night?

Lux asked this science question to a brainy kid who clerked at Chicken City at Two Mile Corner. He bought a carton of Thai-style drumettes, and when the kid handed Lux the steaming box, Lux asked him, "Hey, you're a science whiz, right?"

"I'm studying marine biology at UMass Extension."

Lux thought studying biology at that party school, called a microbrewery by all concerned, ought to be a bitter waste of someone's time. Lux was enrolled in night courses at the Four Cs. Cape Cod Community College was another fifth-rate institution, and he shouldn't be acting righteous. He told the kid, "Well, this isn't about biology exactly, but I've got a science question for you. Let's say we're standing right here at Two Mile Corner, at Chicken City, this longitude and latitude, so to speak. I mean right here, tonight. When is it darkest?"

"The darkest time of night? That's not the number one FAQ I get around here. The usual question is 'Do fries come with that?' or 'Is it lard or vegetable shortening?' But you're asking about your basic global orbit positioning, right?" The kid swabbed the counter and narrowed his eyes, entering a wholly new thought register. He was into it. Math eggheads love a quiz game. "Let's see. The darkest time of night—you mean when the sun is directly on the opposite side of the planet? And it's, like, lunch hour in Bangkok?"

"Lunchtime in Bangkok? You mean, that's when it's pitch black over here?"

"Shit, it's never pitch black. You'd have to be in a sensory-deprivation tank or in the Luray Caverns way below ground with your headlamp clicked off. It's never totally dark anywhere on the planet. First, you have all this man-made light. Cities burn like torches for hundreds of square miles. They can see Las Vegas from the space shuttle."

"They see Vegas?"

"That's right. Even in the middle of nowhere you've got to factor in stars. If it's a clear sky, you've got your whole Milky Way. It's fucking astonishing—it's these cosmic dust clouds. Just wall-to-wall stars. You've got your big-screen and your picture-frame TVs? Well, they're nothing compared to some hard-core, antitech, naked-eye stargazing."

"So it's *never* night, is what you're saying."

"Starlight delivers about seven thousand angstrom units of electromagnetic radiation."

"Angstrom?"

"A Swedish physicist. That's enough angstroms, I mean, that's enough illumination to have high definition of objects, landscape terrain, your trees, your buildings, everything but the fine print."

"I forgot about the fucking stars."

"I guess it could be overcast, but moisture actually refracts light and makes a broader smear. Like when you're flashing your brights on in the fog, that'll throw up an impenetrable wall—or like right here, with all the fryers going, these plate-glass windows get steamed up until they look like they're whitewashed." The kid was fuguing.

Lux grinned at the science whiz, trying to keep calm. "So when do these stars quit, at dawn?"

"Right before dawn it's black as oil," the kid said.

Lux sometimes went surf casting in the wee hours and fished until the sun came up. The colorless sea broke in crescents of invisible black foam until his waders were icy. That predawn dark had a strange, crepey texture, and Lux sometimes felt that the sun might not rise at all if a man didn't try to pray once in a while, or try to add his two cents from some internalized spot. Up the beach someone might have those bright-sticks attached to their poles to monitor a strike; otherwise it was dead black. But Lux was thinking if he went into the nursery with King right before dawn, he'd have to worry about the sunrise catching up to them. Lux had seen some sneaky sunrises squeezing up over the horizon like a row of Day-Glo frogmen creeping out of the ocean. And even before that pinkish tinge, the sky turns a queer silver green, like the wrong side of a mirror. Things start to show up. Apparitions. Once, he thought he saw two men walking toward him carrying a coffin on their shoulders. And inside the box, the schoolteacher. It spooked him good. Then he saw it wasn't two men carrying a coffin on their shoulders at all; it was just the empty lifeguard stool on stilt legs.

He told the kid, "Just tell me one thing. Is there a moon tonight?"

"New moon tonight. New moon means *no* moon. So why do you want it pitch black, you got some bottle rockets or something?"

Lux said, "I've got a romantic date, that's all."

"WHY ARE YOU ASKING a fry cook about night conditions? I'm the one who knows everything about night conditions," King told Lux. "Shit, I'm Nocturnus."

"You sleep all day at Rent-A-Relic and that makes you an expert?"

"After hours I come alive, like Dracula—"

"Dracula on Jolt cola."

"And don't forget my Nicorette," King said. He removed a new piece of gum from its plastic blister.

"Okay, if you're the expert, when do we do the transfer?" Lux asked King. "Remember, Officer Francisconi is on second shift. He's still interested in this. He's eyeballing me."

"Wait until he takes his forty at Tang's Chinese, and that's when you go in that field. It should be faster getting him out than when you put him in, tits up."

Lux imagined the teacher in his present-day condition and wondered how they'd collect the body. Was it all-in-one, or in bits and pieces? "So we wait until it's pitch black?"

King said, "Or maybe wait until Francisconi is off duty. Find out when he's not on the chalkboard, and do it then."

"But they're always trading off. Their schedules are never the same."

"Nickerson says next week is the deadline for that job? I say you wait till the weekend, when they're toting up DUI violations around closing time on the strip. No question about it. Robustus comes out TGIF. Friday night."

"We wait until Friday to go in?"

"Yeah, at zero hour. Dead of night." King grinned.

Lux didn't like the idiom "dead of night." He sat in the claw-foot tub, lathering up with a plastic bottle of peppermint soap. After working in the nursery fields, he sometimes smelled of cow manure or that pelletized nitrogen fertilizer, but he bathed just as much to calm his nerves. His anxiety condition was formless, invisible. It had no clear boundaries, no volume, no outlines, and his muscles were always tensing against a guerilla opponent. The hot water was good.

King sat on the toilet lid waiting for his friend's hygiene ritual to conclude. King could make do with a navy shower every other day. He waited until his long blond hair hung limp and greasy and Lux called him Moldilocks instead of Goldilocks, but King knew that Lux's second-shift bathing habits were essential to everyone's well-being.

Lux said, "I'm sick of Nickerson's mood swings. If I could, I'd be working on my own."

"Doing?"

"Nursery work, I guess. Same but different. I'd be top end, without the glass ceiling."

But King knew that his friend's nerve disorder kept Lux out of an office job. Lux couldn't sit still. "Well, it's better if you work outdoors," King said.

"I'd still be fishing. I fished with Denny, but, you know, the cod disappeared. Then there's always driving that Cape Ice truck."

King said, "Remember that hot day we climbed in back with a quart of Rolling Rock? We sat down on that sofa of ice."

"Like an igloo," Lux said.

"God. That was nice—"

"Ten-pound bags of those nice, clear spools."

"Spools freeze faster than cubes."

"There was that. And remember, I was with DOT, putting down rumble strips on I-495." Lux grabbed the shampoo bottle and worked some into his mop.

"Those rumble strips? Tell me again, how is that done? Are they preformed strips, or are they notched on-site? Was that a cool job or what?"

"Not what you're thinking. I'm standing on the highway with cars ripping past at seventy miles an hour. It's like I'm in a pneumatic tube. I lose my hard hat. The wind plucks it off and it rolls across four lanes into the opposite traffic."

"There's all kinds of outdoor jobs you haven't tried yet."

"I'd rather have suede patches on my elbows and interview college coeds."

"Dean of sex?"

"Not even. Just a normal desk situation."

"One day, maybe. When you're a geezer."

"I don't actually want to live to a hundred." His blue eyes tightened into silvery slashes, a conditioned wince, whenever he remembered his hopeless situation.

The two men waited for the "poor me" moment to come hurtling back at them.

"You're talking to a medical experiment," Lux went on. "They gave me this new trial drug. I'm one week along." He reached for a jar of robin's-egg blue capsules on the bathroom sink and popped one into his mouth. "These aren't tranks. These regulate brain enzymes or something."

"Better living through chemistry."

"I can't tell any difference. But Gwen says yes."

He sank below the surface of the water to rinse his hair. He came up again. “Alden went into Boston to see that suit, whoever, and I’m sitting here soaking,” Lux said.

King said, “*Her* again? It’s like you’re stalking that girl. It’s not cool to try to parallel-park with the widow. I’d give her more space.”

“I’m going pretty slow. Maybe she’ll get to know me.”

“First impressions are important. What kind of impression are you aiming at when you dig up those bones?”

“I think she’ll actually want to know. Eventually. I’m going to tell her. Everything. Maybe she’ll learn to forgive what happened—”

“I forgive you. Gwen does—”

“When she wants to.”

“When she wants *some,*” King said. “Maybe these new pills will work. You have any side effects?”

“Yeah. *You’re* my side effect.”

King grinned. It was a jab he could live with. “I guess you mean side-kick?”

King had been his one lifelong friend. He stood by Lux when Lux’s father left home. His mom told Lux that she didn’t hold it against him when her marriage collapsed, but that it wasn’t easy raising a child with a “syndrome.” She blackmailed Lux, taking advantage of his self-hate feelings, making him pay for what happened. And even his brother, Denny, blamed him. He said Lux’s weird freezing condition was the deal breaker for their folks.

“I got my annual invitation in the mail. NORD is having another soiree,” Lux said.

“NORD? Oh, yeah. NORD.”

“National Organization for Rare Disorders. Just NORD to *us.*”

“Oh, like a Shriners convention or something? Once a year the afflicted rub elbows?”

“Yeah. You know, they circle the wagons. I went that one time, but I couldn’t see the point in it.”

“Safety in numbers, I guess.”

“Well, these NORD people make a distinctive gathering. Like that Fellini movie, you know? That one with the freaks?”

“Never saw it,” King said.

"You never saw a Fellini flick?"

"Not that I'm aware of."

Lux had rented them all from Fine Arts Video. Gwen didn't like foreign movies; subtitles just made her sleepy. But Lux was a fan; he was certain that the Italian director would be sympathetic to his false paralysis and to afflictions like uncombable hair. Lux fell in love with the actress Giulietta Masina, the tragic sprite in *La Strada* and *Nights of Cabiria.* He liked one scene in particular in *La Strada,* when Giulietta finds a stunted, deformed sapling, its two limbs forking at a forty-five-degree angle. The waiflike actress stands beside the tree and tilts her arms, mimicking its bowed branches. Lux often thought of this scene from *La Strada* as he worked alone in his pleaching arbor.

He told King, "Well, if you never saw a Fellini movie, you can't really visualize a NORD event. I'll never forget it, since I was actually there in person."

Lux was fifteen. He sat beside his mother in a reserved annex of the cafeteria at Beth Israel Hospital in Boston. A panel of three physicians was seated behind a Formica banquet table. Their platform was draped with a last-minute dot matrix banner on perforated printer paper that said, "Out of the darkness into the light," the crusading motto of NORD. Lux's family doctor had told his mother that Lux should attend a NORD event so that he could meet other children, like himself, who faced daily life with an "orphan disease."

Lux hated the strange term "orphan disease," since he had never really known his father and he'd always felt unclaimed by that side of the family. The peculiar category of diseases seemed tragically linked to his lost patriarch. Dr. Weitzman explained that an orphan disease is a disorder affecting fewer than two hundred thousand people. Drug companies will never sink money into research for these rare syndromes, and patients must turn to one another and rely solely on local support groups.

The room was full of these unfortunates.

Kids with trunks disproportionate to limbs, and others with grossly incoherent features. Some wore helmets because their skulls were soft, and others wore spinal shunts. Kids sat in abominable clusters of same-age peers. He saw one child who was afflicted with that premature aging disorder, and his pinched face had an uncanny sunken-eyed and beak-nosed resemblance to the beloved marine explorer Jacques Cousteau.

Children maneuvered in combative queues of motorized wheelchairs. One boy was propped on a gurney with an IV drip jury-rigged to a hat rack on casters. Lux looked around for the girl with uncombable hair syndrome, but he didn't see anyone with that unique characteristic. Perhaps she had had the sense to keep away. For a full hour Lux listened to testimonials. He learned about blue diaper syndrome, caused by an error in amino acid metabolism. A baby's pee turns indigo blue upon contact with air.

Lux had to sit through hairy tongue syndrome, cluster headaches, burning mouth syndrome, precocious puberty, a speech about new technology in clubfoot prosthetics, and an update on wandering spleen disease. Lux tried to visualize this wandering spleen. He started to perspire as he listened to doctors describe "jumping Frenchmen of Maine" syndrome, a disorder common to an extended family of Canadian woodcutters.

"Jumpers" have an exaggerated startle reflex. In response to sudden sensory input, a jumper will spontaneously *react.* For instance, if a man held an ax and was startled by a noise or by a sudden movement in his peripheral vision, he might swing the ax at an intruder even if it meant striking loved ones and family members. Jumpers will follow *to the letter* any command that is given, even if they are told to jump off bridges or to chugalug gasoline.

Lux started to worry that he might have this "jumping Frenchmen of Maine" disorder himself. What if his mother startled him while he was shaving at the sink? He performed this ritual at least twice a week now that his beard was coming in thicker. What if she surprised him, as she often did, and he turned around and slashed her?

Lux ignored the testimonials and concentrated on a boy who wore a wood block attached to his boot with toggle bolts. Lux tried to guesstimate the size of these toggle bolts; were they three-quarter inch? How many pennies would they cost per dozen, or how much per pound at the True Value?

Parents told their harrowing stories and afterward sat down in teary relief or prideful satisfaction. His mother was called upon, and she nudged Lux. They wanted him to explain his condition.

"I'm not saying," Lux said.

A doctor tried to cajole the handsome teenager into confessing his burden. Lux thought that the physician looked ridiculous in his snowy jacket like the white smock worn by the pastry chef at Bertolette's Cakes and Buns, where Lux went to buy day-old éclairs. His mother said éclairs always tasted better when the crust was a little stale and chewy. Lux saw how his mother could adopt that point of view, since these day-old sweets were sold for almost nothing.

The doctor was intensely curious to find out what condition plagued such a strapping, comely youngster. What might this young lord be reckoning with? "Tell us your struggle. You're with friends," the physician assured Lux.

Lux looked over the strange faces in the cafeteria seats. He didn't recognize a single person but for their nightmarish distinctions, each a hideous exception to the rule. He looked back at the doctor and said, "You can see for yourself. I don't belong here. I'm in track and field. I do hurdles. I'm on the cross-country team." He got up from his chair and carefully squared it beneath the table. He tapped his mother's shoulder and said, "Let's go."

She took her purse and trailed Lux out of the room. He fled the hospital with his mother and waited to cross the street at an intersection. They had parked the car several blocks away to avoid the stiff fee at the hospital garage, and they were glad to have the walk. At the light, Lux stood beside a blind woman. Her white pole skated back and forth on the asphalt like a record player stylus skipping across a vinyl. When the light changed, Lux turned to the blind woman and said, "Need some help across?"

"Did I say I want help? I didn't say *boo.*"

"I was just asking—"

Her face shifted through a series of peppery grimaces. Her wide-open, unseeing eyes resembled the stony peepers of Notre Dame gargoyles on the cover of his French dictionary. "Fuck off, asshole." She bit his head off and walked across the street alone.

His mother said, "You try to help someone, and this is what you get. Maybe she thought you wanted her pocketbook." Then she pulled his cuff and tried to peck his cheek.

Lux charged ahead. But he froze in the middle of the intersection. A mover was wheeling a giant full-length mirror on a dolly. The mirror was in an ornate rococo frame like the kind seen in hotel lobbies or lavish continental restaurants. It caught Lux, head to toe, in its reflection. He froze as the mirror advanced. As he stopped dead, pedestrians made two rivers around him. Lux couldn't resume walking until the threatening vision had steered past him. But the mover had discovered that the street numbers weren't ascending as he had thought, and at the curb he turned the mirror around. Now the mirror followed *behind* Lux until it overtook him. Lux and his mother walked in a different direction, but at the next corner the mirror tagged up with them again. Lux began to run. He left his mother's side and disappeared into the distance as she watched. He didn't meet her at the car. She had to drive home alone.

When he returned to the house that night, she apologized to him for taking him to the meeting. She apologized at least once a week for the rest of her life. It was the last thing she said to Lux when he visited her at the life-care bungalow at Vicar's Landing Retirement Housing. She told him, "Honey, that NORD day? It was horrible. Will you ever forgive me?"

He told her he would. But the NORD day was his one defining springboard from childhood. The rococo mirror chasing him for blocks was the final crystallizing instant. He was changed forever.

KING SAID, "THAT BLUE DIAPER SYNDROME? Does that last into adulthood? Let's say you're in the little boys' room and your piss is like instant Ty-D-Bol. What would you say to the guy standing next to you?"

"Just keep your mouth shut."

"Silence is golden," King said. "I learned that at my blanket party."

"Your first day in the joint?"

"That's right. They give you a party." King had been pinched for an ATM con and was sent to Cedar Junction. He was home again after only a year inside with good behavior, and his parole officer had King adjusting beautifully to working seven days a week at his uncle's car rental lot. He camped and kept house at its office. King still liked to boast that his ATM scheme had been profitable for the meanwhile. He described how he had dressed in blue Dickies with a name patch on the pocket, an Irish name at that. He pushed a dolly into shopping plazas and mini-marts that had freestanding cash machines amid the hubbub. He told the clerk he was taking the unit for a "new motherboard and some upgrades."

He had a clipboard with an official-looking work order where the clerk would put his John Hancock. King unbolted the console and loaded it on the dolly. Sometimes they were built-ins surrounded by cabinetwork and countertops, and King had to pry off the particleboard trim, Sheetrock, or baseboard. King's little tweak on it was that he was careful to dismantle his prize in slo-mo. He didn't race the clock. In fact once, a cop came into a 7-Eleven and didn't twitch an eyebrow when he saw King working. As the cop supersized a refill for his coffee thermos, King was busy tidying up the plundered area. He swept the sawdust, litter, cash-register paper curls, and rock salt that had collected beneath the appliance skirt, using a little whisk broom and dustpan he kept crammed in his back pocket.

The whisk broom *on his person* was the detail that made clerks believe it was legit.

He wheeled the ATM off-site and rolled it into a van. Without raising any dust, he drove the unit to his mother's carport, where he smashed it open with a maul to get to the tidy cash packets inside. He dumped the wrecked consoles behind his uncle's barn in Marshfield. He had collected seven units before he was pinched. His mug was on some videotapes, but at that time his snapshot wasn't logged into the system and he wasn't anywhere online. Not until his uncle put the fink on him.

Lux liked hearing King's little story, but Lux did all his banking business on cash machines. ATMs allowed him to make anonymous transactions without the required face-to-face. If he found a cash machine out of service, he would have to stand in line at the teller and sometimes he'd freeze: He's waiting to cash his paycheck, but he's standing five feet from the counter as if his boots are nailed to the floor. The teller eyes him. She sees that he looks pretty good. He's the hunk of the day, in fact. Her mixed emotions emerge in a scramble of nervous twitches, until she finally says, "Sir, can you please step aside and allow the gentleman behind you to pass?"

Lux always avoided the one-to-one whenever he could use a drive-up window or an outside kiosk.

Lux asked King about getting a car, short-term. At his release from Cedar Junction, King recuperated from a five-week bout of gate fever by boozing and skirt chasing; then he was happy to take over his uncle's car rental empire, Rent-A-Relic. He acquired junkers, distasteful wrecks, cars that had once been stolen or jacked and nearly demolished. These were doomed buggies with a little something left on their engines, although their cabs might be torn up inside, their bodies dinged and banged, paint jobs blistered, hoods warped, fenders crushed. Doors had to be forced open with a crowbar. Usually the suspension was shot, the chassis had been skewed by a side impact, and wheel alignment was nonnegotiable. Somehow King got inspection stickers for each and every one of them. And King's Rent-A-Relics were in demand at only twenty dollars a day, available upon signing an insurance waiver. King was always ambulance chasing or looking at the newspaper to collect rust buckets; sometimes people called *him,* wanting to sell their piece of shit and watch King drive it away. His office was a tiny trailer lichened all over with Taco Bell wrappers. Nantucket Nectar jars and Coke bottles were lined up on the floor in orderly rows of empties, until there was just a narrow path back and forth from the door to the sofa. King was usually stretched out on the Castro taking a horizontal telephone call, the handset nestled on his belly like a black vinyl kitty cat.

Of course, Lux asked King for a car to transfer Robustus. "It will need to have a trunk that works," Lux told King. "A cargo hold."

"I can do that," King said. "Just acquired a van. Totaled in New Bedford last month. I can take it off the lot."

"A van? It's been totaled?"

"On *paper* it's totaled. It was jacked but the kids cracked up. It was towed from the scene and impounded. Turns out its papers are fudged and its VIN number is faked. Passenger side is mauled, the rear end looks like a Belgian waffle, but it's got plenty of load area. It's sitting there on my lot."

"Have the cops checked it out? Tell me one thing: who owned it before it was jacked?"

"Hey, it's a never-ending-story type thing. Look, I'll give you the truck but I'm not on your go-team to retrieve that body."

"You're not on my go-team? But it's always *us.*" Lux got out of the tub and toweled off. He wasn't finished bargaining. "So Friday night we'll drive it somewhere—got any ideas?"

"Let's burn that bridge when we get to it."

"I'm thinking Vermont. We'll take I-495 to the Mass Pike."

"What about Boston, you know, that Central Artery Project?" King said.

"The Big Dig? It's swarming. It's all lit up with floods. They're working overtime shifts. It's chaos twenty-four seven."

"That's why there's lots of options. They're below ground level, dropping into the geology. They're doing all the digging for us. They're driving pilings, setting forms, blasting trenches. Mixers churning slurry. They're pouring cast-in-place slabs. You can put him in one of these caissons. He'll slither into the ready-mix." King was grinning.

"I've been figuring we should go far into nowheresville. Like Vermont. But first we have to bring it back here. We take it a little at a time." He buttoned his fresh jeans. He tugged a clean T over his head and then pulled on his Polartec. He peeled his socks apart and plunged his foot in one. Newly bathed, he always felt he'd regained some ground, he was a notch higher, he was keeping ahead.

They went downstairs to fry some dogs in butter. King wouldn't eat a lowly hot dog unless it was smothered in Land O Lakes.

Lux simmered the wieners in a triple pat and stabbed them onto a plate for King. He couldn't eat any himself. His Thai-style chicken wings were an undigested pyramid in his stomach. "We've got some of those Hefty Steel-Saks, right, Gwen?" Lux said.

"What do you want those for? That teacher has to disappear, you hear me? You can't bring it back here in a plastic bag."

"She's right. We'll need a duffel or something," King said.

Lux asked King, "So you changed your mind? You're coming in? That's a relief—thanks."

"Oh, boy, *us*," Gwen said.

He hunted through the hall closet, not waiting to hear King and Gwen face off.

"You're not coming back here," Gwen commanded.

"Everyone has a skeleton in the closet," King teased her.

"Fuck you." She threw a wet dishrag on his buttered franks.

He lifted it off and folded it on the table. He nipped a wiener tip ceremoniously between his front incisors just to rile her.

Lux picked through some loose-leaf papers on the kitchen table and found his college textbook *Nineteenth-Century American Literature.* For the past year, while he attended night courses toward his degree in landscape architecture, he had signed up for literature surveys when he needed extra credits. The two career tracks seemed indefinably linked. Lux turned to these books as he did to his pleaching arbors—his secret gardens and green rooms—as an immediate haven of tranquillity from his everyday chaos and disequilibrium.

His text was stained with circles where he'd rested his coffee mug here or there. He felt nostalgia for these telltale rings that he had unconsciously administered just a few days earlier, in happier times, before Nickerson's change of plans had ruined his well-being. He opened the book to the page he had marked with an outfall pipe flyer folded lengthwise into an accordion strip. He started to read a poem out loud to King. "'It was night, and the rain fell . . . but, having fallen, it was blood.' That's Edgar Allan Poe."

King said, "Shit. Did you memorize that for class?"

"Not memorize. *Familiar*ize. Hawthorne, Emerson, Thoreau. Shit, you know what? Professor Tindle says that Emerson dug up his wife after she was buried."

"Tindle said that? The dude dug up his wife? Why'd he do that?"

"To take a second look at her."

"He excavated the little woman, his better half?"

"To take another peek at her."

"You mean to take another poke."

"Could have." Lux grinned. He loved the idea that these famous authors might have had their wires crossed. "Tindle says Poe is like a nineteenth-century Stephen King."

"Every century should have one," King said. He was a fan of the writer who shared his name, having read all the horror paperbacks on the library cart on his tier at Cedar Junction.

Lux said, "Poe wrote that story about the heart that keeps thumping under the floorboards. Shit. That's what's happening to me now. Since we're taking out those cedars there's a time value to this—that's my anxiety attack, exactly. It's going thump-a-thump-a-thump. Poe nails it." He turned to a new page and smoothed it open for King to see.

"You're breaking its spine," Gwen said. She was unable to stay out of the kitchen when the men were knocking heads.

Lux read from the book. "'At midnight, in the month of June, I stand beneath the mystic moon.'"

King said, "Hell, that almost rhymes. That's nice."

"I think it actually *does* rhyme."

King said, "That's pretty good. I'm impressed. All right, Thursday or Friday we drive into that field at midnight. We find your friend. One, two, three. ABC. Moon. June."

6

HESTER PIERSON STIRRED HER COFFEE with the dirty eraser tip of her pencil. "I've got five minutes," she told Alden. "I'm heading out for a home study in Eastham. You don't have an appointment, do you?"

Alden piled into a chair and said, "No, sorry. But it's my lunch hour and I thought I'd come over. I just think if you see my face enough, you'll rubber-stamp my application, right? We can cut through some of this red tape?"

The social worker looked back at Alden with unvariegated brown eyes, the pale color of instant bouillon that had been lengthened for more than one serving. She had seen everything tramp through her office at least once. Alden's desire for a foster child was coming from some emotional turmoil and not from the greedy scheming that other applicants couldn't hide. Emotional need. Greed. Neither starting place was promising. Hester Pierson opened a folder. "Let's see where we are with your application." She peeled sheet after sheet from a notebook of official forms and handwritten notes amassed over the past few weeks.

"We've got your medical report with the chest X-ray, your TB, and HIV, right? You submitted your fire exit plan and the floor plan of your place? It's like a studio, just one main room, right? We've got your safety check sheet. Now, you say you've made day-care arrangements at the Windmill School?"

"They're saving a spot for me, but I also have a playpen at the bookstore. I can bring the baby to work. I have written permission from my supervisor. That's in there, right, with his signature on it? And I've got the car seat so Baby Hendrick can go with me in the Jeep—"

"Baby Hendrick? That baby at the rotary?"

"I have a playpen at work. It's a Graco."

"Wait a minute, Alden. Slow down. Who said anything about Baby Hendrick? People get disappointed if they shoot for a particular baby. Everyone wants a DWI baby or they won't be happy."

"DWI? You mean 'driving while intoxicated'? Are you talking about that can of Krylon—"

"No, no. Gee, I'm sorry. That's an acronym for 'domestic white infant.' These babies are few and far between."

Alden said, "I don't think he's all white, is he? I mean, with that head of hair . . ." Alden hoped he was mixed just so he wouldn't be the premium item that everybody wanted.

The social worker smiled. "Listen. There's another option to consider, Alden. You see that kid sitting outside my office? He's fourteen. He needs a new foster mom."

"I saw him. You mean he's fourteen going on *too late.*" Alden couldn't help noticing the boy. He was a lanky, feral creature with long hair splashed to his shoulders, wearing oversize jeans with wide, fraying hems, as if his dirt bike didn't have brakes and he'd had to drag his feet to stop it.

She said, "Look, I've got the playpen. I'm all set. What's holding everything up?"

"Well, your fingerprints came back, but we're still waiting on the CORI."

"Shit. I already told you, I don't have a criminal-offense history."

"The CORI is just regular procedure, honey. I don't expect it will turn up anything."

"Is it Monty? Is that what's holding it up? Are they using my husband's disappearance against me? Because I didn't have anything to do with it—"

"The baby you want is with a foster family in Marston Mills."

"His father's at MCI-Plymouth? How much time is he pulling for that meth kitchen?"

Hester Pierson said, "He won't get the baby. He's a hothead kid, no more than a baby himself. The cops were always called over to the Cape

Breeze Motel. They found Brooks chasing Layla Cox around the apartment with an electric carving knife. You know, he pulls the trigger, and the blades saw back and forth in unison? He chases her around the dinette set. Lucky for her, the cord comes out of the socket. After something like that, Layla would run over to Princie's."

Alden tried not to smile. Certainly the wild man that Hester Pierson described wasn't going to get custody of Baby Hendrick even if he got out of jail. And they'd never give the baby to the porn retailer or to Layla, who was in a detox unit at Boston City Hospital.

"When Brooks found out Layla was working for Princie's Peephole, dot com, he went over there and smashed up the studio. There were two girls doing live spots on QuickTime. He grabbed them off their markers. He wrecked thousands of dollars of equipment and shut down Princie's Peephole for forty-eight hours."

Hester Pierson seemed to admire Brooks McCarthy for his rampage that muzzied up the porn site for two days.

"My CORI report won't say anything like that."

"But we have to consider your family history. You spent four years in CHINS yourself when your dad went to jail. Foster parenting was your only example, and some adult women like you see it as the easiest option. The instant family. It's not that simple."

Hester Pierson had read some DSS files about Alden's youth. These documents portrayed a patchwork of parental negligence, a series of misdemeanor arrests, and other antisocial irregularities. Alden's father, Dane Baker, had enlisted Alden's cooperation when he organized small cons. He took her with him to supermarkets and chain drugstores on robbery sprees. He told her to bring along her Barbie suitcase, a little pink hatbox tote with a plastic handle. In department stores, he stuffed the suitcase with high-ticket items: Seiko watches, batteries, electric shavers. In the supermarket he stole T-bone steaks, jars of Hawaiian nuts, sardines, and cigarettes. Dane Baker went to the express checker with only a single quart of milk or a loaf of bread. Alden walked past the witless cashier, lugging the heavy Barbie suitcase, its booty straining its cheap clasp.

One time, a security officer at the Stop & Shop observed their routine and alerted the assistant manager. The two men waited at the exits for Alden and Dane Baker to leave the store. Dane Baker eyed the ambush and made a U-turn. He headed for the meat department, where he walked out through the loading dock. He left Alden standing alone with the Barbie suitcase.

The manager stepped up to her and opened the tiny pink tote. To Alden's embarrassment, her father had stolen a package of Italian sausage, their bulbous pink coils circling a Styrofoam tray. She had no idea what was inside these translucent casings—it looked like bloody fat tied up in balloons.

The store manager called her mother, who came and took her home. In the car, Alden remembered that her Barbie suitcase had been left on the manager's desk. She pleaded with her mother to go back and get her prized possession. Alden's mother didn't want to face the store manager again, but she turned the car around. Alden recognized the sacrifice her mother was making. Her mother was always fixing whatever damage Dane Baker had done. Her mother was Alden's savior, but not for long.

Jean Baker left when Alden was ten years old. After a month of strange behavior, little spells of nausea and heartburn, what she had called "tummy troubles," her mom moved out. Dane Baker was annoyed by his wife's chronic symptoms. When Alden's mother pushed her plate away, her father would push it back and tell her, "Jean, don't let this food go to waste," as if he'd paid good money for the meat, when in fact Alden had stolen those chops in her Barbie suitcase.

Alden watched her mother force herself to eat one more bite before getting up from the table. Alden asked her father, "What's wrong with Mommy?"

Dane Baker told Alden, "It's nothing. Your mom has butterflies in her stomach."

When her father dismissed her mother's symptoms this way, Alden was left to imagine these entrapped butterflies, fluttering and circling inside her mother's rib cage.

When Jean Baker disappeared, Alden worried that her mother was sick and had gone to the hospital, but in fact her mother had run off in her first trimester to start a new family in North Carolina. She had met a man at the Wellfleet Flea Market, where people rented stalls each Sunday. Tiers of junk were set up in the first five open-air rows of the drive-in theater. Flea-market Sundays were a tradition for the struggling families on the Lower Cape. It was some people's only livelihood to collect junk and sell it to tourists who were looking for authentic colonial "period" items. Dane Baker had once sold an amber bottle, claiming it was a real antique, but it was just an empty Aunt Jemima syrup container.

Alden's mother had planned her exodus for days, cleaning the apartment and secretly organizing her things in boxes. The night after Jean left home, Dane Baker told Alden to fix dinner all by herself. When she opened the kitchen cupboards to find something to heat up, the shelves were filled top to bottom with pink Hostess Snowballs. There were boxes and boxes of pastel sweets, Alden's favorite treat. Her mother had made a special trip to the supermarket just to stock the pantry with packages of snowy, domed cakes. It was her coded good-bye to Alden. Alden ate Snowballs for a week—breakfast, lunch, and dinner—until Dane Baker thought she'd get sick. She peeled off the cellophane and lined up the cakes in parallel rows. She polished them off, one after the next, just to make him angry when she didn't turn green.

After her mother's departure, Alden was left alone with Dane Baker in one run-down apartment, then another. She came home from school and watched an old black-and-white TV. To get better reception, she swiveled the wobbly antenna left and right until it broke off. The black-and-white TV was her monochrome retreat from Dane Baker's full-color squalor, and she couldn't imagine living without it. So she unscrewed the broken antenna's tiny horseshoe receptor wire, and in its place she tilted her father's old-fashioned safety razor against the VHF connector. The metal safety razor brought in good reception. She invented her own resources with items she found in her father's drawers when he wasn't at home to help her.

Dane Baker came back to find a line of blood drops on the linoleum. The dots trekked from the kitchen all through the apartment. "I was looking for a Band-Aid," she told her father. She had cut herself on the double-edged blade adjusting the impromptu antenna. Alden had fashioned a Band-Aid by folding a dollar and winding masking tape around it until she couldn't bend her finger.

Dane Baker saw his razor tilted against the Zenith. He picked it up and brandished it before her face. "Don't ever fuck with this," he told her. When he took back the razor, the TV screen turned instantly snowy.

Then he saw the bloody dollar wrapped around her finger. "Where'd you find that dollar?" he asked her. "You don't use a dollar for a Band-Aid unless you're the Queen of Sheba. Are you the Queen of Sheba?"

"Maybe I am," she told him.

He stood back on his heels. "Oh, you think so?" he said, instantly outclassed. Then, on second thought, he slapped her fanny once before she slipped away from him.

He came home that night with a gift for her, hoping for a truce. It was an antique baby doll he'd "collected" at the Wellfleet Flea Market. It was a three-faced bisque; its head swiveled to reveal three distinct cameos, each one a separate mood and countenance. Dane Baker told her, "Smile. Sleep. Cry. That's a girl's whole repertoire."

When Alden was fourteen, Dane Baker was arrested for signing second-party checks. He was convicted and sent to the MCI at Cedar Junction. Alden was placed with a foster family who specialized in teen girls. The couple, Naomi and Chuck Voigt, had taken in more than twenty girls over the past five years, and the foster mom gloated about her success record. Alden saw how the woman seemed propped up with every new case she took in. But the woman was just another low-end female getting on the gravy train. Foster mothers expect a good cash stipend when they take in children, but some foster moms request teenagers because teens can do manual labor around the house. Alden's foster mom made her steam-clean the carpets, and before Naomi Voigt returned the rental machine to the Vacuum Mart, she made Alden take it over to her sister's house, where Alden had to clean *her* carpets. The condo had wall-to-wall and Alden was there all day.

Cleaning garages, scouring sinks, babysitting, yard work—that was expected.

At sixteen, with almost four years in the system, Alden came to the conclusion that it was time for her to get out from under the nail fungus of social services. She had saved some money, and she changed all the small bills into hundreds so they would fit under the foam insole of her boot. She had earned cash busing tables at the Chocolate Sparrow and a little extra working as a bird dog or earwig for someone making regular dope connections behind Jimmy D's sports bar. Before DSS could get her reassigned, she was going to take that boot of money, nine hundred dollars in all, and leave town, despite the fact that winter was coming. But Alden stayed in foster care until she graduated from high school. With a grant from CHINS, she went to Rhode Island Junior College, nicknamed Reject by the Ivy League snobs at Brown University. Alden was surprised to see that even its own students would introduce themselves by saying, "Hi, my name's John. I'm in my second year at Reject." Although she was enrolled in college, Alden recognized she was still on the bottom rung. So she transferred to Cape Cod Community College, where she met Monty, who was taking education courses to qualify for his ESL certificate.

Dane Baker served two years at Cedar Junction and was released. The last time she'd heard from her father, he'd been pinched again in Florida, where he had been tarring driveways and carport roofs with the Irish travelers, scamming the oldsters in Fort Lauderdale. He wasn't even Irish, Alden didn't think.

Hester Pierson said, "Dane Baker isn't holding us up, not really."

"Then what? Is all this extra attention because of Monty? Is Monty screwing it up?"

"It's not your fault that your husband is missing. Some women think a baby will fill that gap, but it never does."

Alden said, "Don't you believe in second chances? I like to think of a starfish. A starfish can grow a new arm where one is missing."

The social worker didn't like metaphors cropping up in her transactions. She knew that people who speak in metaphors can't be trusted and are often rejected from jury duty for good reason.

Two weeks earlier, Hester Pierson had driven out to High Head to inspect Alden's shack. When she arrived, she said, "This blowing sand is pitting my windshield." She stood over her Taurus fingering the glass.

"Sand *eats* glass," Alden said without apology. "Some people can't imagine living out here on the dunes. But Sea Call has its CO. It's legal." Alden pitched her home's healthful setting, perfect for toddlers. It was the last perch of untamed ground at the head of the golden Provincelands, a gleaming finial of barrier beach at the tip of the peninsula. Alden said, "It's better than being in town, isn't it? There's no traffic where a kid could get hit. Besides, they say Provincetown is built on a seething layer of septic sludge and toxic leachates; there might be HIV contaminants in the gray water that's discharged unchecked every summer season. Then in the fall they have Fantasia Fair—you know, the transvestite convention?"

Alden tried to appeal to the social worker's "family values." Alden knew that Hester Pierson disdained the nonhetero village at Land's End. The festival was world renowned, but Hester Pierson had said, "It's not the best example for our youth."

Alden said, "So you agree. My dune shack is far removed from all that."

Alden reminded the social worker that her home was a pristine Victorian structure, once inhabited by a *real* Victorian woman whose daguerreotype had been preserved by the Truro Historical Society and was displayed in the museum at Highland Light. Alden had a color Xerox copy tacked to her kitchen cabinet. The photo showed a girl with dark hair, dressed in a white blouse with the puffy leg-of-mutton sleeves popular at the turn of the twentieth century. It certainly wasn't practical attire for trudging over the dunes, not like the Polartec sweaters Alden took for granted. The Victorian woman reminded Alden of Jane Eyre.

But Hester Pierson wasn't impressed by the Victorian cameo on the wall. She said that the landscape outside was like the moon itself. "It's not the safest place for a single woman with an adopted baby. Especially since you don't have a partner, do you? Or is there someone on the horizon?"

Alden tried to imagine this partner on the horizon and she pictured

Conrad's cockpit instruments, the lateral needle hair that shows which way the plane is tilted. She didn't think of Ison or Monty but remembered the bus driver, Lux Davis, who had pelted her with dog chow. More often, out of nowhere, his face was superimposed on mental snapshots of her husband. These double exposures warred, but the bus driver never completely dissolved away. He had duped her at the puppy barn, but something had happened; a sudden bliss erupted as if a vacuum seal had broken on a canister of sunshine.

Since her husband's disappearance, the bus driver materialized when she didn't expect to see him. Once, she had returned to the police station to give them the address of Monty's one sister, his only living relative, who lived in Austin, Texas. His sister hadn't heard from her brother in five years, but she promised to call the detectives if he should contact her anytime soon. As Alden left the station, the bus driver arrived to fill out forms. He was the last person to see Monty, at the bus stop where he had dropped him off, same as usual. He smiled at Alden, embarrassed that he had lied about his privileges at the puppy farm.

Later that spring, Alden learned that the bus driver had lost his chauffeur's license after driving his empty school bus into the harbor in a freak accident. He froze up when he slammed the gas pedal instead of hitting the brake. She imagined that there was more to it than that. Then in August, Lux delivered a dump truck of pea stone gravel to the visitor center parking lot, and he had stayed all afternoon to rake it smooth in each and every parking stall. It was during a late-summer heat wave—no wind, just the broiling updraft from the oven effect of sunbaked gravel. Everything was hot and still. The leaves looked painted on the trees. Grasshoppers in the short grass flung themselves in wide arcs, like squirts of tobacco juice.

Alden felt sorry for anyone working outside in the sun, and she retrieved the stainless-steel pitcher from the podium in the lecture hall and filled it with ice water. She brought it outside, but Lux didn't stop dragging the rake in percussive swipes across the pea stone. He signaled that she should leave the pitcher for him. From her window she watched with agitation until he finally took a drink. He sipped from its wide, sweaty brim, then he tipped the pitcher above his head, splashing his face and shoulders. He tossed his long, wet hair, releasing a silver Mohawk of water.

More recently, when she had ordered her mini–satellite dish, Lux was the one who was sent to her shack to install it. He was out on her roof for a good while, and she wondered if he knew what he was doing. He might be a "jack of all trades and master of none," so she went outside and asked him, "How many jobs do you hold down?"

"More than I want," he told her.

"You know the saying, 'The farmer who likes the harvest but hates the plow has an empty table'? And there's the one about the ant and the grasshopper—"

"Yeah? And 'If the rich could hire the poor to die for them, the poor could make a good living.' "

He had spritzed her with that one, and all she could think to say was, "You still make green animals?"

"That's right."

"Is this dish aimed in the right direction? Is it the way it's supposed to be?"

"I guess you'll never trust me after we saw those puppies. I mean, after we saw them *illegally.*"

"I just want my TV to work once you're gone."

"This will pull in just about anything you want. The Romance Channel, CNN, Animal Planet. And it gets foreign TV. You know, the BBC. You like Italian soccer?"

"Soccer? I don't know. I like that FBI channel. You know that one? They dig up cold cases to find copycat crimes—"

He looked at her.

"Go inside and we'll test your receiver box. There's two tiers on your menu, but you have to wait a minute for info to accumulate," he said.

"Don't I need you?" she asked.

"Need me? No. You have to be *in* there and me *out* here." He seemed nervous, uncomfortable unless there was a wall between them. She imagined he wanted to jump her bones, but this was wishful thinking, an ambush of her impulsive fantasies, and she scolded herself. She went into the shack and punched buttons on the digital control. He called to her, "How's it coming in?"

She told him the picture was good. She patrolled with the clicker. "I've got bull riding—" She punched the buttons again. "And this one has Martha Stewart. No, not her. Just some Betty Crocker. She's making *her own wax paper.* Gee, Betty, get a life—"

"Really," Lux called back.

"Now it's Rip Torn selling something. I guess he's sunk to doing paid spots."

"What's he hawking?"

"*The Millennium Almanac,* that guide to everything." She touched buttons and announced the wide spectrum of junk. "How do you get the international stuff?"

He ignored her question. "I guess everything's coming in," he said. "I guess you're all set." He didn't come inside to watch.

Each time she saw Lux, he seemed too charged up, or he acted melancholy and lingered too long at his tasks, as if he sensed a connection to her but couldn't arrange its fragile tungsten filaments. After installing her dish at Sea Call, Lux came back to tack a sheet of Tyvek waterproofing over a hole in the shingling. Then he stayed to hammer a patch of new cedar shakes in graduated rows. As he worked outside her window, Alden was at the kitchen sink doing dishes. When he pounded nails, she felt twangs and shivers roll up her spinal column, and she liked the sensation. He seemed to know he was having an effect on her, crowding out her thoughts about Mr. Two Turrets. As he patched the hole in the siding, she felt something else tearing open.

Addressing flyers for Hyram's rowboat regatta to the outfall pipe, she had decided to mail one to Lux. At the bottom of the sheet, she wrote, "Meet me for a drink at Land Ho! Want to?" Her handwriting was a washy blur of real fountain-pen ink. She folded the flyer and inserted it in an envelope. She didn't lick the flap but reached under her desk for her purse. She took out her spray bottle of Samsara, a fifty-milliliter *vaporisateur,* and aimed the gold nozzle at the glue strip, spritzing the adhesive with a mist of French musk. She closed the flap and rubbed it with the heel of her hand. A magazine article had said:

"Perfume is an invisible arm that reaches out to the unsuspecting." Yes, in an instant its rich saturant was absorbed and arrested in the number ten envelope. Emotive myrrhs and romance toxins—jasmine, narcissus, sandalwood—were ready to launch as soon as her letter was ripped open. Her target would unwittingly inhale her message, breathe deeply its microscopic bergamot spitballs, ingest its gingered veil.

Then he'd know about her.

In an instant, he'd know. Like the clash of a cymbal or a bullet between the eyes.

The magazine instructed: "Use your perfume of choice in repetitive strikes. Expose your target to your specific erotic *irritant* until he can't ignore its symptoms." She had sent the note but had not signed her name.

When Lux didn't reply, she sent a second message. Inside the envelope she had enclosed a little packet of paper dolls with glossy-coated wardrobes on separate cards. It was something she had found at the Job Lot store, where everything costs less than a dollar. It wasn't a child's toy, but a curvy vixen in skimpy underwear, with six little outfits to cut out. She wrote, "Tell me what to wear on our first date. . . ." But again she didn't sign her name. She wasn't ready to let him know what she was thinking, but she was almost certain he'd know anyway. Sometimes, at odd moments, in line at the Mobil station to put air in her tires, at her Seashore office surrounded by her inventory of birdcalls and thistle seed, or standing naked in front of her bath vanity, his face rose up to the surface like a paper flower unfurls in a tumbler of water. Suddenly she saw him *behind everything,* the way a drawing emerges beneath an oil painting, revealing the artist's original impulse—a picture far more interesting than the finished surface.

She told Hester Pierson, "Sure, I've got someone in mind. I'm not a dried-up prude, if that's what you mean."

"No, of course you're not. But it's ridiculous to be alone out here in the wilderness," the social worker said.

"Alone in the wilderness? That's an oxymoron. Don't you know that living out here, I'm surrounded?" She described her pleasant altercations with wildlife, with both resident inhabitants and noisy, teeming migrations. There was always something in feverish transit. She watched everything from the seasonal showstoppers, bluebirds and red-tailed hawks, to the cyclical exodus of gnats and midges. Midges could get through screening and collected on her ceiling in a shimmering display of pixel dots. Midges didn't bite, but they landed on her face and arms and were quite annoying. That fall, she had watched migrating monarchs in forlorn, skittering queues between rare patches of milkweed. She identified several species of migrant butterflies—a painted lady, a red admiral, a cloudless sulphur, a little yellow, then an endless stream of cabbage whites, Monty's ghost messengers flittering across the empty dunes.

The sea itself heaved with transient populations. Bluefish churned the surface in feeding frenzies, driving schoolies and smelts ashore, where they glistened like silver penknives tossed across the sand. Sometimes at night there were floating mats of gelatinous life, drifting colonies of phosphorescent organisms like tumbling carpets of neon. Coyotes and deer trotted past at all hours. At dusk she saw great horned owls cruise soundlessly above the herringbone sand, and in deep winter she expected to see more snowies.

Hester Pierson wasn't listening to Alden's poeticized sermon, and said, "But there isn't another *human* being for three miles in three directions. And due east, it's just that empty Atlantic horizon. It's insane—"

"I've got my minidish. It gets PBS. I get *Teletubbies* and *Sesame Street.*"

"What's this here?" Hester Pierson toed a trapdoor built into the wide-plank flooring. "Circular cellar?"

"Yes. It's original to the shack."

Before Hester Pierson had arrived to inspect her house, Alden had hidden a surplus of baby items in the circular cellar below the plank floor. Toys, bedding, tiny overalls and sweaters. She had amassed so much pastel junk while waiting for her license that she worried it might appear presumptuous to the social worker researching her application. She stored the booty in the cellar. Built of fieldstone and brick, with a rough-hewn ladder, the circular stairwell was the eerie central aspect of her living space. Its tight sleeve was a vertical drop into pitch blackness if she tugged the trapdoor open by its antique brass ring.

But Alden had left the three-faced bisque doll propped on her bed. When the social worker discovered it, she took a shallow breath and told Alden, "If you ever want to sell this, I might be interested." Hester Pierson fingered the doll's pinafore, trying not to reveal her excitement or that she believed the doll was worth a good deal of money. "That cellar's a little spooky. In a horror movie, someone would crawl out that trapdoor at night."

"Yeah. I've thought of that," Alden said. "Some nights I think I hear things, but it's the wind. The wind is *alive*."

Hester Pierson nodded, amazed at Alden's guilelessness—she didn't try to hide anything. Not even her silly fears.

NOW ALDEN WOULDN'T LEAVE Hester Pierson's office. The woman shuffled papers, looking haggard, with dark, hollowed-out cow hooves under her eyes. Having finished jawboning, the social worker looked at Alden with metered sympathy, as if she was thinking, Here is a young woman who's had nothing but hard knocks, a girl trying to pull herself up by her bootstraps. But it's hopeless.

Alden said, "Look, I work for the National Seashore, you know? They have no complaints about me. I'm not a kook."

The social worker acknowledged that Alden was a responsible worker.

"And I volunteer at the Council on Aging, delivering those Meals-On-Wheels. What about that?" Alden said.

Hester Pierson asked Alden, "Do you volunteer at these organizations just to *fill out* your profile? Is it a means to an end?"

"What in the world are you saying?"

The social worker told her, "Avid volunteerism is sometimes considered to be a mental-health symptom."

Alden explained that she had worked many jobs in the private sector. Before her current position at the National Seashore, she had worked in Provincetown, "gallery sitting" at a high-end art bin. But at an opening for a successful New York painter, a glamorous summer resident, Alden was involved in a little incident. The artist's paintings were small oils that sold for fifteen thousand dollars each. With such portable works, the artist worried about thefts. Each tiny canvas might easily be concealed beneath someone's shirt or slipped into the roomy straw beach bags women toted in summer. When the show was being hung, Alden was out shopping for wine and cheese for the reception and didn't see the artist jury-rig the paintings with booby traps. Each canvas was outfitted with a row of silver ball bearings balanced along the inside lip of the stretcher. If someone tried to steal one, they'd be caught.

At the zenith of the party, Alden noticed that a painting looked crooked. She walked over to the wall to straighten it. As she tapped the corner of the painting just so, the ball bearings toppled to the floor. Tiny silver spheres bounced and rolled in all directions. Alden chased them. A few curious onlookers tipped other picture frames to examine the curious antitheft system until the room was overcome by scores of shiny, bouncing balls. The gallery's loyal patrons were insulted by the painter's suspiciousness, and there were few red dots beside the works at the end of the evening. The artist usually sold out her shows, and she accused Alden of recklessly sabotaging the opening.

Alden told Hester Pierson that she preferred her current job at the National Seashore Visitor Center. It was really just a glorified clerk's position, but she'd never be held responsible for a fifteen-thousand-dollar painting.

"Look," she told Hester Pierson, "I've got all the baby stuff. Everything is just right. I have the Child Craft crib. It's got the regulation slats—"

"I know, honey. It's all top-of-the-line. That's not the point."

Alden held on. "I've got the locked storage area for household poisons. I don't own firearms. Emergency numbers are stickered by my cell phone charger. I've got the brand-new smoke alarm—"

Hester Pierson stood up from her desk and pulled her coat off a hook. She buttoned her jacket toggles and grabbed her car keys from the desk blotter.

Alden saw she was being brushed off. She said, "Baby Hendrick—he's *supposed* to be with me."

The meeting was over.

Alden followed the social worker outside to her Taurus. "I'll call you in a couple days, honey, really," Hester Pierson said.

Alden looked over the hoods of the cars in the lot. The sun was shattering off the chrome trim. She saw the writing on the wall. Hester Pierson wasn't going to telephone her anytime soon. Hester would let her know with a form rejection letter under the scrolling letterhead "Commonwealth of Massachusetts."

7

LUX HEARD A CELL PHONE RINGING. Marty Stokes pulled one out of his jean jacket and flipped it open. They were working in the mountains of pea stone, oyster shell, and cinder, loading a dump truck for a driveway job in Pleasant Bay. Marty Stokes handed the phone to Lux. The secretary, Nancy Silva, had given the caller Marty Stokes's number, and he was annoyed that his number was being passed around to strangers. When Lux got on the line, the caller had to repeat her name. He had thought it was Gwen calling to pester him.

"Alden?" he said. Her face painstakingly materialized in his mind like magnetized shavings on a Magic Screen picture. She was asking him a question, but he got only its tail end.

"You need to go where?" He looked at the blinding two-story mound of oyster shell he was standing on and felt his legs give, or maybe it was the broken bits shifting under his weight. Men can be buried in an abrupt landslide of paving stone. That's what his boss had said when he told Lux he'd have to sign a waiver before he could be hired to haul gravel.

"Can you help me run a little errand?" Alden was saying.

The crushed shell was fresh, still rank with little tabs of oyster meat and connective muscle, and its fumes were overwhelming, attracting seagulls that circled above their heads, screeching, as the men topped off their new load. Marty Stokes signaled to Lux to get off the cell phone.

"Sure, I'll come," he told Alden. He could beg off this driveway job. He'd be glad for any reason.

He told Marty Stokes that he had to run an errand. His aunt wanted him to come over to her apartment in Wareham. "She's got a paper for me to sign. You know, a living will or something." Lux's mother had asked him to sign one before she died, and now her sister wanted the same contract. Marty Stokes grinned, amused at how readily Lux concocted his alibi. "Another hot lunch?"

"You have a one-track mind," Lux said. He tapped the cell phone antenna against the heel of his hand and handed the phone back to Marty Stokes.

Driving Gwen's Tercel to meet Alden, he was held up behind a caravan of shrink-wrapped yachts. The boats were being hauled from the boatyard in a parade to the rotary, and from there they crept to an inland lot where they wintered in their tight wrappings. He inched past a cabin cruiser, its prow straining against its glossy prophylactic. He had an almost-phobic reaction to the spectacle, like the time he was chased by that giant mirror as a boy.

He showed up at the Seashore office to see Alden applying her lipstick. He was glad to see that Alden still wore some makeup despite being the head cheese at that Romper Room of orca mobiles, Beanie Babies, wildlife jigsaw puzzles, and Sierra Club posters.

"God, you must have hit every red light," she told him.

He nodded. "All two of them."

Alden locked her office door and twisted a handwritten sign to face out. Instead of the usual Bakelite clockface with red hands that could be set to the exact time when she'd return, Alden had scrawled, "Back in *One Hour.*" Her imprecise message made Lux recall Zeno's paradox, which he'd learned about in his honors math class in high school. If she doesn't say when she actually departs, one hour from *now* never comes.

Lux climbed into her Wagoneer. Sitting beside Alden, he felt as if he were taking the first step on a treasure map he had studied for years and years. The cuffs of his jeans were fuming with oyster liquor, and he told Alden he must be a sight.

"It doesn't matter what you wear for this."

"Exactly what?"

"This is a covert operation. This is anarchy."

He looked at her. "Oh yeah?" He wondered what she was talking about, but he thought that he would probably do whatever she asked.

Turning onto Route 6, Alden ground the gears, depressing the clutch in a clumsy hiccup. The chassis rattled. Lux teased her. "You ever try out for demolition derby in this heap? It's about ready for my friend King."

"King Johnston?" Alden said. "King was in my science lab at Nauset High."

"You went to Nauset? How did I miss you?"

"I was bumped around a little bit, but I did my senior year right here. You must have been a year ahead or something."

"But you and King were lab partners? Jesus."

"No one wanted to be his *partner* exactly. King broke a lot of glass. He spilled beakers of acid. He liked to watch it eat the finish off the work-table. So how's he doing?"

"He's okay. King is King."

"That's not exactly good news, or it's debatable, isn't it?"

Lux was pleased to see that Alden understood King's complexities. He didn't need to defend his friend. She seemed to like King.

When Alden tried to light a cigarette, Lux plucked it from her lips and snapped it in half. "You should quit."

"Hey, that's twenty cents, asshole." She tipped her head to look at him. Was he going to break all her cigarettes in half?

"I'm trying to quit. So can you," he said. He saw her startled eyes, her pupils big and liquid black. He could drown there, but he looked away. He took her pack of cigarettes and threw it out the window. His spirits lifted when she didn't even squeak. He imagined she was falling into his lap like rain into a rain barrel.

At Hyram's, they found a note on the kitchen table. "Alden, I'm at Land Ho! Item's on porch. Can you take me to Hyannis for my stress test this week?"

"Oh, God, he's at lunch with his outfall pipe cronies. His workshops take place over some manhattans. Who knows what they get accomplished."

"Stress test in Hyannis?" Lux said.

"Hyram's a heart patient. They put him on a treadmill."

"Treadmill? Every day's a treadmill."

She looked at him. His bleak irony was a little bit of a shock to her. Beneath his sometimes-frozen veneer, he was usually sunny. Hyram had even told her that his name, Lux, means light.

"Hyram says it's out here," Alden told Lux, and she pulled him by the arm onto Hyram's back porch. She lifted a nylon tarp to reveal a drab green rock. A loggerhead turtle in its ripening aftermath.

"This washed ashore at Hatch's Harbor. It's beginning to stink. In fact I'd say it's getting into the putrid stage, don't you think?" She was gleeful.

"It's pretty far along," Lux said, happy that its rank odor competed with his oyster shell grime.

Alden examined the sea turtle. "Poor thing. See here? Its flipper was sliced away by a trawler's propeller—or a whale-watch boat. With one flipper gone, it couldn't paddle to the surface for air, or it bled to death trying. The New England Aquarium is autopsying these turtles for the survey."

Lux nodded. "It won't be too hard to figure out what happened to him. This one was struck by a boat. It was a hit-and-run."

"Can you help me put it in the Jeep?" Alden asked.

"Where's it going?" he asked.

"I have to help deliver it to the research laboratory."

Twenty minutes later, they were standing in the parking lot outside the Mid-Cape office of the Department of Social Services.

Lux said, "You're saying you want me to put the loggerhead in that Taurus? They'll have to get all new upholstery."

"That's not my problem. I'm just supposed to leave it."

He wiped his mouth with the back of his wrist, ashamed to be amused by her outlaw idea. "Who's it really for?" he asked her.

"That bitch at DSS."

He was beginning to understand that Alden was a girl who had a lot of problems distinct from the one at the center of everything. Maybe the one big problem that Lux felt responsible for had fractured into a starburst of sister disasters. He'd had the same thing happen to him. His freezing syndrome had spawned a mirror ball of incidents and difficulties. That was the usual.

"Please," she said. Her eyes looked swimmy. She stabbed his waist with her pointer finger, poking him gently. Her wet eyes drilled him, as if to suggest that for the misdemeanor he was willing to enact on her behalf, she understood he'd expect his reward. She would come through with her part of the bargain. She wasn't too uncomfortable with the prospect. At least this was what he was fantasizing. The parade of shrink-wrapped boats still bothered him.

They waited until a visitor parked his car and walked inside the building. When the lot was clear, Alden showed him that she'd brought a coat-hanger come-along. But the Taurus was unlocked as per usual. No one locks his car on Cape Cod. People think the peninsula is charmed. They think that criminals won't cross the canal, fearful of the bottleneck at the bridge on their turnaround. They don't stop to imagine the native scourge, what the locals might be up to.

Lux hauled the vile-smelling carcass from the deck of the Jeep, leaving a tangy smear on the carpet. He placed the turtle upright in the passenger seat of the Taurus, strapping the seatbelt around its ribbed midriff as if it were a child. He told Alden, "This way, all its stale seawater and rotten slime will drain into the seat upholstery."

"Shite. You are bad to the bone," Alden said.

Her slang unnerved him. Or it was the creature, pitiable in its own right, and he felt it might be almost sacrilegious to incorporate the endangered animal in Alden's vengeance scheme. Lux reminded her that police could cite them for premeditated destruction of property, and worse—premeditated stalking and harassment.

She didn't want to hear it from *him.* "Look, I'm not forcing you to do anything. I mean, no one's aiming a weapon between those big blue eyes."

He grinned and looked at the treetops in the distance, enjoying her flirty indictment. He watched a distant airplane, buzzards, little rumba lines of cirrus clouds, to avoid looking at her. He rubbed his hands on his jeans and climbed back into her Jeep, but this time he was behind the wheel. She got into the passenger side and giggled in high-octave spurts and tinklings as Lux circled the lot and turned onto the street. Alden said, "I'm never coming back!"

At the Seashore office parking lot, Lux got out of the Jeep and walked over to his car. At the Tercel, he turned around and waved good-bye.

Alden flattened her palms together in prayer and dipped her face forward in a campy Buddhist curtsy. "I owe you," she said. She was entering the building when Lux called to her, "Have a *Nauset* day!" It was the familiar pun from their high school years, but it thrilled her when he crooned it.

Alden returned the corny blessing. "Hey, you, too. Have a Nauset day."

8

LUX SAT THROUGH DINNER with Gwen and his nephews. He cut his portion of lasagna in half but couldn't eat any. He quartered it, then sliced it into eighths. One minute, Gwen shot him daggers; the next minute her eyes were big and fearful. She didn't want that skeleton turning up in her pantry again. Lux told her that King had promised a truck on Friday.

"I don't want to know your schemes." She covered her ears with both hands. The little boys were oblivious to this back-and-forth, but Gwen asked Lux to spoon some Jell-O salad on his plate so that Nils and Ian would follow his lead and taste their scoop of wobbly raisins and carrot shavings. "I can't get vegetables into them unless it's with Jell-O." Her domestic talk seemed tragic to him, and he tried to oblige her. He spooned Jell-O onto his plate in a shivering dome.

But after dinner he was surprised to see that Gwen had packed suitcases. She had left him and Denny before, but this time Nils and Ian had filled cartons with toys. They had their wooden trains, their armies of plastic men, Micro Machines, space-station vehicles, and Memory cards, all the permanent fixtures of their lives. He tried to calculate Gwen's probable length of stay at her mother's house in Waltham by tallying up the boys' collection. It was enough for the whole winter season.

Gwen put the kids into the car, snapping their belts. She told Lux, "If Denny rings through on the radio, tell him we're in Waltham."

"Does your mom know you're coming?"

"She's ready. But she tells me if I decide to come back here after I calm down, she's never taking me and the kids again. She says I should *never* come back."

"Don't go to Waltham," Lux told her. "I need you here."

"Why can't you leave that teacher where he is?"

"If I don't go in and get it, Marty Stokes will. Then Francisconi will finally know. They find the teacher, they put it together. I was driving his bus. A funny coincidence, isn't it?"

"You think it's funny? Because of a *coincidence* I have to leave my house."

He tried to meet her eye to eye, but she whipped around the other way. He grabbed her elbows but she jerked free. She got behind the wheel of her Tercel. His nephews waved. It wasn't out of the ordinary to them. They loved going to their grandmother's tract house, where the sidewalks were level and their Matchbox cars could be jetted back and forth between them.

He watched his makeshift family loaded up. He told Gwen, "You know I might need the Toyota. If King forgets about me, I'll need a reliable car—"

"You think that poor teacher cares what you drive?"

She gunned the small engine, and it warbled brightly like a dishwasher. She backed up and did a three-point on the grass. He saw the familiar bumper sticker "Chatham: A Quaint Little Drinking Village with a Fishing Problem," and he just felt sorry for her. That sticker wasn't an inside joke, as she thought, but a depressing commentary.

"I'll need this car." Lux tugged the door handle.

She depressed the lock button and rolled the window up, leaving an inch.

"Come on, Gwen—"

"Fuck you. Go fuck your fixation," she said.

"Just watch me," he said. "I'll fuck her brains out."

HE STOOD AT THE KITCHEN SINK beneath the bare lightbulb. He scraped clinging hunks of Jell-O off Gwen's Fiesta plates and loaded the dish drainer. Ever since Nickerson sprang the news on him, the teacher's face kept appearing everywhere, in the scummy dishwater, in the window's reflection of his own mug, in the hooded streetlamp outside. The tape kept rewinding to that bitter day two years earlier.

On that April morning, everything started *as per.* Lux punched in at six-fifteen at Bay State Nurseries. He checked the computerized timer for the automatic irrigation nozzles, which had been on the fritz the day before; then he mixed stinking fertilizer according to specific recipes for the different fields. Starter rose canes need more phosphorus; conifer seedlings need the nitrogen. He spot-tested the soil pH with an insta-kit in Second Field, where he had noticed emerging buds on cherry saplings were showing deformed scales. He helped Marty Stokes fill the spreaders. Then he left the nursery and showed up at the bus lot at six forty-five. He drove two morning routes, first one for the high school, then one for the middle school. Middle school kids are barbarians.

At eight forty-five he went back to work at the nursery until two o'clock, when he left to do his afternoon bus routes. By three-thirty he was finished for the day. Early enough to nap and have a full night of something. Cards, or the dogs at Wonderland Park, or basketball. He was center forward for the Silkworms, named after the beloved guided missiles in the Desert Storm offensive. Lux wasn't an official vet, but the older men adopted him when a player hurt his knee and they needed someone extra. He played with the Gulf vets once a week at the Nauset High School gymnasium, if he wasn't presoaked.

On his P.M. route that Tuesday, Lux was already enriched. He had been using a script for a back strain he suffered unloading a truckload of Dursban, a trailerful in fifty-pound bags. The sacks leaked puffs of insecticide dust each time he slapped one onto the dolly, and he had a splitting headache. The headache made him forget about his usual safeguards for his back, and he didn't bend his knees in correct synchrony with his lifting technique. Since then, he'd been taking Vicodin caplets and knocking them back with a pint. With the kiddies aboard, he was trying to stay a notch above stone blind, but the Vicodin threw him off. Bourbon was a familiar opponent, but the tabs were messing him up. He tapped the brake too hard, pitching the kids off their haunches. They fell back into their seats, spilling notebooks, soda cans, CD players, and headphones. Girls erupted in feminized shrieks, and boys unloosed novice curses in their cracking voices. Lux gripped the steering wheel tighter. He held the wheel at quarter to three, then at two o'clock, then back at quarter to three. The wheel felt spongy in his hands as the bus floated over the blacktop like one of those Tunnel of Love dinghies.

The teacher who monitored the afternoon route walked up the aisle to take a good look at the driver. He aimed his burning eyeball at Lux as if his scalding once-over might help to dry him out. Lux wriggled his fingers in a wormy salutation. The bus monitor sat down in the seat behind him.

The teacher was Montgomery Warren. Afternoons, he rode with Lux as bus monitor. Lux saw the coincidence in the bus monitor's name and his official title. If students asked Lux a question, he'd say, "Ask *Monty,* the *monitor.* I'm just the driver." He'd say, "Ask *Monty,*" the same way you might say ask "Cookie" if you wanted your dinner, or ask "Blackie" to shine your shoes, or ask "Rusty" to sharpen your ax. The students recognized that the nickname belittled the schoolteacher, and they grabbed the opportunity to elongate the ritual and tease it out as part of their daily fare.

Monty Warren made little impression on the feral teens. Lux knew that a school bus was an unhappy arena, like a Roman coliseum. Mean kids teased the children sitting directly in front of them, attacking any outstanding physical characteristics. Kids with a sizable ear shelf or extra poundage or acne flare-ups triggered the lexicon. "Lard ass," "pus bump," "fag," "wigger," "tard." Lux recognized these generic idioms, feverish slurs from kids on the threshold of adolescence. His own classmates had called him "zombie" and "Frankenstein" when they saw him have his frozen seizures.

Monty Warren had been a Peace Corps volunteer in Sierra Leone and had worked for AmeriCorps in the States. For two years he was an orderly at Butler Psychiatric Hospital in Providence, where Rhode Island's "upper crustaceans" send their nervous Miss Debs. Then he crossed the canal to teach at the middle school in Orleans. "Public school is the new third world," he told Lux. "Even on Cape Cod, with all our *Mayflower* descendants, I had to go back to school for my ESL certificate."

The bus monitor carried an insect exhibit that he had brought into school. The teacher was a butterfly expert or something, but it was a hobby Lux couldn't fathom spending precious hands-on time doing.

Lux saw that Monty Warren's butterflies fit his tree-hugger profile, but he'd seen another side of the bus monitor at the local bars in town. The schoolteacher turned up with different trophies and goers, just like a collector. Never his wife. He grazed the pastures at Erin Go Bragh, Yesterday's, the Binnacle, and Land Ho! Lux thought that Monty's swordsman persona seemed uncharacteristic of his milquetoast school-teacher profile.

Lux cornered too sharply and pitched the bus monitor across the aisle, undercutting the olive branch technique Monty was trying on two rowdies in the back seats. Boys palmed lit cigarettes each time Monty walked to the rear of the bus, and when he turned around they flicked the lit stubs at his back. Lux watched his mirror, sighting Monty's bright yellow nylon Windbreaker with the Nike swoosh. The monitor was having a heated moment with a kid, and Lux lifted his foot off the accelerator to back up Monty's verbal threat.

Monty asked Lux to pull the bus over. Lux got up from behind the wheel and walked to the back of the school bus to be enforcer for the monitor. Two boys were smashing each other with closed fists. One of these kids was already bloody. Lux yanked the aggressor off the weakling student and tossed the brute into the aisle. He steered the hothead kid by his shoulders and slammed him down on a bench up front. Then Lux crashed down behind the wheel, gunned the engine, and plowed into the moving traffic.

"You're fucked up," the kid told Lux, leaning over his shoulder. "I'm gonna tell the principal, Miss Sullivan, you keep booze in that Mylanta bottle."

Lux turned around. "Okay, and you tell her you pounded little Petey back there. That will save me the trouble."

More and more often, in midroute, Monty told Lux, "Maybe I should drive."

Lux said, "I guess you have your chauffeur's license?"

"Not exactly."

"Then I guess I do the driving." He paddled the wheel to compensate for his steering miscalculations. Lux's turns were swinging too wide, or they were too tight and his tires squawked against the curb. With each mistake the students cheered as if they had boarded the Corkscrew at Six Flags.

As long as Monty was standing in the aisle, they somehow felt safe.

Lux pulled up short of the usual stops, fearing he was going to roll past. He crushed the brake, and the bus throbbed to a halt. Kids trotted up the aisle and tumbled out. As they scattered, it took all of his concentration to keep the bus dead-still until each child was clear of his fender. Yes, he must be illegal. He didn't think kids would know. Again, he merged into traffic, always a half beat too late. Moving streams were shunted from lane to lane to incorporate his careless maneuvers. Lux crammed the brakes, and Monty's butterfly exhibit crashed to the floor. Schoolgirls dived into the aisle to rescue the diorama, each one vying to hold it in *her* lap. Girls loved Monty. On the school bus it was just gooey thirteen-year-olds, but at the bar rails in town the skinny teacher was always surrounded by new prospects. Lux had seen him in action. Monty's flagrant skirt chasing encouraged Lux to think seriously about the teacher's wife. Without being conscious of trying, Lux had already started the planning stages of his campaign.

But Lux wanted to make sure that the schoolteacher had no intention of defending his claim, so when the last children were dispersed, toting their Rollerblade booties, ripstop nylon backpacks, and classic black vinyl violin cases, Lux kept driving. He passed Monty's usual drop-off.

Monty stood in the tiny stairwell, gripping a silver pole. "Hey—you missed my stop." He cuffed Lux's shoulder.

Lux kept going down the country lane.

Monty said, "No kidding, asshole. You're past my corner."

"I'm driving us down to the harbor."

"Excuse me?"

"Let's have one at the Viceroy." Lux accelerated down Cove Road.

"You've had your share already."

"There's no actual shortage, is there? Since when are they rationing?" Lux wanted to have a beer with the teacher to find out just how much resistance he'd throw up when he moved in on Alden.

The bus monitor climbed out of the stairwell and slammed back in a seat. He crossed his arms. Kidnapped or what have you, it was no use arguing with the madman at the wheel.

Lux steered the bus down a tight drive beside the waterfront. The gravel lane was narrow, obstructed by clumps of wild olive that scraped both sides of the bus, making a racket. Lux edged the bus into a tiny sand parking lot behind a cement-block building. The tavern had no windows and looked like an old transfer station thrown up by ComElectric to house transformers, or like an EPA pump house installed to filter contaminated groundwater, maybe after a submerged diesel tank had ruptured. The tavern was right on the water, but it didn't have bay windows, sunny decks, or the usual bright Styro dock bumpers and nautical decor.

Its concrete slab walls were a faded flamingo pink. More recently, they'd added a row of decorative stencils—a line of royal crowns painted in harsh blue. Monty followed Lux off the bus. "Are you leaving me here?"

"I'm buying you one," Lux said.

The bus monitor looked at the cement-block building. A one-word neon sign flashed audibly above the door lintel, "Viceroy . . . Viceroy . . . Viceroy," without the article. The bar's name alone said "sleaze facility," and as he pulled the bus monitor inside the front entrance, Lux pointed to another sign that said, "Watch your step. Stairs uneven."

Monty addressed the skewed risers carefully and followed Lux into the dark room.

Lux said, "You want a beer?"

"I guess."

"No one's forcing you to have one. I'll take you home right now. You want to go home?" He was sure Monty wanted a wallop as much as he did.

The bus monitor walked through the dark interior and sat down at a small pedestal table. Lux saw that they had at least the one common denominator—a typical thirst after a typical workday. Lux followed Monty to the table and told the bargirl, "Two tonsil swabs over here."

"Let's get a pitcher," Monty said, his mood ascending as he studied the girl's back end while she leaned between the two men to light the tiny candle in a plastic-meshed tumbler. When she went to get the pitcher and two big glass beakers, the men watched her retreat. She wore tight jeans that carved her buttocks into two distinct flesh portions. Lux noticed the pinched seam, but Monty went even further to actually verbalize the feeling. "Tight jeans. Tight hole. You would hope."

The schoolteacher's crude remark must only have scratched the surface of his unrefined thoughts. But Lux didn't like to go public with his fetish gymkhana.

Monty said, "You come here every day?"

"If I knew that—"

The bus monitor laughed with sudden, unmasked pleasure. He dabbed at the sides of his mouth with his thumb and forefinger as if his grin were spittle. "Shit, Lux, you don't know where you are day to day?"

"Day to day? I'm a working slob. I do my morning route, then I'm digging ditches at Bay State. I'm in the field or in the AmTran. I do hard hours same as you, Teech." He took out a prescription bottle and shook two Vicodin into the palm of his hand. He washed them down with his beaker-sized glass. "For a back strain," he told Monty. "I was stacking bags of insecticide all day Saturday."

"I'm against all forms of insecticide."

"Even the EPA-approved ones?"

"Especially those. 'EPA-regulated' is just like saying 'registered gun.' Just because a gun is registered doesn't mean it won't be used to kill someone."

Lux looked at the teacher and thought of all those registered guns. "Well, the aphids are waking up right about now, you know?"

"As they have every year since long before we evolved."

"Good that our bosses can't see us sitting here evolving."

"Yeah, we're going backward to the reptile stage, back even further."

"Yeah. Into single-cell barflies. Good your *wife* isn't here to watch us," Lux said. He had meant to wait awhile longer before asking about her. She was in his head like a noontime dream—wide awake or sleeping—her face flashed before him like a screen saver flares on at each unconscious downtime, just like those candles in the movie sputtering in the wrong progressions.

"How about *your* wife? Does she know you come here?" Monty said.

"Oh, I live with my sister-in-law, in unholy matrimony."

"You mean that you're doing your brother's wife?"

"It's her idea."

"No kidding?"

"Her old man's on a swordfish boat."

The teacher stared mesmerized across the table, the way believers look when they see the Virgin's face in a sticky bun.

"Got a problem with that?" Lux said.

"Shit. I don't care who you bang. Sister-in-law, baby sister, whatever."

The bargirl came back with a new pitcher.

Monty said, "Thanks, Tina." He turned to Lux. "She looks like what's-her-name. Tina Turner."

"I think her name's Kathy."

"Hey, Tina? Kathy? How about some Goldfish over here?" Monty said.

The girl ignored him.

Monty walked over to the bar and took a basket of tiny crackers. He sat down again and went on. "But, hey, you ever notice how blacks use American product names for their babies—you ever see how that goes? My students have names that come right off household items. Girls and boys. There's Sunbeam, L'Oréal, Cascade, like the dishwasher soap."

Lux looked at the candle between them. Its nervous flame twisted left and right in the still environment, almost a vacuum; what would it do in a windstorm? He saw how Monty referred to these children as if they were a curious subset of *Homo sapiens.* Lux saw the race element emerging in his rival's profile. It was just another reason he should rescue Alden.

Monty said, "My theory is that these people have a sense of the musical syntax in words. They're not thinking about what the words actually mean—"

"You're a backward asshole, you know that?"

"One person's 'backward' is another person's 'full speed ahead.'"

"I didn't know they let butterfly geeks into the Klan."

"I've never attended, but I respect their right to assemble. To gather together—"

"That's right, forget about little Cascade, little Electrasol—"

Monty said, "I guess you think it's not the *American* way. We have to *absorb*."

"I thought you worked in the Peace Corps on the Dark Continent and all," Lux said. "Since when do they recruit Nazis?"

"I went there with my *white* girlfriend. You don't think I acted like these United Methodist missionary gonks who get into village life from the ground floor up."

"I guess mud huts *are* the ground floor."

"In Africa, everyone's HIV or full blown. It's called slim disease. They're so skinny, they look like those Peek Frean chocolate straws."

The new pitcher was sweating, but Lux didn't want more. He teased the candle flame with his fingertips. He drew his hand away slowly, lifting its tiny flare higher until the flame was a full six inches tall.

"Jesus, where'd you learn that trick?"

"*The David Copperfield Christmas Special*."

The teacher understood that Lux had winged him.

"You know, your wife's very pretty. It's Alden, right?"

Monty nodded.

"Alden, then. With her on your arm, why are you still in business?" Lux said.

"What are you saying?"

"I see you with different girls in town. How many in your elite posse?"

"Oh, it's just the one, Penny. She's into bugs. We go on butterfly safaris."

"I've heard it called 'getting it on,' but never 'going on safari.' That's good—"

"Penelope *is* good."

"Your wife doesn't like bugs?"

"My wife *is* bugs."

"How's that?"

"She's lost. You know, lost in space? A lunachick."

"Lunachick?" Lux thought of the little girl with uncombable hair. A girl like that is always stigmatized and misunderstood. Of course she'd be called crazy because of her syndrome; her hair spiraling in a hive of curls gave her a wild appearance, like a sun-bleached haystack delirium on a van Gogh postcard.

"Manic-depressive. It's biochemical, but she won't take her medicine."

"So why'd you hook up with her?" Lux said. "I mean, if she's such a mess."

Monty tipped the pitcher into Lux's glass. He looked directly at Lux and said, "Why am I with her? I guess because she's so *hot,*" he said, exaggerating the final consonant before biting it off. He licked his index finger and stabbed the tabletop, making a hissing sound effect, as he watched Lux.

Lux rearranged his legs under the table, kicking a chair away.

Monty went on, "You're really pushing your luck driving a school bus down here to the Viceroy. Shouldn't that bus be back in the lot by now? You'll get your pink slip."

"Only if you report me."

"Oh, that 800 number?"

"You know the one, dial 1-800-SIT-ON-MY-FACE."

Monty had a donkey laugh. But Lux was already imagining trying to park the bus in the one or two tight spaces remaining at the lot, if there were any at all. His route took the longest to complete and he was often late logging in. The last few drivers to come back were forced to drive their bus home. They'd have to park it in front of the house, an inconvenience to the neighborhood traffic. Side streets were narrow, and most everyone's driveway was too tight. You might nose up to the garage door, but the bus ass would stick out over the sidewalk.

There was always an informal race back to the lot, and Lux was sometimes forced to keep his bus overnight, but his place was on the outskirts of town and he didn't have to wrangle with curbside slots. Gwen and Denny's duplex was in the last rural farmland in Eastham, in the last few turnip fields, soon to be developed, but for now he could pull the big yellow barque right onto the grass.

"This bus route I'm driving is just temporary. You know I won a prize last fall for my arbor? I want to get a degree in landscape architecture. Hideo Sasaki was down here on vacation and someone brought him to see my sunken gardens and pleaching fences. You know him, Sasaki? He designed Copley Square in Boston. He said he liked what I'm doing. He said it ranks up there with the Ladew masterpieces and Longwood Gardens."

Monty looked at his watch—a big article with a blue butterfly, small as a shamrock, preserved under the crystal.

"But enough about *me*," Lux said. "That watch must be a babe magnet."

"Oh. Sorry. You were saying you want to be an architect?"

Lux forged ahead. "You think your wife is missing you right about now?"

"I guess."

Lux leaned forward. He said, "She's wasting her time thinking about you."

The schoolteacher blinked once, then let his eyebrows rise slowly into a frozen bridge.

Lux said, "Do you have some kind of arrangement? Or is she in the dark about this safari slut?"

"Hey, what's it to you who I'm doing or who I piss on?" Monty said.

"Live by the sword, die by the sword," Lux said.

"You're just jealous. Your little black book is blank."

Lux told the schoolteacher, "No, I'm just wondering—why are you chasing pussy when Alden's in your pocket? She waits for you at your bus stop, on that corner almost every day—"

"Maybe she's waiting for *you*."

His words startled Lux, and Lux tried not to react, but a smile was organizing. He set his teeth and fought its independent muscle contractions.

Monty said, "Shit. Is this what's behind the reverse directory? You're interested in my wife?"

Lux hated the butterfly collector for reading him right. He pushed back his chair and stood up. He turned his pocket inside out, looking for dollars.

"I've got it," Monty said. He snapped a bill out of his wallet.

Lux left his own cash for the bargirl they'd undressed in their minds. Lux left every dollar he had next to the stuttering votive crock he'd manhandled all during happy hour.

AFTER TWO PITCHERS, they left the Viceroy and climbed back into the empty school bus. Lux had some trouble maneuvering a three-point in the tight lot. The schoolteacher tried to ignore Lux's incompetence and walked up the black rubber mat collecting cigarette stubs left behind by middle school brats, juvie Marlboro men, who stamped out butts with their new Doc Martens. He grabbed a seat pole when Lux jammed the brakes for one lone crow on the blacktop. The bird trotted left, then hopped back to its daub of carrion after the bus plowed past.

Monty sat down behind Lux for the final mile to his stop. Lux pulled up to the intersection and opened the accordion door. Alden was nowhere.

"Let me see that ant farm," Lux said, stalling for time. Maybe Alden would show up to meet her husband, although they were already one hour late. Monty allowed Lux to examine the "Butterflies on Strike!" diorama.

"What's their beef?" Lux asked him.

"Their beef?"

"Why'd they go on strike?"

"They're on strike because of these new butterfly breeding farms. Butterflies are becoming a commodity sold for weddings, baptisms, graduations, inaugurations. They release them willy-nilly—"

"They sell these bugs for weddings?"

"Ten bucks a pop. But it upsets existing ecotones to release butterflies just anywhere. And now they've got biotech corn. Biotech corn produces toxic pollen that kills monarchs."

Lux got a sample of Monty's Green sermon. The teacher was on a soapbox. "I see," Lux said. "So that's why you've got them on their walkout?"

"Or maybe it's because teachers get shit pay for riding with a drunk bus driver."

Lux said, "At the Viceroy you stayed abreast of me, did you not?"

"I guess."

"Everyone wants to go on strike. You see those checkers at Star Market? They claim they get nerve damage dragging items across those scanners. I get nerve damage just *showing up* for this shit job. But I never saw a butterfly behind a cash register. You ever see one?" Lux was talking nonstop.

Monty leaned back to look at him.

"I'm on painkillers that don't even kill pain," Lux said.

"That explains." The teacher stood on the waffle steps, holding his diorama. He said, "You want me to drive it to the lot? I will."

"Don't do me favors."

"Not you. I'll drive because of my nonspecific, global altruism. For the good of our town. For the benefit of mankind."

"You're off duty, monitor, so don't monitor me. Hey, how come Alden didn't show up?"

"I guess she gave up waiting. We're way off schedule. Or maybe it's because I told her about you."

"You told her what?"

"I said you have a canning factory where you chop up girls and put them in a pressure cooker. You *eat* girls. You put their shit in the microwave and eat that, too. I said you're a pervert with the hots for her. She should never meet me at the bus stop again. In other words, Lux, you'll never lay eyes on her. She's all mine." Monty edged backward down the bus steps, watching Lux react. He tried to sprint away.

Lux jumped out of his seat and charged down the waffle stairwell in total submission to his circulating chemicals. He started windmilling toward the teacher. He swung a roundhouse punch and his fist connected. He smashed Monty's nose in one pop; Lux heard its bony bridge snap with the sound of a Popsicle stick. He jabbed again and hit Monty's shelf of front teeth. Two square incisors sailed right and left like Scrabble blanks.

In the lightning attack, Monty hadn't been able to throw up a block. His nose was streaming blood in symmetrical spigot lines, staining his guide yellow jacket. Already his busted lip had started to balloon.

Lux climbed back onto the bus. Adrenaline stole his legs, and he dropped into the driver's seat. In an instant he thought of going back out to console the teacher. He would volunteer to drive him to Outer

Cape Health so a physician's assistant could insert cotton swabs daubed with lidocaine into his nostrils, the routine at Gold's Gym when amateurs go at it.

His anger flared up again. Lux goosed the gas pedal, and the bus shot forward. He nosed it after his drinking buddy.

Monty was tearing along the shoulder in frantic strides. He reached the corner, but Lux steered straight at him. Lux swerved the bus to miss him. Its huge butter-sheen fender cleared, but the rear end sluiced over the curb and knocked Monty down. Its back tires, double sets of big 920s, climbed over the schoolteacher in one rotation.

The rear axle hitched, the wheel jounced, and Lux felt the thud in the steering column.

Lux awakened from one murky dreamscape and entered another.

A nightmare in *broad daylight* has crisp, unarguable features. Suddenly the sky looks searing. The empty fields ripple like electric currents. The swath of blacktop beyond the windscreen is a bottomless ravine ripping slowly open.

"Hey, where are you, man?" Lux called to Monty.

He didn't see the bus monitor on either side of the empty road. He looked into the side mirror and into the wide rearview, which showed the empty vinyl seats. These empty seats had a mocking implication, like a Court TV gallery before the jurors file in with their final verdict. Then an atonal mewling ascended from somewhere. It was a human voiceprint but in a wholly unique manifestation. Lux tried to ignore it, but discovered it again.

Ignore it. Hear it. Forget it. There it is again.

He slammed the bus into park and jerked the door lever. Simultaneously a tin stop sign extended on a retractable arm and shivered over the blacktop. Lux studied its trembling red disk, paralyzed. Then he took the steps in one sinking leap. The bus monitor was on the pavement behind the second axle. He was on his side, his limbs rigid and posturing in a worst-pain scenario. The tailpipe spewed drops of poison effluent over his bloodied face where his nose had been broken—only a minor detail, now, within the terrible whole. Lux saw how his hips were swiveled in opposition to his trunk. When Monty struggled to breathe, his chest couldn't expand. After his premodern, mewling cries, Monty could no longer communicate without any air in his lungs. His imperious school instructor's face had lost its typical expression, and even his surly Casanova smirk couldn't hold on. His face looked like the famous tragicomedic inversion, two ghoulish masks melded together in warring conjectures.

A car rolled past. Its driver had not observed the law and didn't stop for the idling school bus. The car kept going. Lux smelled the rank chemical stench drifting his way from a yacht-building yard at the end of the street. He knew that at four-thirty the workers at Fiberglass Yacht would go off shift and the cars would be streaming past. He lifted the schoolteacher and carried him onto the AmTran. He put the body down on the rubber runner; the long mat suddenly assumed the effect of a conveyor belt tugging beneath his feet.

In his trauma reaction, Lux was still cognizant enough to know that if authorities saw him now, in his fortified condition, he wouldn't be able to explain his innocent role in the dream he was having. He sat down behind the wheel and slowly pulled away.

He looked in the mirror and saw Monty's butterfly diorama left behind on the shoulder of the road. The line of protesting insects was just a row of yellow tissue snips. There wasn't time to go back and get it. Cars were turning onto the street, leaving Fiberglass Yacht.

Lux drove home to the duplex. When he pulled up, Gwen was outside pinning bedsheets on the umbrella clothesline. Gwen wasn't surprised to see him coming home with the bus in the afternoon. He often lost his chance to get the last free space on the lot. So what? Besides, she was glad to see him. She wasn't against giving him a little attention right now; both her boys were napping.

Her husband, Denny, was twenty miles offshore on Stellwagen Bank. The crew went out each time with a milk crate full of dog-eared *Playboys* and the like, and she had told him, "You're happy with pictures because they don't talk back."

She tossed her extra clothespins into a sawed-off milk jug and gave the umbrella clothesline a spin. The wash flew out in a circle of white spinnakers like a landlocked regatta. To Gwen, a household helper was a thing of beauty.

She grinned at Lux, expecting the fresh-ass greeting she had learned to love. "Sissy," he called her, warping its meaning forever in their little trysts at noonday or midnight. She didn't mind the nickname.

She told him, "I know what you want." Then she saw him. For once she looked at him instead of jabbering. His shirt was bloody. "Christ. What happened to you?"

"We're fucked," he said.

"What?"

"We. Are. Fucked."

"Oh, my God. Did you wreck? Did they stop you for DUI?" She knew he was always a little primed when he left her and worse when he returned. What made her think he got sober in between? "I can't believe it. If you've lost your chauffeur's license, that's a chunk of our household income."

When he didn't come back with anything, she knew it was something worse than her accusations. "Did they get King for selling? I knew it. Lux—did he finger you?"

Lux walked back onto the bus and she followed him. They saw the teacher crumpled on the rubber runner as if it was the first time for them both. Monty Warren's jacket was a blazing guide yellow, and its Nike swoosh on the breast pocket seemed brazen at that particular finish line. Lux stopped to imagine that these name brands must turn up on all kinds of victims as they line up to get their toe tags. Underneath the teacher's jacket, his shirt was torn and his undershirt was crunched and twisted like a Fruit Of The Loom cummerbund. Around his neck he wore a house key on a braided plastic lanyard; it only reminded Lux that his drinking buddy wasn't going home. Bloodstains from his leg fractures made an odd red doily effect on Monty's khaki trousers. Lux stood beside Gwen and looked down at his colleague and rival. He couldn't be sure if Monty's neck was broken, but the schoolteacher's bloody face was remarkably smoothed since the last time Lux had looked. The onslaught of pain had peaked and subsided, and his blank face confirmed that the teacher had attained the pinnacle of his altered state. The teacher was dead.

"God. What happened to him? What's wrong?"

Lux looked into her face.

When he tried to brainstorm, he came up short but for that one everlasting theme and impulse—Alden.

"An 'act of God' type thing," he told Gwen. But he was thinking, Why not, in the name of love, couldn't he have done this terrible thing *on purpose?*

He watched Gwen's face as she sifted through probable consequences that included not just herself but her children, too. They had watched a TV movie called *Prison Mommies,* where kids visited their mothers in jail but were kept separated behind a Plexiglas window. In order to talk to one another, they had to pick up telephone receivers.

Gwen started to scream in staccato bursts.

Her voice had a crushing echo effect in the empty school bus, and Lux slapped his hand over her mouth. "You'll wake the boys," he told her.

He stared at the bus monitor's slender corpse, his small frame and tousled clothes almost like a sleeping child's—but his nephews Nils and Ian were never this emptied, this quiet.

Gwen erupted again.

Lux grabbed her shoulders and shook her once. "Be *quiet.*" They gave the bus monitor a silent instant, but it was just the beginning of their unrest.

Lux marched off the bus and went into the house. He found the carton he wanted in the mudroom. He hadn't yet burned it in the oil barrel with the rest of the trash. Barrel burning was on Thursdays.

He held the box in front of him to measure it. TESCO Automatic Umbrella Clothes Dryer. Automatic? The Price Chopper sticker was Day-Glo orange and seemed to blind him in little stabbing afterflashes. The box was four feet high and twelve inches deep. Monty might fit inside it.

He carried the body into the kitchen, and Gwen held the cardboard flap open as Lux lowered Monty into the corrugated two-ply carton, his legs scissored tightly, knees to chin. Folding the teacher's arms inside the box, Lux saw Monty's wedding ring, a wide gold band thick as a locknut or faucet bonnet. Lux held Monty's wrist and tried to tug the ring off to get rid of it, but it wouldn't slide over the second knuckle. He dropped Monty's hand. It creeped him. There is nothing that represents the soul more than the hand, and Lux couldn't touch it again. He imagined a matching wedding ring on Alden's hand, and Lux felt his guilt and lust colliding. He pictured the girl with uncombable hair widowed now, her future wide open.

He went over to the cupboard and lifted out the last little nip to be found in the house. He swallowed the whiskey and put the cap back on the empty bottle. Maybe it would sweat a few drops for later.

He told Gwen, "I'll get us out of this."

"*Us?* Since when?"

He looked at his brother's young wife, still beautiful after two kids. If she gave him a little affection now and then, it didn't really hurt anyone. But he wondered when she would turn against him. He never knew a woman who wouldn't say that a man had taken advantage after she was through with him.

Lux started to walk back outside.

"You can't just leave him here," Gwen yelled after him, her eyes wild. "This is the kitchen! Nils and Ian might find it."

Lux came back and lifted the carton upright in the pantry closet next to Gwen's twisty mop. A deep red map had soaked the cardboard, but without his heart pumping, Monty's bleeding would have stopped. Lux kept slamming the pantry door until the latch caught.

He walked back to the bus. He saw it wasn't just a bratmobile any longer, but an idling monster. He still had more to do. Forensic crime squads might spray Luminol on the rubber grid where Monty had been lying to make blood marks light up in the dark.

He couldn't drive the bus through the All-Towel car wash without looking conspicuous. He'd have to get Gwen's mop and swab it down himself. He examined the twin back tires on the right side—big 920s, huge and dumb. He went to the side of the house and uncoiled the garden hose. It didn't reach. He climbed back into the bus and nosed it up beside the house. He tugged the hose and set the nozzle on jet spray. He aimed it at the herringbone tread. Gwen stood on the grass with her hands clasped over her mouth. She watched Lux work methodically on his cover-up routine. Lux explained to Gwen that in court a cover-up is considered an add-on offense to an original crime. A crime *on top* of a crime. It was getting worse with every bit of detailing he performed. He warned her, "You didn't watch this."

Lux took a bucket of water and the twisty mop and boarded the bus. He swabbed the aisle back to front. The slick rubber mat looked too pristine without its typical surface grime. Lux lit a Marlboro and dribbled the ashes, but it wasn't enough soot to refurbish the newbie-smoker pigsty effect achieved by the end of an ordinary school day. He told Gwen, "If you really want to help, go get your carton of Salems."

She went to get her cigarettes and sat down across the aisle from him. She stared hotly at Lux as she lit up. For ten minutes they chain-smoked two different brands and dotted the bus floor with butts and ashes. They felt dizzy from too much nicotine all at once, but at least the rubber mat was sullied again.

"What about my fingerprints on all these butts?"

"Shit. We should have worn gloves."

"King would have told us that."

"I'm not King. I'm not thinking like a convict. Fuck."

"You're not?"

He told Gwen to go into the kitchen to get the half gallon of Juicy Juice from the fridge. He dribbled the sugary drink across the bench seats and onto the floor where Monty had been lying. The juice spilled red tongues across the rubber mat.

Gwen said, "Aren't you overdoing it? Besides, that body has to be out of my pantry. Right now!"

Lux said, "Denny has the *Extra Dry* moored at Rock Harbor, right?" Lux had heard of a ship in a bottle, but his brother had named his little sailboat *after* the bottle. "We could keep it in the boat until Denny gets back. Denny could help me figure this out."

"The *Extra Dry* isn't a morgue. It's his pride and joy. He won't want you taking that teacher aboard. Besides, it's been hauled out of the water and winterized."

"Shit. He's got it shrink-wrapped again, right? I forgot."

"Yeah. Besides, that body can't go in the galley. It needs refrigeration." She was finding some comfort in practical equations.

He nodded. "I know. It's got to go in the ground." He went in the house to call King. King would know what to do. King ordered videos and reading material from Palladin Press: *How to Make Disposable Silencers; How to Use Mail Drops for Profit; Secrets of Good Credit; Do-It-Yourself Submachine Gun; How to Hide Things in Public Places.* "For academic study only."

King said, "That schoolteacher, no shit? He's tits up?"

"This is what I'm thinking. We'll put it in the field at the nurseries. I turned over three rows with the Bobcat today—we've been transplanting cedars all week." He held out his tarry hands to show Gwen the sap stains on his palms and knuckles. "The teacher can go in one of those rows—for now."

King said, "That sounds all right. First we'll get rid of his prints, and maybe pull out his teeth. You got pliers?"

"Pliers? Shit. I'm not doctoring him."

"I see your point. We just cross our fingers. Wait and see. Like a couple *amateurs*—"

"Fuck you." Lux slammed the receiver down, immediately sorry he'd rebuffed a virtual mastermind.

Gwen had been listening, wild eyed and sobbing. He took her back on the bus to look at the operation. "This will work," he told her. "This is within the limits of possibility."

She said, "Why can't you tell them it was an accident. You didn't kill him on purpose—"

"There are losers in jail who drove over baby carriages *not on purpose,* you hear what I'm telling you? Every DUI fuckup says that." His eyes were glassy; then tears popped over his lashes. "*Not on purpose* doesn't mean shit," he told her. But he wasn't sure what had happened to Monty, or why.

It started to rain. Big aromatic dollops of spring rain pelted the bus roof. "My wash!" Gwen said. Together they tumbled out of the bus to tear her laundry off the clothesline.

She was crying again. She'd have to hang her wash all over the living room. She looked at Lux as if he were the bad weather itself, a gale-force wind peeling the shingles off the house where her babes slept. He tried to calm her, but she twisted away from him. With her arms full of sheets she walked away, stepping on the elastic hems. He knew not to follow her back into the house. Bothered by what King had said, he took Gwen's car and went back to find Monty's front teeth. He looked for the broken nubs in the grass just in time to see an opportunistic crow alight on the ground nearby. It pecked at a white tidbit in the soil, like a morsel of shoepeg corn, and lifted off.

9

ALDEN PEELED THE FOIL OFF a tiny casserole tray and shoved the little dish before Hyram. His breakfast never stayed hot because Alden saved him for last, after taking breakfast to Mrs. Crease on Marsh Road and then to Mrs. Hansen on Cole's Neck. These dowagers sometimes tried to make her sit down, but she told them she had to report to work at the Seashore office by eight-thirty. She actually started at nine o'clock, but she chose to give Hyram all her attention. He didn't mind if his eggs got rubbery.

"How is the old gal, Mrs. *Crease?*" Hyram asked. "Did you make sure Mrs. *Crease* took her Synthroid tabs?" Hyram liked to say the unsettling name and see Alden flinch. But Alden didn't let him bait her. She was too busy spilling her pet peeves about the MSW at social services.

Alden said, "Dane Baker used to tell me, 'Always avoid the middle man. The middle man leaves the door ajar for Murphy's Law. A third partner always steps on his dick.'"

"He said that?"

"He's a fountain of knowledge."

"You mean a urinal of useless information," Hyram said.

"But this time, he's right. Hester Pierson is this middle man who has fouled it up for me. From now on, I avoid talking to her."

"You want to detour the application process?"

"Exactly. Those DSS pencil pushers don't know Monday from Tuesday."

"Civil servant types, you know, they sit there with incendiary slogans on their coffee mugs, but they don't get behind the yoke. But, Alden, they always have the final say." He wished she'd change her mind about getting a foster baby.

"Well, I might just go pinch him."

"Guerilla-style?"

"I bet they wouldn't even know if I stole him," she said. "They don't keep track. I bet they don't know one at-risk baby from the next."

Hyram said, "At-risk Baby Hendrick, and at-risk Alden herself."

Alden shrugged. She told him that Baby Hendrick had been farmed out to a family in Marston Mills. "It's a lie." Hester Pierson wouldn't tell her the foster parents' last name. So when Alden left Hyram to go to work, she charged over to the Hole in One doughnut shop in time to find Officer Francisconi buying a cruller and a pint of coffee milk. The officer was tight lipped when she started asking questions. Francisconi knew about Alden's tantrums at social services, and he was way ahead of her. He wasn't talking names. But he goofed and the name slipped out.

The McShanes, McKinleys, McCoys—what was the name Francisconi had leaked? It was an Irish name. These names made Alden think of cheap white hankies sold by the bale. These foster parents—the McFarlanes, the McPhersons, the McCloskeys?—were taking care of four DSS children already; Baby Hendrick was number five, Francisconi told her.

There must be a score of Irish names in the phone book with local exchanges. Alden couldn't call each one. Instead she asked the clerk at the Eastham Superette if he knew a family with a lot of foster kids. Alden knew it was always the unemployed, the downtrodden, families under economic duress and on the dole who patronized convenience stores. This family would be regular customers. Minimart cashiers were supposed to monitor all sales of scratch tickets to welfare clients and the elderly, and the clerk was relieved that Alden didn't want any Megabucks tickets. "So do you know these McDermotts? MacNeils? McKeens? You know, a really big family? Sort of mixed up?" she asked him.

"Multicultural, you mean?"

"Yeah. All forty-eight flavors."

He told her of a house where he'd seen a lot of piebald children running in and out.

Hyram had promised Alden that he would go along with her to find

Baby Hendrick. He said, "I'll be your uncle from your mother's side of the family. It'll fill in your family profile."

She said, "You? You're not really an asset. You're a famous trouble-maker around here."

Whales and dolphins, coyotes, those were *his* people. But some local busybodies liked saying that Hyram's family connections were a little curled at the edges, a little suspect. Hyram had already told Alden about his three wives. He loved them all for different reasons. From the safety of his bachelor perch, he explained to Alden what had made their separate reigns distinct and memorable to him. Two American girls and one Asian bride he'd met at My Tho, thirty miles outside of Saigon. He had told Alden which one liked gardening, which one did the *New York Times* crossword puzzle with an ink pen; but of course he couldn't tell her what he had really liked about them. One bride's long neck, another's wide hips, and his Ginny, from My Tho—her little dewdrop at the center of everything.

Alden said, "Okay. Come with me but act like a grandpa figure, not Casanova. Just take a stab at it."

"I can do that."

When Alden arrived at Hyram's place at noon, his daughter from Saint Paul answered the door. Alden mistook her for a new Meals-On-Wheels volunteer, and she didn't like another postmenopausal zester nosing about the place. Alden breezed into the house to find Hyram in the living room. He looked shell shocked by his daughter's sudden materialization. He introduced Alden to Sandy, who had just arrived from Minnesota on a surprise visit. His daughter seemed uncomfortable when Alden and Hyram stood abreast to face her, two to one. They were a spontaneous couple that Sandy didn't want to figure out. Sandy was well informed about Hyram's history with young women, a history he might never wish to conclude.

But Alden had never heard about Sandy. Hyram had mentioned only his two sons, who lived on the West Coast. He had told her, "They live as far away from me as they can get without applying for a visa."

Sandy said, "Dad tells me you help him tape his eye shut? Has a doctor prescribed this regimen?"

Alden said, "If you ask me, I think we should be taping his *mouth* shut."

His daughter smiled at Alden, a tight, evaporating grin. "My goodness, what's that racket?" Sandy said. "What's that scratching sound?"

Alden heard it, too. Hyram had not yet lifted the coverlet from Godzilla's birdcage, a morning ritual he usually attended to straight off, before he brewed his coffee. When Sandy arrived at the door, he forgot about the canary.

The bird was making a ruckus in the draped cage.

"Oh, is that your birdie in there?" Sandy walked over to remove the towel from the birdcage. As she lifted the cover, the bird lifted with it, its foot entangled in a loose thread. Each time she tugged, Godzilla was clonked against the bars. Sandy didn't notice and kept battering the imprisoned ball of fluff. The garroted bird jerked up and down like a tiny marionette puppet.

"Alden—she'll kill him!" Hyram jumped up.

"I've got him," Alden said. She reached inside the spring door to rescue his pet. Cradling Godzilla in her palm, she carefully picked at the thread, unwinding his tiny rice feet from their shackles.

"You brained him," Hyram told his daughter.

"Sandy didn't see he was tangled up." Alden defended her, asserting a first-name privilege that went unreciprocated. She was testing the waters. Hyram might have wanted to tell her not to bother.

Sandy looked back and forth between Hyram and the young woman who had adopted him. Sandy was relieved to let Alden assume her caretaker role, but she was the *daughter* who had come all this way from Saint Paul. She described her difficult travel itinerary and how, before the day was out, she would have to reenact it in reverse. From Minneapolis she had flown a budget airline; once at Boston, she had avoided paying for a Cape Air ticket by renting an uncomfortable subcompact to drive one hundred miles to the godforsaken Outer Cape, where her father had retired without having called a family powwow to discuss it. On the last leg of her trip, she had braked for coyotes crossing Route 6 "like they owned the place," and she had almost wrecked.

Alden understood how it wasn't easy for outsiders to cross the

River of Forgetfulness and drive down Route 6, that narrow two-lane stretch, tagged Suicide Alley for its history of head-ons, just to spill out at the rotary circle, face front with the Quitting Time Clock. It was especially unrewarding if they'd come on some bitter family business.

Sandy wanted to take Hyram to lunch, but he vetoed most of the restaurants she mentioned. "Not worth the detour," he said. "Rice meatballs," he explained. "Watered-down ketchup or day-old Jell-O at that place, like a hockey puck. And that one? They just serve watered-down water."

Alden told Sandy, "For Hyram, it's Land Ho! or nothing. It's right on Main Street next to the bank. Believe me, he'll just pick at his food if you take him to the Hearth and Kettle."

"That's right. I won't go to that trough," he said. But he'd go anywhere with Alden.

Alden pushed him down into a chair. She gently daubed cold cream on his eyebrow and cheekbone to remove some telltale adhesive.

Hyram said, "Hearth and Kettle. That's where seniors stack up as soon as they get their Social Security checks. There's hundreds of 'em. It's like a Japanese beetle trap." He made his "please rescue me" face at Alden.

"Look, Hyram, go to lunch with your daughter. I'll come back later," Alden promised.

"No. I'm not going." He wished his daughter would leave him alone. He asked her, "Honey, what do you want? I mean, besides the little catch-up."

Sandy sat down across from him. "Well, you said you would sign off on Mom's insurance policy. You know what I'm talking about. I've FedExed this thing twice."

"It's here somewhere, I guess. Maybe it's in my accordion file over on the sideboard." He pointed to where his papers towered in lopsided stacks along one wall.

"I've got another copy with me. Just sign it."

Alden waited in the kitchen as Hyram looked for his reading glasses and a pen. When Sandy saw he was going to put his signature on the document, she said she agreed it was wrong for her to have shown up unannounced. "I'll just use the powder room. Then I'm going," she said. Her voice was spirited. She was pleased to wrap it up.

Godzilla had recovered and began to make tentative cheeps, hopping perch to perch. He froze on the center bar and with fiery, melodic madness released his familiar note strings, presto and fortissimo, as if to say to Hyram's daughter, It's three to one! and Be gone with you!

SANDY LEFT ON HER JOURNEY BACK to Logan Airport, after having asked Alden where to buy live lobsters that come in a carryall with seaweed and dry ice. She'd take her seafood back to Saint Paul.

"That's a long haul just to get a shore dinner," Alden said when she was gone.

"She'll get a chunk more than that."

Hyram didn't want the reminder of a child, especially in its adult form. "Her life is boring. She holds it against me that her mother raised her. Her boring mother had the chisel in *her* hand. She doesn't actually know she feels that way—she can't identify what causes her hostility toward me. That's the crux of it. She doesn't have the *upbringing* to know why. That's the catch-twenty-two. She hates me because she doesn't know *why* she hates me. A little cash should make her happy."

Alden saw that Hyram compartmentalized his feelings about Sandy and her mother, when he was always telling Alden not to do that with her feelings about Monty. When Alden made excuses and made wistful interpretations of her husband's exodus, Hyram told her, "Stop trying to pick the fly shit out of the pepper." He told her she should ask herself one question: Do you want Monty to turn up alive or dead?

Alden said, "Look, I'm sorry about your daughter. I mean, she's not exactly a Carnival cruise, is she? But I'm going to find Baby Hendrick. Are you coming?"

"Promise you won't try to snatch him?"

"I just want to visit."

"I'll come with you only if you sign on to one of the boats going to the outfall."

"Hyram, I addressed all your flyers. I Xeroxed your environmental impact memo, the one with the tiny print that had to be enlarged. It was a nightmare to get it right. First it's too big, it doesn't all fit. Then I do it again and the margins are wrong. I'm like a fucking secretary to you, but I'm not spending a perfectly good Saturday to drop anchor over a sewer pipe."

"But we want more women. Women on leaky draggers always crank up the tension in the press."

"Forget it. It's almost winter. I don't want to sail out there in gale-force weather."

"We'll put you in a survival suit. My yellow oilskin jacket will be big on you, but you'll look like a daffodil."

"Look, it's great what you do for the environment, but—"

"*You're* my environment," he said.

"Who says I am?"

She didn't like it when he was sentimental. She liked him hard as nails.

Hyram left the house without tying his shoelaces because his ankles were swollen worse than usual. Alden stooped down to knot them. "Look at you. You're wearing an unmatched pair of oxfords. One black, one brown."

"Oh, Christ."

"That's a geezer thing, not having the right shoes. I'm going to put you in the Manor. Geezers have to have round-the-clock care."

Threatening seniors with the Cape End Manor was a strategy used by wicked caretakers, but Alden was just teasing. She knew he wasn't ready for a nursing home, not yet. Just the other night, he had given a commanding briefing at town hall, protesting the National Seashore's decision to give dirt bikers access to the fire trails crisscrossing the moors and Provincelands. Dirt bikes threatened the berms protecting pristine wetlands, and bikes didn't always stay on the trails.

At town meeting, Hyram spoke against using violent measures to curb the motorbike invasion. He said he didn't encourage the practice of stringing monofilament fishing line across fire roads to flip bikers off their Kawasakis and Suzukis. But Hyram took the time to explain, in step-by-step detail, the demonic procedure, the how-to, as if instructing reckless activists to follow suit. He seeded the idea to flip bikers off their dirt bikes, right there in town hall, and on record.

"I didn't go so far as to hand out spools of fishing line."

"But someone brought a crate of wire spools to the meeting. Tell me, it wasn't you who arranged that? Did you think of those teen boys who might wipe out on their bikes? Like that scraggly kid I saw at DSS. He could be one of your victims."

"If he pedals over the last red eft or dusky salamander, he deserves what he gets."

"You love slimy newts and tree frogs. What does that say about you?"

She enjoyed jabbing him, and he loved it, too. He tried to take her mind off her errand. Alden followed the scanty directions she had pried out of the minimart clerk. She drove until they saw a little house with three different swing sets in a row. This grouping of multiple swing sets in distinct stages of rusty disintegration was a dead giveaway that children lived on top of one another as if in an orphan bin.

And the yard was busy with a slew of raffish neighborhood bratlings; some of the brood must be the unfortunate foster children. The kids were riding faded plastic Hot Wheels in the driveway, their ribbed tires making a racket. Others zoomed in and out of T-bar laundry lines shooting Nerf guns, mostly the broken article. Alden parked in the drive and climbed out of the car, the instant target of a flurry of Nerf darts.

Baby Hendrick wasn't anywhere to be seen.

Hyram was instantly surrounded by mites as Alden walked after a young girl who looked like she might know something. The girl pretended to ignore Alden until she asked, "Is Baby Hendrick inside having his nap?" The girl turned on her heel and ran up to Alden, happy to be asked something about the newcomer to her household. Alden had guessed right: this one was at the top end of the hierarchy and was probably a busybody.

"He's at the doctor with earaches," the girl said.

"Earaches? Both ears?" Alden asked.

"His nose is running green goo."

"When did this happen?" Alden said.

"Came that way," the girl said, stopping to blot her own nose with her sweater cuff. The girl had a bad burn on one cheek.

"How did you get that?" Alden asked. "Was that a curling iron?"

"I was fixing my hair for the Little Miss Moby-Dick pageant," the girl said, although her hair was limp.

"Is your mom or dad at home?" Alden said.

"No."

"Who's in charge of all of you?"

"I'm in charge," the girl said, her voice challenging Alden to disagree.

"And what's your name?"

"Toya."

"LaToya?"

"Not *her.* Toy-a."

"Oh, okay. Can you show us the baby's room?" Alden asked the tiny self-elected kingpin.

"He sleeps in his crib in Mrs. McGuire's room."

"Can you take us to her room, then?"

"For what?"

"We're supposed to see who sleeps where."

"You want to see where *I* sleep?"

"Sure. We want to see where Toya sleeps."

The girl walked them inside the kitchen through the littered carport. The kitchen was tidy, but the laminate countertop had several burned circles, as if someone had put a fry pan on the counter when it was searing hot. Once might have been understandable, but there were many burned circles, intersecting rings, as if the cook of the house didn't understand the elementary law of cause and effect.

The girl pulled Alden by the hand, and Hyram trailed them into the living room, where a naked man was passed out on the sofa. The sleeping man had had the decency to place a white motorcycle helmet over his cock and testicles for the sake of the children left in his charge. The white helmet dome looked as if a huge puffball mushroom had sprouted from his mossy groin.

The little girl didn't miss a beat and tugged Alden down the hallway to the master bedroom. Alden looked back at Hyram with genuine distress over the disheveled world they had stumbled into, as if Hyram could do something about it. Together, Alden and the girl inspected the baby's bed, a portable playpen. Alden said, "This might be the brand that's been recalled. See? These fabric sides can collapse and smother the toddler occupant." The DSS had not yet approved Alden's application, but it seemed to have allowed several infractions to go unchecked here at the McGuire household.

Hyram told Alden, "Once you're in the system, they probably don't bother coming back to check for quality control."

"I guess not. It smells funny. Like a flea bomb." Alden opened louvered closet doors as if to search for termites or worse vermin.

Toya showed Alden her own room, two tiers of bunk beds against opposite walls. The room had the tight, crowded feeling of a chicken coop or cattle chute. There was a scruffy throw rug and a few worn stuffed animals with lumpy forms, but no colorful posters, pajama bags, or high-end toys, no LEGO Technic sets or video games. Again, Alden studied the girl's burned face, tipping her chin left and right. "So tell me how you got burned."

"I told it. I was fixing my hair for the Little Miss Moby-Dick pageant in New Bedford. But now I can't go since I got this." She circled her finger in the air beside her sore cheek.

"That's too bad you missed the contest," Alden said, "but your hair looks nice. Some people have to *iron* their hair to get it flat like that." She squeezed the girl until she squirmed. Hyram saw an immediate resemblance between the two. Hungry waifs that want the upper hand. But the little one was skin and bones, her shoulders like interlocking coat hangers beneath her cardigan.

"Are you her daddy?" she asked Hyram, pointing to Alden, who was snooping in bureau drawers.

"That's right," Hyram said.

Alden shoved a drawer shut. "Hyram, you don't have to lie to Toya. *She's* not the enemy." She told Toya, "He has enough daughters he can't do anything about."

The girl nodded her head in exaggerated hitches up and down. She was used to the reigning confusion of her mixed-up household, where adults never made sense. The naked man was shifting on his sofa springs. When they tiptoed back outside to the Jeep, two kids were sitting in the front seat, staring out the windshield, ready to go. The little girl guide was clinging to Alden, entwining her skinny arms around Alden's waist, and reaching up to tug Alden's chin, trying to get her attention again. She begged Alden to take her home. "I'm good," Toya said. "I do the most chores. My chores are dish drainer, Clorox the toilet, videotapes in the alphabet, fish tank, pet dish, tie socks in pairs, sweep carport—" The girl kept going.

"*Find someone who wants to be found,*" Hyram told Alden. "Forget that other one."

Alden looked away from the girl's burning eyes as she pried the child's fingers off. She finally succeeded by giving Toya a dollar to distract her, much to the distress of the other children. Alden had no other small bills and asked Hyram.

"I've only got twenties."

"Liar," she told him.

"I tell the truth."

"Oh, I guess twenty bucks is too much," she said in a gnawing voice.

Hyram didn't reach for his wallet. Alden found an old pack of Doublemint gum on her dash and handed out the remaining sticks. She watched the kids bite down hard on the brittle stubs. The pack was God knows how old. It had been baking in the sun.

Driving home, Hyram told Alden to stop at the Bridge Restaurant. "You really should have had lunch with Sandy," she said.

"Lunch with Sandy is always animal, mineral, vegetable. Nothing distilled."

He ordered drinks at the bar, and they fell into a booth by the window, where they could look out and see the canal bridge. Alden searched for the extension ladder she had often seen propped against the suicide fence, compliments of the Corps of Engineers, who supervised bridge painting on the Sagamore span.

She said, "See that abandoned ladder, like a farewell stairway to the highest cables? It's an open invitation. Come one, come all."

Hyram thought that her moody spells were happening too often. She used to bounce into the house and chatter like a finch. Godzilla tried to compete with her. Hyram liked her that way. Lately she was dipping in the other direction. She more often used her dreary radar instead of wearing rose-colored glasses.

Hyram looked out the window but saw nothing. "Alden, that's not a ladder, it's a serrated shadow, an optical illusion. Honey, there's no ladder there. It's your imagination."

"It *was* there. Everybody saw it."

"It's not there now."

She stirred her gin with her pointer finger.

"Don't be such a princess of doom and gloom. So what if you can't get this baby. Someday you might have one of your own."

"One of my own? Claiming blood ties is a kind of save-your-own-soulism. I just think a baby should be with the person who really wants him."

"Alden, this search for a baby, it's just a diversion, a reprieve from the upheaval of the last couple years. You don't really want a kid. What would you do with it?"

"Spend less time with you."

HE SAT IN A KITCHEN CHAIR as she taped his eye shut. Then he put on his reading glasses and pawed through his newspapers on the sideboard. Alden told him that when he wore his reading glasses with one eye bandaged and out of service, he looked ridiculous. "Poor me," Hyram said. "Poor everyone."

She tried to leave him with his newspapers, but he turned on the TV. An action movie was starting, with typical footage of larger-than-life good guys in a face-off with larger-than-life villains. "Hey, want to watch this? It's that Kennedy in-law, what's his name, the behemoth with the German accent."

"I'm tired," she said.

He didn't whine or make her feel guilty when she walked out the door. In mutual respect, she didn't let the storm door slam.

She sank behind the wheel and drove away, turning off at High Head, heading onto the dunes. Farther into the eerie dunescape, an owl cruised parallel to her Jeep, chasing a rabbit flushed from a thicket by the Wagoneer. Alden was happy to oblige the snowy. Bunnies were plentiful. It was early in the season to see snowies, they usually arrived in January. Logan Airport had a big problem with snowies in midwinter, when the owls hunt the open grasslands that divide the airstrip. She watched the owl in midplunge, its wings troweling the sand as its talons seized the cottontail. Its thrashing wingbeats left behind the telltale "angel" imprint. Alden often discovered these angel memorials on the dunes, but Hyram had told her not to feel sorry for the victims. "These are just ghostprints on the food chain, that's all," he said.

10

ALDEN WAS UNPACKING A NEW SHIPMENT of critter jigsaw puzzles—multipiece sets of interlocking tentacles, whiskers, and antennae—when Ison phoned her at work. "Have you had a change of heart?"

"Sorry," she said. "No difference."

"Well, maybe you could just tell me your plans?"

"My plans? What plans?"

"You know—," he said.

He wanted her to recite the heated litany that she had once composed just for him. Instead she lowered the receiver into its cradle with careful precision. Disconnecting, she felt instant relief and secret revulsion, as if she had just propped a flower in a moldy crypt.

The phone jangled again.

Each time she answered, she declined his invitations. But Ison seemed to want to enact the exchange even without her participation. His excitement seemed to be waged and measured by how quickly she hung up on her end. He usually rang at specific windows in his office schedule, and she knew when not to answer her line.

Then she wondered if it might be Conrad calling another time. His invitation to take her to lunch on Nantucket after shooting aerial pictures from that Diamond two-seater sounded almost good to her now. But she remembered that Conrad was off cape, learning to fly a commercial jet. She pictured her old friend sitting in the cockpit of a giant Boeing 737 as it plunged across the tarmac and lifted off, as helpless as an ant washed downriver on a maple leaf.

Ison left a message on the machine explaining that he and his wife would be down to open their vacation house for the holiday season. His wife had come ahead to make pinecone wreaths. "I'm driving out this afternoon," he said. "Sarah needs my help with the wire frames, but she likes doing the wreaths herself. That keeps her busy. Maybe I can see you? What about early tonight or on the weekend?"

Alden tried to ignore his invitation and looked back at her computer screen, lit with the current FBI Ten Most Wanted list—a daily habit she no longer tried to hide from customers who came into the store and stalled near her desk. She went to www.fbi.gov every day. She had bookmarked several "true crime" home pages. She liked to read the profiles and reverse directories for fugitives the FBI wanted to track down. Splashed open on her desk was the Metro Section of the *New York Times* with a paragraph about an unclaimed body. Maybe it was Monty. But it was just another missing someone. Alden had once seen the famous "coffin shot" of the Lindbergh baby, a cult photograph tacked to a wall at a frat party at Brown University, where she had gone slumming with her classmates from Reject. Things were quite different since the days of Lindbergh's baby; search operations had become privatized. Search companies advertised their services on the Internet, and one had asked Alden for her credit card number before they would take her name and information. Firstsearch.com specialized in "reuniting lost loves and missing family members." She had dumped some cash into it before seeing how it might be just another telemarketing operation.

Alden discovered several missing-persons Web sites. She had even found the telephone number 1-800-AUTOPSY. But without a body, no one could be sure what had happened to her husband. She learned of a national clearinghouse for victims of amnesia. She could log on to www.amnesianet.com or call their hotline at 1-888-AMNESIA for a recording about unclaimed persons who had turned up with the memory disorder.

She visited amnesianet.com at least once every other day, but the descriptions never exactly matched Monty. She had lost hope that Monty's disappearance might be the result of a simple crack on the head, or whatever it is that jump-starts the amnesiac's blank passage as if a delete button had been hit.

If Monty was alive, he must have had full recall or else he'd have been profiled on the amnesia hotline sooner or later.

When Alden looked at the current FBI Ten Most Wanted menu, she noticed disturbing coincidences in the crime statistics. A man accused of bludgeoning two people to death had the last name Mallet. In another column, a report said that a missing child's shoes had been found in a panel truck marked "Piedmont Interstate Transit." The child disappeared from *Oxford,* Mississippi, and his shoes were found in the same panel truck parked in *Hightop,* North Carolina. The shoe motif sent a shiver through Alden. She had started to wonder if butterflies emerged as a motif in Monty's disappearance.

As soon as she had discovered her husband's dalliance, Alden had stopped thinking of butterflies as lovely innocents. She imagined that if hell exists, there would be *butterflies in hell.* Hell would be swarming. Orange viceroys, monarchs, and queens—these specimens were like the jagged flames bouncing across the skies of hell.

Her husband was still missing.

His disappearance was gaining a cheap B-movie feeling the longer it went unsolved. But Monty wasn't a pushpin or adhesive dot on an FBI chart. He was a nobody.

She browsed princiespeephole.com, just to take a look at its pop-up window. "If you are not of legal age to view adult material, you must leave this site now." Alden wondered where Layla had left Baby Hendrick when she worked the "Live Fuck Shows" and "Live Nude Chats" listed on Princie's drop-down menu:

- ☐ Teen Pink
- ☐ Amateur Pix
- ☐ Pregnant Teens
- ☐ Fisting
- ☐ Pissing
- ☐ Latinas
- ☐ Shaved

Alden thought a printout of the menu would be ammunition if she went back to DSS to campaign for the toddler. Princie's porn outlet was the same old, same old, but it was odd to see that it ran its Web site right here on Olde Cape Cod, the first nexus of Puritanism in the New World. Then a customer found her desk, so she clicked back to www.fbi.gov.

The customer asked, "Does this *Field Guide to Deciduous Trees* include 'box elder'?"

"Box elder is anything in the maple family," Alden said.

The woman lifted her eyebrows, impressed that Alden knew this right off the top of her head. "My skin test said I'm extremely allergic to box elder. Since I retired here last year, I've got bad sinuses."

Alden said, "This time of year it's molds that are the worst allergens. Molds reign. It's because of these wetlands. We've got a terrarium effect. Glacial kettle holes are fed with springwater, and we've got cranberry bogs, quaking bogs—"

"Quaking bogs?"

"Florida has molds, too, but the intense sunshine regulates spores. Here, the climate is temperate and that's usually spore friendly. The Southwest is your best bet. New Mexico or Arizona. Now that's good sinus country."

Alden was twisting the knife too much. The customer bought the guidebook, upset that she had chosen the wrong location for her retirement.

By late afternoon, Alden was ready to close shop when she looked out the window and saw him.

He stood at the entrance to the Nature Trail for Sight-Challenged Visitors, nicknamed the Blind Trail by the regulars and park rangers. The cinder path was strung with a heavy nylon cord studded with rubber washers that enabled visually impaired nature buffs to hike down a quarter-mile walk through a bird sanctuary.

Alden sometimes used the trail during her office breaks. She felt lucky if she heard a hermit thrush. Its lilting flute notes drifted in two parts: first it was the sound of broken glass being swept into a metal dustpan, and then, with the second cascade, the glass tumbles into a waste tin. Where the more-difficult trails branched off in all directions, braille plaques warned blind hikers to turn around to follow an identical rope in reverse, back to where they had started at the visitor center's parking lot.

In his big-shouldered Italian overcoat and gleaming loafers, Ison looked out of context in the coastal setting, like a banker with amnesia. Alden looked at his face for any sign of contrition or remorse about his dirty phone calls, but he looked the same as always—unruffled and confident. Unrepentant. He seemed absurd in his elegant business clothes compared to the usual tourists, nature buffs in khakis and hiking boots, long-distance cyclists in spandex tights with padded fannies, and seniors in lemon yellow golf sweaters. Ison's expensive overcoat looked out of place in the wooded glen, but Ison himself wasn't out of place in such a coat.

He loitered on the Blind Trail. Loitering was its purpose, after all. Year-rounders often walked the nature trails, which were dotted with cautionary signs: "Do Not Pick the Sea Lavender" and "Report Stranded Sea Turtles—Do Not Move Animals from Site." In warm weather, familiar oldsters sat on the few stone benches set up near the picnic grounds. A few of the signs in this area had been misprinted and were never corrected or replaced. They said "Con*ver*sation Area," not "Conservation Area," and the regulars who jawboned on the benches joked that they were just following government orders.

Alden monitored the traffic on the Blind Trail. People turned up unannounced. It was Ison now, but last week it had been the man from Parents of Murdered Children, someone she had met at a session of bereavement counseling. Alden had attended one meeting in her half-and-half state: unofficial widow or jilted wife? The grief counselor had said, "Alden, you cannot complete the grieving process if there remains even a smidgen of optimism." He had told her how his ten-year-old son was killed in a car accident when his in-laws cared for him one weekend. The child wasn't in a seat belt. "That's murder, if you ask me," he told Alden. Holding his son's death against his wife's parents had ruined his marriage. Dating this man was like being rescued from a shipwreck by a hero who arrives in a leaky boat, with snakes climbing in over the gunnels. In her off-center condition, she had run into one bad character after another. There had been a flurry of suitors after Monty's departure, but Alden trusted no one but Hyram, who, at seventy-two, seemed wholly distinct from the prowlers who showed up on the Blind Trail.

Once, she thought she saw her father, Dane Baker, at the entrance to the trail. She hadn't seen him for three years, not since his arrest in Florida with the Irish Travelers. Alden sometimes received letters from her father stamped "ATTENTION! THIS IS FLA. DEPARTMENT OF CORRECTIONS INMATE CORRESPONDENCE. The sender is not authorized to enter into credit contracts." Once, he wrote to her with a proposition. He asked if she wanted to take hormone injections so her eggs could be "ripened and harvested." He told her they could sell her eggs for thousands of dollars to infertility specialists on Park Avenue. He knew someone who would set it up. At least Dane Baker was safe behind electronic doors, but Ison and the nut from Parents of Murdered Children were still at large.

Alden was always relieved to see familiar faces at the picnic tables. Boatyard workers stopped their duties patching hulls with fiberglass, or scraping and sanding prows, and came to the cypress grove to eat their sack lunches. Once, she had recognized the bus driver, Lux Davis, who came with a crew from Bay State Nurseries. His wavy black hair had reached his shoulders. She imagined taking her kitchen shears from the magnetic knife holder and tackling his head as he sat on a stool, dark, silky clumps landing on the floor in a circle around her. But the local boys weren't eating lunch outside her window this late in the season. Stone benches were cold.

With Ison waiting outside, she had another cigarette, against rules. Loose tobacco flecks fell across her breast, and she tamped them with her fingertip. Tobacco was like gold dust in its final, threatened era. She had once seen a documentary that showed fresh tobacco curing, big, droopy leaves creased like yellowed pillowcases. She imagined reclining against those tarry pillowcases for a little nap, burying her face in them.

Then she unpacked a new carton of paperweights—beetles, mantids, spiders, secured in Lucite domes. People loved to get nose to nose with a black widow spider safely arrested in an inch-thick slab of plastic. Its beautiful red hourglass almost looked fake, as if it had been stenciled on. Maybe these were ordinary spiders doctored to look like the more-infamous specimens.

She looked out the window again. Ison waited, shivering. He hunched his shoulders and tucked his hands inside his cuffs, just for dramatic effect. "I hope you freeze to death," she said. But then she saw him take out his cell phone and punch a number. Her desk console erupted. Even though she had expected it to ring, she jumped.

"Just talk to me for a minute," he said. "No strings attached." Alden couldn't leave her office without walking past him anyway, so she agreed to meet him on her way out. She grabbed her jacket and left by the back door, which automatically locked as it swept shut. Hearing the lock catch, she panicked and waited for a moment at the concrete lip of the loading dock. Ison circled his arm, and she went down to face him.

"Just hear me out," he said.

"You can't hang around on the Blind Trail. You aren't blind." She brushed past his shoulder and started walking up the trail. They walked up the cinder path in awkward silence. She could have pointed out the saw-whet owl perched ten feet away in the crotch of a white oak. She could always find it if she combed the landmarks. Alden guided seasonal "owl prowls" and "sunrise hikes" sponsored by the Wellfleet Audubon. She knew where to look for different owl roosts, finding telltale signs, like the whitewash splashed on tree trunks and the accumulations of "pellets"—little knots of fur and feathers, beaks and bones, insect chitin, the undigested matter regurgitated by owls at rest. These compact puffs of silvery fiber were soft as a rabbit's foot, and she carried one or two in her coat pocket.

She asked him, "Isn't your wife making pinecone wreaths? You should go home and help out."

"I'm no help."

They went a little farther into the deepening wood. But he stopped on the path and toed at something under a chokeberry bush. "Look," he said. "What's that?"

Alden crouched down to see what he was talking about. She reached through the brambles to find some magazines cinched in a neat packet, like a stack of schoolbooks tidied in a strap. She recognized its booty. "Oh, shite. I guess some kids stashed their smut."

"Eureka," he joked.

"Look, this must be somebody's secret stash," Alden said. "Kids ride their skateboards out here to horde their *Playboy*s in the woods." She wanted to dismiss it as nothing.

"But these aren't Hef's rag. These cost a pretty penny. Too expensive for kids."

He pulled one from the stack and handed it to her. He said, "What's in the table of contents?"

"*Table of contents?* I don't think these magazines have a contents page."

"Just tell me what's in these pictures," Ison said. He was standing close behind her. He waited for her to begin.

"Why should I?"

"I want to know what *you're* seeing, in your own words—"

"My words? Oh yeah, I get it. My words."

"I want you to be a part of this."

"This treasure trove?" she said.

She understood that Ison had hidden the magazines under the chokeberry bush himself. As he waited for her to cooperate, he rested his hand on her shoulder with a bit of pressure. It wasn't a real threat, but a weirdo benediction. Behind a shelter-belt of cypress, they were tucked away from sight, but she heard her boss's voice as he walked to the parking lot with a research assistant who wanted a lift home.

"Okay," Alden said, "in this photo, the guy is wearing a catcher's vest. He's a Met, I think. It looks like the girl is borrowing his bat—" She looked up to see a nuthatch angling down a length of tree trunk, its tiny arrowhead shape a welcome distraction for an instant.

"Tell me the next one. Go ahead."

She looked at his face. He had put on his sunglasses and she couldn't see his eyes.

Ison had opened his belt. He quizzed Alden about the pictures. He didn't want answers but liked *asking* more questions. His handsome face twitched; tiny fissures rippled his cameo as he progressed. His fine features couldn't hide the spikes and tremors.

Alden remembered Dane Baker's story about a small church

somewhere. The church was whitewashed every year, but within a few weeks the paint started to blister. The clapboards had never been seasoned correctly, and the sap started to bleed each summer season. Like clockwork, little bubbles and welts broke through the smooth surface. The church blistered and peeled, its paint tearing off in patches like diseased skin. Dane Baker said that this strange phenomenon was symbolic of all the people in church each Sunday who claimed to be free from sin. He said it was like that painting in *The Picture of Dorian Gray,* which he'd seen in a TV movie. He had never actually read the story; his education was limited to cons, booze, and the reliable getaway.

She still held the magazine and she slapped its pages shut. "I'm out of here," she told him. "It's not up my alley, you know? Sorry."

"Wait a minute, Alden," he said. "Why don't you let me get you a new commuter booklet? You can come to Boston, or when I'm down here on weekends with Sarah, we can find a new hideaway—what do you think? I saw a cute string of bungalows—"

"Hey, I'm not a side salad, okay?" Alden held the owl pellet in her hand; its furred nap had a tragic softness that almost made her tears roll.

Ison dropped his voice to a deeper whisper. It was like a grief-struck voice, but he was an impostor. "Alden, you knew I was married. What can I do about it? You can't have hoped I was available." He pronounced the word "hope" as if he were lancing a boil. "I thought with these pictures we'd be on the same level."

He was saying Alden had "halfsies." She had enacted her equal role.

Alden collected the pricey magazines that littered her wildlife sanctuary. She walked back in silence to the Seashore Visitor Center; Ison followed a few paces behind her. She threw the magazines in the Dumpster behind the loading dock. He seemed annoyed that she had tossed the expensive stash, but he didn't reach into the bin to retrieve his investment, at least not there and then. He asked her again to reconsider their relationship.

Alden told him, "Don't negotiate with me. Don't waste your time." She walked up to the parking lot, where her rusted Jeep was parked just two spaces from Ison's gleaming sports coupe. Her Wagoneer looked like a beat-up vehicle from behind the Berlin wall. In Eastern Europe these relics were rebuilt many times over from odd parts hoarded over decades of the cold war. Alden took pride in maintaining a car that should have been retired long ago. She felt righteous sitting down in her heap, until it wouldn't crank. She waited, her face flushed, as Ison's car purred away. Then she tried it again.

11

BRIGHT MAPLE TREES HAD SHUT OFF their sap lines and were letting their canopies sink. Leaves fell in a continuous stenciled shower curtain effect as she circled the rotary and drove past the splintered Quitting Time Clock.

The air had changed. It smelled of grass mowed one last time before men drained the oil from their Toros and Lawnboys. It smelled of chimney fires, of creosote and high-priced cherrywood. She was sure Ison had already bought his split of logs in a shrink-wrapped plastic tote with built-in handles. These "weekender" fire totes were sold at the entrance of the Super Stop & Shop.

Without Monty or Baby Hendrick, she was left out of the loop of domestic chores and comforting autumn traditions that are de rigueur for happy families. Her self-pity was a fiery mix of shame and injury, as if she had stubbed her toe on furniture or banged her head on a cupboard. Her tears welled up and plowed down her cheeks.

She saw the season was changing before her eyes. Two weeks after Halloween, there were still some decorations left on stoops, on fence posts, on rooftops. Out of nowhere, in the rising dusk, she saw several overstuffed pumpkins, taut plastic globes, like piñatas just waiting for a party.

Alden pulled into the Eastham Superette to buy a pack of cigarettes. She saw Lux Davis in line as she asked the clerk for her Pall Malls.

"Nicotine fit?" Lux said, letting Alden step up to the cashier first.

"Yeah."

"Those things have ammonia added to them, you know? To enhance your addictive response," he said.

"You should visit the grade school with that story. It's too late for me," she said.

"It's not too late until they find a spot on your lung."

"Hey, since when are you the visiting nurse? You some kind of white knight or something?" She plucked his loose pigtail of tangled black hair off his collar and let it fall back down. "Maybe you've got a Samson thing, is that it? Long hair helps you save the world?"

He looked back at her in sidelong glances. If he kept his eyes on her too long, he might freeze like that and never be able to look away. But he noticed her wet eyes and said, "What's going on with you?"

She wiped her cheek with the heel of her hand, trying not to use the backs of her knuckles like a Shirley Temple. Tears of indignation were double-sized, quivering drips that pinched loose each time she blinked. Humiliation brings forth colossal waterworks, and she was embarrassed to have Lux see her like this, after her exchange with Ison. Her husband had called her tears "sorry water," quoting one of his middle school pets. But who should be sorry? The victim or the perpetrator? Her husband's leave of absence was the root problem that had spurred her commerce with Ison. Monty was responsible. Maybe both men were. All men, she thought.

She tried to smile for Lux, but she thought of the three-faced bisque doll her father had plopped in front of her. "Smile. Sleep. Cry." That was her life in a nutshell.

"Hey, are you okay?" he said when her tears didn't stop.

"I'm fine," she told Lux. "Just mad as hell."

"Mad about what?"

"Just some love troubles, that's all. Nothing to call the authorities about."

Nothing to call the authorities about. He imagined Francisconi talking on the phone with Alden. "Must have been a big blowout," he told her as he paid for his pint of orange juice and twisted off the cap. He swigged from its widemouthed bottle; its citrus scent was a soothing breakfast smell.

"I should drink orange juice instead of buying a pack of Pall Malls."

"Yes, you should. So who's giving you grief?" Lux asked her as they left the store. He gave her a circle of space. But she kept inching forward as he backed up.

"You wouldn't know him," she said. "He's not a year-rounder. He's got a vacation house down here."

"Not a native, you say? Well, that's what you get, Alden, when you cast too wide a net. The what-have-you, the trash fish population. It's a lot safer choosing a familiar face," Lux told her. His awkward words had crystallized before he could douse them. He lifted his orange juice to hide his famished expression.

Alden said, "The *trash fish?* The *what have you?* Yes, that describes him pretty good."

Lux listened to her interrogatory chirps, like a little bird turning up lost in his forest at last.

She asked him, "Who makes you the expert about tourists? You ever date one?"

He thought it might finally be happening; the fuse was ignited on each end. The outfall flyers and those paper dolls sent to him anonymously were really sent by her and were not just apparitions. He looked at Alden, trying to decide if she was saying "Come here" or "Go away."

Does she want some company or not?

Was she going to be a cock tease or a legitimate torment?

Loneliness was like a soap film on some women. A bell jar. A cartoon cloud that drilled rain on them. He could always tell when women had been knocked down. But since he actually knew what had happened to this one, he didn't want to be too reckless, or too careful, either.

She stood beside her Jeep. "You on foot tonight?" she said.

"Gwen has the Tercel."

"You hitching?"

He saw she wanted something. The transportation quiz was just a preamble. If she was inviting him for a ride, the fuse must be hot. The fuse was sparkling along.

Alden said, "Get in. Hurry up. I don't want everyone to see me drive off with someone—*someone like you.*"

Lux sat down in the Jeep beside Alden. He was moving forward on his treasure map. With a scale of "one inch equals a million miles," he felt he was closing in on the lockbox of his lifelong hope and wonder. He cranked down his window. Alden explained that ever since they had hauled that sea turtle in the back deck, the odor had lingered.

She drove around the rotary.

"I've got to fix that clock," he told her. "It'll be a bitch replacing mature plants. It's a nightmare. Thanks to you."

"Hey, I wasn't the driver. That girl was doing paint. She should be locked up in a mummy crate." The next thing, she was telling him about Baby Hendrick. "He was so cute, but he's white as a jar of paste."

"Sounds like an iron deficiency or something. Or maybe he eats lead paint off the windowsills. Maybe it's HIV. Babies lose traction fast."

"No, he's just fair complected. You ever feel you are destined for someone?" she said.

He pushed the sun visor up. He didn't want to look at his hungry eyes in the sliver of mirror. He thought of his mother's description of the girl with uncombable hair. Yes, he felt destined for someone. The girl *who looked like the girl* who had grown up in his mind. He told her, "You should just get a dog or a reliable boyfriend. Babies are a pain in the ass."

"That's what Hyram says."

"He must know something."

"Yeah, I guess. My mother left when I was ten."

"No kidding? My dad walked out on us." He didn't know why he told her this. "I had those seizures. So my mom blames me."

"Your father left home because of that? Shit. We're doomed. If our own parents can't tough it out, who would?"

He knew she was talking about her husband.

"But your dad's in jail," he said. "At least you know where the fuck they are when they're nicked and tucked up."

"Thank goodness. Doesn't the state have to notify you before they let them out?"

"They notify their assault victims, that's all. I don't know if they give the heads-up to their lousy kids. There's nothing like a little concertina wire between you and your loved ones to help you reevaluate."

"I guess," she said.

He saw he might be talking over her head.

Then Lux noticed a cruiser creeping up behind the Jeep. It trailed them for two miles as they rolled up Route 6. The cop car was tight behind them, kissing their ass like a shark sucker fish that attaches to the side of a great white. Lux looked in the side mirror and thought he saw Officer Francisconi behind the wheel. Francisconi was a *Walking Tall* hallucination Lux suffered now and again. He told Alden, "Nice and easy until we lose our friend, okay?"

"I'm crawling."

"Just act normal. Act as if you know where you're going."

"I know where."

He would guess she was actually flirting. "So tell me," he said. "Where do we go in this nowheresville?"

THEY KNEW THAT THEY WERE DOING A CRIME.

The heavy plastic bags leaked on the pavement and splattered their trouser cuffs as Lux helped Alden load the back of her Jeep. All six mushy spheres were the familiar orange plastic sacks sold in True Value hardware stores. Filled with leaf litter and lawn clippings, they formed crude Halloween pumpkins that families displayed on front lawns all over town. The stolen jack-o'-lanterns bulged, almost bursting, as Lux forced them aboard and slammed the tailgate shut. Alden eyed the overstuffed pumpkins, thinking only of their booty of sour compost, maggots, and spiders.

But the decaying sacks reminded Lux of the teacher's scissoring arms and legs as his body tumbled into the open hole at Bay State Nurseries. The nightmare candles sizzled up and down. He brushed his hands on his jeans and grinned at Alden to cover up his boomeranging panic.

Alden looked at him and said, "What's the matter? You did the dirty deed with the turtle, right? I thought you men love pranks. Thank God. Because I couldn't do this by myself."

They worked in the dark. The moon had just completed its garish harvest phase, and the new moon was a disappearing act. Lux searched the horizon for its black-on-black disk, a deep velvet monocle or eye patch with a silver rim. He thought this antimoon far more handsome than the oversize latex ball he had seen last October.

Alden got back behind the wheel. They cruised past Snow's Library and turned down Tonset Point Road. She recognized Ison's neighborhood because Mrs. Crease, on her Meals-On-Wheels roster, lived out this way. Coasting down the lane, Alden switched off her headlights and rolled right up to Ison's trophy house. She stopped beside Ison's top-end sports car, which was parked beneath a naked rose arbor.

Lux got out of the Jeep. She sat alone for a minute to get up her nerve. Her sinus headache was pounding and she pinched a decongestant pill from its foil backing. An instant later, she couldn't remember if she had actually swallowed the pill. She tried to count the puckered holes left in the foil, but she couldn't keep track. She took another tab. She often double-dosed this way, and her nerves were jangled.

Here was the famous house with two turrets on opposite ends. There was a glassed-in porch in between. Inside the solarium, a purplish grow light was burning. Alden wondered if Ison was raising pot, just like a lowlife, and the idea tempered her hatred for him, but only momentarily. When she tried to peer in the window, she saw an ultraviolet bulb suspended above a tray of exotic houseplants. Ison was forcing bulbs, or maybe his wife raised those sulky African violets. Taking a closer look, Alden recognized the tightly pleated fists of seductive ranunculus flowers. The grow bulb gave the stippled glass a furious blue tint as Alden considered the fussy hobby for a moment. It must be bothersome to raise tropical blooms that are unhappy from the get-go. Potted plants suited embittered spinsters, women with difficult living habits, routines of furious privacy and fussy solitude. A high-strung woman is often called a hothouse flower, and it isn't a compliment. She wouldn't want to be like them. But when Alden considered her hard luck with men, she thought there might be some wise rewards in choosing to reside in a greenhouse. Alden's mind was always swarming with polarized theories about different love habitats and their probable consequences. She remembered the governess Jane Eyre and the meager options presented to *her.*

Lux warned Alden that the plush two-seater was probably locked. She tugged the door open anyway, half expecting to trigger the alarm's chirps and sirens, but nothing happened. Lux lifted the tailgate of the Wagoneer, and together they transferred the necrotic cargo from one vehicle to the other. Alden worked directly, like a laundress shifting clothes from a washer to a dryer.

Stabbing the plastic skins open with a penknife, Lux sifted the wet leaf litter over the luxury dashboard and front seats. Tart mulch filled drink holders, the CD drawer, the little armrest hollows where Ison's wife had left a lipstick and an emery board. Alden helped shake out the orange bags until they were emptied and the prim car interior was fully obscured with moldy oak confetti. She teased out the contents from the final pumpkin bag, careful not to spill a scrap of her formidable Dear John statement, as Lux nudged the car door shut. The debris rose to the tops of the passenger windows, covered the dash, and darkened the low windscreen.

She stood back to look at what they had done. Lux offered up a wolf whistle in solidarity, until she shushed him. In a moment of contrition, she panicked and thought that they should sweep it all out. But there it was. Unquestionable. Austere in its one unarguable interpretation. Seeing the leaves piled high and layered in, Alden remembered an art installation she had once viewed with her husband during a weekend in New York. It was an exhibit of human hair swept up and collected from the floors of barbershops throughout Manhattan and put in a room of its own at the Whitney Museum. The artist's statement explained his premise: man's unmistakable neutrality was revealed in a limited chart of "human earth tones" represented in the piles of clippings. Her husband had said that these filthy protein skeins with cuticle flecks and scalp dust—blond, brown, gray, shorn and mingled together in benign tufts and ringlets, a hair rope that tied us one to another—just illustrated how the gene pool can be polluted. Monty always had some final word about the risks inherent in mixing diverse populations. But Alden looked at the tangled human mess and saw nothing more threatening than a possible allergic reaction like the one she suffered with cat hair.

Just that night, Alden had thought she saw her husband's face, backlit in a bus window. It was the Plymouth-Brockton coach that did the

Wash-Ashore Route from Boston to P-town three times a day. Of course it wasn't Monty but another man whose profile echoed some aspect of her husband's imperious face.

Seeing the luxury hot rod crammed with autumn's grandeur in rapid decay, Lux told Alden that it was a perfect blow to any man's id to have his car's interior destroyed with compost. Then he described the bloody fish gurry he'd once seen dumped on someone's front seat after a draggerman's love spat. Ison's car was a close second.

As an unexpected bonus, Alden noticed a wolf spider crawling in a diagonal line across the inner windshield. In her wildest dreams she hadn't imagined such a fat one. "This is perfect," she told Lux.

"It kind of says 'Fuck you,' doesn't it?" Lux said as they stared at the teeming terrarium on four wheels.

Suddenly she wanted full credit for their vandalism. She told Lux to wait and she strolled up the flagstone sidewalk and rang the doorbell. She noticed the new wreath on the front door, its pinecones frosted with artificial snow, and she imagined Ison's wife had worked her little hands to the bone making the hokey item.

After a moment, Ison himself appeared at the door in his bathrobe with a peculiar makeshift sash: he had strung a vinyl extension cord through the belt loops and knotted it, its pronged end swinging. That surprising detail almost derailed Alden from her attack mode. The extension cord sash made Ison almost seem human, and it jolted her sexual recall. She felt a familiar internal shiver, the little washboard tingle from ascending O-rings of tight muscle. She didn't want to think of it.

Ison wouldn't turn on the porch light. He pushed open the storm, one index finger raised to his lips so that Alden wouldn't speak too loud and bring his wife to the door. He whispered, "Who's there?"

"Oh, please. You can forget the act," she told him. "It's me, of course."

Ison knew her voiceprint in the darkness. "Alden—" He feigned agony, his words dripping with clotted honey that she could almost taste in her own mouth. She turned on her heel and trotted back to her Jeep. She piled into the driver's seat. She slammed her door, and Lux slammed his. She was pleased that Ison heard both doors latch and would know that she wasn't a solitary crone on a rampage. She had an escort. She rolled the Jeep around the arbor and drove off, right past the violated sports car. She hoped Ison's wife would find it right away and the two of them would have it out.

LUX'S CLOTHES WERE LAYERED with soured snips, pine needles, and bracken. The Jeep smelled woodsy, like a rustic Tyrolean cabin. Alden started sneezing. Lux handed her his handkerchief.

"God. You carry a real handkerchief? That's pretty good," she said.

"My mother taught me. I use it to wipe my knife blade so it won't get rusty."

"Really? That's what it's for?" Then she saw he was teasing her.

He stared ahead, smiling, waiting for her to squeak.

She didn't give him the pleasure. All evening she had felt a charged current, even more than she'd felt the time he'd hammered her shingles at the shack, and she felt her muscles vibrate, from her knees up to her trunk. It wasn't just the camaraderie of their impulsive scheme, but a ticklish, itchy sensation, like the feeling when she sawed a thread between two back teeth. "You have any dinner yet? Are you hungry?" she said.

"I could eat a chicken-fried horse if you had one."

"I haven't done my shopping this week, but I can make you a sandwich at my place, okay?"

"Don't go to any trouble," he said. But he wanted trouble with her. "What kind of sandwich are we talking about?"

HER HOMEBOUND ROUTE ACROSS the dunes was black as pitch. She tried to find the new moon, but its mysterious blot had sunk below the horizon. She had triumphed that night with Ison, but she felt a mounting anxiety about the landscaper. She was sure he was next to torment her.

They got out of her Jeep to hear the waves untangling. "Horse manes," they were sometimes called. The surf sounded different each time she listened, but it *always mocked the landlocked* and their petty problems. Waves crashed, pounded, suctioned and raked the pebbled sand. Even in a calm, the waves were an audible *swat, swat, swat.*

Her shack was lit up like a golden box.

"Is that a hundred-watt bulb?" Lux asked her. "That's not safe in this firetrap." He sat at the tiny pedestal table, waiting for her to doctor four slices of bread. After a moment he said, "How's your dish working?"

Alden said, "It's excellent. I watch episodes of *Filed Away* and *Unfinished Business,* you know? You ever see that show *Filed Away*?"

"I don't think so."

"They have victimologies, unsolved files, cold cases. Profiles of missing persons."

He couldn't look at her without wanting her instantly. It took every speck of his intellect and will power to sit still in his chair. When he tried to inhale, he was breathing two saw blades.

He stared at the sandwich on his plate. He realized he was famished and could have finished both halves of his peanut butter and jelly in three or four chomps, yet he waited for her to make her own version. As she scraped the jar with a knife, he lifted one half of his sandwich to explore the jelly seam with the tip of his tongue. When she sat down, she gave him *her* sandwich and took the one he had already licked. He thought she did it on purpose.

She watched him across the table. He looked like a man who wouldn't be daunted if faced with the tedious chore of constructing a perfect geodesic dome.

"Thanks for your help tonight," she told him.

"Any time. But if you don't mind me asking, what's the story with that suit? Is that your type—a banker?"

"He operates a business on the Internet—"

"Oh, he's a day trader? Their scam goes 'Buy, lie, sell high. Pump and dump.' That's how these tourists buy their trophy houses."

"Not the stock market. He sells wilderness tours."

"A travel agent? Oh, Christ."

She said, "He was just intermission, not the movie."

Lux saw she was uncoiling more wire from the spool, but he wasn't going to let it ignite. Demolition experts take weeks setting up, notching beams, removing existing plaster, windows, fire doors, until the structure is down to its bare brickwork. Then *kabloom.*

But Alden was unloading her feelings. She said, "It's one thing he's married. But then he turns out to be one of those sickos. You know, those guys who whip it out at bus stop shelters? I've seen them parked outside of Bally's Fitness Center. They sit in their cars just to see girls walk past in Jogbras. You can see their neckties crink, crink, crink, as they whack off. Those guys are everywhere."

Lux watched her shoulders heave and relax. She wasn't lumping him into her description, but he felt lumped in.

"You still waiting for Monty to show up?"

"I don't know. I guess." She didn't want Lux to dissect her brain. "Let's not go there, okay? *Do not pick the sea lavender.*"

"Excuse me?"

"I don't want to talk about *him.*"

"He was cheating on you."

"Shite. Does everyone know I'm a doormat?"

"He's not coming back."

"How do you know that, pray tell?"

"I've got crystal balls."

His joke unnerved her. She said, "So do you want to join Hyram's protest group sailing over to the outfall pipe? He needs more crew, people who can navigate so he won't end up in Newfoundland. Hyram's having a meeting this week."

"Isn't that tunnel almost finished? I mean, they're never going to shelve it now, no matter what Hyram does out there."

"You mean those fucks at Massachusetts Water Resource Authority? They'll have to deal with the public this time. Hyram says there was a group in the Northwest that stopped a power plant in Seattle after it was already online. Hyram's been on national TV, you know."

Lux said, "TV shows *like* to profile losing causes. If it's TV worthy, it's a done deal already."

When she sipped her milk, he watched the silky, almost imperceptible muscle current as she swallowed.

He stood up to get the carton of milk to refill his glass.

She watched *him* adjust his step in that telltale gait of a man whose dick has jumped ahead of the negotiations. She scolded herself for letting herself picture him in that condition. "You want a beer instead?" she asked. "I've got a bottle of Genius stout. It's been around. What's the shelf life on that?"

"On Genius stout? I don't have a clue. Don't you mean Guinness?"

"Oh, right."

He looked at her, trying to see if her pun was an act. She couldn't be such an innocent. "I'm kind of sober," he told her.

"Oh yeah, sorry. Have the milk." She said she'd drive him back to the duplex, but she didn't get up from her chair.

He picked up a can of Dust-Off, a cylinder of compressed air that Alden kept handy to clean her laptop keyboard and Nikon camera. He came back to the table. He aimed its pinprick wand at her face, and her bangs lifted.

"Hey, don't waste that."

"What constitutes waste is a personal opinion, same as thrift. For instance, aren't you going to finish that?" He pointed to her sandwich crusts.

She pushed her table scraps toward him and he popped them into his mouth. He wiped a daub of peanut butter off the rim of her plate.

"Hey, you should read the 'Miss Manners' column," she said.

"'Good manners are made up of petty sacrifices.' That's R. W. Emerson."

"No kidding?" She lifted her chin a half inch higher. He saw he was hitting a nerve. The wrong one.

He held the Dust-Off and spritzed her with iced air.

She watched his face, his dead-ahead, unblinking stare that she couldn't meet. He squirted her again. His playfulness had evaporated and now he was serious. He stood up. He took her wrist and led her across the floor to the antique iron bedstead that he had prized for weeks through the Victorian window.

On the table they had left their glasses coated with whole milk, and the shack smelled of sweet dairy, strawberry jam, and woodsy grime from their misdeed as Lux pushed her onto her bed.

"What have you got in mind now?" she said, one beautiful eyebrow arched higher. But she seemed to know what was coming next.

She was lying straight as an arrow on the antique three-quarter mattress, not a full bed, but there was plenty of room for the two of them. She smoothed the palms of her hands across the damask coverlet on either side of her hips; its worn cotton nap felt soft as doeskin. She waited for Lux to fall down beside her.

He stalled for time, wanting to prolong the thrilling instant when he arrived at ground zero on his treasure map. He picked up a bracelet he found on the night table. He told her, "Put this on first." When he tugged her wrist, he saw that the inside of her forearm had repetitive white lines, parallel scars left behind from secret melodramas she'd enacted when she was a teenager. Forensic manuals called these scars hesitation marks, and they were most commonly found on shook-up girls from higher income brackets.

He was about to ask her about the "cry for help" written in braille across her tender skin when she grabbed the gold herringbone chain. "This is an *ankle* bracelet, stupid—from my tenth-grade sweetheart," she told him. She had kept it since high school, when girls dressed in retro disco clothes and displayed their gold anklets entrapped beneath tight panty hose mesh. She wasn't the type, but she had worn the ankle bracelet for her boyfriend. For other men she had done more foolish things. For one she had shaved her pubic hair and for another she had switched her antiperspirant stick because he told her that his sister used the same brand. "So what?" Alden had said.

"You can't smell like my *sister,*" he had told her.

It was soon after she switched brands that he broke off with her, as if it had been his sister's scent all along that had drawn him to her.

Lux tried to fasten the chain around her ankle, having a little trouble with its gold prong.

Alden looked into his face and smiled.

She looks pretty comfortable, he was thinking.

But he felt wild, disheveled, his clothes hoary with leafy specks and snips of grass, like the god Sylvanus. He kicked his jeans across the room. He sat down on the bed beside her. He held the tiny can of Dust-

Off and threatened to squirt it. She grabbed it from him and read the label. "Hey, the *warning* says that this causes frostbite." She recited the instructions. "Always use in upright position."

"That won't be a problem," he said.

She liked his self-mockery and she pushed her trousers down and pulled off her sweater. Bare breasted, she propped two pillows behind her head to watch what he would do next.

He took the Dust-Off and aimed the pinhole wand up and down her nakedness, carving indented lines on her skin and scrolling a tight seam of air across her nipples. He probed her belly button with icy blasts from the can, like invisible fingertips.

She started to succumb to the diaphanous, airy foreplay, overwhelmed by his charming games and by his muscled physique. She thought, This is the body of a man who can lift a sea turtle with one hand like it was a sack lunch.

Lux asked her, "You glad to be rid of Mr. Two Turrets?"

"Like I said, he was just filler until Monty comes back."

"Filler? I can do that." He rode the heel of his hand down her shin. He unclasped the bracelet from her ankle, and in the same seamless gesture he inserted the chain into her wet slit—with short probes of his index finger, the way a magician stuffs a scarf into the handle of a cane—and slowly finger-fucked her. She scolded him, but he wouldn't stop. Soon he had convinced her that he knew what he was doing. She kept still as he touched her, until her orgasm pulsed over his knuckles. He tugged the bracelet out of her body, its gold weave encased in a moist, glassy straw.

This is how he took control of her every thought.

His cock plowed her inner thigh and he entered her, taking measured, deliberate jabs to sink past her tight petal-remnants.

But in another moment she resurfaced, breathless, and said, "Lux—what have you heard about Monty?"

He halted in midglide and looked into her startled eyes, her pupils large and dilating. "What have I heard? Nothing. Not now."

"Oh, never mind. I don't care. Don't stop," she said. She stared into his face, then closed her eyes. Her lashes were distinct and beautiful, like deep brown saffron threads.

Once more he urged his hips, still cautious and worshipful. He kissed her in short, aggressive nips; a smear of strawberry paste rimmed his mouth and they both tasted it.

But again Alden was jarred from her louche amnesia. In the tiny shack, beneath the hundred-watt lightbulb, her delicious staggers of sensation were overwhelmed by a recognition that cut across the dream effect of their skin-to-skin contact.

She shifted beneath him. He felt his jelly sandwich, a sweet mush, rematerializing at the base of his pharynx. He kissed her instantly to distract her. He rolled onto his back, tugging her hips to keep her on top. She yelped, then gurgled at his mastery.

She closed her eyes and smiled as he joggled her. "Goddamn you." She bounced. "Really. I don't care where—he—is."

Lux tugged her hips, until he couldn't get any deeper. "I know this," he said. "I know where *you* are."

HE WOULDN'T LET HER DRIVE him back to the duplex. He said he wanted to walk. The moonless night was an attraction, he joked. "Coyotes are our friends." He wanted the sensation of leaving her tucked in. After so many nights watching her routine, he wanted to take charge. He covered her up. He handed her the bisque doll, the way a parent offers a teddy bear to his baby daughter. "Oh, God," she said, pushing it away. "I can't sleep with this."

When she was alone, she stretched in her sheets and rolled from her back to her tummy, pleased that her cotton damask was still warm from two bodies, not one. She pictured Ison's sports car crammed with oak and maple tatters. An inventive brush-off, in its successful carry-through, gives an underdog a warm-all-over feeling and a peck of self-confidence. But Mr. Squishy's eerie homunculus challenged the harmony she felt. The unsettling figurine and the three-faced bisque doll engaged in a contentious sulk from opposite sides of the room. She feared she would have her recurring nightmare about Monty: He's playing the keyboard in the empty summer resort, his hands inserted beneath the polyethylene drop cloth. In the chilly tavern, zombies from the movie *Carnival of Souls* begin their ballroom dancing.

She dialed 1-800-AMNESIA just to listen to the update. She no longer cared if the stats matched Monty, but listening to the amnesia recording had become an addictive sleep aid. She waited for the tape loop to begin, then rested the phone against her pillow, letting it drone. When that didn't put her to sleep, she dribbled her anklet-string across her breasts, remembering how Lux had teased her with it. She dragged its textured chain, its warm emollient gold still as powerful as ever.

She plumped her pillows and pointed the clicker at the TV. Her reception drifted in and out in ghosting waves of snow or pepper. She would ask Lux to come back to adjust the dish.

12

IT WAS STILL FOUR HOURS UNTIL LUNCHTIME in Bangkok, and the countdown to their crypt invasion had begun. He called King to make sure he was bringing a truck.

Lux told him that he wasn't thinking of Vermont any longer; he was thinking about the Cape Cod Canal. He saw its chalky green ribbon snaking from Buzzards Bay to Sagamore. As a kid, he had fished with King from its rocky jetties, where the current was dangerous. Once, some men were drowned when their waders filled up with water and the drunken slobs couldn't unbuckle their boots fast enough. After that, his mother wouldn't let Lux go out there with King. King went alone.

King said, "The canal? We put him in the canal, and he'll be coughed up with the eelgrass down in Wareham or Mattapoisett, just like those dudes that fell off the rocks. It's better to put him back in the ground."

"What about this? I'm thinking vernal pool."

"You mean one of those puddles at the bottom of a kettle hole? That's where coyotes make their dens. Near potable water. Forget the wilderness idea, we need a substantial crypt. Ready-mix or something."

He got off the line with King and called the Audubon hotline to leave a message for Alden. After the beep he said, "Alden? Alden, we've got to talk—" But midway he choked. He hung up the receiver.

In the meanwhile Lux thought he'd better go find his friend Tindle in case King spooked and didn't show up with a Rent-A-Wreck loaner. Lux might need Tindle's truck. To get to Tindle he'd have to attend a meeting. Lux didn't see any other way.

Lux had joined AA briefly a year ago, but he stopped going to their soirees. He was keeping sober without attending meetings, but he told Tindle, "All that knee-jerk ritualism creeped it for me." Each meeting started with a progression of memorized cues and prompts.

"I'm Frank. I'm an alcoholic."

"Hi, Frank!"

"I'm Carol and I'm an alcoholic."

"Hi-i, Carol!

"My name is Rick. I'm a drunk."

"Hi-i, Rick! Good to see you, Rick!" The membership sounded like a brainwashed hallelujah chorus of boozers and pin jabbers. The typical assemblage of AA church-basement inhabitants just recalled the pivotal NORD gathering Lux had shunned years before. Lux wasn't a joiner. But during the first weeks he was sober, he had shown up at the library room at the Seaman's Institute, where he did some evening meetings. He did his meetings at Seaman's instead of at the student union at Four Cs Community College, where he had just started attending night classes. He was earning credits in order to be admitted to the program in horticultural science and landscape architecture at UMass, but he still wasn't sure he was "college material."

Lux had met Tindle when Lux showed up fortified at his first evening class, an entry-level course with the forbidding title American Transcendentalism. The adjunct professor, Jim Tindle, was a "friend of Bill," and it was Tindle who took Lux to his first AA meeting.

The professor took some extra time with Lux after class, helping him adjust to the ebb and flow of the literature course. He sat knee to knee with Lux in torturous seats in the back of the classroom. The plank chair had a particleboard armrest that curled around Lux's waist and imprisoned him behind a miniature desk that looked more like a chopping board or cocktail tray. The chair made him claustrophobic, but he and Tindle sat like that under the blinding overhead lighting long after the other students were dismissed.

Tindle convinced Lux to try to stay straight long enough to read the first assignment, one story from the Hawthorne collection. Lux went home and read "The Minister's Black Veil," about a man who walks around wearing a handkerchief to hide his face. Lux thought Tindle had assigned that particular story because a mask was suggestive of Lux's refusal to acknowledge his alcohol problem.

Lux and Tindle discussed the class assignment sitting side by side at the bar rail at Land Ho! Tindle was sipping tonic water while Lux was doing shooters with Rolling Rock chasers. He didn't like Tindle's attempts to steer him off the bottom shelf. Lux purchased straight shots of whatever was the house brand. He thought he heard Tindle saying "Come on, try J & B," but Tindle had said, "HP."

Lux said, "HP? Is that single malt? Is it bourbon?" He explained to Tindle that his mom had taught him that there's no difference between Stock fifths and more expensive name brands except for the *taste.* Its *taste* isn't important. Taste isn't even on the pie chart for booze artists.

Tindle said, "No, son, I'm not talking about which *shelf* you're on. I'm talking about finding your higher power."

Lux had been teasing the professor. He knew about the "higher power" idea. He had heard about that culture club firsthand from some of its card-carrying members who worked with him at the nurseries. Marty Stokes was a friend of Bill's. But Lux wasn't interested. Tindle recognized Lux's typical label jabbing, but he saw that Lux liked talking about the Hawthorne, even in a stupor. Lux read a little more Hawthorne, and started on the Emerson, which was harder going.

Tindle used the lit class as a springboard, and finally he squired Lux to his first AA meetings. Lux stayed off the sauce for a week, then a few more weeks, until he was one month sober.

When Gwen saw him reading a book, she said, "Why are you ignoring me?"

He told her, "If you see me take this bookmark out of this book, that's a pretty good signal you should leave me be."

She grabbed the little column of paper and tore it into snips. She was trying to sit on his lap, as she often did. Sitting on his lap would lead to kisses and further. He'd tell her, "You're a bottomless pit." Pinching his textbook under his arm, he walked her to the bedroom. One night, he went back to the text instead. He asked her to make some coffee.

"Coffee? Since when do you want coffee at this time of night?"

They hadn't been very comfortable together with the schoolteacher pushing up daisies just two miles from their duplex. It got worse with Gwen when Lux signed up at the college and found his new friendship with Tindle.

"You trying to improve yourself?" Gwen said.

"I think I am."

"You can't improve on something that's worthless."

He shut his book and looked at her, but he didn't rise from his chair. "Thanks for your vote," he told her.

She threw her shoe at him. Then its mate. She peeled off her blouse. She tossed all her clothing into the ring.

She'd get her way eventually, but when she was in bed with Lux, Gwen seemed to know he wasn't thinking of her at all. He was in love with the teacher's widow. Gwen was certain she saw it happening. "You're going insane," she told him. "That girl doesn't even know you're alive."

Gwen knew from Lux that his only other long-term girlfriend was the woman with complex tattoos. He had told Gwen that sleeping with that one was like climbing onto a Persian carpet. If not for Gwen, he had no prospects.

"I don't need your charity," he had once said.

"Charity? I'm just about a martyr," she said.

Lux went back to his book. He started to attend some meetings as he tackled more Hawthorne, the Emerson, the Thoreau. When he sat down to read *Moby-Dick* his nerves were jangled, like Lindbergh must have felt on his first transatlantic flight. He maneuvered the twists and turns of Melville's technical explications of threading harpoons and celestial navigation, and for that he had to be stone-cold sober. Tindle was taking him to meetings twice a day. The Sunrisers met at 6 A.M. at the United Methodist church annex. The Sunrisers were local contractors, security personnel getting off their night shifts, housekeeping staff from the Treadway Inn and MidCape Sheraton, some workers from the fish-processing plant, students, anyone who needed to attend meetings before hitting the lumberyard or fish piers or punching in.

Adjunct college profs don't earn very much, and Tindle made his living as a carpenter, running a good renovating outfit with a four-man crew. He rebuilt whole houses; Mansards and Victorians were reborn "as was." He had a milliner's studio where he made Victorian doors from scratch with all the gingerbread trim and beveled glass. He did pantry window cupboards, banisters, balustrades, honeycomb lintels, and mantels to die for. In his spare time he made notable reproductions of Windsor chairs with authentic joinery, locking tapers and hand-rived spindles, arms and bows. He showed Lux his workshop and the cherry, oak, and maple he used for carving chairs. Lux said, "That's nice wood. I guess we have something in common. But I like working with the live article."

Tindle led meetings at the Four Cs student union, but Lux didn't like doing his meetings with kidsters. These college boys, hardly much younger than Lux, never shut up about their keggathons and brew-shooting contests, where they'd pierce sixteen-ouncers to chugalug the ejectile stream. These jocks showed up the day after a hateful wee-hour binge on bonfire night, but few returned to a second meeting.

Yet Lux had listened to one kid's story. The student described how he had worked his way through college doing two shifts at a KFC franchise in Fall River. In a drunken stupor he had climbed onto a countertop to get a box of plastic coffee stirrers from a high shelf. The kid was so faced that coming down he stepped right into the Friolator. He was wearing steel-toed Timberlands, and the boiling oil filled his work boot until his foot was chicken-fried. He couldn't get his boot unlaced fast enough. He was in the burn unit at Hasbro Hospital, but they couldn't save his dog. He was in rehab for months, learning to use his new prosthetic foot and getting pinned on morphine. The kid's deadpan delivery was impressive. He avoided extra flourishes. The story was whole on its own.

Lux was impressed by the Friolator story he had heard at the college, but he soon found out that every meeting has a Friolator story. These Friolator stories were archetypal in the AA narrative; there were hundreds of classic linchpin events that graphically illustrated the program doctrine. These booze artists recounted the same stories nightly, in perpetuity, but Lux saw it was like trying to wrap insulation around a melting ice cube or like losing the spoon while stirring the applesauce. Every drunk knows that the next installment is only one golden inch away.

Lux had never confessed *his* Friolator tale because it could put him in jail.

Despite the kid in the Timberlands at the college meeting, Seaman's Institute was more Lux's crowd—lobstermen, bridge painters, linoleum installers, postal employees, ticket clerks and greeters from the Steamship Authority and Hy-Line Cruises, where they get video feeds from Wonderland Greyhound Park and Suffolk Downs with full-card simulcasting. There was an old geezer from Otis Air Force Base who claimed he helped the navy deliver the A-bomb and that's why he couldn't stay straight. There weren't too many kidsters in this seasoned tribe. Not too many women, either.

Women drunks unnerved Lux. It wasn't sexism; it was deeper than sexism. It was momism.

WHEN GWEN HAD GONE, Lux met Tindle at the 7:30 meeting at Seaman's Institute. It was once a seventeenth-century flophouse for merchant marines who set anchor in Nauset Harbor and left their tall ships to have a night with waterfront harlots. Historic buildings like this one, with its floodwater marks dated on the first-floor foundation—"Hurricane 1938"—gave Lux the sobering feeling that many had come and gone before him and his hitch wouldn't last long.

In the library room, Lux found Tindle at the coffee urn with some brand-new faces looking up at him like scrubbed headlights. Anxious for instant salvation, these novices had familiar, tortured foreheads. These tortured foreheads were the bar code of the boozer clan. Lux empathized with these newcomers, who were looking across the Patagonia of their first sober twenty-four hours.

Because Lux had stopped attending meetings, he had never mastered more than two of the Twelve Steps and was there for the body count only. Tindle said that as long as Lux wasn't drinking, it didn't matter in what small increments he moved toward self-knowledge. "Sobriety is the means, not the end," Tindle said.

Tindle had reservoirs of patience. He thought that Lux's false paralysis syndrome might be cause enough for his drinking problem, but Lux's unorthodox living arrangements with his brother's wife might be making Lux feel guilty. A thing like that must eat at you.

Lux had never told Tindle about Monty Warren, but he was ready.

He thought he might need to borrow Tindle's 4x4 truck.

The automobile is at the business end of every scheme. He'd have to bring Tindle into it in case King ditched him.

Lux sat down next to the college professor and Victorian-house wright. The combined force of these divine occupations was encouragement enough, and the dam burst. Lux confessed. The story just started to sluice out; it crashed ahead in a wild expository madness like hip-hop lyrics. He told Tindle about Monty Warren's corpse buried in the cedar rows at Bay State Nurseries. He whispered, "It's got to come out. We're transporting it to another site—destination unknown."

"You say you have a body in there?"

"For about two years. It might be just bones."

Tindle listened, his eyes locked on Lux. "Back up," Tindle said.

"How far?"

"When did you bury this teacher?"

"Before I got sober."

Tindle was relieved to know that the event had happened prior to their acquaintance—before their little heart-to-hearts and their respectful bond had been made in the classroom at Four Cs.

Tindle said, "You're saying you had an accident, or was it more than that?"

"I've been going over it in my mind—"

"Shit, don't you know? Was it a blackout?" Tindle used the fearful word. The blackout phenomenon was something Lux had never wanted to acknowledge. In a blackout anything can happen. You could steal from your mother, cheat your best friend, see God and the devil superimposed on the mug of your father, who comes walking back after fifteen years. Lux tried to explain what he thought was the truth, but the room was filling up. He whispered to Tindle, "It's why I finally got sober."

"That's right. You did it. Who would have thought you could?"

The men turned in their seats to face each other, connecting in the way that happens between addicts, pilgrims, boat people, POWs, inmates from Alcatraz, all the wash-ashores who commune after a deathly crossing. They were sober; anything else was inconsequential. The only thing that mattered was the elementary sequencing pattern of staying straight *day after day after day.*

One member emeritus was happy to see Lux come back to the fold, and he elected him to run the meeting.

"I don't think so," Lux protested. "Shit, give me a break."

Old-timers heckled him, pressing him into the role. He stood up and started the meeting *as per.* "I'm Lux. I'm a drunk—"

Chirps and gobbles like a turkey farm at sunrise.

He paused to let their mushy greetings subside.

"I see some neonates here. Which Dr. Detox wants to adopt one of these bottle babies?" He played the role of prodigal son as the circle settled in.

"Sit down, zombie," someone teased.

"Criticism is the highest form of regard," Lux said.

"That's right. Opposition is friendship." Tindle enjoyed these meetings the way a nanny likes to watch her charges play in the park using strategies she has taught them. Despite Lux's poor attendance, Tindle could take a little credit for Lux's confidence at the podium.

"I'm one year without a taste of anything," Lux said. "My job is good at the nurseries. So I won't rehash the night I drove the school bus into the harbor."

They knew he'd lost his job as bus driver and liked the cartoon. But he retold it, a routine they expected, syncopated with their pockets of laughter and blistering love talk. Mark Skillings said, "Poor harbormaster—he was almost retired when he sees that bus topple off the jetty. Maybe it's got babies on it. He gets his heart attack instead of a gold watch."

Lux protested, "They said his cholesterol was four hundred. It wasn't my fault. All those fried oysters. But I'm not driving that bus route anymore—"

"Lux, we've heard it and we *love* it."

Lux nodded. "I'm not behind the wheel. Not in the driver's seat.

Count your lucky stars. Your sprouts are safe. But it's my fourth year at Bay State. I'm getting into some nice shit there. I make trees hold hands like a strip of paper dolls. I twist the tips of their branches, and these green gypsies are dancing in a line. I'm in charge of the whole operation. Stop by sometime and look at my creations."

The membership was confounded by the offer. Lux was extending a genuine invitation. Bringing a roomful of post-embalmed brethren, most of them acting manic on dry drunks, into the showplace of Bay State Nurseries—his boss wasn't going to like it.

He told them, "You know, I tried to go alongside the program, I thought I could stay abreast of it, on the *outside, looking in.* But now I want to try this thing called the surrender tradition."

Tindle looked at Lux. He didn't know where Lux was going.

Lux read aloud from the handbook. " 'To *surrender* means not to be protective of others. To *surrender* means to stop trying to control others. To *surrender* is to stop denying. To allow *others* to feel their *own* consequences.' "

Lux looked deep into the room, past each upturned face, bridge painters and linoleum installers, past the attentive circle and farther, as if he could look through the wall behind the coffee urn and see the twinkling harbor. His voice dropped two registers. He said in a husky admission, "You see, there's this person. She doesn't know what I've done to her. With my understanding of the surrender tradition, I'm supposed to tell her the one thing that could kill her—"

Tindle popped out of his chair and went up to Lux. He tried to stop Lux from engaging in his long-awaited Friolator confession. But Lux went on, "I just have to face her and tell her *everything*. Right, Jim?"

Someone said, "Tell her what you need to tell her, man. It's her cross. Don't deny her that burden, because it's really a gift."

A third party chimed in, "You either *give,* or you *slave.*"

Lux nodded. Give or slave. It was making sense to him now. But Tindle announced, "Hey, have to split. We're leaving early. Sorry, folks."

Lux didn't budge. The room laughed, then fell hushed. Everyone was trying to gauge the handsome statue. He stood before them in a T-shirt, his muscles defined and rippling, like he was wrapped in a golden rope swing. Hands as big as a blacksmith's oven mitts. Dark, wavy hair in a snarl of shoulder-length fronds. Piercing eyes, blue as glass cleaner.

Their sugary, good-natured jeers and nickering made him come to his senses all at once. He said his good-byes. "I'm Lux. I'm a drunk. Fuck you. Go wipe your ass on a tea towel—"

Tindle started pushing Lux toward the door. Lux didn't resist. He grabbed his jacket from the coatrack by the exit, knocking a picture frame from the wall, a painting of tall ships from Chatham's precious yesteryears when more men were drowned each year than died of natural causes.

Lux sat in Tindle's truck, trying to explain Alden Warren. "This connection just keeps intensifying," he said.

"You mean the widow? You think she's your problem now? But you were drunk when it happened."

"Love-drunk."

"In love with alcohol." Tindle tried to get it back on track.

"Do you think she'll accept the news? I mean, I guess she'll just freak."

"You fell for the teacher's wife? That's like Shakespeare's *Richard the Third.* He courts his victim's bride, Lady Anne. It's that famous 'coffin seduction' scene in the funeral procession."

"He comes on to her during that?"

"Richard is a hunchback with a withered arm. He gets her to accept a ring. He's a cripple who gets his jollies asserting his power."

Lux listened to Tindle's instant synopsis, his heart in his throat. "So, does this Lady Anne fall for the guy who offs her husband?"

"That's right. It's the same in that film *The Trouble with Harry.*"

"What's that?"

"A Hitchcock classic. They dig up a body four or five times. In that one, too, the gravedigger gets the victim's bride."

"No shit? Are you saying it's a literary theme or something—"

"Maybe for Hitchcock, but this is real life."

Lux pressed the heels of his hands against his eye sockets.

Tindle said, "Look, you're saying it was an accident. That's what it was, and that's what you'll tell her. This girl is your ninth step in one shot. She's all of it. The whole shooting match. But what's my role? This isn't in the Twelve Traditions."

"I'm not asking you to lift a finger. After we get Mr. Bones, I have to find Alden. I've got a history with her that's growing a long tail. I've got to face the music."

"That's right. Face the music, and the calliope stops. Once you tell her, that runaway carousel stops spinning."

"I want to tell her. I wanted to *yesterday.* Maybe I'll need your truck."

13

TINDLE DROVE LUX TO THE FORT HILL PARKING LOT, a scenic overlook above the Million-Dollar Marsh. Stargazers came out there. Lovers and lonely hearts alike parked before the breakwater jetty to watch the moonglow on the water. There wasn't a moon this night. But in the near distance, Lux saw several white swans at rest in a tight circle on the water, like fluffy meringues on a silver pie sheet.

King pulled up beside them in a late-model white panel truck, its backside caved in from a rear-end collision. As King swung around in a circle, Lux saw the business logo stenciled in huge letters on both sides of the van. "Jesus, what the hell is he driving?"

Tindle read the lettering. "G.O.D. Guaranteed Overnight Delivery."

Lux saw the courier's pledge, which promised "delivery overnight or your money back," and the toll-free number 1-888-G-O-D-TO-GO. Lux said, "Shit. Why don't we just get us a loudspeaker."

King got out of the Rent-a-Wreck truck and walked up to Lux's window. "You like it? It's cherry except for its back end. These solid-panel vans can accordion. Ass-bashing these boxes can't be forgiven, but it runs good."

Tindle was smiling. The van looked totaled.

King looked at Tindle, stung, and asked Lux, "Why do you need me? You got *him.*" But they all climbed into the G.O.D. truck to talk over their plan. Lux sat between his friends. Tindle reached across his lap, extending his hand to King. But Tindle withdrew his paw when King just squinted at the AA maestro, unreceptive to the formality. King's close-set eyes took some getting used to, like a spider's frontal vision centered on a tidbit of something.

Tindle was trying too hard. The prof wanted to fit King into a niche, but there wasn't a niche at hand.

"You get arrested for armed robbery?" Tindle finally asked King directly.

"Rape," King said.

"Oh, Christ," Lux said.

Tindle cocked his head. "Oh, I see. You did time for sexual assault?"

"Nope. They couldn't prove I committed the rape. My lawyer tells them if she got undressed and *folded* her clothes and put them on a chair, and *I folded* my clothes and put them on a chair, does that look like a rape?"

Tindle said, "A lot of rapists and killers were habitual neatniks. Bundy. Dahmer. Leopold and Loeb. They were immaculate, they used hair pomades and lavender water. They *always* folded their underwear and rolled their socks."

Lux told Tindle, "He's jerking your chain, Jim. He didn't rape a girl."

"Your Nissan have all-wheel, Jim?" King said.

"It's just got the four-wheel," Tindle said.

King said, "Oh, shit. We need the *all-wheel.*"

"This van have all-wheel?" Lux said. "No? So shut up."

"Yeah, but it's got God power, right?" King said. "Jim's tub would get stuck. She's too loaded up. He's got a thousand pounds of toolery in back. That Tuff-E is stocked and he's got that built-in table saw."

Tindle said, "That saw is custom. That's bolted to the bed. It goes on the job with me. We can't do much about it." Tindle opened his Nantucket Nectar and passed it over to King.

"No, thanks. Fruit juice is for monkeys."

Lux said, "Since when?"

"I won't touch it," King said.

"You drink battery acid, I guess," Tindle said.

"I don't drink fruit juice unless I'm hospitalized."

Lux saw it was going to be uphill. But Lux needed King for badass injections. He needed Tindle to rubber-stamp the transfer and to give his churchy thumbs-up. But his two friends together canceled each other out.

"You got garbage bags?" Lux asked King.

"I still have that equipment bag I pinched from Nauset High School."

"You stole that duffel from the high school?" Tindle said.

"It came full of stuff I wanted."

"Is the zipper good?" Lux said.

"It zips," King said.

The men were silent as they visualized the bus monitor. Lux had found a library book that explained the five stages of decomposition: Fresh, Bloated, Decay, Post-Decay, and Skeletal. Blowflies are the first to begin the work, and their maggots have three molts as they chew into the corpse. Then there's hister beetles, rove beetles, and centipedes, mites, and earthworms. Ants or wasps often make hives in skull cavities. Lux assured his mates that everything should have come and gone by now. "Soft tissue disappears. It will be bones, hair, leather. And whatever synthetics he's wearing." Lux thought of Monty's guide yellow Nike jacket. Then he thought of Alden. He sometimes saw her wearing his mother's satin bed jacket, a delicate item that his mother saved for her occasional commerce with men. He thought of Alden in that jacket, her hair lofting over her shoulders in gorgeous kinked clouds, like his childhood heartthrob, the girl with—

Tindle watched Lux's secret reverie wax and wane across his sharp features. Tindle said, "You're obsessed. You're Richard the Third incarnate."

"Who's that?" King said.

Tindle said, "Shakespeare."

King said, "Oh yeah? Shakespeare, kick in the rear, happy New Year."

"You don't like Shakespeare?"

"Oh, him? You mean pinprick, pencil dick, the insect fucker?"

"Give it a rest," Lux said. "Let's move it."

King said, "Right. Why are we waiting till midnight? It's black as pitch."

"I say let's do it," Lux said.

King said, "TGIF." He squirted the windshield washer and flipped on the blades until the glass cleared.

He rolled away into the dark and flicked on his headlights. The lamps bloomed momentarily, then dimmed. Their funnel beams shrank to nothing and disappeared. Next, the dashboard lights faded away and they couldn't see the dials.

"What's with your battery?" Lux asked.

"Fuck. It's the alternator, I guess," King said.

"That's just perfect," Lux said.

"Cops will pull us over if we're driving without lights," Tindle said with a lector's authority, or like a preacher who says, "God knows all human endeavor is doomed without faith's illumination."

"Jesus, ladies. We'll be there in a minute," King said, and kept it rolling into the black.

THE CEDARS LOSE THEIR HEADY SMELL AT NIGHT. In sunlight their needled tiers would mentholate the air until Lux felt his sinuses clear. They walked into the open field. The G.O.D truck hummed like a walk-in refrigerator where they'd left it running on the gravel track. If they shut it off, it might not start. Tindle stood by with the loppers while Lux troweled off the surface mulch and began to dig with his spade.

"You sure this is the right place?" King asked.

"Sixth one in from this end," Lux said. "This is the spot. I'm ninety percent sure."

"You could be digging in the *ten* percent that says you're a hundred percent *wrong*."

"It's not the regulation six feet, so we'll be finding it soon." Lux used the plural, although the other two men were standing there doing nothing.

In the dead black, Lux couldn't see much and worked by sound. He loosened the clay pack. He heard the blade edge tear into the tamped peat. Then he heard the muffled plops as moist clods tumbled off the spade's flat bowl. He levered clump after clump. He remembered all too well the soundtrack he had heard when he buried the schoolteacher. Loam had sifted over the TESCO clothesline carton, first a pattering, then a thudding, until the cardboard was blanketed and the sound went mute.

Then his spade scraped against something more than roots. The blade struck, and the object squawked like a spirit cry. He shoveled off the loam and saw that the TESCO box had vanished. In its place there was a presentation of bones. Around the muddy form, the silt seemed extra silky, made twice rich with worm castings after two years of their secret business.

The three men crouched to scoop dirt with their hands. King flicked on a Maglite and pinched it between his knees as the trio pawed soil away from the remains. The surprising yellow parka emerged like a midnight sun. The Nike swoosh inched across the breast pocket like a white worm.

Beneath the blazing jacket, the bones were cobbled together with a queer organic wallpaper, like shrink-wrapped skin. His clothes were gone except for the Gore-Tex jacket and his boots with waffle soles. They brushed the dirt away until the whole corpse surfaced. The bones were marbleized. The skull was still attached to the spinal stalk, clipped at its axis by a tab of petrified leather.

But when King pulled the corpse from the opened trench, the skull rolled off its shoulders. Lux picked up the moldering head and quickly set it down again.

The magnitude of that surprise stalled them for an instant.

The yellow jacket flopped open and Lux saw the teacher's house key on its plastic lanyard woven between two ribs. The Maglite caught the sliver of notched metal that had once been the key to Alden's house. Monty had once explained to Lux that some of his students were latchkey kids, and they had to wear their house keys looped around their neck or clipped to their backpack. In PC solidarity, Monty started to wear his own key on a neck chain.

Monty's occasional moments of compassion confounded Lux, who wanted to remember the teacher as the playboy he was—Alden's doom. Lux tore the key from the skeleton and plunged it in his pocket.

They collected the ladder of bone rubble, and King said, "Monty, dude—looking *goood.*"

"Tune off, will you," Lux said.

"Your voice carries," Tindle said, but he was grinning at King's irreverence. A little bit was called for.

Lux held the duffel bag open as King dropped the schoolteacher's jumbled bones like a clatter of collapsible TV trays. He zipped the bag before they saw the skull perched by its lonesome. Lux tried to open the bag again but the zipper was stuck.

Tindle whispered, "Cruiser."

A Crown Vic turned into the east end of the field.

King tucked the skull inside his jacket and snapped the rivet buttons.

If anyone should have had the burden of a chin-to-chin with Monty's skull, it should have been Lux.

Tindle told them, "I'll get this." He lifted the equipment bag and walked over to King's van. He put it behind the driver's seat. Lux heard its cargo clacking as he quickly raked the dirt over the crypt hole and tamped it with his boots.

The Crown Vic rolled up beside the G.O.D.-mobile and its flood swelled open. An officer got out of the cruiser and walked up to the driver's side of the empty van. The officer called into the dark, "Nickerson?"

Tindle called back, "Heigh-ho."

The three men left their tools on the black ground and walked over to the patrolman, who waited beside King's clunker, encircled by the dizzying flood.

"Nickerson have you working tonight? Who's foreman here?"

"I am," Lux said. He recognized the constable. It was Francisconi nosing around. He wondered how Francisconi had second-guessed him.

Francisconi aimed his light at Lux's lapel so he wouldn't blind him, but he had pinned him. "You get overtime to be out here at night?"

"I wish," Lux said.

Tindle spoke up, "We're not on the job. We lost a kitty."

"Whose pet would that be?"

King said, "I just got him. It's a white kitten. I didn't know that white cats are usually deaf. But that's the problem, I guess."

"It can't hear you call it?"

"No. I got it for my girlfriend, but it had wanderlust."

Francisconi said, "These little cats like to hunt. They're ratters. They get in a drainpipe and end up on the other side somewhere. But boys, it's not safe walking around these fields in the pitch black—you could fall into a hole." Franciscoui didn't look at Lux directly, but Lux worried he had seen them digging in that cedar row.

"A cat won't stray if it's neutered," Tindle said.

"That's right. Snip its onions, and what's the point of carousing?" King said.

Lux was amazed at how his friends had meshed to create a workable shield.

The officer recognized King. "You operate that portable junkyard—what is it? Rent-A-Heap? Is this delivery van from your lot, or is it a personal vehicle?"

"It's not a distinction with me. I drive whatever is sitting there."

"I guess you have the paperwork for this disaster?"

King hopped into the G.O.D. truck and pulled out his registration.

The officer scrolled his tiny penlight over the documents and handed them back. Then he penned the animal control officer's telephone number on the back of his own business card. He handed the card to Lux. Lux saw that Francisconi did underwater welding when he wasn't wearing his badge. "Rudders, propellers, anchor ports, and ripped hulls."

The officer said, "Better look for the cat tomorrow. Hear what I'm saying?" He pounded the fender of the truck in a tom-tom rhythm and said his good-byes. He sat down in the Crown Vic and backed out of the field, slowly rolling through a few muddy craters.

King said, "I see what you're saying about Francisconi. He's trying to brainstorm. Yes, indeed. You're bothering him. Let's just fax the MCI and tell them you're coming. You'll be going up the old dirt road—I'd hate to see it. Pretty boys are the property of Mr. Cone."

"Mr. Cone?" Tindle said.

"Mr. Cone gets first dibs on freshmen," King said.

"Oh, that." Tindle didn't want to hear more.

King said, "I say we don't off-load tonight, since Uncle Nabs is sneaking around. We sit still somewhere."

"We can go back to the duplex. Gwen took off, so it's okay. The house is empty." Lux remembered the bitter scene in the driveway when she had told him she wasn't throwing him a life preserver.

Lux went to get the tools. He found the spade, but the loppers were missing. "Shit. They can't walk off on their own."

"I've got them," Tindle said.

In the loamy clods, a wedding ring. Lux didn't see it.

KING DROVE OUT OF THE FIELD, but at the Fort Hill scenic turnaround above the ghostly swans, the G.O.D. van died. King tried to crank it, but it wouldn't start again.

They both turned to look at Tindle, sitting between them.

"Sorry, boys. You can't use my truck for a meat locker."

"Come on, Miss Nancy, just give us a lift to the house," King said.

"I don't have to do jack shit," Tindle said. Lux saw that his warm-hearted mentor, Bill's friend, who had guided him through a survey of transcendental masterpieces, was through with him.

King said, "Tindle—that rookie uniform saw the *three* of us. I believe he can count to three. Leave us here with Mr. Bones, and when that genius comes back he'll be asking what happened to you."

They waited.

Tindle said, "Now or never."

They piled out of the G.O.D. truck. Lux picked up the duffel, fearful the long bones might snap in half and jab him. He put it in the back of Tindle's truck, beneath the table saw sheathed in plastic. They climbed into the cab after Tindle without another comment. When he looked up again, Lux saw King had put the skull, face out, on the dash. King told Tindle, "Hey, you got your own Jolly Roger. Who needs foam dice when you got this?"

"Are you fucking crazy? Get rid of that," Tindle said.

Lux told King, "I guess you want to go back inside? They're plumping your pillows right now. It's toothbrush day."

King pulled the skull down and handed it to Lux.

Lux opened the glove box, and a book fell out. Lux saw its Amazon bookmark flutter loose somewhere, and told Tindle, "Sorry I lost your place." He read the title: *Pocket Guide to the New Millennium: An Unauthorized Time Capsule.* But the skull wouldn't fit in the glove compartment. Lux held it in his palm; it wasn't heavy, but it wasn't weightless, either. It had an inscrutable heft, as if a soulful afterthought still adhered to its bony mask. Lux feared Monty's specter might pop out and start to chatter like those cartoon spooks who materialize and begin a soliloquy. He could almost hear the schoolteacher preaching to the kids on the bus, "You pitch zingers now, but you'll be friends again tomorrow."

Lux was totally creeped by the skull, by his growing reverence or *affection* for it. Its big black orbits seemed to pin him with an echo of the bus monitor's burning eyeball. He wasn't thinking of the cruiser, or prison time, or the tiny allotment of luck he had left. For that one minute, he wasn't thinking of Alden. The movie candles stuttered up and down.

Tindle was careful to drive the speed limit to Gwen's duplex. King picked up the paperback guidebook. "Does this almanac have the tide charts?"

"I don't think so," Tindle said. "This isn't an actual almanac. It's that best seller about the year two thousand. Last year's news."

When they arrived at the duplex, its dark windows reminded Lux that it would be just him and Robustus to share housekeeping duties. He wasn't going to enjoy it. King climbed onto the bed liner and reached for the duffel. He handed it to Lux. They walked into the house. Tindle wanted to use the "facilities."

They all wanted to wash their hands.

Lux rested the duffel on the coffee table, beside Gwen's bowl of plastic fruit. King was acting like Carl Comedian. He walked into the kitchen and put the skull on a pedestal cake plate, beside a wedge of Gwen's famous devil's food. Together they stared at it in wonder.

Then Lux searched under the kitchen sink for a can of WD-40 or for Gwen's Final Net hair spray. She had volunteered her hair spray when Lux assembled the TESCO umbrella clothesline and its aluminum pole wouldn't fit into its collar base. He needed a lubricant to ease the zipper teeth on King's duffel so that he could put the head in the bag with the rest of it all. The head on its own was giving him some trouble.

He couldn't find what he wanted and he greased the zipper with a stick of butter until he got its lock tab to glide back and forth. He took the haunted article from the cake plate and tucked it under the sleeve of the glowing parka. The Nike swoosh on the Gore-Tex body bag surprised him again. He was reminded that everyone, pros and amateurs, major-league lineups and farm team rosters, friends of Bill, and even that freaky NORD assemblage, everyone had the one thing in common. Boots on or boots off.

He heard a racket outside, a small engine chugging. King had climbed back on the truck to start up the Honda portable generator that powered Tindle's table saw. Tindle needed the generator on building sites that hadn't yet been hooked up with electrical service. Lux went out to the driveway. King had removed the tarpaulin from the ten-inch Craftsman table saw and was checking it out. "This is awesome," King said. "I learned how to operate one of these in shop therapy at Cedar Junction." He picked up a piece of two-by-four from a bucket of scraps in the pickup, mitered corners and stub ends that Tindle saved for shims or to use as kindling in his woodstove at home. King flicked the switch on the motor and the blade started to spin. In the pitch dark, he ripped a board up the guide until it was halved like a bar of soap. "Cuts like butter," King told Lux. Just for amusement, King ripped several pieces until Lux could smell the fresh cedar dust.

King was shouting over the racket, "Dudes in shop made dollhouse furniture. CD towers. We made those beveled plaques that say 'Home Sweet Home,' anything to send back to the folks." King grabbed a scrap of pressure-treated pine. He fed the plank into the purring wheel and it shrieked when the teeth made contact. He pushed the block of wood farther up the table. He hit a knot and his hand slipped into the saw teeth. The murderous blade didn't differentiate. Three fingers shot against the rip fence before King knew anything.

Lux shouted, "Hey, flip that off!" when he saw King turning away, leaving the machine unmanned. Lux didn't understand the problem until King stumbled backward and whipped around, holding his bloodied hand between his knees.

Tindle must have heard their startled yelps erupt and he charged outside. He saw what he thought he would see.

In the dark, the blood was black as motor oil. It sprayed across Lux's jeans as he pulled King inside the house. Beneath the overhead light, the wound spilled a crimson swash across the wall-to-wall carpet until Lux grabbed a pillow slip from a mound of laundry and wrapped it around King's hand. King lost his legs and swayed in a circle. Tindle pushed him into a chair so he wouldn't faint and fall down. "We got to put him in the truck," he told Lux. "This needs an MD."

"You think we should leave this duffel or bring it along—"

"Let's go."

"We leave it?"

"Go. Just go."

Lux shoved King down the walk and into the cab of Tindle's truck. Then Lux climbed in back to look at the saw and examine the wood scraps. He found the missing fingers in the cedar dust, three white parsnips without their blood source.

"What should we do with these?" Lux cupped the daubs of flesh; all three were severed past the second knuckle.

Tindle said, "Hold on. Wait here." The prof went back into the house. He came out with a jug of milk. He presented the mouth of the plastic bottle to Lux. Lux fed each digit into the tiny spout, one at a time. He heard them plunk in a bottom inch of milk. Tindle snapped the cap on.

"BEAUTIFUL," AN EMS TECHNICIAN SAID when Lux handed him the bottle of rosy pink milk. He told Lux, "You were thinking ahead. This makes all the difference."

King tried to sit up. He asked Lux to move his truck from the Fort Hill lot. Rangers patrol Seashore lots after midnight, or Francisconi could find it sitting there. Lux found the car keys in the pocket of King's bloodied jeans.

"Don't forget it," King said as he fell back on the rubber pillow, his face glossy white as fondant.

A medic asked King to rate his pain on a scale of one to ten.

King said, "I can't do the math."

Lux told an EMS flunky, "Fuck, you're crazy. Where's your hospitality? Break out the morphine."

From Hyannis Hospital, King was transported to Mass General in Boston, where surgeons could attempt to sew his fingers back on and reconnect the nerves and muscles. Lux and Tindle watched as they loaded King into a hospital shuttle bus with state-of-the-art gizmos and built-ins to monitor King's temperature, oxygen levels, heart rate, and blood pressure and his indoor-outdoor consciousness during his ordeal. "You have the fingers?" Lux asked the driver.

A medic said that in order to avoid a mix-up, "Fingers stay right with the patient. At all times."

As the ambulance drove away, Lux saw King on the gurney, the milk jug propped beside him, sloshing like a Lava lamp.

14

OFFICER FRANCISCONI COMES INTO THE HOLE IN ONE at the wee hour of 2 A.M. Patti Roderick is behind the counter. Her boss is in the kitchen loading the dough machine, cutting rings, frying batches, and filling trays for the surge coming in. She says, "He's a robot. You can't talk to him or he loses his rhythm, you know, he forgets where he's at. He's got four tubs frying at once."

"It's not rocket science," Francisconi says.

"That's what I tell him."

The doughnut tycoon brushes through the saloon-style door with another silver sheet of fresh items and disappears again. Patti goes to work squirting maple frosting on the naked article with a pastry bag, its aluminum nozzle cupped in her hand, its bulging sack tucked inside her elbow. Francisconi thinks the room smells like his baby's milk-sweet breath when she was a small infant. He pictures his wife and little daughter at home asleep. Maybe he can get on afternoon duty after doing midnights for two months. His chief doesn't think of switching anyone before his rotation comes up, unless someone makes a point of asking. Francisconi didn't want to press the issue in case he wants a favor later on, in the dead of winter, like the time he took his wife to Florida and the chief hired a "special" to fill in for him.

Patti slides the doctored tray into the rack beside knots of fried dough with chocolate icing and confetti sugar specks. He imagines his own girl working in this doughnut shop one day, on her summer vacations from high school. She'd like to shake and dribble those jimmies on cakes. She'd fit right into the operation. It would be past his retirement mark when his daughter works here. Unless he adds to his twenty if he makes detective.

Early-bird business starts when long-liners and a few last-gasp dragger captains stop in for boxes of assorted dozens. Crews are already at the harbor sorting gear and checking cables, chains, and doors before they steam out. At daybreak, building-boom contractors line up for their coffee. Truckers and bus drivers come in whenever they shoot up Route 6. It's the one reliable spot to tear off a bite.

"One of *you* is always first to get here," Patti tells him. "You're a cliché. Uniforms and crullers."

"Civil servants need coffee, too."

"Who does?" she says, unfamiliar with the distinction he was making.

He stirs his coffee until it cools down. He's thinking over what he saw that night. Lux Davis and that zero King Johnston. The older fellow, Tindle, operates a *This Old House* operation, but Francisconi doesn't know how he might fit in. Francisconi ran the registration on King Johnston's van, and just as he thought, it was a piece of fancy paper-hanging. His license check and M and W on King Johnston was pro forma; King wasn't exactly *missing*, but King might be *wanted.* King's day job wasn't enough entertainment for him, but when Francisconi called it in, Sheila said that King had nothing current on-screen.

But Francisconi had been watching Lux for months. He saw Lux going out to High Head at odd hours. That's where Miss Bride Interrupted had set up house in one of those historical shacks after her hubby took off. It was Sea Call or one of those mournful names. They all sounded alike. His chief had wanted those lean-tos torn down; they attracted vagrants and teens who started unauthorized bonfires, tearing up the hundred-year-old planking for kindling wood, without getting their bonfire paperwork from town hall or permission from the park service. Then the busybody preservationists from the Peaked Hill Historical Trust decided to restore and winterize the eyesores and rent them out.

Francisconi had seen Lux and Alden together in Alden's beat-up Jeep, and Lux was out on the dunes so often, he must be doing her. A couple of different nights, Francisconi had waited at the turnoff at High Head, where the road turns to sand. Without any hardener on the unpaved road, he couldn't drive the cruiser onto the dunes without bleeding the tires. He couldn't respond to his radio calls without air in his tires, so he left it to the park rangers to patrol the back shore in their Land Rovers and ORV buggies. They told him that they never saw trouble at Alden's shack. Alden was okay.

But from the turnoff, Francisconi saw a good show. More than one prowler, it seemed, was interested in the little shack. He stopped Conrad Ellis, still wearing his blue blazer, driving out to Sea Call after his last puddle jump. "What are you doing out here?" he asked the pilot. Conrad said, "I took a wrong turn leaving the airstrip. I guess I'm beat after doing my Logan turnarounds." Francisconi knew it was bullshit. And once, he recognized that fellow who worked as a grief counselor at the Mid-Cape Outreach Center. The man's own son was killed in a wreck. It wasn't exactly protocol to visit someone after midnight, he didn't think. She liked a cross section, all right, unless it was a pileup of sightseers. She was a pretty thing; no doubt she would have toms contending for a perch at her window.

He saw Lux Davis come and go on foot even when it was blowing hard. Once, Davis had his tackle box and saltwater rod, but the other times Francisconi saw him, he wasn't fishing. Not for bass, anyway. He was walking back from Alden's shack. He looked like a man with a problem, all right. He looked like a man with a secret he wanted to *unlearn.*

Lux Davis had changed his lifestyle since driving that big AmTran school bus off the boat ramp into the harbor. After that, the kid made a 180-degree turn to sobriety. Now he was going to college at night. He was getting write-ups in the *Boston Globe* about his jobs in rich folks' million-dollar backyard gardens. Lux was some sort of genie with a green thumb. Nickerson knew he had a cash cow and brokered subcontracts for Lux, skimming a profit off the top. He was pimping the whiz kid. Even the town wanted to hire Lux to fix the green clock at the rotary, and Nickerson was going to gouge them pretty good.

Francisconi is thinking he might ask Lux to make a green poodle or something for his wife's birthday. He should have asked Lux for the price list for something like that when he saw him in the field. Maybe they could go around Nickerson. But he forgot to ask when he saw the trio acting nervous. Lux looked miserable in the lying game, as if King Johnston's lie wasn't a good fit for him. He needed a bigger one.

No, if a kitty was lost out there in Nickerson's fields, as Johnston was saying, they would have heard it squeaking.

Again he wonders how much it would put him back to get his foundation plants trimmed and snipped to look like FAO Schwarz stuffed animals. He hopes the price tag on those smaller masterpieces might work into his budget somehow.

He takes his cup of coffee and climbs back into the cruiser. He rolls around the rotary and cuts off Route 6 at Hay Road. He drives past the duplex on Snow's Road where Lux lives with his brother's family. They have the right side of it, but the other unit is still empty. It isn't prime property. Housing is scarce, but a dump like this isn't inviting to summer folk or to respectable year-rounders. Buyers want bay views and picket fences.

The duplex is blazing, its house lights left on and the front door wide open. There isn't a car in the driveway. With the front door agape, he can see right into the living room. There isn't a sign of life except for licks of smoke scrolling from a central chimney stack. The furnace must be chugging to keep up.

He radios the tower. "Seven hundred—Baker seven."

"Seven hundred. Yeah, Baker seven?"

"I'm at Forty-six Snow's to look at a suspicious entry."

"Copy, Baker seven."

"Am I keeping you up, Sheila?"

"Baker four is bugging me. Now you."

"Shit, don't you love midnights?" he tells her. "Midnights. Midnights. Midnights."

He gets out of the cruiser and switches on his flashlight. The bluestones leading to the front stoop are drizzled with blood, blobs still fresh and satiny. He's careful where he steps as he follows the trail into the house. There are blood spatters in the foyer and liberal splashes on the wall-to-wall carpet in the living room. He calls out, "Officer—anyone home?" Nothing.

He takes out his latex gloves and snaps one on, tugging it over his wrist. He plows one fingertip across the stains that soak the acrylic nap. It looks like bleeding from a laceration, but it could be a stabbing. The pattern doesn't have the typical pulsing arcs of staggered arterial flow, but it looks serious just the same. The blood marks are confined to the living room, front hall, and stoop. They must have gone somewhere to get help.

Going room to room, he finds nobody. The family is missing. The husband might still be away fishing. Long-liner crews are going out past the season each year, even after the weather turns. He finds the kids' room is a typical mess, as if they had been dragged off in the middle of a tangle. Even his daughter's room looks like a cyclone hit it, day to day, but these boys have WWF posters on the wall. There's a mattress pulled onto the floor so they can plunge off the top bunk to imitate their favorite wrestlers and have their own "Nitro Smackdown." Maybe that's how someone got hurt. But there isn't any blood upstairs. He hopes it wasn't the little ones who had had the accident in the living room. But he has his radio on his belt and he would have heard if Rescue had been sent out here. He keeps the volume down when he visits the Hole in One so it won't be a nuisance, but he hadn't heard any calls to the duplex on Snow's Road.

15

TINDLE DROVE LUX TO FORT HILL and let him off at the blacked-out van. "Sunrisers tomorrow. Seven-thirty meeting?" Tindle said.

"A meeting? That's five hours from now. Shit," Lux said.

"But you need a meeting." Tindle had gone the extra mile and expected Lux to cooperate.

"Yeah, maybe," Lux said. He got behind the wheel while Tindle clamped cables on his battery and connected them to King's truck. Lux tried to imagine that some of the prof's good faith and inner light was transferred with the charge. He cranked the ignition and it turned over. He'd need more than a two-year battery to get him above the rising water he was in now. He drove out of Fort Hill. As he accelerated, the lamps were furry and then quit altogether. He could drive back to the duplex without headlights unnoticed—if he was lucky.

He followed Tindle until Tindle split off; then Lux rolled three miles in the pitch black. He remembered the kid at Chicken City. Angstrom units. Full moon. New moon. Nothing. No stars or heavenly bodies to help him, but his eyes adjusted. Alden had told him the folk names for the lunar cycles. A full moon in October was the "harvest moon." He'd heard that before, but November was the "beaver moon." December had the "cold moon." He followed the extinguished map, thinking of Alden. She was a golden aura before him, like those cone lights in museums that illuminate a walloping diamond on a pedestal stand, or a precious Egyptian cartouche. He followed her golden image home.

He saw the duplex. The two levels of yellow windows against a mystery background had a homely, tattered look, like punched-out slots on the Nativity calendar his mom used to tack on the mantel each

Christmas season. He remembered his mother's face, deep in concentration, as she pricked cranberries with a needle, stringing garlands for their scotch pine. Then he saw the cruiser. It was coming right at him. The officer noted his dead beams, and the blueberries started twirling. Lux pulled into his driveway and waited for the cruiser to turn around. He knew the frontal that was coming. He cut the engine, flipped the visor down to look in the mirror, and slapped it away again. He squared himself for the one-to-one, but his heart was thudding, *noir, noir, noir.* He saw the B-movie candles spitting, *as per.*

He remembered the cake plate where King had left the muddy noggin beside the slice of devil's food. Lux had zipped the bony helmet in the duffel, he was certain. But here it was—the nightmare he'd been having. He was glad that Gwen had gone to Waltham. His nephews would be sound asleep and Gwen would be sitting in the kitchen with her mom, discussing her bad experiences. At least she wasn't here for the shakedown.

Officer Francisconi edged the Crown Vic behind the van. He got out of his vehicle and walked up to the G.O.D. truck. He leaned inside the window. "Looks like you had some trouble tonight. That's a lot of blood on your carpet. You all right?"

"I'm okay."

"Who was hurt?"

"King, you know King Johnston? He was using Tindle's table saw. Lost three fingers. They took him to Boston in the emergency shuttle."

"He was transported to Boston? From where? I didn't hear the call."

"We were driving him to Hyannis."

"Without electric?"

"We took Tindle's truck. This one here has a moody alternator. It lives and dies. We were tearing to the hospital, but halfway there King passed out, so we stopped at the firehouse in Yarmouth. Their EMS took him the rest of the way and we followed in the truck. Shit, they're cowboys, you know? They were weaving through the road bats on Suicide Alley like they were snowboarding. When we hit town, they were rolling onto the sidewalk."

"I bet King was royally bitching and they couldn't wait to deliver him."

"I guess. At Hyannis the doc said they aren't set up for that kind of accident. Decapitated fingers—"

"You mean *amputated.* The other means his head is severed."

Lux didn't want to picture it twice.

"King have insurance? Because that'll be microsurgery. Teensy nerves and muscles, that's a specialist."

"We had the fingers in some milk." Lux was chirping. He heard his wired notes and he tried to control his voice.

Lux stepped down from his seat to face the officer.

"I worried it was one of your sister-in-law's kids," Francisconi said.

"No. They're at their grandmom's. It was King."

"He find his girlfriend's cat?"

"Oh, yeah, she got it back. You come out here about the cat?" He saw Officer Francisconi wasn't in a hurry to leave.

"This van isn't legit. I looked it up."

Lux said, "It was impounded or something. King knew all about it. He got it from the repo lot in Fall River. It was in the cage, you know, where they keep abandoned Denver boot mysteries and junkers, all the stolen bicycles. They auction them off—"

"It's got lousy paperwork. I'm thinking King didn't tell you right. Did you know you were driving with funny registration? And this is a stolen vehicle?"

"King learned its autobiography. I don't know shit."

"Well, that courier was in Attleboro. It closed shop. Sold its vans, but this one was jacked. King shouldn't have it. It's borax. I guess we'll be talking to King about it when he's feeling better. This gets towed to the barracks. Leave the keys in it."

"It's all yours. I can't use it—it won't crank once you shut it off. But listen, I've got to get the Woolite on that carpet before it sets." Lux started up the path, but Francisconi was coming along behind him.

Lux said, "Oh, you want to help me scrub that rug? I'll trade you Gwen's apron for your forty-cal."

Francisconi rested the heel of his hand on his teensy holster and laughed. He pumped Lux's shoulder as they walked up the path. "Try club soda on that rug—it might work. Just one question for you. What was King sawing up into little pieces? Good thing he wasn't playing with a chipper."

"A chipper?" Lux lifted his eyes to see Francisconi's tickled expression. The officer was enjoying it. Midnights get boring.

Francisconi said, "King deconstructed ATMs for a living. So, now, what was he sawing up?"

"He was trying to make doll furniture or something. He learned how at Cedar Junction."

"Learned about dollhouses? Taxpayers think they're making exit signs and vanity plates but they're getting home ec? If we were in Texas—"

Lux didn't want to hear about Texas and its death row statistics. He walked inside the house. The officer came after him.

The kitchen was blazing. Lux double-checked for King's little joke on the cake plate, its black orbits big as mouse holes, but it was hidden away. Francisconi walked into the living room. Lux tagged up and stood beside him, his chest hammering. They looked at the damage to the rug. The duffel was tucked under the cable-spool end table, which was littered with King's Nicorette wrappers. Francisconi picked up the wadded foil. "Whose dream gum?"

"Opium? Nope. That's just King's nicotine Chiclets."

Francisconi was being playful, but Lux was freezing up.

Lux was having one of his slowdown spells when Francisconi's speech seemed to decelerate and grind to a stop. In his frozen standstill, Lux heard the officer's voice at an exaggerated volume; each phrase was severed and distinct from the next, each word disconnected from the one preceding it, each syllable too eternal and punctuated by rebounding silences.

"Well, you better get to work. It's gruesome," Francisconi said, and he turned to leave. As he walked through the kitchen he said, "Hey, you have a sweet tooth? Me too."

Francisconi had found a bowl of leftover Halloween treats. Nils hoarded his trick-or-treat booty in a mixing bowl and curbed himself to puritan samplings. His brother, Ian, ate his loot right out of the pillowcase in the first twenty-four hours.

"Help yourself," Lux said.

The officer took a minute to choose, combing his fingers through the candy bars and jawbreakers. He took a peanut butter cup. Lux walked him outside. Francisconi sat down in his cruiser. He said, "Sure glad no one died but the broadloom. It's shot. Kent's Carpet World has its January sale coming up, if you can wait till then."

LUX STOOD AT THE WINDOW as the cruiser disappeared up the road. He waited one minute longer until his nerves were sorted. Then he lifted the carryall nightmare and went upstairs to find a secret hiding place. He wasn't going to bunk in the same room with it.

He opened Gwen's armoire in the upstairs hall. He saw her summer dresses, loose shifts and jumpers. He placed the duffel behind a long chiffon skirt; its silky fabric rustled frail protests as he reached in. He was thinking Gwen wouldn't like coming home to see her house wrecked, and he went to find a sponge and a can of carpet foam. He worked on the drizzled carpet, but the stains held. Gwen was a neatnik. He'd have to pull up the carpet and buy a new remnant. He hadn't forced her out, but he was glad she was missing this. If she was finished with him, he wondered if she'd keep her mouth shut.

He stretched out on the sofa, trying not to sink past slow-wave sleep and to keep ahead of his REM nightmares. His wide-awake visions were even worse.

FRIDAY MORNING, LUX TELEPHONED Mass General and talked to a nurse. She told him King was doing all right, considering he had had his amputated "phalanges" pinned and wired, and his "*flexor sublimis* and *flexor profundus* tendons," "digital nerves," and "digital arteries" painstakingly reattached with nylon sutures more delicate than human hair. As he listened to her description, he fingered the tightly braided snips of Monty's whistle lanyard, which he had kept in his pocket.

The nurse said, "King looks good. At least it wasn't his thumb. The thumb is the grasping hub. It *opposes* and gives you your dexterity."

"Nurses don't get enough credit," he told her.

Police hadn't come for the G.O.D. truck. He left it in the driveway and went on foot to the nursery. Nickerson told him he had the go-ahead on the green clock. They could prep the site that morning, before returning to the field to ball up the rest of the cedars for the Seacrest job. Lux was sent to the rotary to remove stumps where the broken trees were beyond repair. After the roots and branches were carted off, Lux could do his magic act with survivors. But the emerald seven was gone.

The empty hole on the clock dial needed new trees large enough for Lux to trim and sculpt them into the missing numeral. Nickerson didn't have the mature stock and had ordered English yews from Sylvan Nurseries in Westport. They'd be delivered the following morning. Lux worked with Marty Stokes preparing the trench, mixing loam and compost with 10-10-10. Crows collected in the trees, looking for salamanders, beetles, and worms upturned in the excavation. Lux thought of the crow that had made off with the teacher's incisor. It might have gobbled it up or hoarded it somewhere, the way a rat stockpiles the little trinkets and souvenirs of its ingenious rat world. Next he thought of Tindle's story about Richard the Third and how he stole his bride from a funeral procession. Monty should get a funeral and burial. Right here. At lucky number seven.

He worked with Marty Stokes to finish the crypt. It was a legitimate operation, but the timing was perfect for Lux's illegitimate purposes.

The hole in the clock was a gift from God.

Even the local police helped out. They had placed orange cones along the shoulder of the road. The town manager had told them that traffic shouldn't intrude on the project, that the clock was under a deadline.

It started to come together. The Quitting Time Clock was a fixture, almost a sacred spot, and Monty would have his new comfort station in a place of honor. The beloved landmark welcomed one and all—not just wash-ashores and lost souls like Mr. Two Turrets, but VIPs like Senator Kennedy and Representative Barney Frank, economist and publisher Marty Peretz, and the world-renowned retired Harvard dean Henry Rosovsky. More than one of the above-mentioned summer slouchers had hired Lux to plant rose of Sharon saplings or hydrangeas or to realign and reset stones in a temperamental flagstone walkway. The rotary clock was good enough for them, it was good enough for the schoolteacher. From that spot, Mr. Bones could wrangle with eternity and all its little unburst blisters.

Lux needed to have a car. He borrowed Marty Stokes's cell phone to call Punchy's Garage. He told Punchy about the G.O.D. truck and asked him if he'd give it a tow over to his grease pit and take a look at it.

When Lux showed up in the garage bay, the van was on the lift. The place was a museum of Punchy's wacky muffler art, exhaust-system sculptures of all kinds. When he wasn't rotating tires or changing oil, Punchy welded junked parts and pipes into kooky aluminum figures. "Catalytic converters make perfect heads, you see?" he told Lux.

"You're right. This is a nice one. Who is it supposed to be?"

"Lady Di. See her tiara? Galvanized barbed wire."

Lux said, "I thought it was Christ, you know, with *his* crown of thorns."

"Jesus didn't have boobs last time I heard."

Punchy told Lux that his car trouble was red squirrels. "When it gets nippy, your red squirrels make nests on warm engine blocks. They'll chew through hoses, belts, and wiring."

"Squirrels ate the wiring?"

"They gnawed your ignition cable and bollixed your vacuum diaphragm. You know what to do about red squirrels? First you catch them in a Havahart trap and then you drown them in a rain barrel."

"What's the damage to *me?*" Lux said.

"I thought this was King's piece of shit."

"Actually, they're saying it's supposed to have a sheet or something."

"That sounds about right. If King has his paws on it, it's got a past history."

"Never-ending story."

"No shit, genius. Let me show you something."

"What's up?"

"This tub has been customized, look here." Punchy lifted a floor mat. He tugged a strip of duct tape loose. "See? Under this tape it has a false floor—see where it's soldered? These rivets aren't factory."

"No kidding?"

"You want to take a look inside? I'll torch the seam."

"No, thanks."

"Are you crazy? I bet there's a little stash here. I bet it's a pharmacy, or maybe some artillery. That's what it's for."

"Not interested."

"Does King have any idea what he's got here? You should find new friends," Punchy said. "You and me. We have *talents.* We don't need drug lords and slobs like King Johnston." He explained to Lux how he felt that they shared a connection with their outside art. He said that he welded junked parts and Lux worked on trees, but they each made masterpieces out of ordinary items.

"Just fix the fucking truck, will you?" Lux said, counting out three twenty-dollar bills and stuffing them in the vest of Punchy's overalls. Punchy shrugged and went to work on the gnawed ignition cable. Then he used the Dryvac to clean the squirrels' nest, fluffy rings of beach grass, leaves, and newspaper snips from the manifold and piston skirt. Punchy said, "These nests will catch fire. Red squirrels are demons. But you ever see a chickadee nest?"

"I don't think so," Lux said.

"Chickadees make nests from chunks of sphagnum moss and rabbit fur. They swoop down to peck the bunny's rump and pull its fur out."

"No shit?" Lux knew that no one could live on Cape Cod without these affections cropping up. Even Punchy, who was always soaked in motor oil, had an Audubon sticker on his tow truck. Just how long would their Land's End paradise survive? Lux hoped he wouldn't outlive it.

"You really want to drive this if it's pegged?" Punchy said.

"Yeah, I'm going to be driving it. I've got a delivery to make."

"I guess you kind of want to get picked up? Is this a cry for help or something?" Punchy said.

"Yeah, I need professional help. Fuck you." Punchy's third degree hit a nerve. Lux sometimes wished everything would stop. He saw how a bunk at the MCI was almost better than being at large, better than his day-to-day uncertainties, looking over his shoulder ever since he hit the schoolteacher. He understood how geezers who are finally paroled and set free want to turn around and go back inside.

Punchy was saying, "No man is Teflon forever." He told Lux that he was walking a thin line between bad luck and tough luck, between worse luck and disaster.

As Punchy jawboned and waxed into typical poetic roadblocks, Lux gave himself a deadline: Robustus goes into the clock as soon as the moon rises. If there is a moon or not.

16

HYRAM REFUSED TO RIDE THE SENIOR SHUTTLE. "I'm not getting on the bus with Mrs. Crease," he said.

"You'd make a sweet couple," Alden said.

"Her and me? When hell has a thermostat."

Alden agreed to drive Hyram to his stress test. She promised to come back to get him in time for the outfall pipe meeting at his place that afternoon. Alden wanted to wait at the heart center during Hyram's ordeal, just to hear what the cardiologist would tell him. Hyram wasn't watching his diet or taking his meds. But Alden had been asked to attend an informal hearing at the Barnstable County District Court. The car accident at the rotary was under investigation, and Alden was summoned to the meeting. It wasn't an official subpoena, but Hyram said, "Show up. Answer questions. Don't overexplain."

"Explain what? I didn't do anything wrong."

He said, "The town fathers are upset that the clock is wrecked. The *Cape Codder* editorial says that the patrolmen were asleep, that they should have been directing traffic. That's why they're being so orthodox, calling everyone back for this hearing. Just act nice to the uniforms."

"Do you think I need a lawyer?"

"No. But you could have brushed your hair. It's kind of wild and flyaway. You might have dressed up. I mean, when you wear a skirt you're irresistible."

She tugged her fingers through her windblown hair. But it was too late to change from her trousers and her Chippewa mud boots, rubber slip-ons with leather shanks. Earlier that morning she'd walked into the

Million-Dollar Marsh to count hawks for the register. A fleur-de-lis of thistle burrs edged her pant cuffs.

"At least my shoes *match*," she said.

Hyram lifted one foot and then the other to see if his oxfords were a pair. He'd also brought along his sneakers in a paper bag for the treadmill.

"Mrs. Crease wouldn't browbeat me like you do," he said.

At the courthouse an officer showed Alden to a seat in the front of the gallery. She sat down beside the man who had rear-ended Layla's compact. He was wearing his foam collar. The tight cuff cinched the man's beefy neck, which reminded Alden of a pig-in-a-blanket cocktail wiener. Officers from the Orleans barracks and one state trooper attended, but Alden was surprised to see Layla Cox herself in the front row. She had been released from detox, but Alden didn't know if she was still being held at the county jail. She didn't wear cuffs or ankle chains and she wasn't dressed in an orange jumpsuit, like the jailbirds that picked up trash along Route 6, getting a little sunshine for their trouble.

Sitting beside Layla was a guy who might have been a public defender or a detox counselor. Then she remembered where she had seen him. It was the man who pulled the cross on casters up and down the highway. He was tall and lanky, like a basketball goof, but he had dressed in a sport jacket for the occasion, instead of jeans and a knee-length muslin Jesus robe. His hair was in dreadlocks, long fuzzy swags of burred blond like strips of upholstery stuffing.

Alden didn't know why he was there.

The investigating officer asked Alden, "Where were you standing when the accident happened?"

"I was on the traffic island."

"When the cars collided, you were on the island?"

"That's right—"

Layla sounded off. "No way. She was running across. I had to slam my brakes."

"You say Alden Warren was directly in front of your vehicle?"

Layla went blank, as if she'd been asked an SAT question.

But she had recognized Alden's name. This was the person who had been inquiring at DSS about Baby Hendrick. The two women locked eyes. Alden saw that Layla had not been able to remove every speck of gold paint; a trace of glitter still edged her nostrils.

The witness in the foam collar looked at Alden and said, "You were out in the middle of all that traffic."

"That's when the pickup struck the Nissan," the dreadlock-coiffed cross hauler said.

"Excuse me," Alden said. "I didn't see *you* out there wheeling your cross."

The man in the foam collar said, "But *I* saw *you.*"

"Am I sitting on a red-ant hill or what?" Alden said.

The officer said, "Okay, folks, let's calm down. We're here to poll witnesses, and from a tally of your subjective statements we can assemble the common perception and get an objective analysis of events."

Alden said, "Isn't the 'common perception' that the driver of the Nissan was DUI?"

"Did you make eye contact with the driver?" the officer asked Alden.

"It was foggy. You know how bad the fog gets right there next to the boat ramp—it just rolls right off the water onto the highway."

A patrolman confirmed that the conditions were very poor at the rotary. Other officers nodded their heads, smiling with unmasked pride. They had all had personal experiences with the aberrant climatological episodes on Cape Cod.

In the wrap-up, it was noted that if anyone had played a significant role in the accident, in its cause and effect, it was Layla herself. The toxicology report had come back with a lot of high numbers in her blood panel.

"Waste of people's time," Alden said as she signed an attendance sheet. She was getting up to leave when Layla charged up to her. "Waste of time? Oh, rilly? You were the whole cock-and-balls fuckup at the rotary. I got rear-ended and they took my baby."

The cross hauler started pitching his two cents. Yes, people like Alden and the National Seashore were always "trying to micromanage." They were "poisoning waterfowl, clearing land for hot-air balloon landings, building bird-watching boardwalks over marshland, when they should mind their own business."

His verbal trajectories were mind boggling. But Layla put her face into Alden's and said, "That's *my* baby, Miss Shoehorn. So fuck off."

Alden saw Layla's gold pores glittering. She said, "What kind of mother sniffs paint? What kind of mother are you?"

"I'm the real one," Layla said.

Everyone started to rip and tear. The court deputy said, "Folks, this isn't the appropriate setting. If you want to discuss these other issues, it'll have to be off courthouse property."

Alden said, "I'm not going off courthouse property with *them.*" She watched Layla nuzzling the stilt-legged fundamentalist as he walked Layla out of the room, ducking his head at the door lintel.

"Who is that?" Alden asked.

"That's Layla's boyfriend," the court deputy said, leading Alden to another exit on the opposite side of the courtroom.

"I thought her boyfriend was in jail."

"Brooks is in jail. This is the new one, Mike Perry. He's the guy who installed Princie's Peephole online. Right here on the Outer Cape, if that doesn't turn your stomach."

"My stomach's fine. Are you saying that the man who carries that big cross is Princie? They're one and the same?"

"Princie's not his real name. He's like the CEO of that smut site. Yeah, he's Princie *in person,* I guess."

She asked the officer if the court was finished with her and if she was free to leave.

He said, "If you were standing on the shoulder when the accident happened, like you're saying, then we'll have to try to live with that."

She saw that the officer wasn't convinced she *was where she was.*

HYRAM WAS DELAYED AT THE HEART CENTER, so Alden went back to the Seashore office to transcribe the Audubon hotline, 349-WING. She had let it go for a few days. Some people listened to "relaxation" tapes, ocean surf, summer rainstorms, recordings of falling water, crickets, wind singing through a screen door. Transcribing the hotline messages had an equally calming effect on Alden, and she felt the tight band across her shoulders begin to relax and her motor nerves shifted down to a slower gear. Then she thought of Toya. She imagined the third-grader sitting beside her, writing the bird counts in the ledger with her earnest, people-pleaser workmanship.

These messages were canned and Alden was glad she didn't have to make chitchat, but she liked hearing the familiar voices of the birders and seniors, who seemed full of warmth for her. She imagined that they might even have some respect for her. She was the bird accountant for all of Land's End. The tape had the usual congratulatory messages, gabby tree huggers excited about their hairy woodpeckers returning now that they'd hung suet balls. One old gal asked Alden about her Thanksgiving plans: would she be delivering Meals-On-Wheels or working in the soup kitchen? If Alden was free, she was invited to join them for the "common feast" at Our Lady of the Harbor.

Alden wrote down the sightings and filled the bird registers she was monitoring. One male Eurasian wigeon in North Chatham, three hooded mergansers, a glaucous gull at First Encounter Beach, one horned lark on Fisher Road in Truro, winter wrens, golden-crowned kinglets, pine siskins. She printed the sightings distractedly, smudging the ledger.

Next she heard, "This is Sally Dine on Old County Road. Good news! The deer have come back to my salt lick . . ." She wrote down five more entries. Several callers protested new plans submitted by the Army Corps of Engineers to rid the power lines of cormorants. Hundreds of these macabre shorebirds roosted on parallel high-tension wires behind the Stop & Shop parking lot, visible to tourist traffic on Route 6. Cormorants have no protective oils, and the flock collects on the power lines with their wings extended wide open to dry their feathers, an unsettling silhouette reminiscent of vultures. The town wanted them gone. The Army Corps of Engineers planned to install PVC pipe sleeves on the cables. The PVC pipes would rotate each time the birds tried to roost, evicting the cormorants from their ComElectric perches.

She was almost finished, but there was a personal message at the end of the tape. "Alden?" She instantly knew his voiceprint. His rich, euphonic whisper had a lingering effect on her, like vibrations in a bell tower that resonate long after the clanging chimes have stopped. She felt its percussion in her pelvis, an abdominal shiver, the same shiver she had felt in her bed when Lux told her, "I know where *you* are."

But Lux was cut off, or he had hung up. The next message said, "Alden, baby, we've got to talk." It was Ison.

17

ALDEN CHOPPED CARROT STICKS at Hyram's kitchen sink. She arranged cherry tomatoes and celery sticks around a bowl of hummus dip. Outfall volunteers expected little snacks and enough cider or Rolling Rock to get them through two hours of Hyram's brainstorming and his hot-sauce ridicule for anyone who wasn't throwing his shoulder against the wheel.

The living room was already swarming with do-gooders and the din was getting louder. College kids, geezers, even the crone who had accosted Alden at Snow's Library, blaming her for the seagull massacre. It was a big turnout. Alden thought of the misleading sign outside her office, "Con*ver*sation Area." The same sort of free-for-all chin-wag was in progress in Hyram's parlor.

She heard someone talking about a summer resident who wanted to excavate two inground swimming pools on his property, one freshwater pool and one saltwater. He needed permission from the Cape Cod Conservation Commission to pump seawater from nearby Little Pleasant Bay. The expensive system operated synchronous intake valves that would keep saltwater circulating, siphoned back and forth from the tidal inlet to the swimming pool, like a churning lobster tank. Someone said he was "very pushy" at a zoning board meeting. Alden stopped scraping a carrot when she heard it was Ison they were talking about. Each new McMansion was a leprous scourge on pristine natural vistas, and natives liked to complain about the build-out, even when they were making their money pouring foundations, digging Title V septic systems, framing houses, shingling, roofing. But duplicate inground swimming pools set a new record for gauche and ostentatious behavior. She wanted to tell them that, of course, Ison needed to have two of everything, two turrets, two swimming pools, two *women.* They were saying he would need to get an environmental impact statement before he could get a building permit. She gouged another carrot with the peeler as she listened to the fiery gossip about Ison. She was thinking how he had impacted *her* environment without a permit.

Volunteers took every available chair. The rest sat on the floor Indian-style in a circle around Hyram, who presided over an open cooler of Rolling Rock stubbies. Hyram's stress test had been uncomfortable for him, but he wouldn't tell her details. She had told him to take it easy, maybe postpone the meeting, but Hyram was already reading a sheet of boat assignments with the names of the vessels, their captains, and how many volunteers each boat could ferry. He had charts spread out on the table, where he penciled in the exact location where the nine-and-a-half-mile noxious pipe abruptly ended and released its 370 million gallons of effluent every day. It was where the last three hundred right whales wintered, in the plankton-rich waters of the bay. Hyram said, "Nitrogen from the outfall will affect the Cape Cod Bay food web. And here's the new projections from the Lobster Conservancy. They'll be testing the larvae, postlarvae, and young of the year for lethal effects and sublethal effects like larval malnutrition." The room hushed when Hyram spouted scientific jargon, their eyes glazed over like middle school slackers. Captains wanted the honor of having Hyram onboard, and they had to put slips of paper with the name of each vessel into a bowl. Hyram would sail out with the winner but promised to sail back with a different captain. Hyram said if they stayed in a tight flotilla they wouldn't need more than one navigator for the voyage across Cape Cod Bay.

Boats would leave MacMillan Wharf, Rock Harbor, and Wellfleet to sail westward to Plymouth to meet up with boats coming up the canal. "How many knots do we average? Dinghies with outboards are slower. I won't wait for stragglers," the captain of the *Linda B.* said.

"We don't leave anyone behind," Hyram said, pouring scalding water on anyone with a big head. "If it's blowing or there's chop, you admirals will just have to tow the corks and croutons."

Alden brought the tray of vegetables into the living room.

Everyone took carrot sticks and stabbed them into the hummus dip before Alden could even sit down.

Alden handed a stranger a paper napkin. "Thanks," the woman said. Then the woman stood up and told the group, "Can I have a minute? I'm Drew Mazur, and I'm recruiting more people for our efforts against these 'butterfly weddings' happening in Boston. You've heard of it?" She wanted volunteers.

"Butterfly releases should be banned," she said. "People think it's a 'green' touch to free these swarms in the hundreds instead of throwing rice or pitching their mortarboards into the air, but butterfly releases threaten the natural populations. The Xerces Society has proof it disrupts the migration routes of monarchs and painted ladies. Breeders ship thousands of butterflies FedEx each season. They ship in the dead of winter when it's too cold to release them."

She had come to Hyram's with her propaganda in neat ziplock packets, like a Welcome Wagon lady who gives out coupon books to newbies. "Here's our e-mail and telephone," she said, handing out her Xeroxed sheets. "There's a high-profile wedding on Saturday at the Public Garden. You know that sitcom star from Dorchester? He's getting hitched. There will be more than the usual press attending. If we pull it off, it could get picked up. It's a national story."

"I heard about that wedding. It's that dreamy kid actor who went to Emerson? Ellery Baker?" a college coed burbled. Then she slapped her hand over her mouth, embarrassed to have revealed her interest in the budding beefcake.

"See?" The butterfly activist glowed. "These stars stir up a lot of attention. They bring in FOX, New England Cable News, Channel Seven—and that's an NBC affiliate. The time line and meet-up locations are written down. There's a map and instructions about parking. Don't use the parking garages. We have designated certain restaurant alleys near the wedding. We can swoop in and swoop out before anyone gets towed."

Butterflies redux. Monty had saturated Alden with this touchy information about butterfly weddings. She had finally started to forget his obsessions and pet peeves as everything about him grew more and more fuzzy, but here it was again. "Butterflies on strike!"

Alden looked at the Xeroxed info sheet and was surprised to see it was signed by Penelope Griffin.

"Penelope Griffin is organizing?" Alden pounced on the newcomer with her burning question.

"Penny? Oh, yes, she spearheads this whole operation. She'll be there on Saturday."

Alden had thought Penelope Griffin was long gone. For several months her nemesis had been off cape and out of mind. Suddenly the wraparound mural was rolling again. She was right back where it started, face-to-face with Miss Griffin at the police station, with Monty still nowhere to be found.

"Since when is Penny back on cape?" Alden said.

"She's in Amherst. She teaches at Smith."

"Conservation studies?"

"It's math, I think."

"No kidding? Math is a mystery to me," Alden nattered onward, losing her grip.

"What does your outfit do at these weddings?" Hyram said, looking at Alden. One corner of his mouth had an attractive little crinkle, a familiar expression that warned Alden: Take everything with a grain of salt.

The stranger said, "We try to paintball the bride. Or dump the cake. Anything to get their attention."

Hyram said, "You're trying to get people arrested, is that what you're saying?"

"No, just simple D and D, *disrupt and depart.* We've already done two weddings and a couple's golden anniversary. No one has been arrested."

Hyram told her, "A golden anniversary? How about funerals? Bar mitzvahs—maybe a bris?"

The stranger smiled at Hyram with a faraway look, as if she was mulling over his suggestions.

He said, "There's a butterfly crisis, sure, but we've got the fishing industry from the Merrimack all the way to Block Island, so, honey, we have to move on with our meeting."

The woman said, "Of course. You have a big day coming up." She thanked everyone for taking a minute to listen. She looked at Alden. Of course, she couldn't know about Alden's connection, but Alden felt she did anyway. "See you in Boston Saturday?" The woman seemed to be saying, You should come to Boston in memory of your husband; Monty expects you there. She turned at the door and waved her leather glove at Alden.

THE MEETING REACHED ITS FEVER PITCH when everyone had had enough beer to achieve a full-throttle do-gooder buzz. Alden tried to hurry people out. She saw Hyram was tiring. Penelope's name on the butterfly docket had left her paralyzed, and she hadn't noticed when Hyram's face had turned pale and ashy. She looked at him now: a gloss of perspiration on his upper lip and forehead reflected the overhead light. The meeting had been long and raucous, and when his troops were gone, he told her he was having a little discomfort.

"You having chest pain?" she said.

"A little pinch, that's all."

She found his nitro patches in the bathroom cupboard and she helped him plaster one strip on his belly. "Maybe I need two," he said.

"Let me call Dr. Glass for you. Please?"

He said, "I just need to put my feet up. I'll watch something." He reclined on the sofa and she gave him an extra pillow. "Find me an infomercial. I like those."

"God. You'll watch anything."

"My chest is tight. It relaxes me."

Alden wanted to call the doctor; but once, Hyram had become really brassed off when Alden had telephoned his physician. Hyram had recited the rules of their liaison. She was never to interfere with doctors, the VA, his lawyers, his brokers, his magazine subscriptions.

"Your magazines?" she had said.

"Your job is just to serve me those TV tray dinners. That's your skill set. Understand?"

"My skill set? Okay, I won't call the doctor. I'll wait until I have to get a priest."

"Back off, missy!" he had shouted.

But she understood that Hyram didn't want her to acknowledge what was happening to him. His health was declining. *Life is a rope bridge with both ends on fire.* He loved Alden's company because she could distract him.

She obeyed her friend and didn't contact Dr. Glass. She placed the telephone on the sofa beside him as he watched TV. A few weeks ago, she had programmed the speed dial so that all he needed to do was punch one or two buttons, one for Alden, one for EMS. Then she left him.

ALDEN RAN INTO THE STOP & SHOP after leaving Hyram. She wanted to have something exotic to serve Lux the next time he came to her shack. She wandered up and down the aisles, selecting some ripe cheeses and table crackers. Then she thought these items weren't hearty enough for a hardworking landscaper. She picked up a can of Three-Alarm chili. When she turned around, she was surprised to find little Toya sweeping the aisle with a kitchen broom, its long handle still in its cardboard wrapper. They were several aisles from the household items. Toya had been sweeping her way up and down the supermarket rows. Her look of serious concentration as she chased paper curls and snips of litter was adorable to Alden.

Alden said, "Toya—you sure are busy."

"I like to sweep," the girl said without looking up.

"I could use you at my house."

Toya lifted her face to see if Alden meant what she said. Alden saw that the little girl's left eye was angry, with a deep bruise like a halved prune under her lid. She'd been clocked.

"I'm missing school because of this," Toya said, rubbing her head.

"Because of that shiner?"

"Not that. I'm home for three days because the school had a lice test. Me and Raphael. They won't let us back until we comb the nits."

"But what happened to your eye? Who hit you?"

"Kendall slammed the door, and the knob hit me. See this? My new Rugrats wristwatch?" She turned her wrist to show Alden. "Kendall got it for me after he did it."

"Who's Kendall? One of your sibs?"

"Kendall rents from us."

"Was Kendall that man on the sofa?"

"Not him. That's Sewell. Kendall lives in the downstairs apartment."

Alden understood that the McGuire household might have a slew of wastrel patriarchs living off the DSS cash pot. Toya held her arm high until Alden fussed over her Rugrats wristwatch. A woman found them in a huddle. Alden stood up straight to greet Toya's foster mom. Mrs. McGuire looked ready to set to, but Alden was first to weigh in. "How did Toya hurt her eye?"

"Are you from the Yarmouth office? I filled out the report already."

"You wrote up a report about her eye?"

"That's right. Who are you?"

"What about that curling-iron burn? It still looks raw." Alden tipped Toya's chin side to side. "Sweetie, does that still hurt?"

"She picks her scabs," the woman said, tugging Toya's elbow and taking the broom from the girl. She stroked Toya's long hair with a grim and too-calculated gentleness, Alden thought. Toya looked back and forth between the two women. Mrs. McGuire told Alden, "Is this a home-study visit? Finding me here in the Stop and Shop? You have to show me your ID."

Alden said, "I'm not DSS. Oh, please—" But Alden surveyed the overstuffed grocery cart. Mrs. McGuire was buying economical family-sized items. A twenty-five-pound bag of rice. Generic apple juice. Store-brand cereals in plastic bags. Forty-eight-ounce cans of cheap noodle soup and plastic bins of no-name cookies. "Did you see they have crates of clementines? How do the kids get their citrus? I guess you can't splurge on clementines for foster kids?"

Mrs. McGuire recognized that Alden might be more than she wanted to handle one-on-one. She pushed her cart down the aisle and didn't look back. Toya trotted behind her, but then she turned around and came back for her broom. She started sweeping beside Alden, unwilling to follow her foster mom.

Toya said, "You still want Baby Hendrick? His real mom came to visit him."

Alden said, "Did she take him?"

"I don't know. Maybe—"

"I didn't think she was supposed to get him."

"You want *me* or him?"

Toya's rhetorical question jogged Alden's sleepy obsession. She was flooded with delicious stimuli standing face-to-face with the little girl. Her hunger was wide awake. Alden said, "Sweetie, of course I want you." She took Toya's broom and propped it against a rack of jams and jellies. She steered Toya into the next aisle, between two refrigerator cases. They walked behind the deli counter, where a clerk was slicing honey ham for a woman. "Too thick," the customer said. The clerk shoved the ham log into the machine one more time. "Like this?" the clerk asked the customer, holding up a paper-thin circle of meat.

"Not there yet," the customer said.

Alden pulled Toya through a door with plastic strips hanging from the ceiling to separate the chilly storeroom climate from the normal temperature inside the Olympic-sized superstore. They zigzagged between crates of milk and cottage cheese stacked on dollies. They entered the stainless-steel theater where two butchers were hosing scraps from furrowed worktables. Alden found the exit onto the loading dock. A few drivers were smoking beside a Stop & Shop tractor trailer. She jumped down to the pavement and reached up for Toya. Toya looked down at Alden. "You want me to jump?" Alden watched the little girl's expression shift from confusion to wonder. When she lifted Toya off the platform, the girl automatically clutched Alden around the neck and cinched her legs tight around Alden's waist like a sock monkey. Alden hugged her before setting her down. She took Toya's hand and together they ran behind the strip mall complex to the parking lot. They climbed into Alden's Jeep.

Alden helped Toya buckle her seat belt. Shoppers loading their cars nearby didn't notice her. She was like any young mother. The place was always crawling with half families, whole families. Matrons en masse. It was Momsville.

Alden goosed the gas pedal, just nudged it enough to roll it away nice and easy, without any spectacle.

18

LUX LEFT PUNCHY'S GARAGE and drove back to the duplex. He telephoned the hospital. King was in a semiprivate room, and through the receiver Lux could hear King's roommate already bitching. King had "survivor's euphoria" and was talking nonstop, pestering the geezer in the other bed. "I have to piss with my left hand. So I don't pee on my bandages. I'll never be able to zip up with that hand. It's all backward. Like driving in the UK."

"Hey, your fishing reel cranks on the left side of your UglyStik. Let's say when you get discharged from the hospital, we take our rods and go out to Race Point for striper."

"You can go for striper—I'm going for *candy* striper."

"Oh, nice, you'll give that night nurse a nightmare. But listen, the crypt hole is ready."

"Where?"

"Robustus sub viridis tempus."

"Please, not your high school Latin—will you translate? Where are we talking about?"

"Under the green clock."

"No shit?"

"Quitting Time."

"That's genius. You aced it, man."

"He's not planted yet."

King said, "I would help you, but, you know, my fingers are throbbing."

"They're hurting? That's good, isn't it? That must mean the nerves are alive."

Lux didn't want to picture King's severed fingers in Technicolor. He tried to hide away in the hat shell dome of his erotic fantasies, where performing onstage it was . . . Alden in her tiny iron bed. But just that morning he had awakened on the sofa after dreaming that Gwen had come home to find him in *her* bed. She told him, "Lux, it's *you* I love. Not Denny." She planted kisses up and down his bare back until he jumped to his feet, the bedsheet snagged on his erection.

Gwen's dream confession had scrambled his nerves and confused him again each time he thought of her. To fight it off, he wanted a shower. He wanted to feel its needle spray against his eyelids, his tongue, his lips.

After he dressed, he took the duffel from the armoire and tugged its zipper open. He grabbed a couple of Gwen's dresses off their hangers and wadded them into silky scrunchies to muffle the noisy skeleton. He stuffed the pastel heap on top of the bone rack. He wanted to walk away from the carnage, the various knobs and spokes of Robustus, but he zipped up the bag and put it back into the G.O.D. truck. Even with the duffel stuffed with Gwen's dresses, he heard the TV-tray clatter of its contents, and his heart chugged. He got his tackle box and put it in the truck. He tossed in his saltwater rod, and King's UglyStik, next to Nickerson's spade. He needed the spade; the rods and tackle box were a smoke screen. But he liked to think that one day he'd throw his line in the water. He'd have his old routines back when the worst was over.

He rolled out of there in fifteen minutes.

The dark was coming on, but the bank stayed open until 6 P.M. He avoided the drive-up teller, fearing that the G.O.D. truck would be a spectacle in the peep-through window. Instead, he went inside and stood in Chrissy's line. He wrote a check for cash. "You've got enough to cover this, but not much else," she told him.

"You won't let it bounce. You know me."

"Yeah, I know you. But I don't run the show," she said.

"For some lucky someone, you're the *whole* show, I bet."

She smiled at the compliment; then she blushed and rubbed her button nose, trying to decide if Lux was coming on to her after all this time or if he was just being nice. Yes, he thought she was adorable. She wasn't trying to corner him or trying to make him owe something. She wasn't putting the touch on him. Their connection was wholesome. Then again, every time he saw her she was behind a granite counter. She had a foot pedal to buzz the police station.

After doing his banking, he drove the G.O.D. truck down the same route he used to drive the school bus. He turned in to the puppy farm with his wad of cash. He walked through the kennels, breathing in the spicy fresh puppy dung. The pens hadn't been hosed yet. He asked the kid attendant, "Any of these ready to go?"

"That litter there is only seven weeks; they've got another week to bulk up."

"If I give you a deposit, will you save one?"

"Could."

"And over there—those yellow ones, what about them?"

"Those are goldens. They're already sold to the Pet Luv chain. But you don't want a golden—they're schizoid. Take a sheltie."

Lux picked up a black-and-white pup, like a mini collie dog with a pointy snout, but still a puffball. Its belly was distended and tight after its evening gruel. "Are these shelties like those Frisbee dogs you see on the beach? They leap seven feet high and twist in midair to catch what's flying at them?"

"You're talking about a border collie; these are like that, but these are minidogs."

"These have shots?" Lux asked.

"Shots. Wormed. Kennel cough, the works."

"How much?"

"For you? Six hundred."

"Six? Fuck you. Who put you in charge? That's twice what you'd get from Pet Luv."

"Three times."

"You prick. I'll give you two."

"Four."

Lux pressed the puppy into his face and breathed its fluff, thinking its narcotic puppy smell would buffer his "ninth step" confession to Alden. The sheltie wagged its reedy tail like a little peace pipe. It nipped his T-shirt with its needle teeth.

He counted out four crisp Benjamins, crumpling each one so they didn't stick together. He would bring Alden back to pick out her favorite one from the lineup. The rest would be shipped in crates to pet malls. Lux lifted a water bowl from an empty pen. The stainless-steel bowl was so big, the puppy could room in it.

The kid said, "Shit. Just help yourself to accessories, why don't you? Hope she's ready for a dog. Women don't like to wipe up after they piddle."

Lux hit the bottleneck where Route 6 funnels into the rotary. He snaked in and out of stacked-up sightseers only to find that traffic was stopped behind a further parade of shrink-wrapped sailboats and cabin cruisers emptying from the boatyard at Fiberglass Yacht. His heart drummed and his palms leaked sweat on the steering wheel. He rubbed his hands on his jeans, but again they were wet. He decided to postpone his secret business until traffic had thinned. He turned off the crowded circle at his first chance. He drove to the minimart in Eastham to waste a little time in the aisles. He microwaved a slice of pizza until it was a puddle of cheese, having no intention of eating it. He paid for a pack of cigarettes and the bubbling wedge of pizza and went outside to sit in the truck. He smoked three Winston kings, one after another.

The shrink-wrapped procession was gone when he drove back to the clock. He steered into the muddy track where he had worked with Marty Stokes earlier that day. He cut the lights and rolled a notch past the gaping hole for number seven, making certain no passing traffic could find him from that angle. When he climbed down from the cab, a wind was coming up. He had left his quilted mac at the house, or it was in Tindle's truck. He was soaking with sweat, and the cold was eating through his shirt seams. He crouched down to unzip the duffel. He parted Gwen's swirl of dresses to find the teacher's skull. As he lifted it out, the wind whistled through its eye sockets and ripped it from his hand. "You fuck," Lux said as it rolled a few feet away. His curse was swept off. He walked after it and scuffed it forward with his boot like he was setting up a soccer shot, having lost his reverence for it.

Next he unloaded the porous relic—ribs, spinal stalk, and femurs, all bridges and causeways—into his lap. The headless trunk still wore the jacket. Lux realized the jacket couldn't stay, he'd have to take it off the teacher. The nylon jacket was indestructible and would never dissolve away. He'd have to see if it would burn in the trash barrel. When he jerked the jacket sleeves loose, brittle bands of desiccated muscle snapped in pieces like uncooked egg noodles, sprinkling fossil tabs across the marl. The skeleton was breaking up, no longer the sum of its parts but the parts alone. Lux rolled the coat to the opposite shoulder to peel it down the bony arm.

The guide yellow jacket was stiff with a mineral scrim, its crusted collar soaked in layers of sandy grit and chitin, but its color still flamed like a kitchen window in the early dark. Monty had told Lux he had bought the coat because butterflies are *attracted to yellow.* On his safaris with Penelope Griffin, butterflies would actually alight on his arms and shoulders. Monty explained that when he wore the jacket, the tables were turned. The specimens he sought would actually pursue *him.* Lux stopped to picture the teacher pulsing with little wings as he deboned the jacket.

Lux thought again of the crow that made off with the teacher's incisor. Then he looked for Monty's wedding ring, the size of a locknut or washer bonnet. It must have been lost somewhere en route. Lux wanted to believe that this was symbolic. Alden was freed from her marriage pledge. Monty couldn't hold on.

With Nickerson's spade, he worked a deeper sink within the prepared bed he had dug with Marty Stokes. He guesstimated the breadth and height of the bone pile. Then he carefully stacked the ossified stalks into the hole—backward, forward, making a squared heap, until he couldn't tell where he should place the head. Which end was pelvis or shoulders in the laddered rubble? He didn't need to know.

He listened to the traffic circling, fearful someone would stop, but the cars kept moving. The transfer was complete. Monty was in the depths of the clock, in permanent time for the hereafter. Lux carefully backshoveled the sandy loam and packed it down until it looked like the trench he and Marty Stokes had readied for the English yews that would arrive in the morning. They'd be using block and tackle to lever each massive root ball into the secret crypt, where its harl would uncoil and entrap the schoolteacher. No one would be the wiser.

He climbed into the van and inched back onto the rotary, sparring with moderate traffic. He had circled once already when he remembered he'd left behind the duffel stuffed with Monty's jacket and Gwen's dresses. He rolled around again to go back for it. Lux realized too late that he must have looked fried, all mops and brooms, making wacky, unnecessary circles around the rotary. Only drunks and tourists circle the rotary repetitively—you're lost or you're a lush.

Therefore a trooper materialized right behind him as he parked behind the clock.

The G.O.D. truck was probably a novelty to the mountie, or Francisconi had put the word out.

The trooper stepped up to his window. "This is a service drive, just for the clock. It's not public access."

"That's right," Lux said. "I work with Nickerson. We've got some English yews coming in tomorrow. I left my duffel."

"That there?" The trooper walked over to retrieve the item, taking careful steps in the fresh soil as if worried about his spit shine. He came back to the window as Lux reached for the suspect registration card, but the trooper didn't seem interested. Lux waited for him to unzip the bag and search through its ridiculous heap of textiles, but the trooper handed him the duffel through the window. He told Lux that he wanted to check the van's taillights and blinkers because of its bashed-in ass. The trooper walked behind the G.O.D. truck and waited for Lux to cooperate. Lux tapped the brake pedal and flicked the turn signal, left side, right side. Lux watched his rearview to see the officer's uniform warm up, black out, warm up. The signals worked fine, but Lux was reduced to a sweatpile of nerves.

The trooper came back to the window. "If this is a refrigerator truck, where's the unit?" The officer aimed his light into the way back and eyed King's saltwater rod. "That an UglyStik? That has a graphite core, right? God, I want one of those. Those are nice," the trooper said, holding his citation pad. But he wasn't writing.

"It belongs to my friend. He splurged on it."

"What are you getting this late? Blues or striper?"

"Just catch of the day. For my own consumption."

"Okay. You're all set." The officer waved him loose. Lux thought that the trooper acted a little too *divine,* happy as a dog with two tails, when usually these guys were stone faced. He watched him walk back to his cruiser and sit down. Lux saw him kissing his radio as if he was telling Francisconi, "We have liftoff."

Lux didn't wait to find out.

LUX DROVE ONTO THE DUNES at High Head and followed the fire trails out to Sea Call. The Provincelands sandplains are unpredictable; the hummocks shift from year to year, according to wind and gale. The landscape has a mind of its own. At the foot of dangerous dunes, the Seashore posts signs that say, "Keep Off. Live Sand." He made one wrong turn and had trouble turning around in the loose pack. Rocking the van only made a deeper sink. The treads carved into a layer of black magnetite. Lux had forgotten to bleed the tires. His run-in with the trooper had derailed him. "It's the little details that turn around and bite you," he could hear King scolding him.

He tried to dig out with Nickerson's spade, but sand sifted back as he shoveled each side of the wheel well. Live sand was indifferent to human toil.

He could see the dark outline of Alden's shack from where the G.O.D. truck had foundered. Alden wasn't home yet after Hyram's meeting, but Lux was happy to wait for her. He tried to run the heater, but the van wouldn't turn over. Punchy had jury-rigged the ignition cable, but there must have been another angle to the problem. Lux would be sure to tell him an artist wannabe shouldn't hang out a service shingle.

Then he saw the high beams of a National Seashore Land Rover following the switchbacks two dunes over. These rangers patrolled High Head at all hours—a throwback to the days when pirates and smugglers made landfall with their booty at midnight, after intercepting merchant ships. He tumbled out of the van, dragging the duffel. He'd been lucky with the trooper, but rangers search coolers, traps, and toolboxes, looking for scrubbed lobsters or whatever they think you're poaching from the Seashore. He couldn't be sure that the ranger wouldn't swoop on him for driving the repoed van. He decided to ditch it there. It was King's never-ending story, not his. He remembered Tindle quoting a French poet who had said, "A poem is never finished; it's merely abandoned." He might forget the van, but Lux understood that he wasn't finished with Robustus. He still had the jacket.

To avoid a heart-to-heart with the ranger, Lux trudged down the steep leeward side of a dune. He sank into a catbrier thicket to get out of the wind, but the wind found him. His teeth were chattering. Lux hugged his knees to his chest to wait out the ranger's inspection. After a few moments, he saw the Land Rover's taillights ascend the next dune over. It stopped at the G.O.D. van, where the fire road forked back out to Route 6. The ranger would have his look-see, and Lux could freeze to death just sitting around. The wind was slicing. It occurred to him that Monty's nylon jacket might be a reliable Windbreaker.

He unzipped the duffel and tugged the jacket out. The idea of actually wearing it caused stomach acid to sizzle abruptly in the back of his throat. But Lux made a fist and pulled one yellow sleeve over his arm, and then the next. He shifted his shoulders, adjusting the crusted collar. He zipped it up to his throat. He cautiously fingered the embroidered breast pocket, as if the Nike swoosh were a snake that might curl around and bite him. But the coat blocked the wind.

He stood up and tacked back and forth over the dunes in parallel lines. He plowed his way into zones, latitudes, and geometries where the ranger couldn't see him. Trekking through deep sand was taking its toll on him. Too exhausted to lift his feet, he carved a helix of zigzag lines across the shifting surface.

The ranger had departed, leaving an orange sticker plastered on the windshield of the G.O.D. truck. The notice warned that the truck would be towed at the owner's expense by the park service, with additional fines, if "the disabled vehicle isn't removed within 24 hours." The sticker had a list of local towing services and their phone numbers, including the phone number for Punchy's Garage.

Lux tried to rehearse what he would say to Alden. If only he had the puppy for a bread-and-butter gift, his confession would be easier to saddle-soap. He remembered his frozen spells in high school when he couldn't formulate a simple sentence if the teacher asked him a direct question. He understood why he wore the ghost's jacket. It was worth a thousand words to him.

19

ALDEN STOPPED AT THE EASTHAM SUPERETTE and brought Toya inside. "What would you like to eat, some ice cream? Come over here, look at these shelves of chips. There's pretzels or candy."

Toya's pupils dilated like big black blueberries when she understood that Alden was serious. Alden was not taking her back to the McGuires'. Alden steered Toya by the shoulders into the next aisle. "Let's see. What about these cupcakes?" Alden took a package of her sacred Hostess Snowballs and handed it to Toya. Toya cupped the little package as if it were a bar of plutonium. Alden said, "Go ahead," and she criticized Toya's foster mom's habit of buying only bargain-bucket bulk foods until the girl was certain that the little cake was *hers*. She was in paradise now. She started to peel the wrapper off. She bit into the cake as if challenging someone to snatch it away.

Driving onto the dunes at High Head, Alden crested a hummock and her headlights scrolled over a silvery apparition. Where the fire road forked, a panel truck waited, its engine cut. Toya shrieked in surprise when she saw that the white Econoline van had "G.O.D." stenciled on its side. She had never seen the word "God" in any other context but the one she knew. Alden wondered who the prowler was and pulled up to the van to see that the driver's seat was empty. Perhaps the driver was in the way back. It was a courier truck touting "Guaranteed Overnight Delivery." When she understood the acronym, it immediately took the edge off. The truck might have tried to make a drop-off at her shack. She had recently ordered books on the Internet. In preparation for her foster-care license, she had bought some titles about child rearing by the scholars Robert Coles and Ashley Montague. She had also ordered a picture book for Baby Hendrick, *Pinkerton, Behave!*, a story about a wayward family pet. Perhaps this G.O.D. truck was subcontracted by a larger courier. FedEx and UPS refused to deliver to locations on unpaved fire roads, where unlevel dips and gullies spilled packages off their shelves.

But the unusual van looked too banged-up to be in active service.

She saw that the truck's front axle was buried in sand up to its wheel wells. She got out of her Jeep to ask the driver if he wanted to use her cell phone, but he must have hiked back to Route 6. She looked into the cab. There wasn't much to see except for an empty dog bowl on the passenger seat.

Toya called from the Wagoneer, "Don't leave me here. It's spooky."

Alden climbed back into the Jeep and squeezed Toya's bare knee, icy beneath her thin jumper. She drove up to her shack. "Here we are."

Toya looked at the desolate sheet of dune sand in every direction but one. Then it was the big black sea, bigger at night than in daylight.

They could hear the surf pound.

Toya said, "Do waves come up to the door?"

"Only once every hundred years."

This didn't reassure the little girl. Toya said, "Does Mrs. McGuire know where I am?"

ALDEN POURED A GLASS OF MILK FOR TOYA. She washed Toya's face with a new Barney washcloth and gave her one of her own jerseys to wear as a nightie. She tucked Toya into the trundle bed built into the window seat. She had already made up the bed and kept it ready with the pillows plumped. *You must have an extra bed ready at any hour.*

"I never slept in a drawer," Toya said, a little concerned.

"It's cozy, isn't it?"

"You know that witch with the sugar house? She had Hansel go to bed in that drawer."

"And what are you implying?"

"I'm 'plying nothing. I like this drawer. It's snuggly." Alden saw Toya's tough facade straining to overcome her more-childish, vulnerable instant. Toya ceremoniously removed her Rugrats wristwatch and put it on the windowsill. Alden offered Toya the three-faced bisque, but the doll seemed to disgust the girl. Alden twisted its head in a circle, demonstrating its three distinct aspects, and told Toya, "Smile. Sleep. Cry." Toya couldn't appreciate it as an antifeminist statement nor see the humor in it. For Toya, a self-disciplined little people pleaser, it was all too real.

So Alden sat down and read from her Buck-A-Book copy of *A Child's Garden of Verses,* but the little poems seemed cloying and long outdated, and Toya was more interested in Alden's satellite dish.

"Tomorrow you can watch TV."

"Now?"

"You should try to sleep."

"Maybe I can't."

"Listen to the waves," Alden said, turning off the fringed lamp beside the girl's bed, and she tiptoed across the room.

DRESSED IN HER NIGHTGOWN, Alden stood at her kitchen window. A figure was silhouetted on the hill, a black cutout against the Atlantic mirror. He wasn't one of the scientists who came out there twice a year to set up weather-monitoring equipment—those geared styluses that ink rising wind speeds over graph paper and Taylor charts. He wasn't from the U.S. Fish and Wildlife Service, men who came to roll out snow fence in checkerboard grids to protect the plover nesting sites.

The prowler was lugging an overnight bag as if he expected to sleep over. He wore a hooded parka with its storm collar zipped up high over his chin. The hooded outerwear reminded her of the police sketch of the Unabomber. When she flicked on her porch light, his coat blazed bright yellow. It was what mountain climbers might wear when leading Outward Bound novices into treacherous gorges. Her husband had purchased a coat like this. He had said it attracted butterflies.

This wasn't Monty. It was Lux.

She pushed the door open and stood barefoot on her stoop, her thin nightgown swirled and lifted in the wind like a giant buttercup in a Lewis Carroll illustration.

Lux stopped still when he saw the vision. He wanted to stake his claim on land and sky, beast and bird, heather and heath, everything in the twenty-foot grid of glacial till that remained between them.

"You spending the night?" she called to him.

He walked forward in stiff, unsteady strides.

"Where did you get that coat?" she said. Her spine tingled, as if ice beads of an abacus were aligning on a spindle, a column of her wildest intuitions and far-fetched equations finally adding up. But she couldn't find an easy explanation for why he was wearing Monty's jacket.

Lux stepped onto the porch and stood before her, weaving. He was losing his legs and he grabbed Alden. He pulled her close, right beneath his chin. In their standstill, she tipped her head back to look at him.

"Shite, what's the matter with you? Are you having that seizure thing? Are you all right?"

"Alden—" He gripped her elbows. "Alden, I want to tell you—"

"Tell me what?"

He said, "You are so *tiny*—"

"Excuse me?"

"You're tiny."

"That's a new one. That's pretty good, the best come-on line I've heard in a while."

He pinched his thumb and forefinger together, as if holding a speck of magic dust. "You are—*this*—tiny. I know how that feels, Alden, but I'm in charge now."

"O-kay," she said, adopting a teenage mall rat's tone of mocking tolerance for his queer display of affection. "Why are you in that jacket?" she said. "Is that jacket—"

"I was freezing waiting for you."

"It's filthy. How could you put it on?"

"I'm cold. I'm shivering. I can't come up with the words." He dropped his raw face into his hands.

His non sequiturs had tumbled out, almost pure nonsense, but she felt a caul ripped away, a stone rolled from the mouth of a cave, a broken wing suddenly mended. She didn't want to follow his logic to find its source. When he looked at her again, his unrelenting stare-down torched away her confusion. She was convinced by the tears that glistered and lit his face.

She pulled him inside the shack. "We need to be quiet. Toya's asleep."

He saw the child in the trundle bed. "*Her?* Where did she come from? I thought you wanted Layla's kid."

"No, this is the one I want."

"I bought you a puppy. You won't need kids now."

"Really? Where is it?"

"You can have your pick of the litter. I've got it on layaway, paid in full, actually. When did you get the girl?"

They looked at Toya asleep in the corner bed. Alden whispered, "Lux, are you staying here tonight?"

Alden didn't ask any more questions about Monty's jacket. She was putting a kettle on the burner and finding a tea strainer. She was *happy* to see Lux. He fell into a chair and dropped the duffel. Seeing Toya installed, he felt like his prom date had bought her own corsage and his token of affection wasn't appreciated. "Is there something to drink?" Lux said through his fingers.

"I'm making tea."

"You still have that quart of Guinness?"

"You don't really want a drink, do you?"

"Someone should have a drink."

"There's Bombay Sapphire. It was Monty's." She walked over to the cupboard. The floorboards seemed soggy, giving with each step she took. She crossed the trapdoor and it felt like rubber. Lux's confession had finally hit her. "I can't come up with the words," he had told her.

She reached for the bottle of gin. She walked back and handed it to Lux.

He twisted its cap. A juniper musk filled the air like tree surgery, a blitz of chain saws tearing him up.

She saw him struggle with the jeweled blue bottle. She took it by the neck and kneaded his fingers loose. His grip was halfhearted. "Lux, you don't really want a drink, after two years—"

"I guess not. But you could pour one."

"You won't let me smoke, but you want me to drink?"

She sat down with the teapot and filled a mug for him. She blew gently across its steaming surface a few times to cool it. She set the mug on the table and turned its handle toward him, making every effort to comfort Lux, which made him feel worse. He tugged his hands through his loose hair and looked at Alden. She seemed to be waiting for his further instructions. She seemed to trust him. She seemed to *love* him. He decided he didn't need to tell her the school bus details for *her* sake. He was being selfish to want to unpack his own carry-on luggage in front of her. It was AA horseshit to confess your burden and hand the baton to your victim.

He shivered convulsively, his shoulders dipping back and forth. Alden went over to the deep zinc utility sink that doubled as her bathtub. She started running hot water.

She pulled him over and unzipped the ungodly item he was wearing, tugging the zipper from his chin and slicing it down. He let it fall to the floor. She lifted open the trapdoor and kicked Monty's jacket into the root cellar. They heard it slither down the ladder. "What's this?" she said, pointing to the duffel.

"Stolen property," he said.

She tossed it into the black hole after Monty's jacket.

Lux stepped out of his shirt and jeans.

"Get in," she told him. "But be quiet—don't wake her."

He sank beneath the water.

She scrubbed his back with a silky cake of oat-flour soap, splashing her nightgown. "Thoreau would approve," Alden joked. "The well water. The oatmeal suds." She tried to encourage him.

"Oh, God. Oh, no. You're beautiful, Miss Wilderness," he said when she showed him how unnatural things came naturally to her.

ALDEN SAW SHE HAD A MESSAGE banked on her cell phone. She punched it in, fearing it was Hyram. She'd forgotten to leave the ringer on and wondered if he was feeling worse. But it wasn't Hyram; it was Mrs. McGuire. Her message said, "I know you've got Toya. I don't see any reason to tell Hester about this mix-up, do you? Just bring her back."

Alden made Lux listen to the message.

"Shit. She must be in a tight spot," he told Alden, "to call over here instead of just calling the cops."

"Her kids keep showing up at school a little worse for wear. I bet she's on probation."

"She'll have to admit that she lost Toya at the Stop and Shop," Lux said. "I mean, Toya has to be in school Monday, right?"

"Not until her nits are gone."

"Her nits?"

"The school is strict. She had her Rid-X treatment, but she can't go back to school until we get all the eggs off her head. They attach to the roots. After the treatment, these eggs are supposed to be dead."

"How do we know they're dead? I don't exactly want to get lice," he said.

"I'll buy one of those little combs tomorrow."

SKIN-TO-SKIN IN HER TINY IRON BED, he told her about King's accident.

"Was it his wedding ring finger?" she asked.

"His ring finger? You think King will ever need it?" But he was thinking of Monty's bony fingers.

"I don't need mine. I lost my wedding ring in Hyram's In-Sink-Erator," she said.

"No shit? You lost it down the drain?"

"I said so."

"So you'll forget about him?" He spooned his hips against her buttocks. He kissed the back of her neck through her tangles of sorrel hair.

"Do me a little favor?" she said.

"I can do you a *big* favor," he told her.

She pried herself loose. "No. I mean tomorrow. I have to go to Boston."

"Boston?"

"There's this wedding."

"You're invited to a wedding? You want me to babysit the girl?"

"No, we'll take Toya with us. We can visit King first. You want to?"

"I work in the morning."

"The wedding is at two o'clock."

Lux thought that by noon he should have sunk the yews and tidied up the crypt after the covert funeral. He said, "Who's getting hitched? Let's have a double wedding."

She couldn't suppress a smile sawing the corners of her mouth. "A double wedding? But this is a protest thing."

"Who's protesting? The bride? The groom? Maybe the ex-husband?"

She knew he was teasing, but he looked different, instantly agitated by her plans. He pinned her arms at her sides and straddled her; his eyes drilled her with a hungry "gimme" expression.

AT SUNRISE, FRANCISCONI WAS STANDING at the window peering through the divided light. A Ranger Rick had ferried him to the shack in a tow truck to get the van, but Alden's Seashore colleague was holding back and seemed embarrassed to barge in on her. Francisconi stamped the sand off his boots, but Alden didn't invite him in. She feared he would see Toya, who was taking her turn in the zinc tub with bubble-bath suds spilling over.

Lux covered for Alden and went outside to face the officers. Francisconi told Lux, "You're not following directions. You were supposed to leave the van for us. Now I have to take you into town and write you up."

"We have to go into town?"

"Don't get asthma yet. We're towing it in. Since Johnston's in Boston, I guess you're the lucky fuck."

"Who says?"

"That van was jacked. It's an active case. It was never in the repo pen at Fall River or New Bedford. You think King knows that? Either way, we're taking it off his hands."

"That's fine. Why do you need me? I'm putting trees in at the clock this morning. I'm hired by the *town,* same as you. The clock's a priority, right?"

"I saw those trees come in on a flatbed this morning. That's where you're headed? Well, you'll be a little late."

Lux heard Alden shushing Toya, who was asking questions in little chirps, so he walked the officers down the fire road to get them out of range. Francisconi said, "You got anything in the van before we hook up?"

"Yeah, I got something in it."

"I thought so," Francisconi said.

They trudged the two hundred yards to the abandoned relic. One whole panel side was spray-coated beige from blowing sand.

Lux drummed the fender with his fist, and the crust of sand collapsed to the ground. He climbed into the cab and grabbed the dog bowl. He saw that the floor mat on the passenger side was askew and the secret compartment had been forced. Someone had cut through the sheet metal with a keyhole saw and crimped it open with a pry bar. Punchy must have come out overnight to help himself. Lux hoped it was worth his trouble. He pulled the mat over the false floor and jumped out of the van.

"Is that it? That dog bowl?" Francisconi said.

"What do you think, I've got a pound of something? A jelly-bean jar of Ecstasy? I'm straight edge, you know that."

"Yeah, we know."

"I don't saw my fingers off."

"Not yet."

"So you'll give me a lift to the rotary?"

"Okay. We write you up on Monday. You find us. Don't make us find you."

Alden walked out to them carrying her retro Comet coffeepot, a much-prized item at the Wellfleet Flea Market. She rested mugs on the hood of the tow truck and started pouring. The ranger came over with his thermocup for a refill.

"Ever hear of automatic drip?" Francisconi asked her, examining the dented aluminum carafe with its white oxidized splotches. The officer seemed perplexed by her rustic life in a shack that had few modern conveniences. It was his opinion that Miss Bride Interrupted belonged in a split-level house on a cul-de-sac, where neighbors could keep an eye out for her.

But the November morning was gorgeous. The Atlantic disk blazed with veins of sun, like a gold coin too big to spend. Everyone looked at the sea. Alden always felt that in the daylight, things never seemed as problematic nor as hopeful as they appeared in the half-light. She had tried to put Toya in the cellar, giving her a lantern and a box of powdered doughnuts. She had explained to the little girl, "We don't want the policeman to find you here, right?" She lifted the trapdoor and showed Toya all the plush stuffed animals and crib toys she'd stowed away for Baby Hendrick. Toya wouldn't cooperate. "These toys are for babies," she said, refusing to climb into the gloomy hole.

Alden said, "If that cop comes back and sees you, he'll take you away. Just sit on the ladder, right here."

The girl was white. She shook her head and started to sob.

Alden let the trapdoor slam. "Okay, okay, we'll put the TV on. But you sit right here in the shack."

"Don't leave me alone."

"I'm coming right back."

Yet once Alden had walked outside with the coffee, the girl started caterwauling. She had quite a voice box for such a little thing. But an easterly was blasting, and standing with the men, Alden couldn't hear Toya's complaints unless the wind died for an instant. Francisconi and the ranger didn't seem to notice the girl. In a minute, Francisconi handed his cup to Alden and climbed aboard the tow truck. Lux gave her *his* cup and the icy dog bowl, his eyes alarmed. He must have heard the child getting more and more frantic. He crowded Francisconi into the cab. The winch started to scream. The paralyzed heap drizzled sand as its rear axle lifted and its wheels were freed.

20

ALDEN CALLED MASS GENERAL to ask about their visiting hours. Lux did want to see King before they crashed the wedding. She ironed Toya's oversize jumper and gave her some tights and a pink sweater to wear underneath it. "Where are we going?" Toya asked her. "Are we seeing a wedding?"

"That's right."

"Can I be flower girl?"

"Maybe you can. Just put your shoes on." Alden was distracted, thinking about the butterfly release and seeing Penelope Griffin again. She pictured Monty's worktable, where he left his specimens from the fields he had visited with Miss Griffin. His plastic ziplock bags of crescent-spots, hairstreaks, duskywings, cloudywings, metalmarks. She hadn't allowed herself to recite this litany for some time, and its poetry came back to her haltingly, but with full force.

They got into the Jeep and Alden drove to get Lux from the clock. The big English yews were planted in a rough seven, but he hadn't snipped and wired them yet. Lux explained, "They're in shock. We'll wait until spring to trim it out."

"In shock?"

"Wouldn't you be? They need to be dormant for the winter, you know, to get used to their little niche." His explanation sounded wistful, as if he, too, looked for his niche.

Toya was scratching her head, and Alden wondered if she still had lice. They stopped at the Mobil station, and while Lux put thirty pounds in her tires, Alden ran across to the CVS to buy a tiny comb for nits.

Toya was asleep in the backseat when they drove off the Cape, crossing the canal bridge at Sagamore. The bridge painters had knocked off and traffic was flowing. Alden said to Lux, "Look, there's that ladder. Can you believe that the Army Corps of Engineers just leaves it behind each time?"

"Yeah, I guess they need a ladder to get up to those cables."

"I'm waiting to hear that someone had to try it."

"You tip off from this height, and the water is hard as slate."

"So what good are suicide fences if you've got a ladder?"

"I don't see anyone trying that ladder right now."

"When you drove that school bus into the harbor, some people thought you were trying to self-destruct. Like it was a cry for help or something."

He didn't like being stereotyped that way twice in the same twenty-four hours. "I was faced, that's all. Vicodin and alcohol. If you ask me, every day it's Chutes and Ladders." But he remembered the instant when she had soaped his back with that foamy oatmeal cake and how the world looked better. *Girls* and their Irish toiletries—Gwen had the same weakness for scented soaps. He told Alden, "Think of it like this: *I'm* your suicide fence."

She liked his love talk. "You're my suicide fence?"

"What are friends for?" he said. "I know you'd do the same."

"Just give me some warning," she said.

They rolled over the bridge, and Alden looked down at the steel ribbon of water. "You have to turn around," she said.

"Turn around?"

"Go back. We have to move that ladder."

"We *have* to?"

"We'll carry it off the arch and leave a note for the corps. They should be more conscious of people's problems, people's day-to-day temptations—their uncontrollable impulses."

"Like swiping a ladder?"

"It won't take long."

He parked at the boarded-up information booth at the Sagamore rotary. Toya was asleep, her adenoids purring from a stuffy nose. Alden covered her with an old Navajo rug that Dane Baker had handed down to her, telling Alden she should never go anywhere without a car blanket. Dane Baker had often slept in his vehicles, especially when traveling between destination points that were yet to be confirmed. Alden was certain Toya wouldn't wake up, but she made Lux lock the car doors.

They hiked up the sliver of sidewalk onto the bridge. The aluminum ladder was at the top of the arch. It turned out to be heavier than it looked and awkward to maneuver, especially when Lux pulled one way and, in her impatience, Alden tried to wrestle it out of his hands. She finally allowed Lux to be comptroller and foreman of the operation. He told her to back up the narrow sidewalk and give him room.

Sidelined, she stood at a distance. She shifted her weight from one foot to the other, crossed her arms, tipping her shoulders in pouty, little-princess slouches.

Lux ignored her. He tried to unhook the claws of the ladder from where they snagged a cable. It was too heavy to lift off in one motion, so Lux rocked the contraption to lever its weight onto him.

He teetered it, partnered it, and waltzed it free. It tumbled unmoored to the sidewalk, squawking like a scaffold.

Then he grabbed *his* end and waited for Alden to lift the dead-opposite rung. They limped unevenly down the west side of the span. Traffic slowed to look at the vaudeville. They left the ladder beside the "Desperate? Call the Samaritans" billboard, but Alden didn't have any paper to leave a scolding note for the bridge crew about their bad habits.

"It's self-explanatory," Alden told Lux. "This tells them: 'Stow the ladder!' "

"That's what it says?"

"I feel a lot better. Think of the lives we're saving. Thanks."

He knew that Alden's wacky save-the-world agenda was genuine, warmhearted volunteerism. But he recognized its obsessive-compulsive disorder symptoms, like his own unmasked furies if and when an episode surfaced all of a sudden. The tortuous if-and-when scenario always hung over him. He remembered sitting beside his mother in his grade school cafeteria, trying to eat his sandwich in methodical nips and smidgeons, from left to right—on the diagonal—crust to crust.

He told Alden, "No problem, baby. Let me know when you want to move something else. Like that guardrail right there—I could adjust that. You want it curled or uncurled?" He was smiling, but he rubbed his shoulder where he'd been clanged by the ladder.

WHEN THEY HIT THE SOUTHEAST EXPRESSWAY heading into Boston, there wasn't any rush-hour traffic. On weekdays an HOV commuter lane opened and closed with zipper-teeth barricades twice a day—once for incoming traffic in the morning, and again for the outbound surge at night. A driver must have at least three people in the car to use the high-occupancy vehicle lane. One time Alden had been funneled into the tight zipper opening before she knew it. Finding herself in that cinched-in motorway had made her panic. She was swallowed up in a pulsing esophagus and expelled into a policed merge area at the edge of the city.

The cops flagged her when she plowed through the HOV lane, her passenger seats empty. They gave her a ticket. Her heart was still pounding from her claustrophobic trip in the segregated traffic tube. Wasn't it bad enough that she was all alone, without her own carpool society, without friends or relations?

Her husband was missing.

Did they have to write a citation?

With Lux and Toya in the car, her instant family, she wished it were rush hour and they could use the HOV lane with impunity.

At Mass General, Lux parked in the fourth tier of the hospital garage. Alden said, "Let's remember where we leave the Jeep. Caddie on its right, Toyota on its left." But then she realized that when they came back, the Caddie and Toyota could be gone, replaced by different vehicles. To calm herself she tried to think of that comforting quotation from a nature tome: "In flux there is *constancy.* In change there is *regularity, precision.*" Caddie right here beside her Wagoneer, but in an hour, maybe not.

Lux watched her nervousness as she swirled around to get her bearings, trying to memorize the concrete ramps and landmarks. "God, you're a hick," he said. "Relax."

"A hick?"

"Okay, you're a country mouse," he said. He said he'd remember the numbers stenciled on the garage floor.

Alden said, "These numbers never make sense to me."

"It's not Chinese," he said. "Calm down." He hugged her shoulders and steered her into the hospital. On the elevator, before they could stop her, Toya punched every button.

KING WAS IN BED WITH HIS INJURED ARM taped to a splint, a wood plank that looked like a breadboard and kept his mangled hand stabilized. Toya shrieked when she saw the leeches attached to King's sutured fingertips. He told Toya, "Honey, it looks worse than it is. It doesn't hurt."

"Are those real leeches, like in that movie *African Queen*?" Alden said.

"*These* are real. I bet those weren't," Lux said, bending down to get a better look.

King said, "When everything gets reconnected, the arteries start to pump blood, but the veins aren't bringing it back yet. These buggers drain the pressure off."

Alden said, "This is modern medicine?"

"For pain management," King said. "I've also got this IV drip. With the morphine and the critters, I'm doing good."

King was used to a lot of sightseers any time the nurses brought in a new beaker of leeches. Medical students ambled in to study the procedure, and then came curious hospital staffers of all stripes and sizes.

Lux teased his friend, "If your fingers don't heal, they'll give you a hook."

"Right. I won't need jigglers or celluloid if I have my own can opener."

"Or you can go out on the *Cee Jay* to gaff tuna and live honest." He didn't tell King about the G.O.D. truck getting repoed that morning or about the minor annoyances with Francisconi at home, and the red tape unraveling around their necks.

King's sister arrived with a full bucket of fried oysters from Legal Sea Food. King tipped the carton toward Alden, asking her if she wanted to try one. "No, thanks," she said, her stomach flip-flopping.

"I'm never too sick to eat a lobster, squid rings, or mollusks," King said, and he made a production of choosing a fat oyster. "I bet these are Wellfleet." His sister smoothed a paper napkin under his chin as he reached into the mound of fried oysters with his left hand.

After sampling a few morsels, King was worn out. He leaned back against the pillow and closed his eyes. He opened them with exaggerated force, trying not to drift away. "Shit. Sorry, folks."

King's sister said, "He gets woozy like that, right in the middle of a visit."

They heard an infant crying. "Is this near the nursery?" Alden said. She remembered Dane Baker's scheme to sell her ripe eggs. She wanted to get going. Alden kissed King with sisterly affection, and said, "Have a *Nauset* day."

King looked at her from his rumpled sheets. He was grinning or wincing.

ONE CORNER OF THE BOSTON PUBLIC GARDEN had been transformed, decorated with cornucopias of waxed harvest fruits, tiny striped squash, curled-necked gourds, and baby pumpkins. On the duck pond the famous swan boats were tucked away under plastic tarpaulins in preparation for the snowy season, but winter was still unthinkable. Guests were seated in rows of folding chairs draped in mint green canvas skirts. A long carpet had been tacked down to make a sherbet-colored aisle through a blanket of fallen leaves. It was too blustery to be called Indian summer, but a circle of propane heaters made it feel like shirtsleeve weather.

Penelope Griffin's info sheet had explained what rows they were supposed to sit in. An insider who was on the groom's guest list had reserved some chairs. Lux and Alden didn't have any trouble mixing in. Toya was an adorable smoke screen. She and Alden might be bohemian friends or relations, or Hollywood colleagues of the sitcom beefcake. Still dressed in work clothes, Lux could have been a gaffer, a stuntman, or a camera technician, if not a real costar. Security personnel weren't checking invitations, as they might have at a city hall wedding where guests had to walk through an electronic altar before attending the main act.

Weddings always sparked Alden's imagination. Here was a couple, *starting out.* God bless them. But she had a built-in anxiety about the wedding ritual, too. It came from the recollection of her own ordeal reciting her vows beneath the Registry of Motor Vehicles banner that had said "Be an Organ Donor."

Then it was Penelope Griffin.

Monty's last hurrah was walking toward her in the flesh. Penelope was just as tall and ethereal as before, but her prim smile made her look like a demonic Julie Andrews in a Goth remake of *Mary Poppins.* She gripped Alden's hand and tugged it up and down. "Alden. I'm so glad you showed up."

"I thought I should come," she said.

"In honor of Monty?"

"Yes. I guess that's why I'm here."

Lux looked back and forth at the two women. Penelope kissed Alden on both cheeks. Alden blushed. This butterfly protest was a tribal ritual of some kind for these two ladies and had nothing to do with him. Gate-crashers usually get their comeuppance, and he knew it would be safer to be sitting beside King with his wrist corsage of leeches.

Penelope sat down beside Toya, who was coloring in a comic book that Lux had found in a rack at the hospital. The picture book had cartoon-character diseases: stick figures of hepatitis B, tuberculosis, and *E. coli* germs. As guests were being seated all around them, Penelope reached for her carryall, tipping its flap open so that Alden could see the aerosol cans of Rust-Oleum. It wasn't Layla's golden spritzer, but a murderous red tint called Fire Truck Enamel. Alden believed that its blazing cadmium red would wreck a wedding dress mightily.

Penelope showed the weaponry to Lux and explained the plan.

"Shit," Lux said. "Are you out of your mind?"

"Don't be chicken," Alden said.

Penelope told him, "It's not a pipe bomb. It's a little spray paint. It's just symbolic."

Lux said, "Alden, we're not actual wedding guests or legitimate bug activists. What's it called, the Xerces Club? Fuck that. Let's go." He stood up.

Alden ignored him and turned to Toya, who was still scribbling in her coloring book. "You're really good at staying inside the lines."

"I know," Toya said. "When can I have some cake?" She had seen the elaborate tiered wedding cake decorated with rolled-out fondant icing, like jeweled and beveled wainscoting.

"The cake will be later," Alden said.

Toya looked at her as if she no longer believed Alden's promises.

Ushers walked between rows to distribute glossy cardboard packages only slightly bigger than ring boxes. Alden cupped one in her hands, expecting to feel something—a faint vibration, a thump, or a scratch. But the package was weightless and inert as if empty. Guests were instructed to hold these containers until the exact moment after the nuptials were concluded and the groom had kissed the bride. At that instant and no sooner, the boxes were to be opened in unison.

"Here goes," Penelope said when the familiar Wagner kicked in over the loudspeaker system.

The bride was beautiful. She walked down the carpet in calibrated steps, in perfect jet-lagged syncopation with the formal march. The groom looked lean and rugged as he emerged at the rustic altar between pyramids of winter squash.

In less than ten minutes, the couple had said their vows and were united. Instantly the sitcom groom sunk into his task. He kissed his lovely ball and chain with a little too much Hollywood, tipping her backward until her knees buckled. Guests squirmed and broke into applause. When he surfaced to face the crowd, his smile seemed pinched, as if he had found no relief in his over-the-top enactment. He seemed to know a kiss wouldn't help him now. Yet that kiss had signaled the guests to unfold their paper containers. There was quite a hullabaloo as women shrieked playfully, in giddy fear and repulsion for *any* insect, no matter if it wore Chanel piping and brocade on its wings. Men were chivalrous and swatted the liberated insects away from their wives and sisters.

Two hundred monarchs and viceroys pulsed at eye level, their orange wings licking like a gas grate. The chill air was slow to trigger their metabolism, and the sleepy insects faltered and dipped in uneven spasms. The drunken-winged cloud lofted and sank, moving feebly in a westward direction, in one disorganized cohesion across the Public Garden.

Blackbirds or starlings swooped across the open lawns, as if to investigate the catered snack. But birds won't eat insects with garish coloration. Orange and yellow markings usually mean bitter tidbits, maybe even poison. The birds banked and seesawed through the veil of intruders, doubling back to their perches in the park's huge specimen trees. One sizable ginkgo towered above the wedding benches, its vertical yellow wall of foliage like the rusted prow of a battleship. Alden was beginning to feel claustrophobic in the tiny Public Garden. Although it was an open-air setting, the municipal park had an austere aura of confinement that she knew must be the result of its being micromanaged and top heavy, and all of its specimens were labeled with Latin identifications, quite opposite to the wilderness free-for-all she was used to at the National Seashore.

"Okay," Penelope whispered to Lux. "We move up through the reception line. We take our places. When we get there, you hit her once or twice across the bodice. Bing-bang."

"Me?" Lux said.

"Will you do it?" Alden said, her voice shrill. "It's simple 'disrupt and depart,' right, Penelope?"

"What?" Penelope said, as if she'd never heard the doctrine before.

"'Disrupt and depart,' that's what your colleague told us at the meeting."

"Oh, right. Whatever. But come on, let's get with it," Penelope said, standing up.

Alden told Lux, "You'll do it? Please—"

He looked at Alden. Her face was suddenly unfamiliar, like the face in a locket that didn't belong to him.

Lux knew that love involved a back-and-forth of necessary ultimatums, but this one wasn't familiar to him. This wasn't a temper tantrum or the typical emotional extortion that Gwen might inflict on him.

When she saw him thinking too hard, she turned to Penelope and said, "He doesn't want to."

Penelope turned to Lux. "He'll do it for Monty," she said. "Your old drinking buddy, right, Lux?"

Lux thought that no one but Tindle, Gwen, and King, three everlasting thorns in his side, had had that privileged information.

He watched the wedding couple realign in a ceremonious about-face to begin their surrender dirge up the aisle. The groom waited for his partner to arrange the taffeta wake of her dress at the turnaround, its heavy train like the tail of a thunder lizard. A few butterflies drifted down to alight on the altar and across the sherbet carpet, holding their wings open in the "basking position," trying to absorb a little heat from the sun. Oblivious to the stragglers, the newlyweds trampled the insects into gold powder.

Penny started shaking the can of Rust-Oleum in her hand to prime it. Lux heard its mixing bead clattering. To him it was the sound of an accelerating female hysteria.

The reception line was clogged behind the hosts of *Entertainment Tonight;* then it was reporters from *Boston* magazine. As she waited, Alden loaded up a Chinette saucer with bite-size quiches, little salmon puffs, and water chestnuts wrapped in bacon strips with toothpick skewers. She handed the plate to Toya. Toya nibbled a tiny quiche, the size of a peanut butter cup, and said, "Ick—what is this? I want some of that cake."

Lux told Alden there was still time to turn around and go home, but Penny urged Alden forward in line until they all stood directly before the bride, the bride's mother, and her new mother-in-law. What a formidable triad it was. It might be a difficult balancing act, even for the guileless bride, but the girl had a resilient doormat expression.

Seeing her in juxtaposition to the bride, Lux realized that Alden might be a confabulation of his own making, the girl with uncombable hair or the Fellini actress he had loved, Giulietta Masina—someone who existed in one crumbling context or another. *Just for him.* Alden stood on the edge of a big abyss, but she was on the same side of it as he was. He had promised to be her walking guardrail, but when he tried to hold her back, she ignored him.

They approached the tableau of matriarchs in the receiving line.

Penelope elbowed him, jabbing his second rib until the pain flared like a firecracker. She proffered a can of paint. He refused to take it. But she had her own cylinder hidden in her jacket sleeve.

She crowded behind Lux, digging her fingers into the waistband of his jeans. She pointed the Rust-Oleum at the bride and depressed its tight button. The aerosol made a viperine hiss as she sprayed looping red lines that bled fatter on contact. She circled heavy crimson leis across the bride's eyelet-lace neckline.

Then she fogged both matriarchs. Lux tried to pry her hand from his jeans, which were sinking on his hips. They careened, knocking against the table that presented the wedding cake, six tiers in all. One could see that the cake, suddenly disassembled, was just a facsimile of the actual confection that would be served after dinner; the layers were Styrofoam beneath rolled-out fondant icing. It was a thousand-dollar item just the same. When he shoved her off, Penelope bumped a propane heater, jarring it off its pedestal stand. Flames shot out like a rocket.

Penelope dropped the Rust-Oleum at his feet. She trotted off, leaving Lux and Alden behind. Alden saw that Penelope was pinning it on them. She pulled Toya's arm, tipping the girl's plate of finger sandwiches. She called to Lux, but a phalanx of wedding guests had suddenly encircled him. A man shoved Lux and dropped him to the leafy grass carpet, kneeing his back. Both the stupefied and the clearheaded bystanders cheered at the masterly takedown.

Cameras were rolling. It was the Channel 7 news cam, or a video feed for those Hollywood tabloids. It was going to be a six o'clock segment, part city desk, part feature story—a little romp with Boston's Keystone Kops.

Penelope was nowhere, but someone chased after Alden and Toya, suspecting their connection to the melee. As she ran with Toya, Alden looked back once, surprised to see that it was the groom himself only a few paces behind her. She stopped short and turned around to face him. Toya sat down on the sidewalk pavement, disoriented. Her jumper buttercupped and revealed her panties. She started to whimper. Then she started to bawl.

The TV star asked Alden, "So—who is that guy? Where'd he come from?"

She told him, "He's just a bystander."

"I think not."

"He didn't do it. Did you see that tall woman? She did it." But Penelope had disappeared.

They watched his bride, her dress streaked like ribbon candy, flanked by the matrons who would bracket her life from there on in. The three women got into a waiting car. But the sitcom star didn't join them. He seemed resistant to escorting his new wife or to attending to immediate events in the bend in the road before him.

Two police cars rolled into the park, steering through flower trellises and garland dividers and around the propane heaters that bordered the half-acre wedding site. An officer got out of a cruiser and took charge of the wedding guest posse. The cop cuffed Lux with a vinyl band, cinching it tight. Alden saw that these handcuffs weren't much different from the closures that come with Hefty trash bags, which must have made it even more embarrassing to Lux. The officer put his prisoner into the backseat of the cruiser, keeping his hand on Lux's head in the typical flatfoot's benediction so that Lux wouldn't bump his noggin.

The groom came to life and started waving to the cops. He seemed to think he had nabbed the bookend to the messy crime. An officer seemed to understand the groom's pantomime and brisked in his direction.

Alden tugged Toya to her feet. They started to run. From the west gate of the Public Garden, it was only a few blocks to the Mass General parking garage where they had left the Jeep. Toya was whimpering as Alden pulled her elbow. Silver strings of saliva fell from Toya's mouth as she continued to bawl. Alden pushed her along the path. Pedestrians looked hard at Alden.

Toya brightened when they came upon the famous bronze ducklings, the same frozen parade of honkers Alden had seen from her tryst suite with Ison. Toya went down the row, patting each petrified duckling. They were directly before the familiar doorway of the Dearborn Hotel, where a police officer was clearing all pedestrian traffic. Alden wanted to ask him where Lux might have been taken in the cruiser, but the officer was too busy. She watched him tear a strip of yellow plastic tape from its sawtooth dispenser. The serrated edge had nicked his fingertip. As blood prickled up, he blotted it on his steel blue cuff. Despite his minor injury, he had secured a plat of bare sidewalk. The boldfaced words "POLICE LINE DO NOT CROSS" ran nose-to-tail in a candy wrapper effect.

"What's this operation?" Alden asked him.

"We've got a jumper," he said.

Another officer joined them. He said that it wasn't an actual suicide attempt, but a hotel guest on the seventh floor was throwing items—small appliances, table lamps, and oddball collectibles—from an open window. Pedestrians were funneled into the street. Some people edged the curb, stopping to watch the insty-landing strip of empty concrete. It was a real show.

The officer told Alden, "A bride-to-be is up there making threats. They gave her a big, surprise shower—a whole crowd of friends and family brought wedding gifts—but she wants out. The party girl is going berserk."

"Shite, is that a bread machine?" Alden saw the accordioned appliance and next to it a Krups coffeemaker smashed to bits. As she watched, a shower of napkin rings hit the pavement and twirled across the sidewalk. Alden looked up at the tower's sweeping face, a dizzying mosaic of mirrored glass. The hotel facade was turquoise on top, where it reflected the sky; halfway down, it sponged up the opposite buildings. But several floors up, there *was* a girl. She stood in an open slot, having unlocked the waist-high slider. She teetered on its sill, dressed in a microminiskirt short as a file folder. She waved a solid silver Paul Revere water pitcher. Every Yankee bride expects at least one Revere pitcher. At Shreve, Crump & Lowe, brides can register for all sizes.

The girl tossed it underhand. The shiny pitcher fell end-over-end, hit the sidewalk, and bounced head-high like a dented ball of mercury.

Toya held her ears as it clattered past them.

One patrolman asked Alden, "Are you a guest? You have to use the other entrance." She remembered the many times she had been a guest. She pictured Ison's no-nonsense expression in the darkened room at midday, when he told her instructions as she undressed. "Slow down," he said. "It's not a race." And "Panties off, skirt stays on."

More officers arrived to take control of the site, and office girls drifted in and out to flirt with the meat rack of law enforcement. A vendor walked through the crowd, holding a tray of artsy wood puzzles "for your office desk or coffee table." He demonstrated the universal rubric for connecting the wood pieces. He held a red dowel and a blue block. He screwed the male spindle into the female collar. "Every puzzle piece has a correspon-ding receptacle," he explained to an office Jill, who giggled.

Toya wanted to try the brainteaser.

Just then, the bride-to-be, in her short bolero jacket and micromini, returned with a familiar seafoam Tiffany box. She tore it open and lobbed Waterford tumblers dead center in the empty concrete before her circle of revelers. One by one, the glasses splashed in distinct chevrons of crystal slivers.

Alden feared that she or Toya might get clocked. She wanted to go home, find Hyram, and ask him what to do next. She plunged through the wall of bystanders, happy to leave the Vegas act before its finale. Toya held on, her skinny arms woven tight around Alden, same as always, clinging like a sock monkey's.

21

"HONEY, SHE'S AWOL," HYRAM TOLD ALDEN. "You have to call in and tell them she's safe."

"They'll make me give her back."

"Jesus, sweetie, you better take the first step to fix this mess." His sugary endearments backfired, and Alden refused to listen to common sense.

Toya came in from the yard and sat on Hyram's lap. He carved an apple, piercing sawtooth cuts through its core. He twisted the two serrated halves apart, making two precise pinwheels of fruit. Toya nibbled the masterpiece dolefully, unwilling to ruin his handiwork.

"Where did you learn to do that?" Alden asked him.

"My first tour on a carrier. KP has its empty respites. We didn't have whalebone, so it's not scrimshaw exactly. But we shipped out with crates of soap and barrels of Macs."

"You didn't spend too much time carving soap, I'll bet."

"Long enough to learn how."

She had come over to his place with Toya that Sunday morning to see if Hyram was well enough to lead the outfall pipe regatta. But he was looking a lot worse since the last time she'd seen him. She unzipped a new packet of nitro patches, peeling the plastic off two gluey sheets. She handed them to Hyram, and he patted them in place across his belly. "Hyram, you're pushing it. You can't sail out with the group. You could have an MI out there."

He looked back at her as if she might convince him if she kept talking like that.

She dialed the first person on Hyram's phone tree and told him that

Hyram wasn't sailing with them, but they should steam out as planned. She had a brainstorm. She telephoned Conrad, hoping he was home for the weekend from flight school. His wife answered the line and told Alden that Conrad was still asleep. She said, "His first week training at American was all paperwork, simulators, and math tests. It wore him out."

Alden asked her, "Can you wake him up? I need a big favor."

"And you are?"

"I've got a heart patient who needs to go to Boston."

"Conrad's not doing angel flights anymore. Not for ages, he hasn't."

"It's Hyram. You know Hyram?"

"The Green Grandpa? He's sick? Hold on."

"I'm not flying Cape Air anymore," Conrad told her. "Remember? I'm back in school."

"You have your *Dukes of Hazzard* pencil case?"

"I've got the pencil," he teased her.

"Is your wife listening? Can't you borrow that little plane, you know, that yellow jacket you take up to shoot real estate? Hyram wants to see the turnout at the pipe. It's his baby, you know. You've got to take us up."

"Lunch in Nantucket sometime?"

"That's blackmail."

"Don't tell me your troubles. I mean, not until we're alone."

"You never give up. What's so great about *us?* What do you see in me?"

"Everyone sees it."

AFTER THE WEDDING, Alden had learned that Lux was being held in a city jail called Area A-1 on Sudbury Street in Boston. She had had to come back on cape without him. She had tried to reach him and had pestered the dispatcher all night, but he wouldn't let Alden talk to Lux. When she called again that morning, she found out Lux had been transported to Boston Municipal Court for a hearing. The officer wouldn't say if he'd be coming back to Sudbury Street or to the Suffolk County Jail. But when Alden started sobbing, he gave in. He told her, "The TV buzz on this will make it hard for him before the bench. But if he can swing a bond, they have to let him out."

She didn't know why Lux hadn't called her. If he had had an opportunity to use the telephone, maybe he had contacted King. She called Mass General, but King told her he hadn't heard a peep from Lux. He'd seen the video on New England Cable News. King said, "I can't believe he paintballed that bride."

"It's all my fault," she said.

"You don't know the half of it, do you?"

At Race Point, she climbed into the tiny Diamond single-engine that had hardly enough room for all four of them. Hyram sat beside Conrad, and Alden and Toya sat behind them in one seat, snapped into one belt. Toya was chattering. It was her first time in an airplane, and she asked Conrad everything about it. First she wanted to know how an airplane stayed up in the air. That was all Conrad needed to hear. They were prisoners in the microcockpit and had to listen to Conrad's theories on "lift and buoyancy," "excess lift," and "zoom reserve."

It was a clear day with thirty-mile-an-hour wind gusts. The little plane lifted off, bouncing like a fishing bobber in rough surf. It took Conrad only fifteen minutes to find the flotilla organizing on choppy waters from Duxbury all the way up the coast to Cohasset. It was a circus of small craft and fishing boats steaming north in a wide band, leaving foamy wakes of all sizes.

"Look, Alden—it's magnificent, isn't it?" Hyram shouted over the single-engine's a cappella. "There's the *Princess,* the *Cee Jay,* the *Laura and Nancy.* It's the whole fleet, and God, there's more we don't even know. And look, we've got the Coast Guard escort. Just like they promised. See if they can stop us."

Conrad banked the tiny plane and descended to three hundred feet. He buzzed the friendlies mile by mile, following the coastline. Captains tooted horns and steam whistles and rang bells. Kenny Bassett set off a flare from the deck of the *Sea Grape.* The canister burst parallel to the cockpit window and drifted east in the stiff winds. In the distance, Alden saw the Boston skyline and pictured Lux at municipal court, standing before a judge in his muddy jeans. Or worse, she worried he might be back inside the Sudbury Street jail. Hyram guesstimated what the charges against him might be: aggravated assault and vandalism, destruction of private property, or creating a public nuisance.

Alden fretted that he might not be able to pay his fines. She hoped Lux could be assigned to a morning of community service, maybe stabbing litter with a pole in the Public Garden. There must be a lot of paper scraps after the wedding fiasco. Her mind was racing when Hyram said, "I think I'm going to be sick. You have one of those little bags?"

Conrad laughed, but then he saw that Hyram was serious. He was hunched in his seat, his arms crossed over his belly. Conrad said, "Hey, are you all right, Hyram?"

"It's just a little pressure. Nothing. Keep going."

They approached the site east of Boston Harbor where an argosy of protesters had collected. Even the fireboats were there, shooting water, tall fountains of feathered spray. The offshore sit-in was teeming, a success far beyond Hyram's conservative estimations. Hyram said, "Look, there's the Channel Seven chopper. Just like we hoped." But he was bent over as if he'd been kicked in the stomach.

"I'm heading back," Conrad said, moving his stick and rudder abruptly, making a forceful chandelle turn, the tiny craft throbbing in the quick ascent.

Alden leaned over the seat and rubbed Hyram's shoulders. Toya mimicked Alden and tried to knead Conrad's neck. She had a crush on the pilot. She liked the way he talked with the authority of a *Star Trek* commander. Hyram seemed to get a little better. He said it was all the excitement, or maybe it was the furious dips and hiccups when the plane hit rough air that had made him nauseated.

Conrad said, "You have nausea? That's on the coronary warning list. No second guessing, okay, Pops? Let's get you checked out." He radioed to Provincetown and asked for EMS to meet them at the airstrip.

"Now, that will be a waste of the good doctor's time," Hyram said. He was trying to face it with his typical wryness, but he looked uneasy.

On the approach to P-town, descending over the bay to Hatch's Harbor, Conrad said, "Look there—at ten o'clock. Those are humpbacks, right, Hyram? They must be going to your party."

A pod of whales breached and spouted, heading west in a constellation similar to the outfall regatta. Their flukes slapped the water, leaving paisley swirls of suds. Alden and Conrad watched in silence, absorbing the symbolic instant; here was the reason for all of Hyram's toil and trouble. It might have been too emotional for them all, but when Toya saw the whales, she squealed with excitement—in a percussive counterpoint to their unhappy tensions.

As Conrad made his landing run, Alden saw the cherry bubbles of EMS. Behind that sparkling truck, two cruisers were lined up on the tarmac near the hangar. She was glad that Hyram would be attended to right away. But she didn't like to see the police officers. Standing abreast of the uniforms, Alden saw two women. It was Mrs. McGuire and Hester Pierson.

"Shite, it's DSS. Go around again," she told Conrad. "Lift off, lift off!"

But the gear had touched down, bouncing from the left wheel to the right, until the tiny plane leveled and bumped along the runway.

Toya clapped her hands in awe of the landing, as if she'd witnessed a sword swallower remove a knife blade from his throat unbloodied. She, too, saw Mrs. McGuire.

Conrad taxied right up to the reception line. He unlatched the cockpit door and helped Hyram climb down. Medics took over, leading Hyram to a gurney. Next, Alden stood on the tarmac, Toya's arms wrapped around her waist, her tiny face buried in Alden's sweater. In an instant she pulled away from Alden and ran into the arms of Mrs. McGuire.

Hester Pierson approached with an officer.

It was a new patrolman Alden had never seen before. He took her elbow and tugged her. Alden planted her feet. He had to push her forward with firm but awkward manhandling until she sat down in the backseat of a cruiser. He started reciting familiar phrases Alden had heard on *Real Police Videos* and *America's Most Wanted.* She recognized snippets of the Miranda spiel in his twanging East Boston accent of buried *r*'s and clipped gerunds. She was under arrest, he told her.

"Well, I *guess so,*" Alden said.

Hester Pierson leaned into the driver's side door of the cruiser and told her, "Alden, you'll get some help now."

Alden sat forward against the reinforced window, begging the officer to let her ride with Hyram to the hospital. But the officer didn't answer her. He sat down behind the wheel and hitched up his trouser legs so they wouldn't stretch at the knees and lose their crease. It was a fussy habit, and Alden laughed bitterly. She thought that this one acted uppity, without Franciscon's kindnesses or teasing. He seemed to think she was bewitched—maybe like the infamous Goody Hallett, a fifteen-year-old Cape Codder who in 1715 bedded pirates and helped sink merchant ships.

For an instant the cruiser tagged along behind the EMS and she saw them working on Hyram. A medic applied adhesive disks to his bare chest to hook up wire leads to a portable EKG unit. The EMS rolled up Route 6 on their way to Cape Cod Hospital, but the cruiser veered off. Alden saw that she was being delivered to the police barracks on Bradford Street in P-town, beneath the Pilgrim Monument. The holiday lights had already been strung from the monument's high parapet, big yellow bulbs on heavy guy wires that stretched 250 feet to the ground in dizzying spirals. Each season, the monument was transformed into a towering Christmas tree, visible across the water all the way to Boston. But the wind was making the wires scream. As the officer pulled her from the backseat, the singing cables hurt her ears. She flattened her hands on either side of her face, digging her fingernails into her temples; her wild hair spiraled, tossed and torn by the gale-force westerlies. The officer nudged her, step by step, along the sidewalk. A few pedestrians parted, turning away so they wouldn't have to make eye contact with Alden as she struggled at the doorsill of the Gothic town hall building.

The officer brought Alden into a screened-in lockup, a tiny cage like an aviary, but Alden started screeching. Her sudden claustrophobia made her whole body tremble, and the officer decided it wasn't worth the tangle. Instead she was told to sit down in a little alcove next door to the dispatcher. The room had a dinette table, soda machines, and a microwave. She figured it must be where officers sat down to eat their lunch and have their little chin-wags. A female officer was recruited to watch Alden until the MSW arrived.

"Who's coming?" Alden demanded to know.

"Someone on call, I guess."

"Is it Hester Pierson? Because I don't want that bitch showing up now." She tugged her sweater, cinching it shut. She fondled the big, flat buttons until one popped off.

The matron put a dollar in the soda machine. The crumpled bill glided back and forth repeatedly until finally it was swallowed up. "See anything you want?" the officer asked Alden.

"I just want to get out of here."

"I'd go for the can of juice. The lesser evil," the cop said.

Alden studied the panel. "Pepsi, I guess."

The heavy can tumbled into the trough, making a lonely racket. The officer popped the flip top and handed the drink to Alden. Alden sipped it dutifully and looked around the place. Her button had rolled into the middle of the floor, a little wafer of plastic. The officer saw it, too, but didn't bother to pick it up.

Within the hour a DSS flunky, jazzed on caffeine, arrived with a state trooper who would transport them off cape. The woman talked nonstop to the arresting officer, repeating the same questions in different mellifluous rephrasings, even after he'd answered them. She said, "So it isn't kidnapping, you say? Is it child endangerment? Because that's ridiculous." The officer crossed his arms and leaned against the doorframe, letting her listen to the sound of her own voice. "Alden's been in the system as a minor herself. We *know* Alden. She's loaded up with neglect issues, mother, father, but she wasn't a kid that we labeled irredeemable. She was doing pretty good until now. It's our opinion at Yarmouth that it's wrong to criminalize a victimless event of impulsive mischief. That's really an issue for psych to look at, right?"

The female officer agreed that Alden should definitely have a look-see by a seasoned headshrinker.

When the newbie cheerleader finally led Alden into a waiting van, Alden said, "You taking me where? To county or Framingham?"

"No, honey. That's not happening now. That will be *if* and *when.* First we go to Bridgewater."

"Bridgewater? You're taking me up there? Who says?"

"It's the routine."

"The routine?"

"If you're going to be charged, it's a pretrial work-up. Otherwise it's just a simple psych evaluation. Relax. You'll do okay. It's a long drive—you need to use the facilities?"

Alden shook her head. She couldn't pee on command.

All her life she had heard about the state loony bin. You can't grow up in Massachusetts and not know about the place. It wasn't a regular feature in the Sunday *Globe*'s Travel section, but there was always a story about it, year after year. For the law-abiding masses, it was reassuring to have a state-funded nightmare resort for lost souls. The NIMBY types who lived in upscale Newton, Lexington, and Wellesley liked their funny farm tucked away in a dead-zone small town like Bridgewater. It was the little burg's only claim to fame.

On the drive up Route 6, Alden held her face in her hands. She let her fingernails sink into her temples until she felt the tender skin prickle and sting. She tugged the remaining buttons from her sweater and started to unravel its hem. Finally she asked the police officer behind the wheel, "Did you hear about my friend? Was it a heart attack?"

"You mean the elderly gentleman?"

"Yes. Is he going to be all right?"

He didn't know anything. Alden wondered who would try to get her out of Bridgewater. Perhaps Conrad could do something, but she remembered how his face had changed when he saw the police cruisers on the airfield. His features froze over and he instantly shifted from a good sport to one of *them*. And if Lux was in jail and Hyram was in Cape Cod Hospital, they couldn't come to her rescue. She was ashamed to be selfishly scheming when her loved ones, too, were under duress, with just as much at stake.

The MSW turned around to look at Alden. "Oh, Jesus, honey, what happened to you?"

Alden's skin was raw with welts where she had raked her fingernails across her face. Her tears burned.

22

A SKINNY, NONDESCRIPT OFFENDER crowded against Lux, trying to rush him off the pay phone at the guard box at Sudbury Street. Lux turned one way, then the other, each time the goon pestered him. He was explaining his problems to Gwen.

Gwen said, "You're saying you want to put up the *Extra Dry* for—what's it called, collateral? You want me to be what?"

"Signatory. You have to cosign the bond."

"They want the sales receipt for the boat?"

"Is it in your name or Denny's?"

"His name's on it, so is mine. It's registered in Wilmington, Delaware, you know, because they don't charge sales tax. I don't know if we have the paperwork."

"When is Denny coming in?"

"He just went out again."

"Swordfish?"

"What else would make him go back out? My mother won't lend me that much money. I guess you can use the *Extra Dry* if you promise you're going to show up."

"If I don't make a bail schedule, they keep me in lockup in Boston's Suffolk County Jail. That's worse than Sudbury Street."

"I said yes."

"God, your beautiful," he told her when she was willing to help him. "They gave me an 800 number for a bondsman, someone called Josh Herman. He's at 1-800-7-GET-ME-OUT. He told me the *Extra Dry* would be plenty enough on paper. Then he gets ten percent. That's standard.

He said if it wasn't that TV stud getting hitched, Dorchester's pride and joy, they wouldn't have set it so high."

"Lux, you say the charge is assault? Assault on a bride—you're insane. We're talking five thousand dollars? But it's not that schoolteacher, thank God. Is the schoolteacher still in Nickerson's field?"

"Will you be quiet? Your mom will hear."

"She's walking the kids to the playground."

He pictured Nils and Ian in their puffy winter jackets. He saw the woolly pompons on their hats. He remembered Toya tucked in that drawer, her tiny adenoids purring as he made love to Alden. Gwen asked him again, "The schoolteacher?"

"It's out of our hair. Don't worry."

"Please. Don't tell me. I don't want to know."

"I'll never tell you. I promise." He recognized that Gwen could roll with the punches. She knew more about his demons than anyone, even King.

She said, "You think that bill of sale is in the galley? I can go down to town landing, but someone will have to help me open it up. It's winterized."

Lux felt dizzy remembering how Denny had had his sailboat shrink-wrapped for the winter. The plastic sheeting was sealed with a heat gun until it was tight as a drum.

"I think Denny keeps his papers at the house," he said. "I mean, that's where I've seen some of his papers. In the drawer with the Amica forms. Look there."

"I'll see. Then I call that number? What was it?"

"1-800-7-GET-ME-OUT. They've got a fax. Thanks, Sis," he told her.

"Will you be coming back to the house, or will you be out at that creepy shack?"

"What does that have to do with it?"

"I'm not your dishrag," she said.

"Dishrag? Come on, Gwen, you're my magic carpet."

She giggled in her typical whiskey voice. He felt her wet lips kissing his backbone, counting each knobby facet. But even now, he couldn't be sure if it was Gwen or if it was Alden that jangled his nerves. His spine felt like a vein of ice until he was paralyzed.

IT WAS TWO MORE DAYS UNTIL LUX MADE HIS BAIL and came back to the Cape on a Plymouth-Brockton Wash-Ashore bus. He got off in Eastham between a rock and a hard place. Who would he spend the night with, Gwen or Alden?

He didn't have the fortune or the obligation to have to decide. When he learned about Hyram, he telephoned the hospital in Hyannis. Hyram's crisis had passed, and he was sitting up in bed, teasing nurses. He told Lux, "She's locked up. She took the kid—well, you know that. She was much worse than we thought. I should have seen what was happening to her."

"I just hoped we could work it all out."

"She had some sort of psychotic break, right there in the P-town tank."

"Alden had a crack-up? Is that what you're saying?"

"She gouged her face with her fingernails pretty bad. She tore the buttons off her sweater and tried to swallow them. That's what they say, but I don't believe that part."

Lux remembered the extra button he had kept in his pocket. The button packet, written in three languages, didn't foretell this outcome.

Hyram said, "I guess her life's been uphill for too long. They're trying her on Mellaril and Thorazine. They let me talk to her once—she was slurring her words. Now they won't let her have the phone."

But Hyram himself was no longer in guarded condition. He told Lux that he was waiting for the senior shuttle to pick him up and take him home.

"No way, Hyram, of course I'll come get you," Lux said. "I can borrow Gwen's car." He wanted to connect with Alden's old friend; maybe together they could figure out what to do next.

Hyram said, "Thanks, son, but you know, I think I'll ride the shuttle. I'll take my chances with Mrs. Crease. I've got fences to mend." Hyram seemed to want to avoid further excitement. Lux respected Hyram's desire to use caution, but he knew that the oldster was blowing him off.

Lux crossed the canal the next morning on his way to visit Alden at Bridgewater. He looked for the ladder. There it was, propped high against the portal railing. In high winds, the Army Corps of Engineers were still painting the bridge. They were trying to secure netting under the arch so that any tools they might drop wouldn't crash through car windshields. The ladder was there for good reason.

Lux waited at the security kiosk. A corrections officer asked him for the paper bag he was holding.

"I brought this along so she'll feel more at home," Lux told the officer.

The officer looked at its contents. "Can't bring this inside," he told Lux. "The patient can't have this."

"Why not? She's had this doll since she was a kid. There's no dope in it, if that's what you mean."

The officer couldn't take his eyes off the upsetting three-faced bisque doll, but he shook his head. "This doll's made of china. See? She could smash its head and slice her wrists with a broken chunk."

"Shit."

"This one's under suicide watch. She's got some old hesitation marks on her wrists, so she can't have pencils, Chap Stick, or anything she can file down in a stump and sharpen. She can't see visitors yet."

"If I leave the doll with you, will you let me go in?"

"Sorry." He gave Lux a card. "Here's the number to call. They'll tell you the name of the MSW assigned to her case. You can talk to them."

Lux tried to see Alden at Bridgewater two more times, but they told him it was better to take things slowly. Alden was making some progress; a visit from him might throw her off track. He sent her items she was permitted to have on the unit. Stuffed animals went through the metal detector. When he mailed her a book of *New Yorker* cartoons to cheer her up, its fabric spine was sliced open to make sure there wasn't a shiv. Lux called DSS, but the social worker in charge of Alden's rehab planner and psychological testing never answered her voice mail.

EACH TIME ALDEN OPENED HER EYES, she saw a circle of strangers sitting around a TV, everyone dressed in frightening yellow. Of course, it was the women on her unit in maximum-security pajama tops, the same glowing color Monty had worn for butterfly bait.

Her worlds were jumbled up. The here and now bled into the long ago. The day-to-day was fuzzy. Sometimes she joined the group, but often she stayed in her corner beside a narrow window. If she stood to the left of the vertical casement, she could look across to a parking lot behind a fence of scrolling concertina wire. The window held only a sliver of information compared to her sweeping view of the Million-Dollar Marsh from the picture window at the Seashore office. But she studied the parking lot with the same concentration. It was a busy place for prowlers.

Prowler number one was Princie, dragging his cross on its caster wheel. But then she saw it was a custodian sweeping rock salt with a push broom. If a plane crept across the sky, she was sure it was Conrad going through his gaits, the mushing glide, the stretching glide, the power-on stall. When an MCI transport van arrived to unload prisoners, she saw prowler number two, Dane Baker, with members of his clan, the Irish Travelers.

Then she saw Monty. He'd come back to coax her from her widow's walk. He was loitering on the Blind Trail outside her window, trying to win her back by mimicking a *real* blind man. Holding one arm extended, he patted the empty air in front of him and bumped into the fence. He turned and bumped into the fence again, Charlie Chaplin–style. It was a real Academy Award performance.

She saw Lux. He was walking between parked cars with a baby cradled in the crook of his arm. Her baby.

23

SEA CALL LOOKED DIFFERENT. At dusk its unlit windows were blank without the hundred-watt bulb burning. When Alden had lived here, the one-room shack had been like a golden cell of honeycomb, but now it was empty.

Lux stepped up to the window and stared inside. Through the drear, he saw the daguerreotype portrait of the Victorian girl in her high-necked blouse with leg-of-mutton sleeves. Maybe Alden would like to have it; he could crate it in foam core and send it to Bridgewater. But Lux had always thought that the antique picture was a gloomy artifact. This girl might have lived here once, but that was a hundred years ago.

The rangers had padlocked the door, but Lux pushed a window sash open and tumbled over the sill. The window frame bowed and yawed slightly under his weight. Lux recognized that the jury-rigged shack would never have lasted this long unless it flexed in high winds and kept a little give for any intruding forces.

He stood up in the familiar room and looked around. A row of unmatched coffee mugs hung from nails above the sink, their open brims all facing in the same direction. Alden had always insisted the cups march across in formation. Pounding nails was one of the chores Lux had done for her during their brief romance. He walked across the room to study the little tourist map of Cape Cod Bay, complete with a sea monster like Nessie swimming across the blue water. Once, he had noticed that Alden had drawn two figures on its back, and he had asked her, "Who's riding the monster?" She had told Lux, "That's us." But her remark had seemed knee-jerk and contrived, and he didn't believe it was the two of them she had sketched.

Everything in the shack was where it should be. He opened the heavy trapdoor above the steep Yankee cellar and climbed down the ladder to find Monty's jacket. He found the bottle of Bombay gin and took that also.

Lux departed from the same sympathetic window and closed the sash behind him. He put the gin in the car and from the backseat he grabbed Alden's bisque doll. He walked down to the wrack line to start a fire. Rangers warn that bonfires should be constructed where they will be washed away with incoming tides so that the beach doesn't look like a charcoal pit. He wrapped the doll in the Nike Windbreaker. He doused the odd bundle with some Olde English furniture oil he had found in Alden's cupboard. He struck a match, and the package started to sputter and sing. The jacket was slow to ignite, but he watched the fabric melt onto the hidden doll. Lux saw the "sleeping" porcelain face surface—its apple cheeks, its nose, its lips—and then its mask caught fire.

HYRAM ANSWERED THE DOOR. Lux handed him the big blue bottle of Bombay gin he'd found at the shack. "This is going to waste," Lux said. "Alden would want you to enjoy it."

"You brought me a bottle? My friend, that's so *gin*erous of you. Well, come in, sit down," Hyram said, pulling Lux inside.

They sat at the table, where Hyram was busy sorting through newspaper clippings. He moved a plastic bag of bird food, spilling a mound of tiny millet seeds. Hyram pursed his lips and puffed the kernels onto the floor. He poured a drink for Lux. Lux said, "No, thanks. I'm doing my best—"

"Oh, that's right. I've got Nestea," Hyram said. "OJ or Clamato?"

"Thanks, but I'm not staying more than a minute, I guess."

Hyram said, "You have a court date?"

"Next month. But they pinched that crazy—you know, that Xerces Club lady? They've got her on five of these paintball protests, and my lawyer says I'm a nobody compared to Penelope Griffin. He says I'll do all right."

"Nobodies. Somebodies. Who's better off?"

"My mother used to tell me to straddle the line. You have to choose your society carefully and try to keep one foot *in* the circle and one foot *out*side."

"She told you this? She was a smart woman."

Lux stopped to picture his mother. "Yeah, a nobody herself, in fact."

Hyram said, "But you're a credit to her. That's the truth of it."

"When Alden comes home, she'll need a new setup," Lux said. "That shack is too isolated."

"She'll have to be close in to town to see her PO," Hyram said.

"She'll love that. But we'll make her show up."

"Absolutely."

"The other side of my duplex is empty. I could talk to the landlord—"

"Or she could move in with me," Hyram said. "I've got plenty of room. Maybe she's not ready for her own place yet. Not ready for that kind of obligation."

The two men stared at the table. In silence, their unsuspected rivalry spiked and quickly subsided. Lux grinned at the old man. "Maybe you're right, Hyram. She can start here with you, and we'll see where she ends up."

He left Hyram with the jeweled blue bottle and went over to the puppy farm. There were only two shelties left to choose between, and he took the lively one, although it might be a handful. He drove home to the duplex. Gwen stood in the doorway and crossed her arms. Lux dropped the dog on the lawn and walked to her. Gwen tried to wear her "What trouble are you bringing me now?" expression, but she couldn't master it in that cathartic instant, a sudden Norman Rockwell redux. Nils and Ian had tumbled outside, chasing the pup through the laundry lines. It nipped the hem of a clean white sheet, unpinning it from the rope, and the boys tugged the loose end.

24

LUX WIRED AND TRIMMED THE NEW SEVEN at the Quitting Time Clock. He used his power clippers for grooming broad strokes; then he used snips, wire, and needle-nose pliers until it was perfectly edged. He checked each emerald plane with a spirit level.

The English yews were thriving, as if he'd buried a cod with each root ball, like the Puritans used to do, having learned the trick from the Nauset Indians.

In June, pleasure boats were launched, stripped of their vinyl cocoons. The season was in full swing. There was a dedication ceremony for the refurbished clock at the rotary. Guests and sightseers stood in respectful rows before the site, almost as if at a memorial service, but everyone was dressed in summer clothes—bikinis, beach towels, fluorescent windsurfing wet suits, and yellow golf sweaters. Town managers from Eastham and Orleans both laid claim to the precious landmark. Together they presented Lux with a plaque and packets of coupons from their warring chambers of commerce. The envelopes had gift certificates to local eateries.

Gwen and King shuffled the coupons and bickered about where Lux should take them for dinner. Gwen wanted to dine at the Captain Linnell House, where waiters wore tuxedos and came to the table with sterling silver pepper guns. She was dying to wear the new dress Lux had bought her at Talbot's, but King wanted to go to his favorite clam shack. Lux watched them lock horns and snipe, a disharmonious jangle that could go on for a while. But their tear-up was disrupted by a deafening report, like sudden pistol shots. The Army Corps of Engineers and the U.S. Fish and Wildlife Service were trying a new method to chase the cormorants off the high-tension wires behind the Stop & Shop. Their first attempt, adding PVC sleeves to the wires, had failed, and the agency had decided to detonate charges at thirty-minute intervals each afternoon.

Alden was back at Sea Call and had told him about the drill. She believed that the Army Corps of Engineers would never triumph over the die-hard crested cormorants but that these boys loved using guns. Some of them were Gulf War vets, but at home they got their jollies traumatizing the gawky shorebirds. Alden had been enlisted to monitor the count, to verify whether their numbers were dwindling or holding firm. She was keeping a diary for Mass Audubon and a separate register for the Seashore to gauge if the crude firearms method was worth the ruckus each afternoon. There were always conflicting opinions.

After the speeches, Lux encouraged King to continue his debate with Gwen about the free dinner coupons. He was sure they would find a middle ground. He left them at the rotary and walked over to the lagoon behind the Stop & Shop, where Alden was sitting in a blind.

Alden was pleased to see that her count was higher than the day before, and the day before that. She punched her tiny RadioShack calculator to double-check her figures. Despite percussive interruptions from the air guns, there were actually more birds returning to the high-tension cables each day, until the ComElectric perches sagged under their weight. It was as if in a show of Teamsters or UAW defiance, the cormorants had rounded up their soggy brethren from every nook and cranny. Still more birds arrived in awkward gymnastic landings; their homely conformation and naked throat pouches were exaggerated at close range. Unlike mythic shearwaters and the glamorous snowy egrets, black skimmers, and endangered plovers, these "sea crows" were the plain Janes of the coast—misbegotten deep divers whose soaked feathers became plastered down and had to be sunned after every fishing trip. She added each new straggler to her tally.

Then she saw Lux walking over from the hubbub at the clock. Tuesdays and Fridays, he drove her up cape for her appointment with a woman probation officer. Alden wasn't going to enjoy sitting across from that "dickless Tracy" for a whole hour, times twice a week, times fifty-two weeks a year. Sometimes her life seemed to be an endless succession of these tooth-pulling stare-downs with low-level pencil pushers. But afterward, Lux might stop at the Job Lot store to find discontinued items at bargain prices—maybe some interesting hair combs for Alden, as well as the leak-stop hose washers or whatever it was he was looking for. She waved her clipboard until he saw where she was hiding. She capped her felt-tip pen and put down her survey. The ledger pages ruffled until she found a stone for a paperweight. When she lifted the rock, a shellacked black beetle flew off, swooping right and left in amorous fervor.

She watched Lux pick his way through the brambles and catbrier along the tight shoreline. He was grinning.

"What's up your sleeve?" she called to him.

He shrugged in mock embarrassment. He had shucked his jersey in the heat and he was bare chested. His shoulders straight as a T-bar, his muscles naturally contoured from hard work, he was Sylvanus. He looked as happy as a young monarch who had been bequeathed a beautiful kingdom.

They sat down together on a pressure-treated bench. He showed her his plaque and the envelope of freebie attractions. "Look, here's some tickets to the Melody Tent," he said. "And free passes to the car wash, plus hot wax."

It was his big day, and she had missed the ceremony.

Lux wasn't going to let her hear the end of it. He teased her for taking her job so seriously. He called her "fish cop," "nature nazi," "Miss Wilderness," but she knew he belonged in that untamed parcel right beside her. He was a Land's End year-rounder. He didn't fear its squalls and impenetrable mists, walls of fog thick as dry ice in a meat locker. He liked swimming on the back shore, even when the mung was pulpy as kale soup and the sea fleas were biting. Some days, at the end of her shift, he would cup his hands as she emptied her pockets, sorting the fluffy owl pellets she had collected. Each souvenir of fur and bleached bones, with tiny skulls intact, a mystery never solved but quietly perpetuated. "Bird, mouse, vole," she said, and recorded the owl's innocent victims in her notebook.

"You ready to go to the courthouse?" he said.

"You go. Tell that enthusiast I'm otherwise engaged." But he waited for her to collect her papers and to cap her binocs. She patted her hips to make sure she had her pens and her car keys. "What are you staring at?" she said. He couldn't peel his eyes off her. She could almost feel him searching with his own hands.

Then, from the opposite shore, the gun erupted on schedule. Three blistering cracks.

The cormorants exploded off their perches like Fourth of July fireworks. The flock swelled overhead. A great black chrysanthemum obscured the sky, then slowly melted apart. In minutes the birds saw-wheeled back to the power lines.

ABOUT THE AUTHOR

MARIA FLOOK is the author of *My Sister Life: The Story of My Sister's Disappearance* and *Invisible Eden: A Story of Love and Murder on Cape Cod;* the novels *Open Water* and *Family Night,* which received a PEN American/Ernest Hemingway Foundation Special Citation; a collection of stories, *You Have the Wrong Man;* and two collections of poems. She teaches at Emerson College in Boston.